Paper Lanterns

Christine Coleman

Dear Reader,
I hope you enjoy *Paper Lanterns* as much as I enjoyed writing it!

I'm always pleased to get feedback on my novels, so I'd very much welcome your comments or questions.

If you'd like to, you can get in touch with me via the 'Contact Me' page on my blog: www.christinecoleman.net

With very best wishes

Christine Coleman

ALSO BY CHRISTINE COLEMAN

The Dangerous Sports Euthanasia Society

Praise for The Dangerous Sports Euthanasia Society:

'Delightful, enormous fun and surprisingly original.'
Sara Maitland, The Literary Consultancy

'… wonderfully titled and brilliantly inventive. Telling the story of one woman's search for a reason to live, it manages to be piercingly accurate about our daily lives while very funny indeed.'
Jonathan Davidson, The Birmingham Book Festival

'A surprisingly original story – gripping stuff.' *The Oldie*

'A funny and poignant story about life beginning at seventy five! Great stuff for anyone planning to grow old disgracefully!'
The Pitshanger Bookshop, London

'I loved how Ms. Coleman addressed some serious issues in such a clever and entertaining way. The Dangerous Sports Euthanasia Society is a gratifying and uplifting testament to living life to the fullest, regardless of age.' *Sharon Goforth, Exlibris*

'…big issues within an "easy" read and some lovely characters. I loved the whole premise of the Society' *Dovegreyreader*

'A terrific girls own adventure with a most unusual heroine who will steal your heart. *The Nottingham Evening Post*

'Dangerous Sports has all the hallmarks of conventional chick lit. It's a light read, irreverent, improbable and focused on a strong female character. That's where the similarities end.'
Lillian Kennet The First Post.co.uk

'When you read a really great book the saddest thing you can do is finish it. I loved it – it's a great book.' *Clarissa Dickson Wright*

'This charming and entertaining story is full of memorable characters of *all* age groups, somewhat of a rarity in fiction today.'
Rhapsodyinbooks

Paper Lanterns

Christine Coleman

Birmingham

Published by Novel Press: 44 Wylde Green Road
Sutton Coldfield, West Midlands B72 1HD
United Kingdom
Email: novelpress@live.co.uk
www.novelpress.co.uk

British Library Cataloguing in Publication Data
A catalogue record for this book is available from the British
Library

Cover design by **Mousemat Design Limited**
Ian Hughes, 5 Pilkington Road, Orpington
Kent, BR6 8HR, England
Tel and Fax:01689 862458 Mobile:07941 723024
e-mail: ian@hughes-design.demon.co.uk

Copy Editing by **Libro Editing Services**
Liz Broomfield: http://libroediting.wordpress.com

Printed and bound by **Bookmarque**,
110 Beddington Lane Croydon, Surrey CR0 4TD
Tel 0208 6123400, Fax 0208 6123401

Paper Lanterns

Christine Coleman spent her childhood in the Sussex countryside, and her late teens and early twenties in Dublin, where she learned to enjoy Guinness and climb mountains while gaining a degree in English. She has taught in secondary schools in Dublin and the Midlands, and now works part time as manager of an Adult Literacy and Numeracy programme in Birmingham.

Her career as a writer includes both fiction and poetry. She enjoys running creative writing workshops and giving talks and readings from her fiction and poems to a wide variety of audiences. Her novel, *The Dangerous Sports Euthanasia Society,* was published by Transita in 2005.

Paper Lanterns was partly inspired by an unexpected discovery of a cache of love-letters written in China in the late nineteen twenties by two separate women to the same man. On her first trip to Hong Kong in the early nineties, Christine was fascinated by the contrasts between the busy urban districts and the beautiful scenery of the outlying islands, and since then she has made several return visits.

For more information about Christine and her work, visit her website and blog: www.christinecoleman.net

Copies of *Paper Lanterns* and the *Dangerous Sports Euthanasia Society* can also be purchased via this site.

What Bookcrossers say about Paper Lanterns

'… the characterisation in Paper Lanterns is wonderful. I loved Ann and Vivienne; their voices are clear and authentic, as are the more minor characters of Poppy, George and Dawn … Ann's pain, and her feelings of inadequacy are beautifully portrayed, both as a mature woman and in her 16 year old voice, which is that of so many unremarkable, unhappy girls of that age. As the narrative moves between the 1930's, the 1970's and 2008, the reader becomes as enmeshed in the drama of this family as the characters themselves. I thoroughly enjoyed this novel. It deserves to do well!'   **Bookcrosser**, *Heaven-Ali*

'…The double layered timescale gives a rich depth to the story, as Ann finds herself revisiting places her grandmother knew well, and visiting some of those strong emotions too. We find out the family revelations as Ann does, and find ourselves rooting for her as well as falling in love with a beautiful island and a happy, free way of life. A good read, a satisfying range of characters, an engrossing plot and a new place to learn about - highly recommended.'   **Bookcrosser**, *LyzzyBee*

More Praise for Paper Lanterns

'A fascinating and engrossing novel with an unconventional heroine. I was gripped and deeply moved by this unusual and sensitive tale of an extraordinary week in Hong Kong during which past and present inexorably unfold to upend Ann's world and shatter her certainties. Ann's amazing journey of discovery shows it's never too late for a rite of passage into a happier life.'
Crysse Morrison, author of Frozen Summer and Sleeping in Sand

'A vivid and absorbing tale of family secrets and illicit love, observed with the keen eye of a poet. You can almost smell and taste Hong Kong. Recommended for fans of Margaret Forster and Penelope Lively…. good solid story-telling, great writing, a wonderful setting, believable characters & pacey dialogue'
*Linda Gillard, author of Star Gazing, Short-listed for **Romantic Novel of the Year 2009***

For Teresa, with thanks.

Friday 8th April, 1930, Hong Kong

"… and I had the oddest sensation – as though my soul – my very self – was a bright flame that now was shrinking, leaning away from him as from a gust of wind. And into my mind came the image of how the Chinese protect a small flame of light from being extinguished and at the same time, beautify it, with a delicate construction of coloured paper."

Prologue

Sutton Coldfield 1971

Ann steps out from the dank shade of the railway bridge into sharp April sunlight. She takes a deep breath as she smiles up at the sky, and has to stop herself from skipping along the empty pavement like a child. A moment later, when she catches sight of the man trudging towards her past their front gate, she slows almost to a halt.

He's probably come into the road from the far end. But then again, he could have appeared there just a second ago, through the gap in their hedge that leads from the side entrance of the house.

She edges closer to a nearby garden wall as their paths cross, but he doesn't seem to notice her. He's staring straight ahead and looking as sad as Dirk Bogarde in A Tale of Two Cities when he was doing his 'far, far, better thing' and the whole class was gulping and swallowing their tears.

Ann is thinking of Dirk Bogarde as she pushes open the side gate and ambles across the lawn to the stream and the little island that holds the summer house, with its big cane armchairs and flowery cushions and matching couch – her favourite place at this time of year. Her class has been let out a whole hour early, and Colin won't be home from school yet, so she'll have it all to herself.

Her hand is already on the wooden rail of the footbridge when she realises there's someone curled up on the couch, face to the far wall. The hunched shoulders in the plain white blouse are rising and falling, rising and falling. The breathing is noisy – little gasps interspersed with sort of stifled squeaks. *Mummy?*

Ann's first instinct is to back quietly away. Vivienne isn't one for shows of emotion – except anger, and an occasional burst of laughter. Mummy, crying?

She can't just leave her. She might be ill. Someone might have died. Granny! Is it Grannibelle?

A few silent strides and she's hovering near the couch, shifting from foot to foot. There is no doubt - this is real crying. The sort she sometimes still does herself, under the bedclothes.

'Mummy?' she ventures, then waits, counting to ten. No answer. 'Mummy? Is it Grannibelle? Is she dead?'

Vivienne swings round and nearly tumbles off the couch, 'Grannibelle…?' she exclaims, lowering her legs and sitting upright. She dabs at her eyes with a balled up handkerchief, 'What about Granny? Has she phoned?'

Ann feels her stomach unclench and she smiles in relief. 'I thought…I thought someone must have died.'

'No one's died, you silly goose,' she sniffs, and opens out the crumpled square of wet cotton to blow her nose.

Ann slides her hand into the pocket of her brown school skirt and draws out a small creased hanky of her own. 'I haven't used it,' she says almost shyly, holding it out towards her mother.

'Thank you, Darling,' she smiles up at her, but her voice is small and shaky.

Ann can't help herself: the rare endearment, combined with her mother's obvious distress, is more than she can bear. She leans forward, knees bent, and is on the couch at her mother's side, clumsily flinging both arms around her and resting her cheek against the white blouse front, with its top buttons gaping.

'Don't be sad, Mummy. Don't be sad.'

She's being rocked, backwards and forwards, backwards and forwards in her mother's arms. 'Shhhhh, now, shhhh. It'll be all right. Everything will be all right.'

They sit like this for what seems like an age. The closest they have ever been. Then the sudden, 'Oh! The time! What's the time?' And Vivienne almost pushes Ann to the floor in her haste to rise, 'Colin! Oh God! He'll be waiting.'

She's half way across the lawn when she stops and calls back to Ann, 'No need to say anything to Daddy or anyone. Just a little headache. A summer cold, that's all. I'm fine now, perfectly fine.'

3

When Vivienne returns with Colin, there's barely a trace of red around her eyes, and by the time Edward comes home she's even smiling. The incident is never mentioned again.

Sutton Coldfield 2008 - Ann

Chapter One

So it's happened at last, thinks Ann. After all these years, Vivienne has been traded in for a woman even younger than Stuart himself. Not that he's so young any more. And Vivienne is old!

Ann stares down at the receiver in her clenched right hand, and winces as she straightens the fingers of her left. How typical of Colin - no contact for years, and suddenly he's managed to shift all responsibility for their mother onto her shoulders.

When she catches sight of her tight-lipped smile in the mirror above the hall table, she gives her head a vigorous shake. Vivienne is alone now, thousands of miles away in Hong Kong. Straightening her back, Ann heads for the kitchen, where she leans against the sink unit and gazes out on the almost leafless garden.

What if Vivienne had rung her with this news, instead of Colin? What could she have said to her mother? Edward's funeral was ten years ago and they've not exchanged a single word since then. On the rare occasions that she's let herself picture that event, she's been disturbed by the nagging thought that maybe she could have been a bit more…More what?

No. What right did Vivienne have to be there at all, let alone to set foot in that house? Poor Edward. He'd never recovered from the shock of her desertion.

Ann sighs as she picks up the almost empty carton from the work surface. There's a film of mottled cream around the inside of the top, and she wrinkles her nose as she sniffs it. It must have gone off in the hour or so after Graham had munched through his twenty grams of soggy cornflakes, or he'd have given her the usual lecture on sell-by dates.

Black coffee, then.

A few moments later, she's panting and gasping with her scalded tongue spread wide. As she bends down on one knee to wipe the splashes of dark liquid from the tiled floor, she finds that tears are stinging her eye lids.

No use crying over spilt …

Oh Grannibelle! I do miss you!

Even now, after all this time, Ann finds herself catching her breath when a shadow in the doorway, or a coat on the back of a chair, tricks her vision; those three years when Grannibelle was part of their household and the children were little had been such happy ones.

To give Graham his due, he'd raised no objections when she'd phoned him from the hospital in Norwich to tell him that she was bringing Grannibelle back to their home in the Midlands to convalesce. She'd been shocked to see how frail her grandmother looked after that fall. 'They're all so old in here!' she'd whispered. 'It'll drive me insane if they keep me in much longer.' But she was in no state yet to go back to her own house on the Norfolk coast.

In spite of her poor health, Grannibelle had been good company, her mind still keen and curious, almost to the end. There were many things they talked about that Ann had never mentioned to anyone: the ways she'd developed as a child for keeping the real Ann inside her, after Vivienne made her leave Grannibelle and Norfolk far behind, and go to live with her in Felicity's house with Felicity's daddy; how you had to be tough on the outside to remain gentle and loving inside, like Grannibelle; the importance of keeping one's own counsel; 'Yes, dear, secrets, if you must call them that. I prefer, "discretion". There's far too much of this public therapy nonsense. Selfishness, that's what it is. Self indulgence.'

There had been hints, though, especially towards the end. 'Tell Vivienne I'm sorry,' she said. 'And your poor Grandpapa. What a mess I made of it all.'

Mainly, she'd talked about China - her early life as a young married woman in the late twenties and early thirties. Shanghai, Canton, and then, for a few happy months, Hong Kong.

Ann remembered hearing some of these stories during the Norfolk time. Uncle Harry was especially exotic, because he'd

6

been born in the Far East. 'Not that it's done me much good, though,' he'd laugh when she'd begged to know what it had been like and did he have to eat with chop-sticks and have his hair in a long plait down his back. 'Your Gran insisted on bringing us all back to England when I was only two. Rotten shame. I might've been able to speak Chinese if I'd stayed a bit longer.'

'Why did you all have to come back, if Hong Kong was such a happy place, Gran?' Ann asked during one of Gran's more lucid spells, a month or so before she died. 'And who is Rupert?'

It was a warm day in late March and they were sitting in the sheltered back garden of the house she still thought of as Graham's. Gran was wearing the green quilted coat that she said made her look like a giant caterpillar, and Ann had wrapped a travel rug across her lap and round her legs. She was leaning back against the padded cushion of the reclining seat, her eyes half closed, and a smile on her face. A thrush was warbling from the top of the half-dead apple tree near the compost heap at the end of the garden.

Gran opened her eyes and pulled herself forward a little to sit more upright. 'Rupert?' she said at last. 'Who said anything about Rupert?'

'You did, Grannibelle. You were talking to him a few minutes ago. You'd dropped off to sleep. You've mentioned him a lot, these last few weeks.'

'Oh! Ohhh,' she sighed, then her lips came together in a straight line and she slowly shook her head.

Ann reached out and took her hand. How small it was. The bones beneath the loose, veined skin felt as brittle as a sparrow's.

'I'm sorry, Gran. I've upset you. I shouldn't...'

'It's all right, my sweet. It's all right. Rupert was a friend. A very dear friend. Maybe I'll tell you all about him one day. When Vivienne comes back. Yes. I must have a word with Vivienne, now. Will you fetch her for me?''

Ann thought her mind was wandering again. 'Vivienne left us years and years ago,' she said.

In the event, Vivienne did come back. But she'd arrived too late to put her mother's mind at rest before she died. And now, after thirty-something years, Stuart has given Vivienne a taste of her own medicine.

'She's in a really bad way.' Colin's words. She'd thought at first, he must be ringing from England at this time in the morning, and felt a twinge of disappointment when she realised he was still at home in Denver, Colorado. 'Unfortunately, I've got a terribly busy time coming up over the next few weeks. Heading up an International Conference on Bio-Ethics. Poor Mum. She sounded desperate – as though she might, you know…'

Damn it, Colin. Why tell me? What can I do about it?

Sadness. That's all Ann feels now. For all of them. Including Vivienne.

Ann dials the long series of numbers, and holds her breath, half hoping for the ringing tone to stop before her mother can respond. If it's not answered, she'll wait till tomorrow before calling again.

'Ann? Is that you? What on earth are you phoning me for? Has anyone died?'

'Em, I got a call from Colin earlier…' Should she call her Vivienne still? Not Mummy. That would sound ridiculous. 'He told me about Stuart, Vivienne. I'm so sorry…'

There's a long silence, and Ann is about to speak again when her mother's voice, clipped and cold, strikes at her ear, 'Colin had absolutely no business to say anything. That was extremely remiss of him. And what have you got to be sorry about? You could have had no hand in *this*.'

'Not that sort of sorry. I meant…well, it must be very upsetting for you.'

'Must it? And what would you know about that? I don't want sympathy from anyone. Least of all you, Ann.'

What had she been expecting? A tremulous voice breathing softly, 'Ann, Darling! How lovely to hear from you.' Hardly. But not quite this level of coldness either. Her mother had never been one to display her feelings, even face to face. How was she to find out her true state of mind through a long-distance phone call?

'I was just wondering, Vivienne…' she pauses.

'Ann, I don't want to rush you, but I was about to pop down to the village to meet a couple of friends for a drink – it's seven o'clock in the evening here. You were wondering…?'

'I've been looking at flights. I thought, perhaps… well, I mean I thought I might pay you a visit.' She hears a sudden intake of breath. A gasp of horror? 'I wouldn't need to stay with you, Vivienne. I just thought…'

There's a long silence – the pin-dropping sort. She is still there, on the end of the line, with most of her day already spent.

'I couldn't possibly have you come all this way and not stay in my house,' her voice is brisk, business-like. 'Whatever would people say? So when were you thinking of coming? The weather is reasonably good at the moment – not too humid yet.'

'Well, em, I don't know… I mean, I was only…'

'You said you'd been looking at flights. One usually has to give them some dates to work with.'

Ann gulps. She pictures Vivienne's painted finger nails, and can almost hear a rhythmic drumming down the line. She draws a deep breath, and her tone is calm but firm as she says, 'I found one that leaves next Monday. KLM via Amsterdam. It arrives in Hong Kong on the Tuesday.' No, this sounds too definite. '*If* I decide to come,' she adds in a rush.

'Ann, I know we haven't seen a lot of each other in recent years, but I can't imagine you've changed very much. You wouldn't have telephoned if you hadn't already made your mind up,' her voice is more relaxed now. There's even a chuckle as she adds, 'And I suppose I'll be having the pleasure of Graham's company too? He'll surely not be letting you out to play, all by yourself.'

Ann bites her lip. That taunting voice! It's just too much. 'Actually, no,' she declares. 'He's not coming too. This is something I'm doing for myself. On my own.

9

Chapter 2

Ann draws her knees up almost to her chin, tucking her toes under the brushed cotton of her nightdress. The sheet on the bed in Danny's old room is icy cold. In Graham's view, it makes no sense at all to have the heating on in a room that's hardly ever used. Recently, she's been holding herself still as a basking seal, waiting for the rumbling grunts of his in-breath, a few inches from her ear, followed by the explosive hiss and whistle of the exhalation, so that she can slide from the king-sized bed and pad along to Danny's room for the night, fully justified in her desertion.

It won't take long for this bed to warm up. Meanwhile, the cold brings a comfort of its own. The link with Grannibelle. With Norfolk. Sometimes she dreams about it even now, as if it's still her real home.

When she was little she'd asked one morning at breakfast, 'What are those pictures I see on the wall at night when I close my eyes?' Everyone had laughed. Uncle Harry was staying the weekend with Grannibelle, and of course Mummy was there too like she always was on Saturdays and Sundays. It was funny how grown-ups could be someone's brother or sister or even their child, and at the same time they were Uncle or Mummy. And it was funny how even a granny was once a little girl, and then a big girl and of course she wasn't called Granny then. She was just Belle. In the photo on her dressing table Belle was a very pretty lady in such a beautiful dress she looked like a princess. 'And that's your Grandpa, dear. My poor Jimmy.' Grandpa died in The War, which was when most people died. But her daddy didn't. He died in the sea. Drowned, when she was still wriggling inside her mummy like a tiny, baby seal.

'Not all daddies die, silly,' Felicity told her, years later, 'Sometimes it's mummies who die. Though mostly it's grans and grandads. I expect your granny will die soon and then you'll never be able to visit her any more and you'll have to stay in my house all the time and I'll never have my own dad to myself.'

Grannibelle's house was cosy. It was a bit like a Hansel and Gretel house. It was the wrong colour to be made of ginger biscuits and chocolate, but if you screwed your eyes half shut, you could imagine that some of the stones in the wall were big flat meringues, or small, china saucers. It had been quite strange to come to Sutton Coldfield and find that all the houses were made of reddish, straight-edged blocks. Granny's kitchen even had some of the grey and white stones on the inside wall near to where the big oven was that was always hot. And there was a tiny room just outside, down the passage near the back door, and that had the same walls as the outside did. That was where the Wellingtons and the yellow waterproofs and the buckets and spades were kept. And Ann's grown-up bike that Uncle Harry let go of when he was teaching her to ride and then she was riding it all by herself. And the rolled up wind-breaks and some big cardboard boxes that she could make a den with.

That's where she was when she heard Gran telling Mummy about pretty and plain. 'You're just like your daughter, Vivienne. Tip of the iceberg. No-one can see from your face what's going on in that head of yours,' she said, in the scratchy voice she sometimes used for speaking to Vivienne – like when a stone is stuck on the bottom of your welly and it scrapes on the paving. 'Pretty and plain, you and little Ann have that in common, if nothing else.'

'What's plain, Grannibelle?' she asked when Mummy had gone back to Norwich to work because it was Monday again. 'Oh!' said Gran and her face went a bit funny for a moment and then she said, 'Plain is straightforward and honest. Like you, Darling.' And then she put her hand on Ann's head and stroked her straggly brown hair. 'Handsome is as Handsome does.'

But Felicity laughed and laughed when Ann told her this after the Norfolk Time had finished. 'Plain is a grown-up way of saying 'ugly', Stupid.' Although Ann was too old now for Hans Christian Anderson, the story of the Ugly Duckling was more like a Folk Tale or a Legend and it gave her hope. After all, Grannibelle had been very, very pretty when she was a grown-up in the old photos,

11

and Mummy still was pretty. Men in the street turned their heads to look at her.

It was Uncle Harry who told her about icebergs. What you could see of them from your ship was only like the top part of their head. The more of them that was showing above the sea, the bigger they were underneath. And icebergs were dangerous. And that was why the Titanic sunk. 'No, sweetheart. Haven't the foggiest idea why your Granny said that. Though come to think of it, I can see how my dear little sister, your mama, could be pretty dangerous for a certain type of fellow.'

Ann eases her feet down towards the end of the bed, her curled toes checking the temperature of each new inch of sheet as she gradually straightens her legs and then rolls over onto her back. She stares up at the ceiling and smiles at the sight of Danny's fluorescent stars, still emitting a faint green glow.

How short a childhood really is, when seen through adult eyes. How quickly we forget that for the child, it's never-ending.

For Ann, at eight years old, it had seemed as though the most important part of her life had come to an end when she had to leave Cley-next-the-Sea, and come to live in Sutton Coldfield with Mummy and Edward and Felicity, as far away from the sea as you could get. And though Edward said it was now her home too, it was all Felicity's really – the whole house and the garden and the stream with its little wooden bridge.

There was a deep part where the water came out from a dark tunnel under the drooping bushes beyond the summer house, and an even deeper part just after it tumbled over a ledge of stone and rushed along for a bit before it disappeared under the fence into the next-door garden. That was where the old witch lived with her giant husband and fierce black cat. Felicity told her she'd be able to get back to the sea that way. All she'd have to do was to lie down and she'd float back there in no time.

An ocean's worth of water will have flowed under that bridge since Ann was in that garden last – a good ten years ago - the gathering at Edward's house after his coffin had slid through the doors of the Crem. Party? Reception? Some of these post-funeral events could be jollier than weddings. Not this one, though.

It would have been all right if Vivienne hadn't come. She'd had to be told about it, of course, but somehow Ann had thought she'd have the decency to stay away – or at the very least to make herself scarce after the funeral itself.

Instead of slipping quietly away from the crematorium, Vivienne had jumped into a car with Colin and his wife, Marlene, and there she was, back in the very house she'd walked away from, all those years ago. Ann would have to try to remain civil - Edward had always been one to avoid a scene at any cost.

At the sight of Vivienne, a glass of dry sherry in her slim hand, mingling so easily with all Edward's old friends and colleagues, some even offering their condolences, Ann felt a wave of nausea. Fresh air, that's what she needed. She slipped away from the crowded drawing room into the oak-panelled hall, murmuring the usual get-out, 'Things to do in the kitchen.'

But Vivienne had followed her. 'Ann,' she began, placing her hand on her daughter's forearm.

Ann gave an involuntary shudder, and jerked her arm free. There was a stabbing heat behind her ribs and a sharp-edged lump in her throat.

Vivienne flinched, and then continued in a level voice, 'I know this is hard, Ann, for both of us, but we do need to talk – there's something I really must tell you – something I would have told you a good while ago, only...'

What was it that Ann had said in reply? She remembers the feeling – an overwhelming sense of dread. The need to escape. She must have said something very final to Vivienne because the next thing she remembers about Edward's funeral is Colin asking her if she'd seen their mother leave.

'No,' she'd said, staring blankly round the roomful of chattering men and women in dark suits and dresses.

Ann knows that Louise and Danny must have been there too. And Graham. It was weird how that sudden touch of Vivienne's hand on her arm had wiped them from her mind, as though they'd never existed.

Half blinded and breathless, she'd jostled her way towards the French windows, and stumbled across the lawn to the overgrown vegetable patch beyond the screen of privet with its sickly scent.

'Mummy! Mum-*mee*, where are you?'

Her ears could hear the child's cry but it held no significance for her. Ann was just a girl herself, barely a week from her sixteenth birthday.

A moment later came the shock as her adult brain reassembled itself.

How could she have forgotten the existence of her own daughter? Since Danny's birth, then Louise's, they'd always been permanently present in her head.

They still are now, of course, though not with the same intensity. Absences are a bit like silences, the way they encompass such a range of weight and texture. Louise's absence has grown light, and soft around the edges, pervasive, almost a presence. The regular phone calls and emails from the Brighton campus act as invisible tethers.

Ann opens her eyes and smiles again at the glow from Danny's stars. His absence, teaching English in Tokyo to eager business men, has acquired something of the tight, sharp feel of Colin's. In her dreams, she sometimes sees them both together, aged seven or eight. Her little brother and her own son, twins.

She'd still been ironing Colin's shirts and advising on girl-friends when he went off to London to read Economics at Imperial College. There was no denying that London was impossibly expensive for students; of course it made sense for Colin to move into the spare room in Felicity's Islington flat.

'She's such a laugh,' he told Ann on one of his rare visits home. 'All my mates fancy her rotten.'

'I'm not surprised,' she'd said, suppressing a pang. No one could ever have been said to fancy her rotten, except Max, perhaps. Max-the-Bastard, as it turned out. That was long before her marriage to Graham and it was certainly not an expression he would have used, not even at the start.

In fact, if Graham had fancied anyone on the occasion they'd first met, it would have been Vivienne, not her. It was during the time leading up to the Betrayal. Midsummer, and Vivienne, as usual, was acting as gracious hostess for the annual garden party for Edward's firm of family solicitors. Graham was the son of a client of one of the other senior partners.

At fifteen, Ann was deemed old enough to hand round the trays of sparkling white wine, while six-year old Colin was entrusted with the canapés. This was the year that Felicity moved to London. On an occasion like this, her absence was almost as tangible as her actual presence; Ann was only too aware that she was no substitute in the eyes of the older men who'd been looking forward to feasting them on Edward's beautiful daughter. They'd had to focus their whole attention on his equally beautiful wife.

Graham himself had not made much of an impression on Ann. He'd just passed his final accountancy exam and his proud father had brought him along, perhaps for moral support, in the absence of his soon-to-be-ex wife. At twenty three, Graham was clearly the youngest guest by several years and she'd tried to imagine herself being kissed by him. She felt she might have had more success with this mental feat if he hadn't been standing so close that she could see the fleck of parsley caught between his front teeth, and a couple of tiny scabs on his chin where he'd cut himself shaving.

'I must say, you're very good at your job,' he'd said, as Ann removed the empty glass from his hand and, in one smooth movement, replaced it with a full one from the large silver tray she was balancing on her palm and forearm, elbow wedged against her lower rib.

'Ah, Graham. I see you've pre-empted me. I was about to introduce you to my daughter, Ann,' laughed Vivienne, almost dancing across the lawn in her stockinged feet. 'Do forgive my dishevelled appearance. I started off so well, but the heels of the shoes that match this dress tend to sink into the grass when there's been even the tiniest bit of rain the day before.'

Graham's long, thin face turned scarlet. At first, Ann thought he'd been embarrassed to find that he'd mistaken the daughter of his hostess for the maid, or an employee of a catering firm, and she felt a little more warmly towards him. Maybe he was quite reasonable-looking after all. But when his eyes remained fixed on Vivienne's ankles and calves, and then proceeded slowly upwards, her face hardened. Same as all the rest, she thought as she quietly moved away.

For some reason, Edward had taken a shine to the young man, and Vivienne, too, seemed to enjoy his company. It turned out that he was a keen bird-watcher, like Edward, and often visited Sutton Park, hoping to catch sight of an elusive nuthatch or bullfinch, or over-wintering migrant from northern Finland.

In spite of her contempt for any man, except Edward, who fell under Vivienne's spell, Ann was thrilled when she discovered that Graham had spent several summer holidays on the North Norfolk coast and used to lie on his stomach for hours on end in the sand dunes of Blakeney Point fixing his binoculars not only on the dunlin and redshank, but also training them on her beloved seals as they basked on the sandbank across the channel that carried the swift-flowing water from the Pit all the way round the Point to meet the pounding waves of the North Sea.

This awkward, slightly pompous young man formed a link to her beloved Grannibelle and Norfolk.

Thoughts of anyone but Colin and Edward found no space in Ann's head in the months following the Betrayal. Graham called on Edward one evening, a couple of weeks after Vivienne's desertion but Ann was settling a tearful Colin into bed. As for Edward, he politely explained to Graham that for the time being he had so much work to complete, he must regretfully ask to be left alone until such time as he could offer more wholehearted hospitality. It was thirteen years before she'd seen Graham again.

Chapter 3

Ann shivers as the plate-glass doors let in a blast of chill morning air, closely followed by a threesome of chattering women with red and white neck-scarves, and shiny identity badges on the lapels of their navy jackets.

'Better be going soon, I suppose,' Graham sighs.

Her sudden pang surprises her by its intensity, but before she can reach out for his hand, he's checking his watch and saying briskly, 'No point paying for more than half an hour, at those prices.' Then he plants a quick kiss on her cheek, 'Phone me when you get there, won't you? And don't forget you'll be eight hours ahead.'

She watches him through the glass wall as he stands at the kerb, making sure that the oncoming taxi is slowing down before he steps onto the crossing. He doesn't look back.

She swallows hard, and turns away, rummaging in her money-belt for her boarding pass. As she inhales the smell of fresh pastries and coffee, the mixture of hurt and irritation she'd felt at his parting words is so quickly replaced by a wave of something light and joyful it takes her a few seconds to identify the emotion: she's on her own, surrounded by total strangers, uncluttered by known objects or familiar surroundings - even the flight bag is new. She could be anyone!

The elation sustains her until the descent to Schipol airport. Here, it's replaced for a few moments by something more like panic. She follows a small group of young couples chattering and laughing as they step onto a long strip of moving walkway, where the strange, almost dream-like sensation of gliding distracts her enough to slow her quickened breath.

When the soles of her canvas shoes make contact with the hard floor, she's jolted into apprehension again, but the shop fronts ahead have a calming effect; this bustling, enclosed space could be a shopping mall anywhere, except for the signs and labels in Dutch, and most of these have English translations.

Her cabin bag is becoming heavy on her shoulder, and she goes in search of one of the mini-trolleys she's noticed that other passengers have adopted, weaving them in and out of shops and cafes.

Once she has bundled her bag and waterproof jacket into the wire basket she quickens her pace. The long, wide corridor ahead is almost deserted, its two walkways still gliding noiselessly in opposite directions. Even the waiting areas beyond the series of departure gates are empty. She'll need as much exercise as possible before the eleven-hour flight to Hong Kong, so she strides even faster along the shiny tiles. The trolley is so light it feels as if it would scoot off on its own without her fingers resting on the handle. A metal bar, four or five inches from the smooth floor, invites her foot. A quick glance around her, and her left foot is on the bar, her right propelling her at increasing speed alongside the slow amble of the moving track.

The years fall away, and inside her head she's shouting, *Wheeee!! Wheeee!* The next minute, her trolley is jerked sideways, its handle thudding into her stomach.

'What are you playing at, you stupid child?'

Ann's left foot is already back on solid ground. She spins round, taking in the sight of the other trolley, wrenched from the hands of its temporary owner by the force of the collision. Her face is scarlet. Total embarrassment overrides the pain in her solar plexus.

The man's expression has switched from anger to cautious perplexity – not an errant child - a middle-aged woman. Undoubtedly insane.

'I… I'm so sorry!' she stammers. 'I didn't…I don't know what got into me…' Oh God, surely she hadn't actually been shouting aloud in her exhilaration. 'Here, let me…' she goes on, spotting a plastic carrier on the floor, and stepping past the man to pick it up.

'Leave it!' comes that stern voice, and she draws back, grabbing onto the handle of her own trolley as if it's a life saver.

The man has bent down on one knee and is peering into the bag, muttering to himself as he draws out a package the size of a shoe-box.

Ann allows herself a glimpse of hope – no real damage done if he's been buying duty-free shoes instead of Grand Marnier or apricot liquor or expensive bottles of perfume for his wife.

Kneeling now, he's placed the package gently on the floor and is removing the paper from around a brightly coloured cardboard box. As he tilts it a little, Ann's hope is extinguished by a clinking sound. He removes the lid, pushes aside some bubble wrap, and lifts out the headless body of a black china cow, garishly painted all over with orange and scarlet flowers and lime–green leaves.

For a moment, it seems to Ann that they are united in grief for this ludicrous animal. She's set aside her embarrassment. There's something almost unbearably poignant in the way the man lays down the headless corpse on the upturned lid and cautiously feels around inside the box till he draws out the severed head and places it in his cupped palm.

He's still kneeling as he twists round to look up at her, 'It was a present for my mother,' he says quietly.

Ann feels she should be kneeling too, but remains standing, shifting from foot to foot. 'Oh dear,' she murmurs. 'Oh dear, the poor thing! I'm so, so sorry.' She's not clear herself whether it's his mother she's referring to, or the inanimate ornament.

The man has recovered his composure. He packs the china pieces back into the box and hooks the carrier bag onto the handle of the trolley. 'Don't give it another thought,' he says briskly. 'It looks like a clean break and I'm sure I'll have no problem in finding someone to mend it.'

'But your mother…'

'She won't miss what she doesn't know. I'll get her something else. As I said, just forget it.' He manoeuvres the trolley round and starts to walk in the direction from which Ann has just approached, though at a considerably more sedate pace than hers.

She's wondering whether or not to run after him and insist on being allowed to pay for the damage, when he stops and turns

19

back towards her, adding with what could have been a smile, 'I recommend that you take more care of any vehicle you're responsible for in future.'

Before she can think of a suitable reply, he's reached the start of the next strip of moving track and is striding along it towards the crowded central concourse in the distance. Was that a smile? More likely to have been a grimace. Whatever! It makes no difference to how she's feeling now: completely and utterly stupid.

The next best thing to having the ground opening up to swallow her is the sight of the sign for toilets a couple of yards away from where she's standing.

Feeling less exposed to further humiliation, now that there's a bolted door between her and the rest of humanity, she takes several deep breaths and begins to review the situation. It couldn't have been for more than a second or two that she'd deflected her eyes from the empty passageway ahead and glanced to her left - the man and his trolley seemed to have materialised out of thin air. At least, now, there's a rational explanation: the poor man had just emerged from the toilets, unable to scurry out of the way of the mad creature descending on him like a runaway train.

He'd thought she was a child. Well, no wonder! Only a child or a mad person would go careering around a public place like that. What would Graham say? The mental vision of her husband's expression of appalled disbelief releases a snort of laughter, which she smothers with her open palm clamped across her lips like an errant school girl.

Regaining her composure, she leans over the washbasin and splashes water on her cheeks and forehead, then pats them with a paper towel. Turning towards the full length mirror near the exit, she poses with her foot on the trolley and examines her reflection from a variety of angles, trying to see how she could have been mistaken for anything other than a middle aged woman. A dumpy, plain, middle aged woman with an over-large chin.

That chin! For a moment, Ann is fifteen again. At that stage in her life, she'd almost come to terms with the fact that she was Fat and Ugly. Maybe not fat, exactly. Size fourteen wasn't a total

20

disaster, but her legs were too short, and her ankles wouldn't have looked out of place on a carthorse, as Felicity had been keen to point out, when she wasn't comparing them unfavourably to the legs on the dining room table.

If that'd been all she had to worry about, she might even have qualified as normal, but there was absolutely no point in making any effort to meld in with the in-crowd. Or any crowd at all. Her hair was bad enough – lank and straggly, whatever shampoo she tried, but she might have hidden it under a floppy velvet cap, or a silky blonde wig if it hadn't been for her face. 'Back of a bus would be a compliment,' sneered Felicity, 'at least that doesn't look like a slab of cold porridge. And no, you flipping can't use my Honey-Bronze foundation.' That would be on a good day: when Felicity was in one of her black moods, the taunts would hit the bulls-eye. Ann would take it, literally, on the chin.

All her other features looked too small for her broad face, but her chin jutted out like a shelf. 'You could balance a cup of tea on that chin,' she'd heard her mother say to Edward years ago. 'Oh Vivienne, don't!' he'd said. But he'd laughed, too. There was even a dent in the middle of it, as if someone had been trying to push it in. Grannibelle had liked it though. When Ann was little, Gran used to stroke her cheek and then nestle the tip of her little finger in the indentation. 'Dear Dolly-Dimple,' she'd say.

Once, when the fifth form had been taken to the Art Gallery in the middle of Birmingham to view the work of the Pre-Raphaelites, Ann and a small group of girls, who were sometimes her friends, were hovering near a picture of a beautiful woman with a mournful face and a mass of glorious red-gold hair.

'Look, Eileen, 'said one, 'That's what your hair would be like if you let it grow.' 'Yeh, you should let it get long,' said another, then turned to Ann, 'Pity your hair's so thin,' she said, 'if not, you'd look a bit like that. Not pretty of course, but the chin's almost as big as yours.'

Ann had treasured that back-handed compliment for weeks. Maybe her chin wasn't quite so bad after all. She'd even begun to think of asking Vivienne for advice on what she might do with her own mousy brown hair, but she soon thought the better of it - Vivienne always seemed to be in a hurry these days, or cross about something, and sometimes it even looked like she'd been crying. Probably best to try Eileen or Carol. If she caught them in the right mood, they might tell her how to get it coloured and permed.

Ann gives a wry smile. Louise is the only person who's ever shown any real interest in her appearance, trying to get her to update her wardrobe on their occasional shopping trips together, 'But Mum, your figure's fine,' she'd say. 'You're not fat, just a bit...'

'Shapeless? Short?' Ann would laugh. 'I'm perfectly happy the way I am. Really. Though I have to say I was relieved to see that I didn't inflict my particular mix of physical-appearance genes on you!'

'Five foot four is called 'Petite', not short. And talking of genes, you used to wear jeans when we were little. You still should. It's those trousers that are shapeless, not you.'

What would Lou make of this tracksuit? Dark navy. Cotton-and-something mix. Machine wash at 40. That, and the white cotton polo T-shirt, and the slip-on navy and white canvas shoes come from the More4Less ex-catalogue store at the scruffier end of Erdington High Street last Saturday. The bright green, V-neck jumper is at least five years old. *Dress for comfort* has always been her guiding principle when shopping. Comfort, economy and anonymity.

The only part of her that she's allowed Louise to influence is her hair. Now, instead of trimming it herself whenever it reaches to her shoulders, parting it in the middle, and fixing the straggling locks behind her ears with a couple of hair clips, she goes to the hairdresser that Lou selected for her.

Turning her head from side to side, Ann has to admit that the chatty girl at 'Headways' has done a good job with the unpromising material she's had to work with. The amber rinse looks almost natural, masking the flecks of grey, and the layering has given it more body, while the side parting with a semi-fringe, and the feathery strands hugging her cheeks, have re-shaped the contours of the broad face.

She flashes a grin at her reflection. No need to hide herself away. With all those thousands of people flying in and out of here, she's not likely to ever see that man again. Probably on his way back to England right now.

England. The only ground her feet have ever known; the only air she's ever breathed. And here she is now, in Amsterdam airport, about to find a café where she'll sip a cappuccino at a table on her own. In less than two hours she'll be boarding a plane to Hong Kong to visit the mother she has scarcely seen since the week before her sixteenth birthday.

Hong Kong 2008 - Vivienne

Chapter 4

As Ann edges down the aisle towards her seat, she's checking for the number that will match the one on her boarding pass, with no thought at all of who might have been booked in to the one next to hers, apart from a quick, under-breath murmur, 'Don't let it be a screaming baby!'

A moment later, and she'd be happy to embrace a bundle of bawling triplets in exchange for the person already seated next to the empty space that KLM, or rather, Sod of Sod's Law, has allocated to her for the next eleven or more hours.

There's an impatient muttering behind her as she waits, transfixed, checking and re-checking the numbers as if sheer effort of will might alter them.

He hasn't noticed her yet. He's bending forward cramming something into the pouch attached to the back of the seat ahead. Maybe, just maybe, it's not him, she thinks as she tries to raise her heavy cabin bag high enough to propel it into the overhead locker. This could be possible, if she dared to clamber up onto the seat reserved for her, but what kind of scathing comment would this draw?

'Here, let me give you a hand with that, love,' says a bulky man with tattooed forearms, jumping up from the row directly behind hers.

She smiles and murmurs her thanks, wishing she could ask him to change places with her. But there's no way out of the situation, so she edges herself down onto the blue cushioned seat, keeping her head turned towards the aisle and trying to make herself invisible.

She hasn't had a chance yet to get a proper look at the man to make doubly sure that it really is him - that dark pink shirt looks unnervingly similar, and the same goes for the straight, glossy black hair, and the gold signet ring she'd noticed on the hand that had cradled the cow's severed head.

Well, she'll end up with a permanently crooked head herself, if she sits with it twisted sideways like this for the next eleven hours. Better to grasp the bull by the horns. Or cow, even. She bites back a smile as she glances at the man out of the corner of her eye.

He chooses this very moment to turn his head towards her. Their eyes collide. One whole second ticks by before their words emerge in chorus:

'Looks like we're stuck with...' he begins, with what sounds like a sigh.

'I could ask a stewardess to...' she says in a hesitant tone.

Ann's sense of the ridiculous takes over and she bursts out laughing. It's hard to tell whether his laugh starts at the exact same time, or a split second later.

There's something surprisingly intimate about sharing the same air as a sleeping stranger. Ann feels her cheeks grow warm at the thought and she's glad of the dim light in this airborne tunnel of sleepers, as she listens for the almost imperceptible in-breath and the long, low puff of the out, the man's mouth, a mere few inches from her own.

George. George Austin. He started his working life as an accountant, but changed direction in his mid-forties. Two adult sons, one in the U.S. and the other in New Zealand. Separated, amicably enough, from his wife of nearly thirty years. He'd been stupid. She couldn't take it. He'd attempted to make amends. She'd found comfort elsewhere. Happens all the time, doesn't it?

Regret?

There'd been a long pause at this question, before he'd answered, 'Yes. Yes, I do regret it. Very much.' Another pause, during which Ann wondered if she'd been too intrusive.

He gave a little shrug, then smiled as he murmured, half chanting, 'You don't know what you got till it's gone...'

He lives near Brighton. Has a couple of small shops in The Lanes. Buys stuff in Thailand, Indonesia, Nepal. *Austin's* is the upmarket one: carvings, embroideries, rugs - antique and fresh-minted imitations. *Artyfacts* is more for the day trippers, but along similar lines. His real interest is old maps and prints – mainly of the Far East, and for these he has another outlet – a shop in Hong Kong. Hollywood Road.

He's done most of the talking, though he has tried to extract information from Ann and listened attentively to her brief and much edited account of her childhood, in which she focussed mainly on the Norfolk years and Grannibelle, with scant mention of the mother she is now visiting.

'Lamma Island? Well, that is a coincidence. That's where my mother lives now. I have the use of her flat on Mid-Levels on the main island, but I always stay a few days with her on Lamma when I'm back. I've got business to deal with first, or I'd travel over on the ferry with you.'

At that moment, the woman on George's right needed to be let out onto the aisle, and by the time they'd all settled back in their seats, the conversation switched for a while to favourite films, and then the lights were dimmed and people were tipping back their seats, preparing for sleep.

How relaxed she feels with this man, thinks Ann as the cabin lights come on and the tannoy announces that breakfast is about to be served.

At her side, George stirs, opens his eyes and looks around him in bemusement for a moment. Seeing Ann, he grins, ' Oh – what a sight to wake up to – the mad trolley woman!'

'Good morning, to you, too,' says Ann, smiling back.

When was the last time she'd sat down to breakfast without Graham for company? As she tugs the foil lid from the small plastic container of sausage, bacon and scrambled egg, she realises with a guilty pang that this is the first time she's given a thought to her husband since trying to control her laughter in the ladies toilet at Schipol airport, the previous day.

'That's mine, I think. That red one there,' says Ann, turning to George who is scanning the carousel for his own case. He reaches forward and heaves it off onto Ann's waiting trolley. 'Just make sure you keep to the speed limit while you're driving that,' he laughs.

'Ha, ha. I can see I'll never live that down, will I?' As soon as she's spoken, Ann bends down and fiddles with her case. That comment could seem to imply that she was expecting to see him again. He's spotted his own case now and is edging towards it through the jostling line of passengers. He probably didn't hear her.

Ships that pass in the night. Maybe this is how it is for travellers – total strangers share a fragment of dislocated time, reaching in an hour or two an exchange of thoughts and feelings that would normally take weeks. Still, it's been... what? Interesting, certainly. More than that, though. In a strange way, striking up this temporary friendship has helped her to feel stronger, more prepared to face Vivienne, what ever her mother's state of mind might be.

'So,' says George as they make their way to the queue for the passport check, 'If we share a taxi, we can get it to drop you off at the ferry.'

'That'll be great, thanks. I'll be fine once I get to my mother's place, but since I'm not used to travelling on my own...'

'I'll probably be over there myself tomorrow or Thursday. What's your mother's name? I daresay my mother knows her and she's bound to ask. It's quite a small community on Lamma, especially among the ex-pats.'

'Well, to be honest, I'm not quite sure what surname she'll be using – it could be any one of four! Her first name is Vivienne.'

George's eyes widen, 'Ann... Vivienne! Of course! There can't be all that many English women on Lamma called Vivienne, with a daughter called Ann.'

'So you know my mother?'

'Know her!' he exclaims, his face alight, 'She's my...' He stops suddenly, with an almost imperceptible shake of his head, then gives a quick cough and continues, 'She's a good friend of my mother's. I know her well. So, you're Ann! Delighted to meet you at last!'

And who's he been chatting to all this time, then? thinks Ann. What's happened to the mad trolley-woman, the relaxed travelling companion who laughs so easily? Here it comes again - the familiar leaden feeling of being shoe-horned into a box labelled, 'Beautiful Vivienne's Dull, Plain Daughter.'

According to Graham, the weather in Hong Kong in early March should be somewhere around twenty five or six degrees. Ann has been focussing on following George through the shuffling crowds as he guides her through the immigration processes; she's given no thought to the outside temperature, so the warm air that she steps into comes as a surprise. She's glad that George is there to take charge of getting them and their luggage into the taxi, and to point out the landmarks as they're driven along.

'This part is a bridge from Lantau Island to the mainland,' he says. 'Amazing feat of engineering - in England all this would have taken years, if not decades. The Chinese part of me swells with pride - while the other three quarters of hotchpotch Britishness wonders what will happen if they carry on reclaiming sea from the harbour at this exponential rate.'

Part Chinese! Why should that come as such a surprise?

'Yes, I know,' smiles George as Ann inadvertently turns to study his face more closely. 'It's not that obvious, is it? Apart from my hair, maybe. Chinese people are very frank when it comes to personal comments - apparently, my rather large chin is typically English. When I'm here I feel almost tall – certainly a few inches taller than I do in England. Just goes to show how relative so many of our standard judgements are - tall, short – fat, thin, beautiful, ugly. All culturally based, aren't they?'

Ann has never thought about this before. She's always been clear about where she stands in the pecking order of 'worthy' versus 'less worthy'.

'I mean,' he says, ' look at those huge blocks of flats over there

28

- like vertical ant-hills. Some would say total eyesores. Only a very few years ago that was hillside - now, those few square yards, maybe as much as an acre, are home to tens of thousands, I guess.'

As the taxi emerges from a tunnel and swings round onto another six-lane flyover, George says, 'We're on Central, now. It's not far to the ferry. I expect you'll want to get straight to Lamma. Has Vivienne given you clear directions to her house? It's quite a long haul up the hill.'

'She said the twelve o'clock ferry is the most likely one, so she'll be there to meet it. I'm not to worry about phoning unless there's been a huge delay,' Ann raises her angled wrist. 'Oh! It's later than I thought. Maybe I should ring. Oh dear, I don't know -'

'No need to look so worried,' laughs George. 'I'll phone for you from the ferry terminal, once we're sure which one you're catching.'

They're off the flyover now and the taxi has slowed down, weaving its way through lanes of cars and buses honking their horns, brakes screeching. As it edges out into the centre of the wide road, a green tram comes rattling and clattering towards them. Ann gives an involuntary gasp, but the taxi swerves back out of danger.

George leans forward and says something in Chinese to the driver, who glances over his shoulder with a grin and a stream of high pitched nasal sounds.

'He says he's sorry to have frightened you. Then something unrepeatable about tram drivers. And how he's been in his job for forty years and never had a scratch.'

Ann feels a mix of relief and apprehension as the taxi takes a sharp turn down a side road on their left, and George says, 'Virtually there, now. Should catch the midday one, no problem'

The driver pulls up at a taxi rank beside a sunlit paved area sloping down towards a low, open-fronted building. Small groups of chattering people are milling around a glass-fronted kiosk beside a line of turnstiles. The large signs above these are in English letters, as well as Chinese, but the series of three or four-letter words are undeniably foreign. The only notice that Ann can understand is the one announcing: Outlying Islands Ferry Terminal.

Before she has had time to unfasten her money belt and draw out her purse, George is handing over some folded red notes to the driver.

'Oh, but you must let me...' Her words falter; he's already out of the car. She opens her door and breathes in a tang of salt on the warm breeze as the driver lifts out her case from the boot. And now George is retrieving his own.

'It's OK,' he laughs, 'I'm not coming with you – I'll get another cab when I've seen you safely onto the right ferry for Yung Shue Wan. You don't want to end up on the wrong side of Lamma.'

'It's very kind of you,' she says. 'I expect I could have managed on my own, but it's always nice to be shown the ropes.'

Ann trundles her case behind her down the gentle slope as she follows George, wheeling his own much larger one. How kind he is, she thinks. And what a coincidence, meeting someone who not only knows her mother, but seems to be on very good terms with her. Surely he can't be a replacement for Stuart? George must be, say... three or four years younger than Stuart. How long is it now since he left Vivienne? Ann gives herself a mental shake as she dismisses the idea as absurd: but then a sly voice in her head murmurs, *Still jealous, Ann? Of a seventy seven year old woman?*

'So shall I give her a quick ring now, just in case?' George is saying.

For a split second, Ann wonders if he's read her thoughts. She stops in her tracks, hoping that her flushed face will be seen as reaction to the combined weight of her flight bag and suitcase, 'Oh! Ring Vivienne? Em...Do you think...?'

George has already taken his mobile from his pocket. He raises a questioning eyebrow and she nods and smiles, then watches him tap in the numbers.

'Is Vivienne there?... Oh, when will she be back?.. I see... Right. OK I'll let her know... Like Vivienne? No, not in the slightest. ...Red suitcase. Navy trousers, white shirt.'

She's forgotten, thinks Ann. I've come all this way and she's forgotten!

'I take it Vivienne's not around, then?' she says, and is annoyed to find that her voice is not as level as it should be.

George smiles, 'That was Constantia, her maid. Vivienne has just popped down to the village but don't worry, Constantia will be at the ferry pier to meet you. She'll help you with your bag and show you the way up to the house.'

'At least this Constantia won't be looking for a younger version of Vivienne, will she?' says Ann, hoping that there's no trace in her voice of the bitterness she feels.

Chapter 5

There's no chance of her boarding the wrong ferry; it's already there, waiting, its cargo of former passengers trudging towards the exit turnstiles as she follows a straggle of men, women and children round the corner and down a wide wooden ramp, her suitcase thudding over the raised painted strips set at intervals of two or three feet all the way to the stretch of concrete quayside where the gangplank sways slightly in the swell.

Ann grasps the rail as she treads the moving bridge between solid ground and the dipping, rising floor of the ferry. This motion, combined with the slap, slap of waves and the whiff of salt and diesel acts like a shutter opening for the flash of a second onto a different time and place. The child, Ann, breathes the Norfolk air. That screeching of gulls could belong to the here and now, or to back then, on the rickety wooden landing stage above the bobbing seal-boat in the creek below as the water rises, gurgling and swirling in from the Pit. Ann blinks and shakes her head; this ferry is nothing like those fat-bellied, open boats.

There's a double flight of steep stairs on the left of the entrance space in which she's standing, feet apart, adjusting to the movement of the floor beneath her thin soles. Those stairs would be a tricky climb, burdened as she is with luggage, so she peers into the seating area on her right.

Where should she sit? The huge interior, with its three blocks of row upon row of fixed, blue plastic seats is almost empty. George suggested she find a window seat up near the front, on the left, where she'd be out of the direct line of icy blasts from the air-con. 'They always overdo it at this time of year,' he told her, 'but it comes as a great relief in the real summer heat.'

Following his advice, she settles herself beside a salt-speckled window and peers through it at the choppy blue-green water and the hazy outlines of skyscrapers on the mainland across the harbour. She's conscious of her quickened heartbeat as the engine thumps and chugs into action. In a little more than half an hour she'll be with Vivienne. There is no going back, now.

A moment later, she hears someone rustling along the empty row behind her towards the window. Turning her head a little more to the left, she watches out of the corner of her eye as a cheerful looking girl, with a tangle of blonde hair, piles her numerous, bulging plastic bags onto the seat beside her.

'Oh sod it!' she exclaims, snatching one from the top of the pile and placing it, clinking, onto the floor between her feet.

Ann gives up her pretence of indifference and swivels right round to peer down at the crumpled blue plastic, which her nose tells her is awash with some kind of alcohol, 'Anything I can do to help?' she asks, glad of the distraction.

'Gin,' says the girl, looking up with a rueful grin. 'Not that I like it much myself – more of a white wine girl, me. Having a party, see, and my mate sometimes gets spirits half price.' As the girl bends down again and peers into the bag, Ann is reminded of George at the airport, extracting the headless cow, and finds herself giggling.

'Sorry! Not funny,' she says, biting her lip, 'I think the jetlag must be getting to me. And those fumes. Is the bottle completely smashed?'

'Just badly cracked – reckon I must've banged it getting on the ferry. Leaking all over the place, but hey, could've been worse. Lucky the others seem OK.'

Ann produces a thick plastic carrier from her shoulder bag, and hands it to the girl, 'My children laugh at me, but you never know when things like this will come in handy.'

'Ta,' she says, manoeuvring the wet bag into the dry one. Then she wipes her hand on the leg of her jeans, and extends her open palm towards Ann, saying, 'I'm Dawn, by the way – as in 'bright new'. Popped out in the back of the van, on the way to hospital, just as the sun came up over the hill, Mum said. First and last time I've ever been early for anything! Nice of you to help me. Guess you better come to my party. S'on Saturday. If you'd like to, that is. There'll be all sorts of people – all ages.'

'I'm Ann,' she says, as Dawn pauses for breathe. The girl

33

reminds her of Louise. The way the words come tumbling out. The angle of her wrist as she flicks a strand of hair away from her face.

'Ann? Wow! How amazing is that?' exclaims Dawn, leaving her bags and hurrying round to sit beside her. 'Can't be more than one Ann coming to Lamma in one day. It's your first time here, right?'

'Er…yes.'

'You've come to stay with your mum, right?'

'How…?'

Dawn laughs. 'Nah, not psychic – nothing like that. It's a small place, Lamma. If you're who I think you are, I know your mum. Vivienne, right?'

Ann murmurs, 'Yes, you're right,' and waits for the usual comment about the lack of resemblance.

'Real tough lady, she is, your mum,' enthuses Dawn, 'Bags of energy. Never stops. Poppy's the same – proper game old bird. I'm meant to be in Oz now, but I kinda bumped into Poppy an she needed someone to mind her shop for a coupla weeks and here I am still, more'n a month later. It's so cool, Lamma. Real friendly. Everyone knows everyone. You be staying long?'

'I em. No, not long,' she says slowly.

Dawn glances at her and smiles. 'You must be shattered. Viv said you'd be getting in this morning so I guess you haven't slept much. Me and my big mouth. I'll put a stop in it right now, and let you chill.'

'It's…it's all right, really. You're very kind.'

Ann turns towards the window as Dawn says proudly, 'How's that for a view, then?'

They're still hugging the coast of Central, with its huge tower blocks at sea level glinting in the sun. The buildings perched further up the steep slope of the ridge seem to be only two or three stories high, and these gradually give way to scrubby dark green vegetation.

Dawn remains silent for a while, and as they round the point of the island, Ann starts to notice the other water traffic: sampans, and larger wooden boats with square reddish sails, white pleasure yachts like tiered wedding cakes, and huge ocean-going tankers, all shades of black, grey and rust.

'What are those?' she asks, pointing at a couple of little tug-boats pulling squat, square barges, ten times their size, each with brightly painted metal pillars forming a huge wigwam-like structure at one end, decorated with geometric patterns in greens and yellows, reds and blues.

'Yeh, I like them,' says Dawn. 'It's cool how they paint them. See that one there, by that tanker? It's unloading the cargo.'

Dawn has taken Ann's question as a signal to resume her bubbly monologue, interspersed with an occasional question, and when she announces, 'Nearly there, now,' Ann goes suddenly cold and her heart gives a lurch.

Nearly there! She should have been working out what she's going to say to Vivienne, not taking in the details of the seascape and the ferry and letting herself be distracted by Dawn. How can she rehearse her own words and actions when she can form no picture of their meeting? Will it be a total stranger waiting for her at the ferry terminal? Or will that semi-stranger, her mother, turn up to greet her after all?

'You excited?' asks Dawn. 'Poppy says you haven't seen your mum for ages.'

Now she's close enough to see the long ferry pier jutting out into the still water of the bay, and the small flat-roofed houses nestling on the slope of the hill among tall trees. And there, on the near side of the pier, a tiny collection of wooden shacks on stilts, perched above the water and the rocks on the shore line, and behind these, a small inlet with a cluster of little boats.

'I think I'm a bit too tired to be excited,' Ann says. She couldn't begin to say how she feels about seeing Vivienne, but dread might be closer to the mark than excitement. Better not to think about that.

Strange how entrenched in the brain impressions can be, based on television or picture books, even when words have already painted a quite different view. Not only her mother, but George, too, has told her how Lamma is nothing like the street scenes of the built-up areas of Hong Kong. There are only two main villages on this island. No roads. No building above three stories high. The rest is undulating hillside, rocky bays and sandy beaches.

Ann takes several deep breathes as the ferry draws up alongside the terminal building. She's grateful for Dawn's company as she follows the other passengers across the gang plank onto solid ground and up a similar painted slope to the one she descended a short while ago, tugging her red case behind her; through the turnstile, then out of the building into bright sunshine.

The first thing that strikes her is the row of bicycles that straddles the top bar of the metal railings on each side of the long, concrete pier. She hesitates at the edge of the track as the other passengers stroll along towards the harbour front, some reclaiming their own bike and pedalling slowly, wobbling a little as they swerve to avoid the people hurrying towards the terminal. Will one of these be Constantia? She hadn't realised that Filipinos might outnumber the Chinese. Maybe Dawn knows her – she seems to know everyone. Should she start walking, or wait where she is?

'Miss Ann?' A plump smiling woman in her late thirties is standing a few feet in front of her, 'You are Ann? Mrs Vivienne daughter?'

'Oh! Yes. I'm Ann. You must be Constantia,' she says, holding out her hand, 'I'm very pleased to meet you.'

'Got to dash, now,' says Dawn, stepping forward from where she was standing behind Ann in brief conversation with another young woman. 'I'm due in the shop this avo. Say hi to Viv for me. Been great meeting you, Annie – don't forget, you're coming to my party. By, then, see you later! Oh, hi Connie, see you around.'

Ann feels an unexpected pang as she watches Dawn disappear into the stream of people. *Sweet*. A lovely child. Not likely to bump into her again, though - or maybe, if this Poppy is a friend of Vivienne's…but still, nice to feel that she found her likeable enough to be invited to her party.

'I take your case now. Mrs Vivienne say to bring you to where she sit. Please follow.'

Constantia steps towards the suitcase and Ann releases the

handle gladly. She's suddenly overwhelmed with weariness. What time is it in England now? Somewhere around five o'clock in the morning? Is this what jet-lag feels like, drained of every ounce of energy, and a hollow sensation in her stomach? If only she could postpone her meeting with her mother until she's had a good night's sleep.

At the end of the end of the pier, Constantia waits for Ann to catch up. 'You are tired from the journey, I think?' she says.

Ann nods, and manages a weak smile. She doesn't trust her own voice; the kindness in Constantia's has triggered a stinging sensation inside her eyelids. She blinks and looks around her as the track veers to the right along the waterfront and leads them under a yellow canopy between a shop front on the left with its displays of tanks full of large, colourful fish and, on the right, white-clothed tables overlooking the small boats in the bay. It's like walking through the middle of somebody's house.

'Vivienne sits nearby. She will eat lunch with you at next restaurant. Very good fish.'

As Ann inhales the sweet and spicy smells of cooking her dry mouth is suddenly awash with saliva. It's reassuring to realise that the queasiness must be hunger. The next moment there's a squeak of bicycle brakes, a shrill ting-a-ling and two young Chinese girls on cycles speed by, calling out, 'Sorree! So sorree!' as Ann side-steps out of the way, banging her thigh against the edge of one of the tables.

'Very dangerous – bicycles. Many, many bicycles on Lamma. Also the trucks,' says Constantia, looking concerned as Ann rubs her leg.

'I'm fine,' she says. 'Just a little tired.'

They've passed a few small shops and now Constantia halts at another restaurant with tables shaded by a large canopy. 'Mrs Vivienne, I bring your Ann.'

There's a scraping of chair legs on paving as two men in their early sixties rise to their feet. The woman sitting between them does not rise, but she looks up, puts down her tall glass, clinking with ice, and extends her right hand.

I've stepped onto a film set, thinks Ann. For what seems like minutes, but could only be a second or two, she stares at the woman, her own clammy hand resting on the zipped top of her shoulder bag, the other arm dangling by her side. Vivienne's eyes are masked by dark glasses. Her mouth is closed, one edge tilted upwards in the familiar half smile, a mixture of amusement and detachment. Her sleek, auburn hair, cut in a bob, curves in towards the slim neck, round which is draped a long, gossamer-fine strip of pale lilac silk. It's hard to see from this distance of ten or twelve feet whether the lightly tanned cheeks are as wrinkle-free as they appear.

It's one of the men who breaks the freeze-frame, 'So this is your daughter, Vivienne!' His deep voice has a nasal twang, 'You were a real child-bride, then, eh? I was expecting a girl in her twenties.' In two quick strides he is at Ann's side, 'Very glad to meet you, Ann. No offence, but I guess you must be a little older than that. Here, let me take this heavy bag. You'll be exhausted from your trip,' and before she knows what's happening he's lifting the strap from her shoulder and placing the bag on one of the empty seats at the table.

The other man draws back the chair he has just vacated, saying with a smile, 'How d'you do, Ann? Delighted to make your acquaintance. Please, sit yourself here. Come along, Pete, we'll leave mother and daughter in peace.'

'Righto. Hope to catch you later, Ann.' Pete lopes back to Vivienne's side, saying, 'By for now, then, sweetheart,' before planting a light kiss on her mother's upturned cheek. He then steps aside for the other man, who takes her hand in his and lifts it to his lips. 'Enjoy your afternoon, my dear. Goodbye Ann. Perhaps we'll see you later in the week.'

'Off you go, then, dear boys. Just pop your head into the restaurant on your way, could you? Tell a waiter we'll be ready to order in a couple of minutes. Oh, Constantia - you're here still. Please take that suitcase up to the house, will you? We'll be up later.'

Ann is hovering awkwardly by the empty chair next to her

mother. A mother who hasn't addressed her daughter with so much as single word. She seems more interested in those men. Even the maid is taking precedence over her. Would Vivienne notice if Ann just slipped quietly away? She shuffles backwards till her heel meets a chair leg and she puts out a hand to grasp the top of the curved back, and then lets her eyelids close. Maybe this is all a dream. When she opens her eyes she'll be in her own kitchen. Or maybe...'

'Ann? Oh. There you are! Don't I get a kiss, after all this time?' laughs Vivienne.

'Hello, Vivienne,' she says, keeping her voice steady as she steps forward and places a hand lightly on the thin shoulder. The sharpness of bone through the emerald silk of the shirt sends a shockwave through her own clammy palm. 'Like Grannibelle, before she died,' she thinks and bends forward, clasping the slender, brown-spotted hand and letting her lips rest for a moment on the soft cheek. There are fine lines around its outer edges and below the shaded eyes. She is still beautiful.

Chapter 6

At first it feels to Ann a bit like lunching with the mother of an old school friend, or someone's aunt she's met years back and promised to call on. Putting a visitor at ease, making polite but relaxed conversation is one of the social arts that were expected of a well-brought up young woman, decades ago. Grannibelle succeeded in conveying this skill to her own daughter, but Vivienne never seemed to have any such expectation of Ann, still a graceless teenager at the time of the Betrayal.

No. She must steer her thoughts well away from that episode.

The cool drink of freshly squeezed pineapple and papaya helps to restore her energy levels enough for her to answer Vivienne's questions about the well-being of Graham and the children. A tray of small steaming dishes arrives; spicy tiger prawns, snapper and squid, sweet and sour pork, fried rice and a plateful of a green leaf vegetable that looks a bit like spinach.

'It's called pak choi,' says Vivienne, gesturing towards it with her chopsticks. 'Try it.'

Ann hasn't realised the full extent of her hunger until she inhales the mix of aromas wafting across the table, and finds her mouth is flooded with saliva again. The next few minutes pass in silence, broken occasionally by Vivienne with a brief comment about the food.

'Do you see anything of Colin or Felicity these days?' asks Vivienne at last, raising a napkin to her lips.

'I've had more contact with Colin than Felicity, and that's not been much to speak of either, these last few years. Sad about Colin's divorce, wasn't it?

'I can't really comment on that,' says Vivienne, fiddling with her chopsticks. 'Apart from that somewhat unusual divorce announcement. I presume they sent one to you?'

'Yes, a couple of years ago. It was weird, wasn't it?' says Ann, smiling, 'Something about a congenial 'distance-agreement' between equal partners, rather than a divorce in the traditional sense.'

'I said 'unusual', not 'weird',' says Vivienne, a little sharply. 'Actually, I found the sentiment rather admirable. Far more civilised to remain on friendly terms. If possible.'

'Well, I suppose…' mumbles Ann, turning her head towards the bay, pretending an interest in a small boat that's heading out to sea, its engine spluttering.

It's Vivienne who's keeping the conversation afloat, 'I've not seen Marlene since … oh! Since Edward's funeral.' There's a slight pause, then a brittle laugh as she adds, 'She seems pleasant enough. Quite pretty, in that rather vacuous, perfect-teeth, American cheer-leader way.'

Edward's funeral. The last time she and Vivienne… 'Yes, that was my impression too,' she says, and quickly moves the subject away from that event, 'But still, with two young children…'

'Any marriage break-up has its down-side, as well you know,' says Vivienne dryly.

Ann flushes, 'I didn't mean…' she falters, but Vivienne is smoothly changing the subject once more. It's like a game. 'So, how was your journey, Ann?'

She'll have to mention that she's had a seat next to George on the plane. Vivienne is bound to hear about this from him. Anyway, it'll be interesting to watch her reaction at the mention of his name.

'I spent the flight sitting next to someone who knows you,' she begins.

'Oh?' Vivienne leans forward, smiling.

'George Austin. He's clearly very fond of you.'

Ann is not disappointed by the reaction; Vivienne's smile remains on her face, but it's fixed like a mask. One whole second ticks by. And another …

Ann relents and prepares to speak but Vivienne has recovered her voice, 'Yes. I like him too,' she says warmly. 'His mother, Poppy, is one of my closest friends. She's a great character, though you might find her a bit…unusual. And talking of unusual, what a strange coincidence, meeting George like that. One can find out so much about total strangers on a long journey, I always find.'

41

Ann smiles inwardly at this blatant attempt to discover precisely what George has said to her about their relationship. Reckless now, following her success in unsettling her mother, she continues, 'Oh, that's not how I met him, exactly,' and she gives a lively account of her trolley-scooter escapade, including the decapitated china cow, and George's initial words to her *you stupid child*. She makes no mention the extreme embarrassment she suffered.

Vivienne's peals of laughter are genuine. She even removes her sunglasses to wipe the tears from her eyes, 'Oh, darling, that's the funniest thing I've heard in ages. Poor George! And poor Poppy, robbed of her gift. Though I have to say, a lurid floral animal doesn't really sound like her cup of tea - unless it happened to be a cat.'

Ann almost pinches herself; she keeps her head bent over her plate to hide the ridiculous smile that is playing around her lips as she wonders at her mother's words, *'Darling!* She called me darling!'.

'Do you know..?' continues Vivienne in a tone of surprise, 'I've often felt the urge to do just that – especially at Schipol, but I've never quite let myself. It's not the kind of thing I'd ever have imagined you doing, Ann. Not even as a child.'

'Oh, I'd have been far too afraid of you,' she says, looking across at Vivienne without a trace of rancour.

'Afraid! Of me?' Vivienne's back has straightened and her hands are gripping the edge of the table. 'I suppose I should apologise to you for my total failure as a mother,' she continues with a forced laugh.

'Oh! I didn't mean it like that. It's just, well, I wasn't the most extrovert of children, was I? Or the bravest. I was clumsy, too. Always dropping or breaking things, so…'

'Ann, let's not go on about things like that. We'll have lots of time to talk, over the next few days, and I'm sure you could do with a short rest now. We'll go back to my house and settle you in. It's a bit of a steep climb, I'm afraid, but since there are no cars and no roads, we have no option. It doesn't usually take me more than ten or fifteen minutes.'

Glancing in the other direction at the bustling main street through the village Ann can see that there could be room for cars in single file, but with the shops displaying many of their wares outside, stacked in boxes on a ramshackle assortment of tables beneath colourful banners and posters, red paper lanterns and striped awnings, there's barely room for three pedestrians to walk comfortably abreast down the centre. And that's before they have to scuttle out of the way at the sound of bicycle bells and screeching brakes.

Ann sees that Vivienne is already walking briskly back along the way that she and Constantia had come, an hour or more ago. This time she's noticing how many Westerners there are – a ratio of perhaps one to every two or three of Chinese or Philippine origin. And so many of them seem to know Vivienne, who nods and murmurs, shaking a hand here, touching a forearm or shoulder there, occasionally turning back and gesturing towards Ann, who quickens her pace to draw level with her mother.

'That's the Oasis,' she says as they pass a tiny shop with a glass-fronted counter, and a couple of small tables on the paving. 'Best croissants on the island, and the cheapest. That's Wilson's next to it. Property – to rent or buy. Whenever I have more visitors than I can house, I rent rooms there for them. Younger ones usually prefer it down here anyway. Nearer to the bars.'

For a short stretch, the path becomes a bridge with metal railings on each side, and Ann traces the source of the sudden whiff of ammonia that is clinging to her nostrils: a shallow concrete ditch, smelling of clogged up drains, trickles down to the narrow strip of litter-strewn sand and pebbles. She wrinkles her nose and is about to rejoin her mother when she hears her sudden shout, 'Watch out, Ann!' Just in time, she presses herself against the railing as the rattle and clank of a noisy motor bears down on her.

The narrow vehicle looks like a tall version of a go-cart, and is driven by a grim-faced man in a dark blue jacket, gripping the steering wheel and staring straight ahead as if to say to any pedestrian, 'Live or die - it's up to you!' He's perched at almost tractor height on the pale grey seat of what could have been a discarded chair from the back of some mechanic's workshop and has somehow been attached to the solid metal platform, together with a steering column and a huge gear stick. The major part of the whole contraption is the sturdy, open trailer, like the back of a small jeep, which is piled high with cardboard boxes.

'I should have warned you to watch out for those darned trucks,' says Vivienne. 'I sometimes think we'd be safer here with proper roads and cars. At least they'd have to follow some kind of Highway Code. A law unto themselves, those drivers - most of them anyway.'

As Vivienne pauses and heads to the right, Ann thinks at first that she's making for the baker's just ahead of them. 'No, this way. Up these steps,' says Vivienne. 'I'll show you round all the shops in the village later.'

The flight of steps is steep, and Ann expects Vivienne to pause for breath where the next flight takes a different angle, but her mother appears to be having no difficulty with the climb. To Ann's relief, the stairs give way to a narrow, level path, bordered on the right by a retaining wall of pale grey concrete, festooned with dangling green creepers, and on the left by railings and a view of the flat roof-tops of houses below.

'Watch where you tread,' calls Vivienne, 'Too many bloody dogs on this island. Still, at least that'll be cleared up before nightfall. Without the sweepers we'd all be ankle deep in the stuff.'

Round the next corner, past a cascade of bougainvillea and the sudden sweetness of jasmine, there are more steps. Then a wider, slatted concrete path with a gradient that Ann can feel in the muscles of her calves, followed by yet more, even steeper steps. All are edged on one side by railings in the same regulation dark green paint, and trees or flowering shrubs, and glimpses of gardens with swings and plastic toys, and flat roofed houses, smarter here than those nearer the harbour. Up, up and still up.

Ann's breath is coming in shallow bursts, her tracksuit

trousers are sticking to her waist more with sweat than elastic and her cheeks are burning. How can she beg for a rest when her mother's brisk pace has not altered?

A moment later, Vivienne halts abruptly and points to the greenery on the left of the path, 'Look, the top of that thin trunk – those green fruit? That's papaya – they're nearly ripe. See those enormous leaves, with bunches of green bananas? And that big purple object dangling at the end of what looks like the backbone of a snake? That's a seed head from the same banana tree. Can you believe it?'

To her surprise, Ann finds herself smiling. Her words emerge slowly but uncensored, 'You! It was you who walked me round the garden when we first came to live in Edward's house. You pointed out all the trees and the flowers. The first thing was the stream, of course. And then you took me to the park and showed me how it was the same stream. And it was you, not Edward who taught me the names of the trees there. ...a for ash, b for beech and birch, c for chestnut, and crab-apple, d for... there wasn't a d, was there?'

'Did I teach you that? Oh I'm so glad. I thought it was only Colin.'

Ann banishes her twinge of jealousy. After all, she was the one who'd blocked out this pleasant memory.

'Anyway, we must press on now for the last few yards. My house is just up there on the right. I suggest that you have a good long drink, a quick wash, and then lie down for an hour or so. Not longer, or you'll never adjust to the time difference. Then I'll take you back down and show you the village.'

Ann is barely aware of her surroundings now, as she lets Vivienne steer her through the gateway and along the tiled path to the front door.

Before she knows how she has reached the bedroom, she is letting her head sink down into the pillow and Vivienne's voice from the doorway is telling her that she'll call her within the hour.

She's being more motherly than I can ever remember, thinks Ann. Her warm glow of pleasure is quickly followed by a niggling

45

doubt – maybe it's her own memories that need adjusting? No. Vivienne was never a proper mother. She didn't even like being called Mummy.

Ann is pulling away from the edge of sleep and drifting into the Norfolk time. Vivienne was hardly ever there in those days – Grannibelle was the one who did everything for her, and sometimes Uncle Harry did things too, like teaching her to swim and helping her make a den at the bottom of the garden behind the chestnut tree and even when it rained you could sit in it and not get wet.

Most other families had a man who would be there at breakfast and bedtime every day and all day on Sundays, and he'd be called Daddy. Her own daddy had been drowned before she was born, and 'drowned' meant dead-and-gone-to-heaven, but she knew that he was living at the bottom of the sea and he always came out at low tide to lie in the sun with the seals. When she told Uncle Harry this he said, 'By God, why didn't I think of that myself!' and he started to tell her a story about seal people called Selkies. Uncle Harry was her favourite man, even though he wasn't there very much but there were lots of other men that she liked too - the man at the station who blew the whistle and made sure all the doors were shut tight, and a different one in the ticket office. And the man who delivered groceries for Grannibelle, and the seal-boat man and lots more when you come to think of it.

And then, when she was a bit bigger, there was the man who turned out to be Edward. At first Ann didn't think he was nice at all because he kept taking Vivienne out in his sailing boat, not just on Sundays but Saturdays too, which wasn't fair because on Mondays Vivienne went on the train to Norwich to do her job and usually stayed there till Friday. Vivienne always looked pretty and sometimes she was chatty and laughed a lot and sometimes she hardly spoke at all, but she almost always took Ann shopping on Saturdays and then to a café in Sherringham where they sat side by side on high wooden stools and Vivienne had a pot of tea and a scone and Ann had a Knickerbocker Glory in a tall thin glass, and scooped up the melting bit at the bottom with a long metal spoon.

Chapter 7

'Mmm, delicious!' says Ann, wiping the light pastry crumbs from her lips. 'I never knew that custard tarts could taste like this.'

They are sitting at a small round table outside the tiny shop that Vivienne had pointed out to her on their way back from lunch. A throng of passengers from the late afternoon ferry is streaming down the pier in an almost solid block that quickly disperses into smaller groups striding or strolling along the harbour front towards them.

'Have another,' says Vivienne, pushing the plate of pale gold tarts across the table. 'We've plenty of time. The shops won't close till after seven and I've told Constantia we won't be wanting our supper before eight, so there's no danger of you spoiling your appetite.'

Ann smiles inwardly: 'spoiling ones appetite' ranked high on the list of childhood 'don'ts', somewhere above 'putting elbows on the table', or 'speaking with your mouth full', but well below the totally forbidden 'accepting sweets from strangers' or 'swimming out of your depth'.

'Yes, I know,' smiles Vivienne, guessing her thoughts, 'it's that mother thing, isn't it? Take it from me; one can never entirely shake it off. I expect you're the same with your two.'

No, says Ann to herself. Not at all the same. I have real bonds with Lou and Danny. But she smiles back, saying aloud, 'Maybe. I've never really thought about it. They do sometimes complain about their dad treating them like children still.'

'You're right – I can't deny it, so I won't even try,' Vivienne holds up her hands in a gesture of mock-surrender, and attempts a laugh, but there's a bitter note in her voice.

'What do you mean, I'm right? I'm not accusing you of anything.'

'Not in so many words. But I'm not stupid. I'm well aware that I've been totally inadequate as a mother from the moment you were born – and before.'

47

'But I…'

'Ann, please. Let me say what I have to say,' she pauses, and when Ann catches her eye and nods, she continues, 'I wasn't well at all while I was carrying you. You know that, don't you? I dare say that wouldn't have helped matters – but it was more likely to be the way things were between me and your father at that time. It really started to go wrong when Leslie got a sales job and was out on the road a lot – I didn't trust him one hundred percent – he was…well, let's just say, he had a roving eye. Up till then, he'd been running a business of his own, or rather, a variety of businesses - and then, when he was drowned…'

Ann bites her lip. She's never actually thought of her father as anything more than that – her father, tragically drowned before she was born. Has she really never thought of him as Vivienne's first husband – about the reality of their relationship?

Almost reluctantly, she brings her attention back to what her mother is saying, '… such terrible guilt, I nearly went out of my mind, so…'

'But it wasn't your fault! It *was* an accident. A freak tide, off-shore wind…'

'I know,' sighs Vivienne, 'But our home was in Norwich then. We hadn't formally separated, though I was spending more and more time in Cley with your Grandma. If Les hadn't driven over that Sunday to try and get me to go back with him, we wouldn't have had that row and he wouldn't have stormed off and got drunk …' her voice drops to a whisper.

Ann has to strain to hear her words. It's almost as though her mother has forgotten that she's there, and is merely thinking aloud, 'I have to admit, I knew he was a bit of a rogue when I first met him. Maybe that was part of the attraction. But what a vile temper, when he'd had too many drinks! In spite of everything, I did love him. I really loved him. We had such times - such fun! It didn't make sense, him being dead.' She sighs again, then adds in a rush, 'Ann, I'm not trying to make excuses for being a less than perfect mother, but what with one thing and another…'

'I know. I know…' falters Ann. She hadn't expected to feel like this. 'It must have been really tough for you when I was little. And I did have Grannibelle.'

'Yes. You did have her. She took to you right from the start. In fact, if truth be told, you had more of her than I ever did.' Vivienne glances down at the crumbs on her plate, then she lifts her head with a quick, bright smile, 'Sun's over the yard arm,' she declares, gesturing towards the large red disc above the horizon. 'I don't know about you, but I could do with a real drink. They know how to mix a proper cocktail there.'

Ann hesitates. Maybe alcohol will loosen Vivienne's tongue even more – get her talking about George, or Stuart and their break-up, 'I…Yes. I've probably had enough tea, myself.'

'We'll move on to the Harbour Bar. We can watch the sun setting over the sea. Corny, I know, but it always gets to me.'

Perhaps alcohol wasn't such a good idea after all, thinks Ann. She's still only half way through her first glass of white wine, but it's a larger one than she's used to and it's having a fuzzying effect on her jet-lagged brain. Vivienne has already downed two large cocktails of goodness knows what lethal levels and combinations of alcohol, and has just ordered a third. Her tongue has certainly been loosened, but not on the subject Ann is most interested in hearing about. Her confessional mood has become less soul searching, and now she seems to be set on justifying her own callous behaviour all those years ago.

'Don't get me wrong. This is in no way a criticism of you. In fact, quite the reverse, really,' she is saying to Ann, when the cheerful Australian in frayed denim shorts who's been serving their table, places another colourful drink into her outstretched hand, 'Thank you, Brucie, darling. You take such good care of me. And don't forget to tell me when you've finished with that no-good girlfriend of yours,' she adds with a deep throaty laugh. 'I don't know if I can wait around for you much longer.'

As the young man chuckles and strolls back to the bar, Vivienne says, 'No need to look so po-faced, dear. These youngsters enjoy a bit of teasing. And whatever you might think, I'm not interested in boys young enough to be my grandchildren. I don't even know his name, or I'd have introduced you properly.'

'I thought I heard you call him Brucie,' she says. 'Or are all Aussies Bruce to you?'

'Did I call him that? Maybe they are, then. I didn't really notice. Anyway, what were we talking about, before whatever-his-name-is brought me a top-up of reviving liquor? You must be ready for another yourself, by now. Shall I call him back?'

'I'm all right, thanks,' she says, trying not to sound too prim.

'Very well, then. Where was I? Oh, yes. The eternal subject of Love with a capital L. I believe I was attempting to get you to understand how it was that I ...that I...Well, you know *what* I did, but you don't...you can't...' Vivienne is twiddling the little paper parasol from her drink round and round between finger and thumb, as she stares down into her half empty glass. 'Look, Ann, I could be completely wrong, but I don't think you've ever let yourself be overtaken by blind passion – not for Graham, anyway. Don't forget, I met him at the same time as you did – that tedious garden party of Edward's. He was a nice enough boy, but he didn't exactly ooze sex appeal then, did he? Nor years later, either - though maybe funerals aren't exactly the time for displays of marital passion. You must have been married, what, eight...ten years by the time of Mother's death?'

Vivienne falls silent. There's a tiny pulsing muscle above her tight-set jaw line.

Grannibelle's funeral! Something that Vivienne had tried to tell her...No! Not now. Not yet.

'I'm trying to explain...' Vivienne's voice trails away again as she glances at Ann, then takes a deep breathe, 'Stuart ...what I felt. What we both felt. If you've never experienced that...How could you ever understand? I was swept away, hook, line and sinker.'

Ann juggles the words around in her head, *Hooker. Liar. Stinker!* She smiles in perverse amusement, before saying quietly, 'You don't need to explain yourself to me, Vivienne. It's your life, isn't it? Probably no really lasting damage done. Except to

Edward. And I did my best to make it up to Colin. He's turned out OK, on the whole hasn't he?'

'And you, Ann? What about you?'

'Oh, me? I was fine. Why wouldn't I be? Virtually sixteen – quite old enough to cope. And anyway, you were always rather …'

'Rather…?'

'Let's just say, we didn't talk much, did we, you and me? Look, I really didn't come all the way here to criticise you for leaving me. *Us*. I was worried about you. Colin said… he said you were really upset, so…'

'Upset!' exclaims Vivienne with a brittle laugh, 'Of course I was bloody upset. But that was immediately after Stuart had told me he was dumping me. I'd downed the best part of a bottle of gin, and was wallowing in self pity when I picked up the phone to Colin, poor lad. Didn't take me long to pull myself together. As you'll have gathered already, there are plenty of other fish in the sea. And anyway, it was good while it lasted – or most of that while. Thirty seven years is a long time to hang on to a man you love. I'm not complaining, now it's come to an end. C'est la vie, as they say,' and she starts to sing in a croaky imitation of Piaf, 'Non, Je ne regret rien…'

'It's great that you're taking it all in such a positive way…' Ann falters as she looks across at Vivienne and sees the sardonic smile appear again.

'Liar!' laughs Vivienne, not unkindly. '"Got her come-uppance at last", that's what you were thinking. Go on, admit it.'

She's doing it again, thinks Ann ruefully: turning the tables on me, as usual. At the same time, she has to admit to a grudging admiration for this woman. Nothing seems to put her down for long. And she can't deny that when Colin had phoned her with the news, her sympathy for Vivienne was diluted by less charitable thoughts. But there's one thing Vivienne got wrong: Ann does know what it's like to be swept away by blind passion. She's never forgotten those months with Max-the-Bastard, and she's not about to enlighten Vivienne on the subject.

51

She lifts her glass and defiantly drains it in two large gulps. Then she looks her mother straight in the eyes and begins to laugh, quietly at first, but when Vivienne joins in, Ann finds herself unable to stop.

'What a delightful scene,' exclaims a man's voice, 'Mother and daughter having fun together. Quite charming!' It's the English man from the restaurant at lunch time.

'Hello again, Julian, dear. Good evening, Pete,' gasps Vivienne, struggling to recover her breath. 'I'd ask you to join us for a drink, but I'm just about to take Ann for a quick tour of the village before everything shuts. She's not seen my own little shop yet, and then we've got to get back to the house. Constantia will have a splendid meal ready for us, and I can't risk upsetting her. She sulks dreadfully if I don't show enough appreciation of her cooking – and you both know what a jewel of a cook she is.'

'We surely do,' says Pete, patting his stomach.

'I'll catch up with you both later in the week,' says Vivienne, stumbling a little as she rises to her feet. 'I'd like to organise a little gathering for Ann, here. Just a few friends, if you'd like to come? Poppy, of course. And George is over again for a while. Maybe lunch on Sunday? If it stays fine we could picnic on the boat.'

'Lovely, Darling. Just let us know,' says Julian, then adds, 'Must you really be off now? We'll borrow these seats then, if you don't mind. Keep them warm for you in case you decide on another drink before you head off up the hill.'

'On the other hand,' drawls Pete, 'since you two ladies are deserting us, maybe we'll have found a couple of replacements by the time you get back.'

Boat! Shop! What else? thinks Ann, letting Vivienne take her arm as they step down onto the path and head towards the bustle and noise of the narrow main street.

Chapter 8

It's eleven o'clock before Ann finally snuggles down under the crisp cotton sheet. Her head is floating pleasantly a little way above her curled body which is feeling so heavy with sleep she knows she only has to let her eyelids drop and she'll be ...

Her eyes won't close, though. They're wide open. 'Bet you blink before I do,' says Max, staring fixedly at her from the airline cushion next to hers. The air she breathes is his exhaled breath.

'Funny,' she says, 'I always thought your eyes were blue, not brown. Your hair's got darker too. I rather like it. Why did you leave me, Max?'

'If you start crying you'll have to blink and I'll be the winner,' says Max. His voice is husky and his dark pupils become huge. 'You don't want that, do you? I know what you do want, though.'

Her hand strays down. She wakes at the wetness of her own touch. It's years since Max has forced his way into her dreams like this. Go away, you bastard, she mutters, go away.

She fumbles for the bedside clock; it tells her that she's been asleep for nearly two hours. She's awake fully, now, and on edge. It's the jet-lag, the disorientation, the surprises that Vivienne has been springing on her since her arrival on Lamma Island, one after another. Ann set out on this journey in order bring comfort to her mother. She'd expected to find her almost suicidal in her grief at being deserted by her partner, and what does she discover? Vivienne is doing very nicely, thank you.

She has lots of friends, some of them personable men a good ten years younger than herself. She has her own little boutique selling a range of unusual but inexpensive clothes, both formal and casual: dresses, skirts and tops in glowing silks, embroidered or plain, alongside hand-painted or tie-dyed cottons, or classy linens, all in an eclectic mix of fashions and fabric - Chinese, Indian and European. 'We'll come here again tomorrow and you can browse at your leisure, Ann. It's about time I gave you some presents after all these years,' she said.

And then there's the boat. 'It's what they call a company junk,' she told her. 'Poppy and I bought it together a few years ago. It has two cabins, a couple of showers and a huge area for entertaining. They had something along these lines, I think, way back in the late twenties and early thirties, when Grandma Belle and your grandfather were out here. We have a mooring in Aberdeen harbour. Maybe we can arrange for George to meet us there if we get the ferry across.'

Ann won't think about George just yet. It was a stroke of luck to have found someone so pleasant and easy to talk to during the long flight, and it had certainly helped to have him going with her to the ferry terminal. A brief encounter, that's all it was – or it would have been, if it hadn't turned out that George has some kind of connection with Vivienne – there's definitely a mystery to be unravelled there.

And there's more to find out yet about Stuart's desertion. Thirty-seven years, they'd been together! Something must have happened to cause that break-up – and Vivienne has to be feeling more than she's showing, surely?

Behind her closed eyelids, Ann sees a sudden vivid picture of Vivienne lying curled up on the summerhouse couch, and her stomach lurches with that mix of bewilderment and fear at the realisation that her mother is crying.

Funny, how selective memory is. How is it that she's blocked out almost everything since then but Edward's face when he gives his step-daughter the devastating news, 'She's left us.'?

It didn't happen quite like that, though, did it? It wasn't news for Ann.

There was the time she'd seen that man again, the Dirk Bogarde man who'd passed her on the pavement just outside their house, the afternoon she'd found her mother crying. Had they been trying to break off their affair? Was that the reason for his noble, doomed expression and her tears?

That was in April. The second time was when she'd seen him near the park, by the entrance closest to their road. It was a few weeks after the O Levels were finished. June or July. He was pretending to be watching the ducks on the pool at the edge of the short strip of road that led to Wyndley gate. Ann was taking Colin to the open air swimming pool after school, and he'd wanted her to stop and let him open the bag that had the sandwiches in so he could tear the crusts off his and throw them to the baby swans.

'Cygnets, they're called,' she said, 'No, you can't. We'll save them for the way back.'

It was a scorching, windless afternoon, and she couldn't wait to reach the rectangle of clear blue water. The paving slabs all round it would be hot under her bare soles before she jumped in, and warm on the back of her thighs when she hauled herself out and sat for a while, splashing her feet. Then she'd have to drag Colin out, and get him to follow her over to the prickly grass bank surrounded by trees, where they could sit and eat the picnic tea that Mummy had made them: egg sandwiches and cheese triangles and mini chocolate rolls wrapped in blue and silver foil. Enough for Mummy too, because Daddy was staying late at work and she'd been going to walk there with them, but then she said she'd got a few jobs to finish first and she'd join them later.

How had Ann known that the man was only pretending an interest in ducks? She must have put two and two together after she and Colin had gone through the gate into the proper Park, and a black spaniel puppy scampered straight past them, making for the duck pond. Of course they'd turned to watch its progress. And Ann saw that the man was now striding over the grass on the other side of the strip of tarmac, towards a woman in a flowery skirt and a white peasant blouse and it was Vivienne, coming to walk with them, after all. How pretty she is, thought Ann, half proud, and, for some reason, half afraid.

Soon after this, Vivienne took to going for a run in the park about half past seven or eight, after the evening meal. 'Wait a bit, I'll come with you darling,' she heard Edward say, the first time. Ann was on the landing, about to come downstairs and wander into the garden after reading to Colin. It was always harder to settle him when the evenings stayed light for so long and their garden blackbird was belting out its full repertoire of tunes from the top of the copper beech at the far end of the lawn. It sounded as loud as if a microphone was fixed to the dark foliage near its open beak. The singing would be echoed back from other trees in other gardens. It made her feel melty and sad in a contented kind of way. The whole of her adult life lay ahead, and soon she'd know about all the secret things that up till now she'd been too young to understand.

'Sweetheart, I'm going to run, not walk,' she heard Vivienne say in the bubbling, laughing voice she used when she was playing with Colin. 'We can have a little stroll together when I've got rid of some of my excess energy. I won't be long.'

By the time Ann had reached the bottom step, the front door had banged shut. 'I'll have a walk with you, Dad,' she said.

'Thank you, Ann, but I don't think I really feel like walking now,' he'd sighed, opening the door of the living room. 'You're very kind to your old dad,' he added with a laugh.

She'd sat and watched the news with him, feeling that she should apologise, but not quite knowing what for.

This was the start of a hot spell. Vivienne went out for a run nearly every evening for the next three weeks. Edward didn't ask to go with her again.

Ann didn't know if Edward knew. She didn't exactly 'know' herself. Mummy still looked quite young but she'd had her birthday in January and she was forty! Edward was even older than her. Twelve or thirteen years. Surely people in their forties and fifties didn't...

But the Dirk Bogarde man wasn't very old. Eileen was the oldest in her own class at school and she was going out with a man of nearly thirty. She wasn't a virgin any more. You couldn't be, with a boyfriend that age. Most of the other girls were still virgins even though some pretended they weren't. Would she ever find someone who'd be prepared to do IT with her?

You don't have to worry about that, Eileen had told her. Lots of boys try to sleep with the ugly girls because they're a bit scared of the pretty ones. Ann didn't know yet if this was true. She hoped it was. There had to be some advantage in looking like…like she could balance a tea-cup on her chin.

But her own mother! Bad enough to think of her doing it with Edward still, let alone a man who looked like he could be going out with someone Eileen's age.

If Ann really didn't want to think about it, why did she slip out one evening, and wait by the alleyway that ran along the side of their garden, while Vivienne went upstairs to change into her running clothes?

Why did she follow her at a safe distance, as she entered the park? Why navigate the open ground by dodging behind clumps of blazing gorse with its coconut scent? And why then, when the slim figure in the white tennis shorts, her dark ponytail bouncing as she jogged along the tarmac path, edged by towering banks of ancient holly, why then did she creep, a little way behind, through the almost-caverns created by their thin, twisted trunks? Why, if she really didn't want to know?

The wide path leads straight uphill though the woods and will soon bring them out onto another stretch of open heath-land. But Vivienne doesn't continue upwards – she turns sharp right along a narrow track of hard, packed mud between birch saplings and the spindly trunks of the holly.

That's enough, Ann tells herself. Time to go back.

But she doesn't go back, though it's harder now to keep out of sight. A single large beech affords more cover, and she leans against it, catching her breath. She's played like this with Colin often enough. He was the fox or the bear she was tracking. She knows there're more large trees a little way ahead - sweet chestnut and pine beyond thickets of bramble and new, low growth of holly.

She scurries forward, stooping with knees bent, aware of the crunch and rustle of the beech mast and sharp, dry leaves. She reaches the safe, rough bark of chestnut trunk. Peers round.

Jerks her head back. Heat rushes up from her chest to her face. She feels sick. Icy cold.

She has no idea how long she's been standing there, numb. Gradually, the whispers and murmuring that she hears as

57

background noises like the wind in grass, grow louder, become audible words. Her mother's voice,

'Darling, I can't. You know that,' a long pause, another whisper, then, pleading, 'What we have is so wonderful, can't we just keep it this way?'

The man's voice is just as she'd imagined, warm and deep. If a blackbird was suddenly turned into a man, it would sound like this. 'Don't cry. I can't bear it. You're right. I'll stop asking for the moon. It's just...'

A brief silence. More whispers.

'You know it's not *him*, don't you? Not Edward. It's my little boy.'

'Bring him with you. And the girl. Anything you want. I'll do anything...'

'Stop it. Stop it!' she's almost shouting now. 'You know it's impossible. For God's sake, he's a divorce lawyer - he'll know exactly what to do...'

My little boy. That's what she said. Ann is merely 'the girl'. It's Colin who's keeping Vivienne from leaving.

Chapter 9

'Ann!' calls Vivienne, ' It's Graham. You'd better come down and use the phone in my room.'

'What time is it?' croaks Ann as she lurches into Vivienne's bedroom.

'Nearly ten o'clock,' says Vivienne and hands her the receiver before leaving the room and shutting the door behind her.

'Sorry if I've woken you, Ann,' says Graham, 'I thought you'd be bound to be awake by now, and I wanted to catch you before you went out for the day.'

'That's OK,' she mumbles, trying to stifle yawn. 'I must have slept right through. What time is it with you? Oh my God, it must be about two in the morning! Couldn't you sleep?'

There's a brief silence, broken by a long sigh from Graham.

Ann tries to speak, but her tongue is glued to the roof of her mouth. Her voice, when she finds it at last, is almost a shriek, 'Is it Lou? Danny? What's happened?'

'Calm down,' says Graham, sounding petulant, 'It's nothing to do with them.'

Ann collapses onto Vivienne's bed. The receiver is still in her hand but it's several inches from her ear and Graham's voice is not trumpeting in his usual telephone way. When she realises that he's telling her something about work, she feels a spurt of anger, but before she can voice her feelings his words begin to sink in, 'So he said that they've most regretfully got to let me go. The bastard. Never did like the jumped up little sod.' He's being fired, she thinks in utter amazement. Graham's been given the sack. Graham! After all these decades of irreproachable service. And he's only two or three years away from retirement.

'Oh Darling,' she says, 'How dreadful for you. I can't believe it!'

'Have to say, I've seen it coming for a few months now. Just didn't expect it to happen like this. Thought they'd maybe shunt me off into a siding and keep me on low grade stuff for my final few years.'

What can you say to someone from this distance? If she'd been at home, she'd have flung her arms round him in a hug.

'Hello! Ann! You still there?'

No, she thinks, she wouldn't have been able to touch him, or bring him any comfort, not straight away. 'Yes, I'm here, Graham. I'm just stunned, that's all. I had no idea the firm was in such trouble.'

'Maybe if you'd bothered to take more notice of me when I attempted to give the odd hint or two...' he lets his voice trail away into another sigh.

'But you never said a word! Nothing that indicated the slightest...'

'Precisely. I rest my case. You didn't notice a thing. As usual. Too concerned about yourself and your new friends at that centre for illiterates.'

Not the moment to ask him, yet again, not to use that word about the people she works with! 'But Graham, when did...?'

'I don't suppose you even noticed, did you? The fact that I've been coming home much earlier these last few weeks? You didn't, did you?' He goes on, relentlessly working himself into a rage at her for his mistreatment by those he could not rail against in person. 'Or if that did actually penetrate your awareness, you didn't think of putting two and two together and - '

'But Graham, I did...'

'Did notice? Or did think?'

'Yes. I mean...'

'Oh, what's the use of talking anyway? There's nothing you can do to change the situation. This call will be costing a fortune, and we've got to start watching the pennies in earnest now. This has upset all my careful plans for budgeting for my retirement. I just thought I'd better put you in the picture right away.'

'Yes, Graham. Thank you. It can't have been an easy phone call to make.' Or to receive, she adds silently. 'Still, I'm sure we'll manage all right.'

'I suppose so,' he says, his tone less belligerent now that he's

60

managing to make her feel bad.

Maybe she'll be able to let this call drift to a halt, 'Well, anyway, I hope you got the message on the answer phone. I wanted to let you know I'd got here safely, but I didn't want to ring you at work.'

'Wouldn't have made too much difference, as it turns out,' he mutters, then gives a bitter laugh.

She's struggling to find suitable words to fill the lengthening silence, when he adds, 'So when is it you're due to come back, then, Ann? It'll be my last day this Friday.' Another long pause, then with unconvincing heartiness, 'It would be nice to have some company at the weekend.'

Oh Lord! Just when she's beginning to enter into a communication, of sorts, with her mother. And there are a still mysteries to be solved, not to speak of her new friend to become re-acquainted with.

'Are you listening to me, Ann? I said it would be nice to have some company for the first weekend of the end of my working life.' That bitter laugh again.

It's terrible for him, of course it is, thinks Ann. But oh…that familiar sinking feeling. 'I did hear you, Graham,' she says gently. 'I was just trying to work things out. I mean, when we were planning this you said…'

'*We* were planning! I don't recall being involved in your decision in any way at all.'

Ann clenches her hand around the receiver, 'You were the one who said it would hardly be worth travelling all this way for less than a fortnight, and it was me who cut it down to just over a week. The fact is,' she continues, lowering her voice, 'I am still worried about Vivienne. She's in quite a state. I have an awful feeling that she'd take it badly if I turn tail and run back home as soon as I've arrived. It would seem like a total rejection, so…'

'And my feelings don't count. I understand perfectly, Ann. Don't give it another thought. I'm sorry to have disturbed you. Goodbye.'

'Oh, bloody hell, Graham,' she mutters as she hears the click

61

of the receiver. 'Now what do I do?' She sighs deeply as the guilt seeps in. She shouldn't have exaggerated Vivienne's state, like that. Oh all right then, lied. She shouldn't have lied. Vivienne doesn't seem heartbroken, exactly. But on the other hand…

'Everything all right, Ann?' asks Vivienne, stepping into the room.

After the situation has been explained to her, she says, 'It would be rather a shame if you have to dash straight back to hold his hand. He'll be feeling a whole lot better after he's had some sleep. Things always look their blackest in the small hours of the morning.'

'Thanks, Vivienne,' she mumbles, feeling immediately better herself. 'I expect you're right.'

'I'm sure of it,' she smiles. 'Men are surprisingly similar in some ways, and as you know I've had close experience of a few. Your own poor father was a very different character from Edward, and Stuart was different again, but I could extract more or less the same responses from each one of them, just by using one or two very simple techniques. And, no, I don't mean sex,' she adds with a laugh. 'Come on now. We'll have some breakfast, and then I'm taking you shopping.'

Ann shuffles the hangers along the tightly packed rails, but she can't imagine herself trying on anything in front of the full-length mirror in the tiny, curtained alcove. Every time she plucks up the courage to finger one of the shirts or dresses, the smiling young Chinese woman, whom Vivienne has introduced as Alice, says, 'You like this one, yes?'

She'd looked so crestfallen when Ann had shaken her head that now, if Alice is standing near her when she ventures to look more closely at a garment, she just smiles and nods and lets Alice place it on the growing pile on the back of the chair next to the counter.

'Have you found anything you like, yet?' says Vivienne, breezing back into the shop a good twenty minutes after saying, 'I need a quick word with the owner of the bookshop. He knows a lad who can come up to the house and fix my computer sometime this week. Then I'll be able to send emails again.'

Before Ann can speak, Alice is saying, 'See, Vivienne, all these clothes Miss Ann is choosing.'

Vivienne looks quizzically at the heap on the chair. Ann raises her shoulders and opens her palms. 'Everything is really lovely, but…'

'I know. It can be hard to know where to start. I've got far too much stock, really, but when I'm on a buying trip I tend to get carried away. Alice, put all those things away again, then follow me. Ann, you sit yourself down there for a bit. We're going to start from scratch.'

Ann watches in a daze as Vivienne strides over to a rail near the door, flicks through the hangers, and removes a couple of skirts which she hands to Alice. Every few moments, she holds a dress or a shirt at arm's length under Ann's chin, and, head to one side, lips pursed, examines the effect of its colour on her daughter's skin-tone.

Ann finds that her shoulders are hunched up almost to her neck, with her arms and elbows tucked against her ribs and her fists clenched. As soon as she becomes aware of her posture, she takes a few deep breaths, glancing around to check that no one else has noticed her momentary transformation into a small child.

There had been more to those Saturday shopping trips than Knickerbocker Glories. From time to time, they became nightmare expeditions for new clothes to keep pace with her childhood growth spurts, sometimes having to venture as far as Jarrolds in Norwich. It was bad enough to intercept the glances and raised eyebrows of the slim, superior shop assistants, and their sympathetic tones when they addressed the beautiful Vivienne, 'The little girl is well built for her age, isn't she, Madam? I'm not sure we have one of those in her size.'

But it was worse, far worse, a few years later, on those occasions when Felicity accompanied them to the shopping centre in Sutton Coldfield. 'There aren't any colours that look good on you, silly,' she'd hiss, out of earshot of her stepmother. 'They're only saying blue suits you cos they want to get rid of that vile dress that no one else would be seen dead in.'

'Don't look so worried, Ann!' Vivienne laughs. 'You'll be trying these on in total privacy. I won't peep, I promise. And I'm pretty sure you're going to be pleasantly surprised.'

She's right, thinks Ann. Yet another surprise – and a good deal more pleasant than the one she woke to this morning. No need to think of that yet. Graham will still be asleep. Anyway, as Vivienne has explained, they can stroll along to the bookshop that doubles as an internet café and she'll compose a nice, comforting email to Graham. So for now, she can let herself enjoy the unusual experience of trying on skirts, trousers and tops that are not only extremely comfortable, but that also seem to make her skin appear less like overworked raw pastry than usual. Maybe it helps that she actually feels like smiling at her reflection in this short-sleeved dusky-pink silk shirt and dark blue denim skirt.

She pulls back the curtain and hovers at the entrance, 'Would it be all right to have these?' she asks.

'See!' exclaims Vivienne in triumph. 'What did I tell you? How do you think I've managed to build up such a successful business? It's flair, that's what it is. I can spot the exact styles and colours that'll bring out the best in each individual customer. Now get back in there and try on the rest.'

Three quarters of an hour later, when they leave the shop, Ann has extended her store of clothing by: two pairs of plain cotton trousers, one white, one black; one pair of jeans in soft, light denim; two skirts; several shirts, blouses and T shirts and a shirtwaist dress in plain olive-green silk. 'We'll do our shoe-shopping tomorrow,' says Vivienne. 'We'll get the ferry over to Central and then Kowloon, maybe. You can't come to Hong Kong without at least one trip to the main shopping areas.'

They are on their way to the bookshop café when Ann pauses for a moment to look at the collection of bangles, pendants and ear-rings on the table outside a gift and accessories shop. She doesn't notice the girl chatting in the doorway to a young man in frayed denim shorts, until she hears her call out, 'Hiya, Viv! How you doing?'

Ann glances back towards the street as her mother answers, 'I'm well, thank you, Dawn.'

Dawn! So this must be George's mother's shop. Ann turns and smiles at the girl, as Vivienne continues with a laugh, 'And is that young Bruce you're making eyes at there? I have to warn you, he's spoken for.'

Dawn is returning Ann's smile and Vivienne says, 'Don't tell me you two have met already!' Then she lays her hand on Ann's arm, 'Dawn seems to have a talent for getting to know everyone who sets foot on this island. She's running the shop for my friend, Poppy while the manager is away.'

'You coming in to have a look?' asks Dawn.

'Later, perhaps,' says Vivienne. 'Ann has to send an email first.'

'OK. I better get back to work myself, or Poppy'll be after me,' she laughs. 'See you, then Annie. See you, Viv.'

As they continue their way along the bustling narrow street, Dawn shouts after them, 'Tell her from me, she's a real slave driver, your - '

The rest of her words are lost in the high pitched jabber of voices from an open shop-front.

Chapter 10

Please don't take it the wrong way when I say that I'm worried about Vivienne. It doesn't mean I'm not thinking about you too but if I come home now and then she gets ill I'd feel dreadful.

To be fair, that's not too far from the truth - how can she know what's going on beneath her mother's brittle smiles. As soon as she's finished this email, she can dash off a quick message to Lou and then to Danny, so at the very least Graham might get a phone call, if not a visit, from Brighton, and an email, if not a phone call, from Japan.

There's a sudden burst of laughter from the back of the shop. No mistaking Vivienne's more raucous tone above the deeper chuckle from the man. Mmm... now that's a thought! She's smiling as she types the next words, *Unless I can persuade Vivienne to come back with me for a few weeks instead.*

But the next idea that presents itself follows on with remorseless logic: since Graham isn't going to be tied down to a job any more, why shouldn't he be the one to make the journey?

No! This is her adventure - her chance to find out more, not just about her mother and George, but herself. Things seem to have been happening in her own head ever since she boarded the plane from Amsterdam – and it can't just be the new clothes that are making her feel almost a stranger to herself.

But who knows? If Graham does come out here, things might change for him, too. Maybe they'll actually be able to talk to each other. Really talk.

They are on the roof terrace of her mother's three-storey house, and Ann is tussling with the wooden frame of an old-fashioned canvas deckchair. She's just helped Vivienne manoeuvre a huge parasol out through the door at the top of the steep flight of stairs that leads to the roof.

'We can't use this when it's windy, of course, but it's a real sun trap up here - in the full sun you could burn very quickly, even in this hazy type of cloud. I thought you might prefer to relax here, rather than traipse along to the beach – there'll be plenty of time for that in the next few days, so long as this weather holds.'

'It's lovely!' exclaims Ann, strolling over to the low wall, and looking down across the roof tops of the sprawling village to the sheltered bay with its assortment of small boats, and the low, wooded hill on its far side. 'What's that over there - the other side of the hill?' she asks, pointing towards a couple of tall, thin chimneys.

'Listen,' says Vivienne, and at first Ann thinks she didn't hear the question. 'No, I mean it. Listen for a moment and then tell me what you can hear in the background.'

Ann peers towards the hill. A dog barks from somewhere down in the village. There are snatches of bird song, like the ones she might hear back home on a summer's day: woodpigeons; some kind of tits or finches; and could that be the mewling of a buzzard? Then a distant screech of cycle brakes. The chug, chug of an approaching ferry. She's about to turn her questioning face to Vivienne, when a deeper, more rhythmic noise enters her awareness and she realises it's been there all the time, a muffled thud, thup, thup, thud thup thup.

'Yes, it's surprising, isn't it? The one sound that never ceases, day or night, is the hardest one for the ear to detect. It's from the power station just beyond that hill. For me, it typifies the contrasts that are the essence of Hong Kong. You'll see what I mean when I take you to that beach. Now then, where did we put the cool-box? I could do with a drink.'

They sit side by side in the shade of the parasol, Vivienne with a glass of white wine, Ann with fresh lemonade made that morning by Constantia, who is now off for the afternoon.

'So! Isn't this nice?' says Vivienne brightly, topping up her almost empty glass, 'Just the two of us!'

Oh Lord! What's coming now? Ann feels her heart begin to thud, drowning the background rhythm from the power station. More justifications for her desertion all those years ago? The very thought of a heart to heart with her mother about that terrible time, fills her with dread. *Quick, think of a safer subject.*

But Vivienne is speaking again, her voice unusually low and hesitant, 'Ann, you remember, after Edward's funeral, I tried to...'

'Yes, yes. I know I wasn't exactly friendly. I'm sorry, but I ...'

'No need for *you* to apologise. I understand how you must have felt at the time. No, no – I'm the one at fault. I shouldn't have left it so late – and that was definitely not the time or place to try and tell you something so complicated.' She pauses as she swallows another large gulp of wine and gives a shaky laugh.

Ann only becomes aware that she's been holding breath when she finds herself taking a quick, shallow gasp, before asking 'What kind of something?'

'Don't look so worried, Ann,' Vivienne says in a lighter tone. 'It's nothing too dreadful, but it will come as a bit of a shock. I expect you knew that your grandmother wanted to talk to me before she died. I don't suppose she told you what was in that package she'd prepared for me?'

Ann shakes her head, bemused.

'She must have known she wouldn't see me again,' sighs Vivienne. 'It was full of letters and papers and an album with photos of Hong Kong. I didn't open it till I was on the plane back here. It took me quite a while to take it all in, and then, well, it's not the sort of thing one would discuss on the phone, and I thought, well, I thought maybe I might make a special journey and pay you a visit, but...'

There's a long silence. 'But' indeed, thinks Ann, recalling her feelings at the time. Vivienne hadn't hung around for long after Grannibelle's funeral – in fact, she'd disappeared almost as fast as she had after Edward's.

At last, Vivienne asks, 'What about the album - did she ever show you that?'

'She used to show me lots of old albums when we lived in Norfolk, but there was one that I couldn't find after the funeral,' says Ann, feeling on safer ground, now that there was something concrete to focus on - something that could hold the shock at bay for a few more moments. 'I'd never seen it before she brought it with her when she came to stay with us in Penns Lane, before she died. It was really important to her, I think. She kept it on her bedside table. There were lots of her with Grandpa Jimmy, and sometimes with a different man, and there was this tall, rather horse-faced woman. Ivy, her name was - she was her best friend in Hong Kong. She died about thirty years ago and wanted Grannibelle to have the album as a keepsake. There wasn't anything secret about it.'

Ann sneaks a sideways glance at Vivienne, who is staring down at the glass on her lap, idly running the tip of her forefinger round and round its rim.

'Everything's such a jumble in my head!' she sighs at last. 'When I knew you were coming, I thought of trying to write down the bare bones of the story, but all I've done is read through the contents of that package, over and over. I'll go and get it now.' She draws her feet together, then adds tentatively, 'If you'd like to have a look, that is?'

'Of course,' she says, a little nervously. 'Unless you want me to get it for you?'

'No. My room's a mess. Help yourself to some more lemonade – or wine, if you'd rather.'

Ann stands up and stretches, yawning noisily, then sits down again. Everything feels unreal, as if it's happening to someone else. Her eyelids droop...

'Sorry to be so long, Ann.' Vivienne's voice cuts in to a dream in which George is rowing a boat down the main street of Yung Shue Wan, with Ann perched up in front ringing a bicycle bell, while Graham is wading towards them, shouting, 'Don't you realise it's against the law to paddle your own canoe?'

Ann opens her eyes and sits forward in her chair as Vivienne says, 'The phone was ringing when I went downstairs. Change of plan, I'm afraid. It was Poppy. I'll have to go round to her house for a bit, so maybe you'd like to look through these on your own while I'm gone. '

'Nothing too serious about your friend I hope?' says Ann expelling a deep breath – whatever is waiting for her, she'd prefer

69

to tackle it without Vivienne hovering beside her.

'That depends on your attitude to cats,' she says, with what sounds suspiciously like a chuckle, 'I have to admit, they're not my favourite creatures, but Poppy views them a little differently. I'd ask you to come with me, but I'd rather you met her in more favourable circumstances.'

'Has her cat died or something? '

'One of her cats has died. One of her twenty-seven cats.'

Ann lifts the flap on the bulky manila envelope and gingerly shakes out the contents onto the bed, then laughs at her cautious approach. What possible harm can be inflicted on her by these random pieces of paper?

The first task is to sort them into some kind of order. Here's the letter Grannibelle wrote for Vivienne a few days before she died: *Penns Lane, Sutton Coldfield, September 1995*. How strange it feels to be holding her grandmother's last written communication, the forward-sloping, rounded script almost as clear and firm as ever.

And this one's in a hand she doesn't recognise: large sheets of flimsy blue paper. Four pages - no, five. Six. Each one packed edge to edge with a spidery scrawl, and barely a space between the lines: *The Peak, Hong Kong, 1971*. A small brown envelope contains something rigid - a piece of card. It's a studio photo of a delicately pretty Chinese girl, sitting bolt upright on a high-backed rattan chair, staring solemnly at the camera. With the photo is a scribbled note on a Company-headed memo. Here are two thin papers, folded in half, and then in half again. The writing is so faded as to be almost illegible.

Next, a separate envelope, crammed with another bundle of sheets. Some of this paper is quite thick, a kind of parchment, but the pages are only about four inches by seven. No date, merely the day: *Thursday*. It's all in pencil and the writing, surely…yes! That pencil could have been held in Grannibelle's youthful hand. This letter too – though it's in faded black on a large sheet that feels like tracing paper - or the greaseproof paper Grannibelle used for

70

lining the tin she cooked her fruit cakes in. For the flash of an instant, Ann tastes the cinnamon flavour of the mixture - the texture of the wooden spoon against her tongue.

It's not right. It can't be right to read these.

More letters in the same hand and yet other varieties of paper-size and thickness. The final one of this bundle is by the writer of the letter dated 1971. This one is signed, Ivy Latham, Wuchow, June 1930.

There's one more fat envelope. Ann won't have to read whatever it is she finds inside. All she's doing, really, is identifying the range of contents in the package Vivienne has left with her. These pages aren't from letters. They've been torn from what seems like a child's exercise book – lined paper. There's a small notebook, too. Everything's in that same handwriting again. In Grannibelle's pencil.

Hong Kong 1930 - Belle

Chapter 11

<u>Friday 8th April, 1930 Hong Kong</u>

I will have to impose some control over my thoughts before they drive me mad! What a night I've had - barely a wink of sleep, and it wasn't the sound of Jimmy's snores that was keeping me awake - I was replaying over and over every minute, every second, of last evening's events.

It took all my will-power to remain there beside him. I had the strangest fear that if I crept from the bed, my feet might run away with me! So there I lay, as still as I could, waiting for sleep – or daybreak. The muggy darkness in our room was still as dense each time I opened my eyes, hoping for a glimmer of light beyond the blinds. When the shapes of the chair and dressing table by the window became more defined, and intermittent little chirrups and twitterings reached me from outside I must have drifted into sleep at last, because the next I knew it was broad daylight and the birds were in full song. Jimmy was already in the bathroom, so I had a few minutes to try to collect my thoughts. For a while, these were less feverish and I wondered how I could ever have feared that I might roam the dark streets till I stood outside *his* lodging. I would have done no more than creep out into our garden and pace up and down across the lawn, under the same stars that would be looking down on *him*.

Him. Mr McFarlane. Rupert.

Rupert.

Ivy and I were chatting on the veranda of the hotel where she is staying with her mother, who rarely ventures out. Poor Ivy, I think it must be a little tedious for her at times. Jimmy was to join us for a drink before dinner, but then I received a chit, telling me that he had been delayed at work by some business to do with the office at Canton, and that he was sending a young friend of his to keep us company until he was able to join us. A few moments later, Mr McFarlane presented himself – he had only that week arrived in Hong Kong from Canton, where he, too is employed by the Asiatic Petroleum Company.

When he strolled out through the French window onto the wooden boards, my head was already turned in his direction. He was scanning the small groups seated further along the veranda on his right, and I was immediately struck by his bearing- it was straight-backed, without being stiff, and at the same time, a little hesitant as he shifted from one foot to the other. His profile interested me from the first - the high forehead, aquiline nose and strong jaw with its rather too-prominent chin would make him a good subject for a character sketch. Then he turned and strolled towards us, saying with a tentative smile, 'Mrs Rivers? Miss Latham?'

As he bent down towards me and briefly took my hand, something like an electric current shot through my palm and found its way into my chest, setting my heart pounding. It was his eyes. I still have no idea what colour or shape they are because I seemed to be looking beyond them into – I can't say what I saw – it was more a feeling that I knew him already, intimately, and that he knew me, better than I know myself. That is nonsense, of course. Merely a passing fancy. But even this morning, I cannot get it out of my head.

His manner towards us both could not have been faulted. He was courteous and respectful, and divided his questions equally between the two of us, making no distinction between myself, the matron, and Ivy, the single woman. Nothing in his conversation could have caused offence to anyone who might have been near enough to overhear it. But every word he uttered held me spellbound. Of all the men with whom I have conversed since my arrival in the Orient as Jimmy's bride more than three years ago, he, Rupert, is the only one who has ever made me laugh in genuine amusement.

What is more unusual, though, is the way he displayed an almost womanly understanding of my feelings when he learned of my recent anxiety about little Harry's fever, from which he has now, thank God, recovered. But this is in no way an indication of a lack of manliness. Unlike so many other men who are never happier than talking of their own exploits, Ivy had to subject him almost to an inquisition on his leisure time activities, before he eventually owned up to some small prowess on the polo field and his proficiency as a marksman. Ivy herself, being a member of a ladies' shooting club, found this of particular interest. One more reason for me to put those silly fancies out of my head! What kind of friend would I be to her, if I let -

Friday 8th April, Still!

I was interrupted in my writing when little Harry burst into the room, shouting incoherently, closely followed by Amah, apologising for the intrusion. When I had managed to calm him down, it transpired that he had been upset by the sight of a dead creature in the garden, which to my horror turned out to be a large rat. Though, as I soon discovered, Harry, at two years old, was not upset by the death of the rodent, but because Amah would not let him pick it up and add it to his toy collection!

I decided that fresh air would do me good, since the day was not too hot, so to his delight, Harry and I went for a ride in a rickshaw all the way down Pedder Street to the harbour where we spent a pleasant few minutes, watching sea birds, sampans and boatmen until to Harry's great excitement, the Star Ferry itself steamed up to the pier.

And now, alone in my room once more, with Harry taking his afternoon nap, I am feeling somewhat clearer-headed. Whether this is the result of our little outing, or the very act of writing down my thoughts, I cannot tell.

Writing used to serve as an outlet for my more fevered thoughts when I was young – eager to at last be allowed to join the grown-ups for dinner, while Bessie and Mary still ate theirs in the schoolroom with Miss Appelby.

When I was young! But I am still young. Still two years to go before I reach thirty and yet I feel even older than Ivy sometimes.

Is it the fact that I am a married woman with a child, while Ivy can flirt to her heart's content, knowing there is always a chance that it could lead to 'true love'? Unless of course, her partner in the game is married himself - but for me it can only ever lead to a dead end.

Oh, Belle, you foolish, ungrateful woman, envying Ivy's single state! She will reach thirty before this year is out, and may never have the chance of finding any husband, let alone true love – if such exists, outside the pages of romantic novels.

When I first arrived out here, I was amazed (and shocked) to find that flirting is looked on as a perfectly acceptable form of entertainment – to an extent that, in England, would be considered totally unsuitable for a respectable young woman, married or not. Now, after becoming quite an adept at the pastime myself before Harry's arrival, I find it hard to keep up any pretence of interest in it – or, indeed, in anything else. I see the same people at every social occasion – and if there do happen to be any newcomers, they seem to be turned out from the same mould as all the rest. The men who are in the least bit gifted in the way of conversation tend to be physically unattractive, and those who would merit a second glance have nothing of interest to say.

Jimmy is a good man, but I did him no favour in agreeing to be his wife. Looking back now, it is hard to be sure if I loved him at all, even then. At the start, perhaps, it was his air of quiet authority and maturity – being considerably older than myself, though it was more than likely to have been his uniform that attracted me, he looked so dashing! Once he had served the last few weeks of his commission in the army, would I still have found such pleasure in his company if I had not begun to fear I might be left on the shelf myself, with Bessie two years married by that time, and even Mary at only eighteen, already engaged?

No. If I am being true to myself, I must declare that marrying Jimmy was a way of escaping the role of stay-at-home daughter, the one who keeps house for her parents in their declining years. Much as I love them, I wanted more from life than that. Jimmy was my travel ticket – he had already been promised a managerial position on an excellent salary in the Asiatic Petroleum Company, a highly respectable international business – so here, at last, was a way to achieve my ambition of foreign travel to exotic locations.

If only I had known then what I have discovered since! It matters not one jot where you may be in the world, if the people around you cannot share your thoughts and feelings – cannot extend your mind or spirit. A view of mountains and calm bays or stormy seas; ramshackle house-boats constructed from all manner of materials, home to families of three or even four generations; collections of hovels (many of these on stilts) through whose open doorways a passer-by may glimpse tiny, garish shrines, each with their own fat little god surrounded by pungent smoke; narrow mud streets where hens, dogs and the odd goat or pig roam around among slant-eyed urchins and toothless, wrinkled old peasants of indeterminate gender; large, brick-built temples with their pillars elaborately carved and painted; the bright and finely embroidered silk garments of the well-born Chinese - one might gasp in wonder at any of these on first sight – but then what? No communication is possible; nothing of enduring value is discovered. The only social interaction is with one's own kind. Even our houses bear names such as Rosemont, or The Laurels, and as for their living rooms! These are furnished in the manner of any residence in the leafy avenues of Hampstead or Reigate or Bournemouth, they are swathed in the same chintz, the same tiger-skin rug by the hearth, the same collections of Tatler, or Punch, though a month or two out of date. How quickly that palls!

It was not long before I realised that Jimmy has no hidden depths – no fire. There is nothing in his makeup that my innermost soul can connect with. I sometimes fear I will be driven mad with boredom in his company. Were it not for my darling baby, my little Harry, and Ivy, my good friend, life here in Hong Kong would be sad indeed.

It is perhaps not so very surprising that my emotions were thrown into turmoil last evening. It has been such an age since any man has raised the slightest flutter in my breast. The loss of control I experienced, though overwhelming, was a merely temporary aberration - a quite natural result of the somewhat jaded state I have been in for these last two years. In itself, this is also not surprising since I have been totally wrapped up in my new role of mother, and although this has been a source of great joy, the difficulties of the birth and its aftermath left me in a physically depressed state. When one has been affected in this manner, it is not unusual for a simultaneous lowering of the spirit.

It was Mr McFarlane's lack of pretension, and his genuine interest in listening to Ivy and myself that made him such an agreeable companion. The fact that almost an hour passed before Jimmy joined us might also have contributed to my heightened susceptibility. When we are in company together, I find Jimmy's presence makes me too aware of my public self, of how I might be appearing to him. It was last evening that caused me to become more fully conscious of this fact. One minute I was completely relaxed, and at the same time totally alive, while Mr McFarlane entertained us with a self-deprecating anecdote about his own arrival in Shanghai as a callow boy of eighteen. Then Jimmy loomed above me, drew up a chair and placed it beside me, and I had the oddest sensation – as though my soul – my very self – was a bright flame that now was shrinking, leaning away from him as from a gust of wind. And into my mind came the image of how the Chinese protect a small flame of light from being extinguished and at the same time, beautify it, with a delicate construction of coloured paper.

I spoke but little during our dinner at the hotel. Jimmy himself was in good form, and despite the wide disparity of their ages, his demeanour towards Mr McFarlane seemed warmer and more candid than I have witnessed on other occasions in the company of his male friends and colleagues. Ivy, too, was displaying her more playful aspect sooner than she would normally reveal on a first meeting. She appeared somewhat crestfallen when, by dint of a seemingly casual enquiry as to the date of his arrival in China, we both realised that he is a good deal younger than he appears. I had thought him to be a year or two older than myself, and clearly Ivy had assumed the same.

After the meal, we seized the opportunity of a quick exchange

77

of views as we withdrew to the ladies' room. 'A mere boy of twenty three!' Ivy sighed, 'He will not be looking to marry for a long while yet. A spinster in her thirtieth year will be of no interest to him as a potential wife.'

'Don't use that ugly word, Ivy dear,' I said, laying my hand on her shoulder as our reflections looked back at us, mine smiling, hers, quizzical. 'Age need not be a barrier. You could easily pass for the same age as he.'

'You can't fool me with your flattery!' she said, and gave a hearty laugh.

Even as I spoke, I had known that she was under no illusions. Her face is pleasant enough, but it is rather too long for beauty, and she is unfortunate in her teeth, which are over large for her mouth.

'I prefer to look at life as it is,' she continued calmly, 'rather than as I might wish it to be. Mr McFarlane is not destined for me. At least, not as husband.' Here she turned to me with another laugh, her face alight with mischief, 'We will let him divert us for a while, you and I. He has already displayed an unmistakable interest in you.'

I felt my cheeks burn, and turned towards the door saying with as much indifference as I could muster, 'You are mistaken. Jimmy is a good friend of his. It is natural that he should pay some attention to his friend's wife.'

Ivy would have none of it, and after much girlish giggling and hugging, we agreed that since he will, of necessity, be a part of our circle while he remains in Hong Kong, she and I will flirt with him together. There is safety in numbers, so they say.

Small wonder, then, that I could not sleep last night after this unaccustomed excitement, fuelled, no doubt, by the extra cocktail before dinner, with no proportionate reduction in the amount of wine I drank with the meal.

Once one's mind has been taken over by fanciful thoughts, these become more extreme with every wakeful hour that follows. It takes more than an hour or two of fitful sleep to restore a proper perspective.

This balanced state of mind is now restored. I am once more fully in command of myself. If Mr McFarlane should seek out our company, I will allow myself to enjoy it as a mature married woman may safely do.

I wonder when we will next meet. I shall speak to Ivy today. I am sure she will need no encouragement to renew his acquaintance.

<u>Monday 11th April</u>.
I was not wrong. Mr McFarlane paid a visit to Ivy and her mother after lunch on Sunday. I, too, was spending the afternoon with them, and little Harry was with me. Jimmy was playing golf and lunched at the club. Mr McFarlane also plays golf. I can only surmise that he found the prospect of conversing with two young ladies, in the absence of the husband of one of them, a more attractive prospect for the afternoon.

His behaviour was exemplary. Mrs Latham retired for her nap soon after his arrival, but before she did so, he spoke to her as if he found her company even more riveting than that of her daughter, or her daughter's friend! Little Harry took to him at once, and insisted on showing how far he could fling the tennis ball that I had placed in my bag against just such an occasion. How kind and patient he is. Jimmy will not spend more than two minutes together in entertaining his own son. Ah well. There is no profit in comparisons.

Before we parted company Mr McFarlane had extracted from Ivy an outline of our usual activities during a normal week. When Ivy revealed that due to the somewhat straitened circumstances of herself and her widowed mother, she undertook some teaching duties on a few weekday mornings, he displayed a great deal of interest, particularly, when he discovered that I often accompanied her on a voluntary basis (I think this is not mere imagination on my part!) Dear Ivy. She is not unattractive, but I know that I have somehow managed to retain a great deal of my girlish looks which even the most objective scrutiny in the mirror tells me are still above the average.

I have been out of practice for too long! This game is not as easy to control as I had assumed it would be. I shall need to keep a tighter rein on my warmer feelings, or withdraw completely and leave the field open for Ivy to play a singles match. Or maybe it will be better if I can extend our play to 'doubles' – Mr McFarlane is sharing a house with a man whose wife is on a prolonged visit to England – 'Bing' Broughton. He seems a good sort, and Jimmy likes him too. Another benefit is his obvious devotion to his wife, Daisy, so there is no danger at all of his attaching himself to me.

They came together to our house last evening for a game of bridge. Ivy and her mother came too and Mrs Parker (whom I must confess to disliking, though Ivy declares her to be kind to a fault.) And there, I would agree, for I find it a most uncomfortable fault indeed to have any of one's statements that might hint at a minor criticism of some absent person, interrupted by her exclamation, 'Oh, but I am sure she was acting with the best of intentions…'

Ivy and I were hoping that her mother, who adores bridge, and Mrs Parker, who considers herself an excellent player, would join Jimmy and Bing at the table, leaving Rupert free to entertain us. Unfortunately, Mrs P declined the offer, so we were forced to endure her conversation for a large part of the evening.

But all was not entirely lost – during the game, each time I glanced across to see how it was progressing (hoping that it would soon be over!) I found that Rupert's eyes were drawn to my face, and once, he even winked at me before saying to Jimmy, 'What a lucky fellow you are, to have a wife whose beauty is matched by her brainpower.' (!!)

I half expected some joking put-down from Jimmy (such as: 'You do her wrong – no one can deny that her beauty far excels her intellect') but he straightened his back and gave a smug smile, 'I am indeed most fortunate. Belle is the perfect wife and mother. You have made the acquaintance of my son, Harry, I think?'

'Indeed I have,' said Rupert, 'a fine little man. I'm free for the next few days, and if it's not too much of an imposition, perhaps I could accompany Mrs Rivers if she is ever thinking of taking Harry for a walk. We could stroll around the Botanic Gardens. And of course, Miss Latham would come too, if she is not teaching. '

Before the party broke up, Rupert and Bing invited Jimmy and me to call round for a drink before dinner this evening. Ivy will come too, though her mother declared that two evenings in a row were too much for her these days, and, before Mrs P could spoil it all, the dear woman invited her to join her for tiffin at her hotel.

I wonder if there will be anyone else present at Bing's house. Whatever happens I shall make sure I get the chance to engage Rupert in a tete a tete. He is such a delightful person to flirt with!

Thursday 14th April

Delightful indeed! A most entertaining couple of hours. Rupert did not ignore Ivy, of course, but I suspect he had briefed Bing beforehand to engage her interest for as long as possible. There's a fine conservatory at the side of his bungalow, and we all traipsed in to admire his collection of orchids. I find them sterile flowers myself, but Ivy was in raptures. Jimmy was holding a copy of Punch which he had picked up from a table in Bing's living room, and after a couple of minutes he sat himself down in a rattan chair behind a cluster of large palms, so Rupert and I were able to step out into the garden for a few delicious minutes, during which time he told me he was heartbroken to find that the only woman he could ever have loved (myself, of course!) was happily married to a friend he truly admired, and could never betray. I, in my turn, hinted that my domestic happiness was due almost entirely to the love I felt for my son, but that a recent meeting with a kind and intelligent young man had restored my faith in the possibility of a loving friendship between the sexes, based on mutual respect and intellectual companionship, with no trace of any physical attraction to sully its purity. Deep sighs from both parties. Hands lightly clasped, eyes gazing intensely. Not a word spoken as we stepped apart and walked slowly, side by side back to the conservatory to join the others.

I felt truly alive again for the first time in months!

Jimmy gave a guilty start when he found that I had crept up and was standing beside him. The magazine clattered onto the tiled floor, and Rupert laughed, 'Caught you, old man! It's a capital offence, you know, to prefer the written to the spoken word, especially when the lips from which they fall are those of your own lovely wife.'

'Belle doesn't object, do you my dear? Wait till you're an old married man yourself, Mac. A fellow needs a break from time to time.'

At that moment we were joined by Bing and Ivy, and Rupert smoothly switched his attention to her. I did not mind in the least. It was all part of the game.

She and I had to wait until this morning before we could exchange confidences – I cannot decide whether this caused me more pain than pleasure. We both admitted to finding R's company the most thrilling we had encountered for many a long month – she felt that I would have the advantage over her for his attentions, since a married woman is 'safe' – she will not be suspected of trying to trap him into marriage, whereas a spinster (how I wish she wouldn't use that ugly word!) is perceived always to be on the look-out for a permanent commitment. She declared that she could not seriously consider R as a possible husband, even should he make such a proposal, and that the difference in their ages would not be not the main barrier . 'I've seen it too often,' she said – 'that resigned expression on the face of the wife of a handsome charmer, when he leaves the room a moment after the prettiest girl in the company has slipped out into the garden.'

Well. We shall see. I shall write a note to R. and tell him I wish to have nothing more to do with him.

Or maybe I will not write this to him just yet. Ivy is right – he is more likely to pursue me with greater intensity as the safer option because it is only a game. If I choose to lift my spirits in this way, Jimmy will be the one to benefit. I fear I have been a gloomy companion for him of late.

<u>Saturday 16th April</u>

It has been difficult to find moments of solitude in which to make my entries. A delightful afternoon yesterday. Took Harry to the Botanic Gardens, where he was at first frightened, and then enchanted by the sight of the caged beasts. I have to admit that I find that raw, jungle smell disturbing – but at the same time, strangely exhilarating. Ivy and R. were with us, but deep in conversation with each other for much of the time. I begin to wonder about his intentions towards her. Perhaps it would not be too upsetting if they become engaged – though that would put an end to anything between him and me, beyond simple friendship.

I think it would be for the best.

But not quite yet! Especially after his visit to our house this morning. He appeared surprised not to see Jimmy, but he would surely have known that the golf club would have been the place to find him!

He said he will join us all at Shek O for a picnic luncheon tomorrow.

<u>Monday 17th April</u>

What an amusing outing that was! Jimmy was in good form and being most attentive to Ivy. This gave R the chance to challenge me to a swimming race. The sea was unusually calm and flat and we swam to the rocks at the far end. We clambered out and dried off in the hot sun for a few minutes. Although we were in full view of the others, we could not be overheard. R admired my swimming style, and then, my costume, particularly the way it revealed more of my shapely legs! I tapped him on the side of his leg, just above his knee, and told him he must not speak to me like this. I had given him a harder blow than I'd intended, for the trace of my fingers remained imprinted on his skin for a few seconds. Of course, he then declared that he would treasure that part of his leg for ever, at which I laughed and slid down into the water again.

<u>Wednesday 19th April</u>

Two more 'sightings' of R since Sunday – once on Monday when he and Bing called round to our house on their way out to dine at Bing's club. Jimmy was deep in conversation with Bing about the relative merits of the Shameen district of Canton as a work base, compared to Shanghai or Hong Kong – a conversation in which I would normally join with enthusiasm – but R and I were able to snatch a few minutes and arrange to meet for an outing the following morning.

We met at Kennedy Road for The Peak tram, a contraption that always amuses me - it is more like riding in a lift than a street tram. The rails are so steep in parts as to be almost vertical, and I was able to cling to R's arm – this was not entirely a ruse, though I confess I did somewhat exaggerate the extent of my vertigo!

We set out on our stroll around the summit of Victoria Peak along the narrow and mainly deserted Lugard Road, where we halted from time to time and gazed down on the tall buildings and busy streets of Central district, and the stretch of sea beyond it to Kowloon on the mainland. I felt totally at ease in R's company and realised we had both moved beyond the conventions of the silly game of flirting. How much more satisfying was our total absorption in discovering the details of each other's lives – our interests – our hopes and dreams!   This is more dangerous by far.

I must ensure that Ivy accompanies me on any further outings. How ironic, that playing at the game of being physically attracted to another should be safer than straightforward discussions that might lead to a meeting of minds!

Thursday 20th April

I was more careful yesterday evening, when Ivy and her mother hosted a small party at their hotel. There were two other couples present and we all played charades. Ivy and I took every opportunity of snatching a few moments with R, but I, at least, was involved in my own charade. I can actually feel a kind of protective layer around me when I step back into the role of 'flirt'. It is strangely comforting.

I told R that I thought I had left my scarf (a present from Jimmy) in the tram carriage on our descent from The Peak on

Tuesday. He declared that he would go back at the earliest opportunity and see if it had been handed in.

This secured me a reason for sending him a brief letter this morning, after I had helped Ivy at the Shooting Club. I believe that the tone of this letter will ensure he regards me as nothing more than a flirt. It may even make him despise me a little, for on Tuesday he revealed a far more serious and principled individual beneath the recent, rather flippant exterior. So be it.

But why should we not be friends, he and I? Why do I become increasingly uneasy, the more I reflect upon Tuesday's delightful and innocent outing? It is this very innocence that is the danger – if indeed that is the correct word for our friendship. Innocence is for children – it is linked to a lack of awareness. Naïvety would be a better word, perhaps.

It is time for him to turn his full attention towards Ivy. Most of his attention. Surely I can safely reserve just a little of it for myself?

Chapter 12

Ann stares down at the page. She is struggling to make a connection between what she's reading and what she has always known about her grandmother. She is torn between burning curiosity and a reluctance to read further; so far, nothing too disgraceful has happened. She's never given a thought to what Grannibelle might have been like as a young woman – young once only, as are we all . By the time Belle had become a grandmother, that young woman would have long since disappeared.

Ann stands up and stretches her arms. She crosses to the window and steps out onto the narrow balcony. The warm air envelops her as she listens for the rhythmic sound from the power station. Vivienne was right - it is always there, under the more definable sounds.

How long has her mother been gone? Will she be expecting her to have read through all this material before her return?

Ann turns her attention to the letters she has laid out on the bed. Her fingers stray towards the stiff, thin tracing paper - maybe this is the very one that Belle referred to in her entry for Thursday 20th April.

Thursday

Ah, Mr McFarlane, you are a disturber! What do you mean by upsetting the equilibrium of two highly respectable (!) ladies in their heretofore blissful states of married and single blessedness? And two at once, mind you! And you so young and all. The poor young idlers that we endeavour to teach to shoot must certainly not have got their money's worth this morning and now at our first opportunity (recess) we two rush together to weep on each other's shoulders for what we haven't got and will never get. It's a great bond, this being crazy about the same person. I only hope I'll be able to preserve enough of a sense of decency from the wreck to give her the chance I wish I could take myself.

Does it sicken you to hear me rave? Perhaps if I make an utter ass of myself, you'll leave me be – which is what I want of course. Any idiot can see that that is all I want.

Ivy can't come to dinner on Saturday so if you want to change our places and go have tea with her in the afternoon, it will be all right. I'll take a walk with you on Sunday morning. She is going with her mother to Repulse Bay for Saturday evening so you won't be embarrassed by having us both picking on you at the same time. You'd better write her a chit and invite yourself to have tea with her, and if she doesn't take you up, you can come along here as we planned. Will you bring your friend Bing with you? I mean it. I thoroughly detest you.

Good bye

The only object of this letter was to tell you that I found the missing scarf I spoke of. It was in my bag all along.

Wednesday 3rd May Hong Kong

How foolish of me to rely on the efficacy of writing! It has done nothing to relieve me of this madness – on the contrary, I soon realised that it was having the opposite effect – which is why I have made no entries for the past two weeks. Every word I wrote in my effort to retain control over this supposedly harmless game has only served to strengthen the feelings I was attempting to deny.

Even my choice of writing implement has been based on a false premise – that the marks made by lead on paper, being less permanent than ink, might allow the feelings thus expressed to be erased with equal ease. But the lead itself is a poison and it has seeped into my soul! Is this why I pick up my pencil once more?

I know this is not science, in the way that a drug such as opium can be proved to destroy the mind and body of the addict, even while it is inducing a state of euphoria unattainable by effort of the brain alone. One cannot have spent these months, these years, in the mysterious East without hearing tell of many a poor wretch who has fallen prey to this terrible substance. But what can science tell us about love? Or should I turn to the poets? No. There is no answer for me between the covers of a book.

What I do know is that poison, if taken in a limited amount over a period of time, does not kill outright – does not kill the body, that is, but it saps the will. Without the power of the will, what is left of a person's moral fibre? Without a moral sense, what is there to distinguish a human from a merely animal being?

I am delirious with joy one moment, and the next am plunged into despair. How can I have let this happen? All the times I've played this game and my heart has barely ever missed a beat! Even Jimmy, jealous though he can be, has never felt threatened by another man paying me particular attention in full view of all. I think he even regarded it as an acknowledgement of the superiority of his possession, his wife, compared to those of other, lesser, men! A certain reciprocation from me was a necessary part of the glory he accrued. Indeed, this behaviour would sometimes develop into another kind of a game, for him, once we reached the privacy of our bedroom. Now, though, I can hardly bear to have him touch me. I have managed to find excuses – the monthly visitor – little Harry needing my attention – fatigue.

Things have not been good between us of late. He raises his voice at me in a most unpleasant manner when I make a perfectly innocuous remark about one of our neighbours or a work colleague of his - or worse still, suggest that he has had enough whiskey for one evening.

I've been careful right from the start to give him no reason to harbour the least suspicion towards Rupert. I often drop a little word regarding his fondness for Ivy, and hers for him. I must also take care not to let slip to Ivy quite how close we have become, though she is fully aware now that there is something special between R and me.

We have allowed ourselves no more than a brief embrace, such as a brother might give his favourite sister. His lips have touched only my hand – and yesterday, oh so lightly, the back of my neck.

<u>Friday 5th May Hong Kong</u>

Out of the mouths of babes... What a lucky escape I had! I believe, or at least I hope, that I managed to laugh off little Harry's remark at bedtime. For a change, Jimmy came into the nursery last evening to say goodnight to his son. He'd already had several whiskeys and had reached his affectionate stage, and after he'd let Harry cling round his neck for a moment and plant a slobbery kiss on his cheek, and then had settled him back on the pillow and stroked his hair, he grabbed my hand and pulled me towards him in a big bear hug, lifting my feet from the ground. I gave a mock-shriek and cried, 'Put me down!'

'Yes, Daddy,' Harry piped. 'Put down Mummy.'

Jimmy held on to me even tighter, 'I do believe the little chap is jealous,' he laughed, breathing whiskey fumes into my face as I struggled to slip out of his grasp.

Then Harry said, loud and clear, 'Mummy likes Big Man betterest.'

The next second, my feet hit the floor with a bump. Jimmy sat down on the bed and very quietly and slowly said, 'What man is that, then, old chap?'

Harry must have detected something in my face – or in the sudden change in Jimmy's voice because he wriggled down under the blanket and murmured, 'Harry sleepy now.'

'Oh, I know what he means!' I exclaimed brightly before Jimmy could carry on with his questioning, 'This afternoon, Harry and I were on our way to the Botanic Gardens and we met Ivy walking with your friend, Rupert McFarlane - so they joined us for a while. Ivy was in one of her frivolous moods and it must have been something she said - she knows that Harry has grown quite fond of Rupert – he calls him 'my big man' because Rupert calls him 'my little man'. I have no idea why Harry said that just now. But then, you'll have noticed that Harry often comes out with funny little remarks, now he's started talking so much more.'

I don't know how I managed to keep my voice so light and unconcerned, but it seemed to work. Jimmy doesn't like it if I ever hint that he doesn't show enough interest in his son, so he wouldn't want to carry on with that conversation, especially as he had something more physical on his mind. It seemed politic to humour him when we'd left Harry's room and he took my hand again and headed for ours. My heart was thudding away in my chest, but Jimmy couldn't have guessed that this was nothing to do with what was going on between us then.

I must never, never let Harry see or hear the slightest look or touch or word that might not also be witnessed by Jimmy himself.

And what did Harry see?

Nothing. And everything. I have let myself feel so myself in Rupert's company, so comfortable - and having Harry trotting between us, one hand in mine, the other in his, I was able to pretend we were a family. The three of us. This was a quite different sensation from the way I have felt when we're in the company of others – our surreptitious exchange of glances as we try to manoeuvre ourselves into a position where we can talk more freely – and different again from the other, fiercer thrill of being on our own. On those rare occasions, I have been on my guard – fully aware of the danger.

This was so different. No racing heart-beat – no sweet stabbing pain anywhere. I was barely aware of my own body – there was just togetherness – completeness. So when Harry let go of our hands and ran ahead along the path towards the aviary, it was the most natural thing in the world for me to take Rupert's hand as we followed slowly behind.

Then Harry stopped and turned back towards us. Rupert let go my hand and opened his arms, 'Here, little man!' he called, and when Harry reached him, he bent and scooped him up and held him against his chest. And then, in an equally natural way, I joined in the embrace, nuzzling myself against Harry's back, with my arms around the two of them.

Mummy likes big man betterest! I must tell Rupert tomorrow - if we can manage to snatch a few moments on our own. What a risk I took, saying what I did – what if Harry had piped up, 'Silly Mummy – big man comed and then Ivy comed!'? Two or three months ago his gabble was almost unintelligible - it's only this last month or so that his speech has developed enormously – everyday he comes out with something new. How delighted I was at first – but now - !

Oh Belle, what are you saying! You are a mother. A *mother*!

Saturday 6th May
Jimmy has at last gone out. Thank the Lord for golf and polo and anything else that occupies a man during his leisure time. Even if I cannot see Rupert today, at least Jimmy might work off some of his foul mood before he returns.

Recently he has been finding fault with everything I do or say – or so it feels to me. My housekeeping is not satisfactory – what was I thinking of, giving cook leave to visit his old mother yesterday? Poor Joseph – he was so grateful – it was the anniversary of his father's death – or something of that nature - and now was an auspicious time for whatever it was that had to be done. (I find it intriguing, the way the superstitious practises of the Chinese co-exist quite happily with their Christian beliefs) Since his mother lives in a small village on the mainland, a good distance beyond Kowloon he would not have returned until today, but Sunday being his afternoon off, I told him to stay over until tomorrow evening.

Truth to tell, I love to have a chance to oversee the work in the kitchen – something I cannot do when Joseph is there – he would lose face.

This morning at breakfast (prepared and served by Amah with the help of the new kitchen boy) Harry sat at table with us both, as he often does on Saturdays and Sundays. Jimmy did not hide behind his paper for the entire meal as is his habit, these days - he tried to engage Harry in conversation first.

My heart was in my mouth - along with some buttered toast - so I nearly choked as Jimmy said, 'Would you like to see Mr McFarlane today, Harry ?'

Harry asked, 'Is Mr Macfin Mummy's friend?'

'Yes,' said Jimmy, giving me <u>such</u> a look – which I pretended to ignore as I said calmly,

'He's Daddy's friend, and mine too, dear, and Aunty Ivy's' – then I carried on smoothly, 'Have you made any arrangement for us to meet up with him today, Jimmy?'

'I rather thought you might have done that, my dear,' he replied. I couldn't work out what his smile meant.

'Nothing has been arranged as yet. Would you like me to ask him round for tiffin – and Bing Broughton, perhaps – and Ivy?'

Harry had lost interest in our conversation and was wriggling on his seat – the little round footstool is always placed on the dining chair to raise him high enough to eat from the table – he'd finished his toast soldiers, and he started to rock from side to side, holding his half-full glass of milk in both hands. His interest was caught by the changing angle of the milk in the glass, and before I realised what was happening, he had leant too far, away from me and towards Jimmy's end of the table. I managed to catch hold of his leg in time to prevent him from crashing to the floor on top of the pieces of smashed glass.

Of course he howled at the top of his lungs, and Jimmy, who had been showered in flying milk shouted, 'Damn and blast it woman, can't you look after the brat. Now I'll have to go and change my clothes. I just hope you've seen to it that Amah has kept up with the laundry and there'll be another pair of clean britches ready.'

Does he suspect anything? Or is it just my own feeling of guilt that makes me wonder what he might have discovered?

I'll send Rupert a chit and see if he and Bing will come over this afternoon. It would look more suspicious if I did nothing.

No, I am sure Jimmy has not the least idea. I think his recent bad moods are related to his work – it seems there are a few problems at the Shameen office. What if he were to be told to pay a visit to Canton? If it were to be only a brief stay, would I be allowed to remain here with Harry?

The thought of such an opportunity!

Another picnic party last Sunday. Around a dozen of us (not counting the children) on a boat belonging to a friend of Bing's – we sailed from Aberdeen harbour - such a picturesque place, with all the crowded sampans of the Chinese, as well as the square-sailed junks and a few large sailing yachts.

Rupert was there of course, and Ivy and her mother, and the dreadful Mrs Parker – this time with her equally dreadful son and daughter-in-law, Lucinda, with their little girl, a few months older than Harry but a quiet, wispy little thing, hiding her head in Lucinda's lap for most of the afternoon. How proud I am of my own bright, sturdy little boy!

We sailed right round to the southern side of Lamma island, a very sparsely populated place, and moored off a beautiful isolated beach with a backdrop of tree-covered hills.

There, we picnicked on the boat – a delicious meal of spicy prawns, crispy duck, and a huge variety of other dishes, all with a leaning towards the Chinese, rather than the strictly English, cuisine that Jimmy insists on at home.

After luncheon, some of the adults, including Jimmy, remained on the boat for a while, drinking cold beer and playing cards with the men, while most of the women relaxed on the deck in the slight breeze, under the shade of the canopy.

There was a certain amount of confusion while everyone was deciding what he or she would like to do first. I stayed quietly at the table, cuddling Harry on my lap – he often closes his eyes for a few minutes immediately after luncheon and I was waiting to see how the groups would form themselves.

Jack Duggan, the boat's owner, suggested the card game and invited Jimmy to play, while Jack's wife, Mabel, said she supposed she should take their children, a girl of six or seven and a boy of about five, to run around on the beach and build sand castles, and would the other two mothers, Lucinda and myself, like to join her?

Before I could fully take in what was happening, we had all clambered down the ladder into the dinghy, and Rupert was at the helm, and calling back to the party still on board, 'Just give me a shout and I'll come back for anyone else who wants to join us.'

It was too soon after eating for us to swim, and when we landed, we set out along the beach to find some shade – there were trees at the far end, and a jutting mass of tumbled rocks. Mabel's two children ran ahead, holding Harry's hand, while Lucinda's little girl dragged her feet and whimpered, clinging to her mother's skirt. When we reached the first block of shade, Lucinda spread out the rug under some kind of conifer trees and settled herself down with her child. Mabel joined them, while Rupert and I followed the other children round to a delightful little bay on the other side of the rocks.

We had twenty glorious minutes to talk together while the children played, well out of earshot.

And now, I have only one more hour to wait before I go to meet him, as arranged.

Writing this last sentence has had such a strong physical effect I fear for what I might be tempted to do.

I will not succumb!

Tuesday 9th.
In spite of great temptation yesterday, I stood my ground. My virtue remains (almost!) intact.

Jimmy came home for luncheon today. He was in such a glum mood it made me wonder why I had resisted that opportunity.

Stop it, Belle. You know perfectly well why. That would be the start of a long and very slippery slope, with a precipice at the end of it.

Enough of writing for today. I shall have a good brisk walk over to Ivy's. And then maybe a swim at the club later.

Wednesday

Dear Rupert
Your note came last night and might have been a real letter

because a coolie delivered it right into my own hand – and how I wish it had been! I needed something yesterday.

Don't worry I'm not going to burden you with the intimate details of my latest family row. And if you ever catch me playing the self-pity card, please remind me forcibly that I'm not getting any more than I deserve. Sometimes I lose my "sense of perspective" and think I'm more to be pitied than scorned, but I do honestly try to keep away from that point of view.

From what Jimmy has said, I am fairly sure he took no notice of Mrs Parker's snide remarks about us wandering off together on Sunday. Mabel, bless her, was so grateful to us for taking charge of her two tear-aways, as she calls them. He still seems pleased to have your company, especially since you have taken pains to spend more time conversing with him on all his favourite subjects. And when you weren't chatting to him or Jack Duggan the rest of that outing on Sunday, it was quite the best thing that you were paying court to Ivy. You see why I had to tell her something of the "special affection" between us. I would not have her hurt, for anything in the world.

I gave her your message and we shall love to come Saturday if there is anything doing. I'm not sure about Jimmy yet but will let you know in a day or so. If he doesn't come and you are going to bring us home, will you spend the night, and Sunday? That will at least give me the chance to see more of you, even if we cannot be alone. I wish you were coming for tea today - Jimmy's gone to Kowloon and is not expected back before tomorrow.

Nuff sed!

Belle.

Thursday 11th May

Whatever follows on from last night, I cannot regret letting Rupert know of Jimmy's intended absence. I knew what it would lead to.

No, that is not true. I had no idea of exactly what. I am trembling again as I hold my pen, struggling to find words that can explain myself to my self.

Even after three years of marriage, even after bearing Jimmy's child, I have never looked on his full nakedness, nor he on mine. We undress separately, or with our backs turned from each other. The light is always switched off before the act itself takes place. He has never disrobed me, layer by layer to my skin, so that I stand before him, naked and unabashed as I look into his eyes.

We smile. Then I am helping him with his shirt buttons, and we are both breathing fast and I am whispering his name between bubbles of laughter, and my name has never been repeated and repeated with such tenderness. *Belle, Belle.* For the first time, the biblical expression for the act of love makes complete sense – 'to know' a person. Jimmy has never known me in this way, and I never imagined that my own intimate parts could be a source of joy that set my whole being on fire – body and spirit no longer separate, the one a mere shell for the other. They are one. They are my self. At the moment of union with him, we each became our true selves - one twin self.

We held each other, murmuring, caressing, laughing and crying, for a long time after.

Such bliss. Such sweet self-forgetting - self-knowing. How can this be wrong?

<u>Friday 12th May</u>
Jimmy has had his suspicions raised once again. We were so careful on Wednesday. Harry was sound asleep. I sent Amah home to her own family for the night. Joseph was safely settled in the servants' quarters, and in any event, he would do anything for me.

Who could have been around at two in the morning on Thursday to see Rupert leave? He has his own key to Bing's house – and a gentleman will not ask another what he has been up to. Although I am certain that Rupert is not the kind to frequent a place such as Spring Garden Lane (if what I have heard of it be true), he would let Bing believe such a thing if necessary.

But last evening, when I came away from settling Harry to sleep, I heard a noise from our bedroom, and there was Jimmy, bending over the bottom drawer of my dressing table. He swung round as I entered the room, and his face was pink.

'What on earth are you doing, Jimmy?' I said, angrily.

'Don't speak to me in that tone,' he retorted.

'I have a right to ask what you're doing if I find you rifling through my clothes drawer.'

'Do you, by God! And do you also have a right to keep secrets from your husband?'

I was stunned. That was the moment when I discovered my true vocation - what a wonderful acting career I could have had! 'And what secrets might those be?' I demanded, a mask of righteous indignation concealing my panic. With a huge effort of will, I prevented my eyes from straying towards the rug that lay below the window, hiding a loosened floor board. 'Have I been running up debts in some gambling den? Do I have a cache of opium hidden among my negligees? Is there a bundle of love-letters tied with pink ribbon, nestling in a secret compartment of my jewellery box?' My voice had risen in pitch and volume with each question - I paused for a moment, throwing back my shoulders as I drew in a deep breath, 'Well? Well?' my finger stabbed the air between us, 'Do I get an explanation? Or should I send for the doctor to bring medicine for your poor, fevered brain?'

All this time, Jimmy just stood there beside the half-open drawer, shifting from foot to foot and staring at me like a rabbit caught in the glare of a light. At last he mumbled, 'Steady on old girl. No need to take on, so.'

I stiffened my shoulders again and lifted my chin but before I could speak he had taken a step towards me, holding up his open palms in a gesture of mock-surrender, 'Hold your horses, Belle,' he said with an attempt at a laugh, 'Let me explain – for pity's sake!'

I knew I'd got him, then, 'Please do,' I said firmly but more gently.

He sat down on the bed and before he could draw me down beside him, I sat too, but left a good space between us. First he apologised, and then he took out a folded piece of paper from his pocket, 'This was delivered to me at work this afternoon,' he said.

With a sinking heart I looked down at the message – surely this was a woman's hand - and an educated woman at that. Small, perfectly formed letters, each scrupulously joined to its fellow with a narrow loop or a tiny curving line, and all with a slight, but distinct, backwards slant

> *'Dear Mr Rivers,*
>
> *I have prayed long and hard before taking up my pen to write to you. Were it not for my deep sense of responsibility towards the preservation of moral standards among the English residents here, I should not do so now, but would turn a blind eye to the actions of the young friend in whom you have placed your trust. Those who speak unpalatable truths are rarely thanked for their pains, and indeed, I look for no gratitude. However, as a Christian, I have no choice but to advise you of my belief that your wife is even now in danger of betraying you with another.*
>
> *It is the solemn duty of every one of us to set a good example to the native population, whether they be heathen still, or among those whom God in His mercy has chosen to save.*
>
> *The Good Shepherd keeps watch over his flock. I pray that you will remain watchful, and prevent your wife from endangering her immortal soul.*
>
> *Yours most sincerely in Christ the Lord*
> *A well-wisher.*

When I had read this, I let out a genuine peal of laughter, so great was my relief in finding not a shred of evidence that could be held against us , 'Oh Jimmy! My poor dear love! This is priceless! We must make it our business to discover the prankster who has played this trick on us!'

Jimmy turned towards me, his eyes scanning my face as if trying to read a text in a foreign script. I was laughing so much that tears were running down my cheeks. 'Or maybe…' I gasped, 'maybe the poor woman is totally deranged! It <u>has</u> to be a woman who has written this.'

Jimmy's lower lip began to twitch and a glimmer of comprehension lit his eyes; then the gale of laughter broke.

The danger had passed.

How many lives is a cat alleged to have? How many of mine have I now used up?

Sunday, 14thMay

I knew that the ecstasy of that night could not easily be repeated – but little did I think it could be weeks before I might even set eyes on R again.

Jimmy came home on Friday with the news - tomorrow we set sail for Canton.

It was as I thought - the office at Shameen has fallen into a state of disorder, and Jimmy has been posted back there while the manager recovers from his illness. A bad bout of flu developed into something worse. Pneumonia or pleurisy, I believe. Lord only knows how long we must stay there.

Ivy came round yesterday and helped me start the packing. Although she has known for some time of how things are between Rupert and me, that one, exquisite secret can never be told. She was very kind and sympathetic, but I have to say, to my great shame, for a few moments I almost hated her for it. <u>She</u> was to go to the supper party at the club that very evening, with Rupert and Bing and all the others, while <u>I</u> could not.

Just a few short days ago, when it seemed that Jimmy had already decided not to come with us, all I could think of was how R and I might contrive, with Ivy's help, to have more time together without drawing attention to ourselves and becoming the object of gossip.

Now, though, after the scene on Friday evening - that

ridiculous but damaging letter - it felt as though Jimmy was testing me when he joined us in the bedroom for a few moments and explained that he could not spare the time to go out with us that evening – the emergency at the Shameen office had caused even more work for him here, with the various tasks that must be handed over to others before we set sail.

'But this will not stop you from going, dear,' he said with a smile, 'You must say goodbye to all your chums for me. I shall be perfectly happy, dining here alone.'

How tempted I was! Jimmy has never minded in the least if I have attended a social gathering when he has been either unable, or unwilling, to accompany me. There have always been a few worthy matrons, such as Ivy's mother or even Mrs Parker, with whom I could mingle, for a while, at least – after all, was I not a respectable matron myself?

'Anyone who wants to bid us fond farewells can drop by on Sunday, or wave us off from the ferry pier.' I said at once, with impressive nonchalance, 'I'd rather stay here with you. So long as you won't mind, Ivy?'

Ivy immediately understood, since we had both laughed and trembled together over that anonymous letter, 'Mother will be coming with me,' she said, then gave a little smile and lowered her eyes demurely, 'I'm sure that Bing and Rupert will take good care of us. But what a shame, Jimmy, that you can't both come.'

Shame indeed.

Or perhaps not. With Jimmy glued to my side all evening, it would have been exquisite torture to breath the air that R was breathing, to see his dear face, and yet exchange nothing but platitudes under Jimmy's watchful eye.

All I could do then was wait till Jimmy left the room and scribble a hasty note for Ivy to deliver in person. Of course I do not hate her! She is loyal through and through - and my only hope of hearing news of R while we are away.

How will I bear it?

It is as though I am being punished for what we did That Night. Or is it that some good angel has been sent to rescue me from myself? I do not want to be rescued!!

Until we return from Canton, I must lose even the comfort of writing these pages, since I cannot be sure of finding a safe hiding place in our temporary accommodation. My 'Dearest Diary' must remain here until our return.

Oh, let that be soon!!

Chapter 13

'Ah, here you are! I hope you don't mind, but I've...' Vivienne's voice trails to a halt as Ann jerks her head round, and the bundle of loose pages drops from her fingers onto the faded silk rug at her feet. The two women stare at each other, the rest of the letters scattered on the bed between them.

It takes Ann several seconds to adjust to the reality of where she is. For the moment, her brain must shut away the confidences that have just been shared with her, in what has felt like an intimate conversation with a new friend. She searches for something neutral to say, 'I hope your friend isn't...' she begins, but Vivienne is already speaking.

'It's a bit...em...awkward, really. Poppy's cat...She's very upset. Poppy, I mean, not the cat. The gardener's been told to prepare a suitable site. She wants to give it a formal send-off.'

What is she going on about? Ann is still attempting to assimilate this startling glimpse into the early life of her beloved Grannibelle, and here is her mother, banging on about cats and gardeners! All she wants at the moment is to be left alone to finish sifting through these letters.

'So you see,' continues Vivienne, 'when I said that I didn't want to leave you on your own for too long, and maybe Dawn could help out instead, Poppy wouldn't stand for it. It was quite clear that Dawn would be no substitute for me, her own... her best friend. "Can't you bring Ann with you," she said, so...'

Ann smiles. No wonder Vivienne is looking somewhat sheepish. She's never been one to lavish attention on animals. No cats, no dogs, no sweet fluffy bunnies. A single goldfish was the nearest thing to a pet Ann had ever been allowed. In The Norfolk time, there was a large and lazy tabby called Shortbread, but he belonged to Grannibelle. Colin had a succession of hamsters; the first of these had been bought for him by Ann, not Vivienne, after The Betrayal. 'So your friend, Poppy, has invited me to a cat's funeral?' she ventures.

'That's about the measure of it,' says Vivienne with a rueful smile.

'Will she be wanting hymns and prayers?' asks Ann, trying to smother a giggle.

'This is a tragic occasion, and I hope you won't let me down by making fun of the dead.' Vivienne's solemn tone is belied by the twitch at the corner of her lips, and a moment later they both erupt into laughter.

Regaining control, Vivienne walks over to the window and turns to face her daughter, 'I know it seems funny - both kinds of funny, amusing and peculiar - but I don't want you to get the wrong impression. Poppy is no fool. She's a highly intelligent woman. We all have our little quirks, don't we? '

She really wants me to like this friend of hers, thinks Ann. This mother-of-George. 'I can't wait to meet her,' she says, rising to her feet. 'Do you want me to come right away?'

'No hurry. I'll make us a cup of tea. Forty minutes or so? It'll take the gardener quite some time to get everything ready to Poppy's satisfaction. So long as she knows we're coming, she'll be fine.'

There's a sudden, heavy silence as Ann bends down to pick up the scattered pages, and Vivienne's eyes scan the bedspread, strewn with paper scraps of revelations.

Ann straightens her back and stands very still, concentrating on shuffling the papers into order. She glances up, then down at her hands again. At last she murmurs, 'Maybe I should finish reading these?'

Another silence, then, in a bright, brisk voice, 'Yes. Do that. I'll go down and put the kettle on. Come and join me when you're ready.'

As soon as Vivienne has left the room, Ann picks up another letter from the bed. This one is written in ink that has faded to brown. The hand is not Grannibelle's.

Monday 3rd July

Dear Mr McFarlane,
Mother and I are now in Wuchow till Monday next, visiting her brother, my uncle Wilfred, a retired missionary. Before we left Hong Kong, I sent you a chit asking if you could perhaps come over to us because I had a message from Belle for you. Since you didn't respond, I gather you didn't receive it.

Did you know that they all had the flu very badly? Little Harry was critically ill for a while. Belle was ill herself at the time. You can imagine what she went through. It is possible that you had news of their illness via your office – if so, you must have been sick with worry yourself. I copy here for you the letter she wrote to me, dated Wednesday, June 21st

"Dear Ivy, it has taken me a long time to get over the flu, but I tell you that the flu was the least of it. And now I must go back in time a little and tell you why you haven't heard from me before this. I was in our cabin, on the steamer to Canton, and had just finished writing you a letter, when there was a knock on the door. It was little Harry, followed by his amah looking very pale and tearful. She was clearly unwell, so I let her lie down on the couch for a while and then was distracted by Harry saying he wanted to see Daddy.

Before we left the room, I quickly blotted and folded the letter and placed it in an envelope. I have thought of nothing but R since I last saw you, and this letter to you was full of my outpourings and foolishly indiscreet. While I was on deck with Harry, looking for Jimmy, he had made his way back to our cabin. It may be that he was still suspicious at that time and was actively searching for evidence, for I am certain that I sealed the envelope securely.

Suffice it to say, he opened the letter and read it and there <u>was</u> a scene. He was going to leave me in

Canton and go back to Hong Kong to commit murder, I reckon. I was paralysed with fear and that scene was enough to make me realise that after all, my little Harry must come first and I can't do anything that will make his life the least bit more difficult than any life must of necessity be. It is too late for me to take another path, and I am thinking of no one but him and Jimmy now, and this is easier to do here than it would be in Hong Kong, so maybe it is a blessing that we have had to remain here so long.

Jimmy wanted me to send R's picture back, and to ask him for mine, so here it is. (R's face would be no longer discernable if my lips had left their imprint with every kiss!) You can tell him that I really don't need his picture anyway. It is no plainer than the one I carry in my heart. I want him to know that I am happy enough. Happier, that is, than I have any right to be, but I know perfectly well that this is of a quite different order to the kind of happiness that I would have had if he had come in to my life before it was too late. If you ever have a chance you may tell him this, but I am not going to write to him myself. I told Jimmy that I did love R, but that I loved him (Jimmy) more than anything in the world. Perhaps this may become true, one day. I had so little chance to find out how much I really do love R But I think I know. It would be better for me if I did not. Please always give me what news of him you can in a casual way."

Mr McFarlane – Rupert - I am so very sorry that things have turned out as they have. Though of course, it comes as no surprise to me that Belle has put her son's well being above her own. Although I have never experienced the love a mother must feel for her child, especially, perhaps, her first born, I believe that she could not have endured the pain of losing him. I am sure that Jimmy would never give him up.

I enclose your picture, and if you will send me the one of her that you have I will send it on. Better still, pay us a visit and bring it with you, when we return to Hong Kong. I know that Belle will be eager for direct news of you.

How are you? You looked very pale when I last saw you at the Parker's, soon after Belle's departure.

Are you intending to stay in Hong Kong? Send me any news of yourself you would like passed on.

I am very happy and well, though mother is not in the best of health. Wuchow is a pleasant spot although not a metropolis! I shall not be sorry to return to Hong Kong on Monday next.

Sincerely,
Ivy Latham

Hong Kong
Thursday 20th July

Rupert dear, it's quite true that a woman can kill her conscience much deader than a man can kill his, otherwise I should not be writing to you today. If one has a dead heart, a dead conscience more or less doesn't matter.

We arrived back here three days ago. Jimmy waited until we were on the boat before he told me that you had been transferred back to Shameen for a few weeks – and that by the time we docked at Kowloon, you would be gone. Somehow, I managed to retain an air of calm as he broke the news. I told him that I was pleased he would be spared any possible embarrassment in having to meet you at work or socially, and that although I no longer have any feelings for you, it would be hard for me to avoid your company entirely, since we were well known to have been on friendly terms and others might sense an awkwardness between us that might set them wondering.

Rupert dear, in truth, I cannot say if I would indeed have found the strength to stay away from you. Already, I have been

106

twice to the Botanic Gardens. I knew you would not be there, yet every man of similar height and build I saw approaching made my heart leap with hope for a brief instant. And then, each time, the painful aftermath which I will not bore you with. Nor how I felt yesterday when I walked down your road and stood for an age outside your house. Although I half-hoped he would, it is better that Bing did not see me and invite me in, for I don't know what you may have already disclosed to him about us – maybe nothing at all.

I am a dutiful wife now. Forever, I think, except for such a slight deflection from the path as this, and I'll admit there is a certain amount of self-satisfied pleasure in duty well done – trite as the sentiment may seem. Now that Jimmy and I have had it out and he is convinced that I am not absolutely rotten he is doing all he can to make up for his past behaviour. I believe that in his way he truly does love me. I should be happy – but my dear, dear I am not. Every time he kisses me I can scarcely keep back my cries to you. I'm not going to see you any more and I can't bear to think of it. There is a great hole in my heart – you have the piece that was dug out whether you want it or not.

Did Ivy tell you that Jimmy mutilated my "family album", the one we straightened up, remember? Removed forcibly every photograph that contained your physiognomy. But he overlooked that one of Bing and you on the top of the boat at Lamma, so I at least have one of your ears and a little bit of your shoulder and your right elbow!

Isn't Ivy a good sport and a dear? I don't know what on earth I'd do without her. I do wish that you would convince her that you never liked me at all and that you really set out to marry her – that you admire (as I know you do) the way she cheerfully shares her skill as a markswoman with the offspring of those who will never quite belong, either to the British community, or to the society of high-class Chinese. I mean I wish you _could_ do it. Really I do, dear. Because you've got to marry somebody, sometime, and it might as well be a somebody who would furnish you with enough excitement to keep you from being bored to tears.

I am so glad you went to see Ivy while we were in Canton. Because she wrote me lots that you said, and it helped. She must have told you that Jimmy requested a transfer back to London. It has been granted, and we leave very soon. But of course you must know this through your office – even if Ivy has said nothing of it.

Shall I write to you when I get home? Nothing could stop me if I thought you wanted me to but it is a desolate thought that I'll never have another word from you.

I remember every moment of 'our night'- not only the actions, which I try not to let myself dwell upon, but also every word we spoke. I think we both knew in our hearts, even then, that it must end sooner or later. I am glad that neither of us could know this <u>was</u> the end. Before you left, you spoke of how long it might take for us to get over this. I hope you won't take long – and I hope I never get over it. It's very unmaidenly, or at least unmatronly, for me to admit all this, I'm sure. When you don't realise what you've missed in life until it's too late to have it, what matters it how brazen a hussy one becomes?

The three weeks left to me here in Hong Kong are creeping by. I didn't know days could be so long. Do you believe in the much hackneyed mutual telepathy? Two days ago at the tiffin table little Harry asked when you were coming again and that night he insisted on including you in his prayers. Well I include you in mine, such as they are. The best love I have – the only one with a thrill in it – is yours. Please keep it until you get a better; that better one is waiting for you somewhere.

This is my last letter to you for the present and it's my good-bye too, and I'm heartsick Rupert dear. I never knew I would care so much. My dear. My dear, why did you come to me so late?

Tuesday   July 25th 1930 Hong Kong

The heat is truly unbearable here. Worse even than Canton, though that was bad enough. I long for England, yet I am in dread of the journey. I have now missed too many weeks to be in any doubt. Over and over again, I've calculated and compared my dates, trying to convince myself that this is nothing out of the ordinary.

After Harry's birth, it was almost a whole year before my cycle began again, and for the first few months there was a great discrepancy in the length of time between the start of each bleeding. But the last four or five events appeared with the regularity of clockwork, as they did before my pregnancy. Even before the journey to Canton, and Jimmy's discovery of my 'affair', his needs in that direction had been less frequent. His own bout of flu, followed by Harry's and mine allowed for a long postponement of a fully physical 'making-up' between us, and that eventually took place at a time when the usual low, back-ache seemed to presage the already late arrival of a bleed – which even now has not yet occurred. And, I must face the fact, will not.

Wednesday the 10th of May is a date I could never forget. That night, I crossed over into some kind of parallel existence, a hundred times more real than my ordinary life. I was far beyond anything as rational as a cold calculation of the risk. R himself made but a half-hearted gesture towards 'safety' and I did nothing to encourage him in that direction. Now, with a calendar in front of me, it seems more and more certain that Jimmy's absence for that one night had chanced to fall in the middle of my most fertile time.

It is fortunate indeed that the activity following little Harry's innocent remark, 'Mummy likes Big Man betterest' now means that Jimmy will have no real cause to question my dates, if what I fear is indeed the truth.

Fear? Do I fear this, or is it my dearest wish that the baby now growing inside me is Rupert's?

No. NO! To be reminded daily of what I have lost - to live with this for the rest of my life? I cannot bear it.

Hong Kong 2008 - Poppy

Chapter 14

Ann is sitting with Vivienne on her small paved terrace in the shade of a spindly papaya tree. The cane chairs remind her of the summer house in Sutton Coldfield, all those years ago. She wonders if Vivienne would remember those few moments when she had stroked her daughter's hair –'Shhh. Shhh. It's all right. It'll be all right.' Unlikely. Those were her own memories. Vivienne's head would have been filled with thoughts of Stuart and the complications of that situation.

What must Vivienne have felt, reading these intimate, posthumous disclosures from her own mother, on the plane back to Hong Kong after the funeral? Back to rejoin the man she'd chosen with no thought for anyone else. *She* had not put her small son's welfare before her own desires. Her teenage daughter wouldn't even have entered the equation.

Ann glances up from the slice of lemon she is squeezing with the back of a spoon against the inside of the tea cup. Vivienne looks away with an almost inaudible sigh and begins to push at the cuticle of her left forefinger with the nail of her right. *No,* thinks Ann. *No I bloody well won't make it easy for her. It's up to her to broach the subject. What can I say?*

'Are you all right, Ann?' asks Vivienne at last. 'I mean, I expect it's all been rather a shock. If you've read it all.'

'All but Grannibelle's last letter to you – and a few more journal pages. And the one that her friend, Ivy wrote to her. I'd had enough by then. Bit of a shock? Yes, I suppose you could say that.'

'So you know, now? You know that your Grannibelle wasn't quite the upright, virtuous person she'd led us to believe?'

There's a sharp crack as Ann slams the spoon so hard against the saucer that the cup seesaws into the air and smashes down onto the terracotta paving slab. 'Don't you *dare!!* Don't you dare talk about Grannibelle like that!' she spits out the words like bullets as she jumps to her feet.

Without a glance towards her mother, Ann has stepped past the fragments of china and onto the sparse grass of the tiny strip of lawn. In two strides she has reached the white-painted wall and stands beside a huge, brown-and-yellow glazed pot in the corner, where an almost leafless climbing plant has twined itself along a trellis of greying wood. She peers down through the small square gaps, over the topmost leafy branches of a tree in the garden below, across descending rooftops down, down to the far end of the ferry pier, along which are scurrying tiny figures towards what looks like a miniature of the vessel that brought her to this island the previous afternoon.

Her lips are clamped and her nails dig into her clenched palms. She's holding herself very still, her head precariously balanced on her rigid neck as if any movement might jolt the dark pool of her thoughts. Once the swirling debris has settled, she'll be able to see more clearly. Grannibelle's image will re-assemble itself. Everything will fall back into place.

'Will you come too, Ann? You can stay here if you'd rather not. Poppy will understand. I really do have to go now, myself, though,' Vivienne's voice sounds disembodied, muffled, as if she's speaking from the inside of a long tunnel, 'May be it will be better if you stay. Better for you and for Poppy. Let's just leave it till you've had a good night's sleep.'

Sleep! Thinks Ann. So that's what it is! More jet lag than shock. That's why her brain is now swaddled in cotton wool. Since she won't be able to think clearly for the time being, she might as well allow her mother to take control.

Following Vivienne out through her high wooden gate, Ann is surprised to find that they are turning to the right. She'd got the impression that Vivienne's is the last house, the very top of the hill, and that the concrete path would soon peter out. But although the track does level off for a while, and then dips down as it rounds a corner, it soon curves steeply up again between tall dark trees on

111

one side, and rough grass and shrubs on the left, giving a brief glimpse of the sea.

The physical exertion seems to be clearing her head, restoring her ability to choose. Those letters, together with Grannibelle's notebook, are filed away in a separate part of her brain; she'll need time to assimilate these revelations. Meanwhile, she can let her curiosity take over: what is she going to make of George's mother – and what will this Poppy woman make of her?

Vivienne is walking briskly a couple of yards ahead, and though she does slow down a little when the path is at its steepest, Ann makes no attempt to catch up; it's not merely her physical tiredness that is holding her back.

Wait for me, wait for me, little Ann would call, trudging along the shingle at Cley, on the way to Blakeney Point. It was always Uncle Harry or Grannibelle who would stop and turn, holding out an encouraging hand, never Vivienne - she'd already be too far ahead to hear her child's wailing voice above the crash and hiss of the sea. As soon as Uncle Harry's old Morris Minor had rattled to a halt at the muddy car park, Vivienne would be scrambling up the bank of shifting stones. She'd pause for a moment at the top of the ridge, raising her bent elbows, then stretching her arms in a wide arc as if in a huge yawn, before disappearing over the edge: first her legs in their cream cotton slacks; then her navy-blue windcheater and last of all the crown of her head with its dark streamers of hair tugged and tangled by the wind. By the time Ann and Grannibelle and Uncle Harry had reached that same spot, Vivienne would be striding along, a hundred yards or more ahead, as near to the seething foam as she could get without wetting her thin black plimsolls.

Now, though, when Ann raises her eyes from the path as it levels out once more, she sees that Vivienne has stopped in the shade of a large clump of bamboo, the green stems and pale yellow ones as thick as a man's arm, and is looking towards her, a quizzical expression on her face.

'Nearly there, now,' she says, 'it's just round the next corner. Don't be too taken aback by anything Poppy might say, will you?

Even though we've been friends for years, she can still come out with things that surprise me. She's a little... volatile, should I say? Heart of gold. Kindness itself, to her friends – generous to a fault. But not a person you'd want to offend. So...'

Here we go, thinks Ann. She's afraid I'll let her down. 'So you think I'll ..?' she begins, keeping her voice steady.

'Offend her? No, of course not. It's just... Well, for one thing, she's half Chinese, as you probably know.'

'And what's wrong with that?' So far, the only people she's seen her mother conversing with as equals have been white. Ex-pats. Poppy, George's mother, is supposedly her best friend.

'Oh!' laughs Vivienne after a moment, 'Nothing! Of course there's nothing wrong with that! All I'm saying is that the Chinese can be very outspoken, and although Poppy, at times, is more English than the English she doesn't pull any punches when it comes to speaking her mind. What I meant was, she might say things that an English woman wouldn't dream of saying. She wouldn't intend to give offence to a guest in her house – it's just that she has a slightly... How shall I put it? An almost child-like frankness – if you know what I mean?'

So it's Poppy she's afraid will let her down, not me, thinks Ann. The idea is so novel that she almost laughs. Vivienne actually cares about her opinion of her friend! She finds herself warming towards this woman who can unsettle her mother's hitherto almost unshakable poise.

The tall, flat-roofed house is similar to Vivienne's but larger, detached, and the white painted stucco is specked with more of the greenish-black mould that seems to be a feature of most of the buildings Ann has seen since her arrival on Lamma. 'It's the humidity,' Vivienne explained as they'd trudged up the steps and slopes that morning. 'However often you scrub them, it always comes back.' Like hers, this garden is enclosed by plaster-clad walls, five or six foot high, but the wide beds of earth edging these walls contain nothing more than the occasional clump of straggly pampas, or some such grasses. What might once have been a lawn is mainly cracked, dry mud.

Ann follows her mother along the tiled path at the side of the house. She hears the voice before she sees the speaker - redolent of the Home Counties, a 1960s BBC news reader, a Joyce Grenfell replica, remonstrating with a naughty four-year old. 'No, no, no! What are you thinking of, Ignatius? That won't do at all. It needs to be at least three foot deep. And wide enough to hold the basket.'

Can this be Poppy? More English than the English! Ann hesitates before she rounds the corner of the house. Expecting to see a tall, thin-faced woman, she glances around and beyond the small group on the brick-red terrace: her mother, just a few steps ahead, her back turned; a stocky Filipino man who could be any age between early forties and late sixties, resting on his spade beside a small heap of earth; and a huge, Buddha of a woman who is slowly levering herself upright from her inspection of the hole.

'Vivienne, you slacker! At last!' she exclaims, firmly removing any doubt about the connection between her rotund figure and that voice.

Ann barely has time to take in the details of the black hair piled like a rook's nest on top of her head, and the floor-length garment of purple silk, before one small foot in a gold and silver mule appears from beneath the whispering hem, then disappears again as the other foot steps forward a few more inches. Ann stares, transfixed. The feet are tiny in comparison with the glimpse of puffy ankles, not to speak of the huge body they must carry, and for an instant, Ann thinks of bumblebees – how their ability to fly supposedly contradicts the laws of thermodynamics.

Vivienne has stepped to one side, saying, 'Here we are, then. Poppy, this is…'

'I know who this is,' booms the voice, 'Of course I know who this is! Could I ever mistake that chin?' and Ann looks up at the broad face looming towards her. The skin is pale as dough, apart from a large circle of rouge on each cheek, and the scarlet, cupid's-bow lips that are pursed upwards in a prim smile. Before she can dodge to one side, the plump hands have clasped hers and pulled her forwards.

The next moment her face is half buried in smooth fabric draped across something as yielding as a pillow – the upper part of an enormous stomach – or maybe the drooping bosom? She feels herself go rigid, then tries to wriggle away, but Poppy's forearms have clamped her too tightly. 'Ann! My Little One!' she chortles, 'I never thought I'd live to see this day.' One of the hands is stroking her hair, over and over, from the crown to the nape of her neck, while the voice, lower now in tone and pitch, babbles on, 'My pretty little one, my munchkin.'

For a moment, Ann lets go of her conscious mind, aware of nothing but the unexpected sensation of comfort and security; then her mother's laughing voice jolts her back to reality, 'Poppy! That's my daughter's head you're stroking. Not one of your precious cats!'

Vivienne steps forward, releasing her from Poppy's embrace, muttering something that Ann can't quite catch. Then she takes the older woman's hand, almost pulling her towards the patio doors, with Ann following close behind.

At first, when she sees the pattern of muted colour through the glass, Ann assumes it's a wide border at the bottom of the heavy curtains that have been pulled across to keep daylight from the room inside. The hanging fabric has been shifted slightly as the two older women squeeze in through the gap in the sliding door. Maybe closing the curtains is Chinese custom, a mark of respect for the recently dead cat, she thinks. *Cat!* The giggle she's attempting to suppress now becomes a choke of horror: those shapes are the swarming bodies of cats, scrabbling at the plate-glass.

'Quick, Ann!' exclaims Vivienne. 'Come in, come in. Mustn't let the cats out yet.'

This has to be a dream, thinks Ann. Her brain is struggling to impose some kind of logic onto the blur of information that is filtering in from her senses of smell, sound and sight. Cat, definitely: a not-unpleasant, slightly fishy smell of food on exhaled breath, overlaid with pine air-freshener; a low, rumbling grumble of little motors, interspersed with plaintive mewling. Gradually her

115

eyes adjust to the gloom, making out shapes in various tones of grey, with occasional glints of green or yellow a few inches above floor level as thin rays of filtered light are reflected from what must be eyes. Then the curtains are drawn back letting full day-light surge into the room.

Twenty seven cats, her mother had said earlier. It is beginning to look as though she hadn't been exaggerating. Poppy is standing knee-deep in a purring mass of stripes and blotches: black and white, brown and black, cream and ginger. 'Come and sit here, Little One,' she says, gesturing towards a huge, egg-shaped cane chair, suspended by a thick chain from the centre of a metal girder running across the ceiling.

At first Ann thinks she's addressing one of the cats, but Vivienne puts a hand on her shoulder and gently propels her forward, 'You're remarkably honoured, you realise?' she laughs. 'It's the only place in the room that the cats steer clear of. They don't like the way it swings when they try to jump onto it.'

It's not just cats that find it difficult, thinks Ann, struggling to wriggle her buttocks up on to the swaying seat. 'Poor little Munchkin! Your legs are too short,' exclaims Poppy wading towards her. Ann quickly turns to face the dangling chair, grips the sturdy cane sides and, in the nick of time, manages to raise one knee onto the padded edge and launch herself from the wooden floor with the ball of her foot. Her sudden movement makes the chair swivel wildly round and round on its chain as she collapses, giggling like a school girl, onto piles of embroidered silk cushions.

With Poppy and Vivienne on either side, steadying what feels to Ann like a wicker cage, the room slowly stops spinning. 'I am so sorry, Ann! Vivienne, please assure your daughter that I was offering her my own favourite chair as a way of welcoming her into my house at last. Ann, dear, you do believe that don't you?'

Ann leans forward, biting her lip, and turns her head from Poppy to Vivienne and back again, at a loss to find what two such different women could have in common: her mother, poised, slim, detached; and Poppy, so very…*Wild* is the first word that comes to mind. Wild, as in, not tamed, not confined by convention. Ann's own journey to this place has been equivalent to Alice's headlong tumble down the rabbit-hole: Poppy is a cross between the Red Queen and the Duchess, with a pinch of that anarchic TV witch Danny and Louise used to love.

Poppy reaches out her hands towards Ann, opening her mouth as if to speak. 'Hadn't we better be getting on with the ceremony, Poppy?' puts in Vivienne hastily. 'I don't want to rush you, but isn't that what we came for? Ann is completely exhausted, as I'm sure you can see, so...'

'Of course. How silly of me. I was getting quite carried away in the excitement of meeting the dear girl at last. I have to say, my sweet,' she adds, smiling at Ann, 'your arrival has helped to soften the blow for me. Poor little Pebbles. We must lay him to rest without further ado. Come along then, Vivienne. Help Ann get down from there while I go and fetch Dawn.'

'Dawn's here already, is she?' asks Vivienne.

'Of course! Someone had to stay with Pebbles while I supervised Ignatius. She's upstairs in the drawing room.' Ann scrambles down from her seat and turns to watch as Poppy picks her way through the scatter of cats towards the far wall, bending from time to time to stroke a furry, upturned head or raised back. She's surprised to see a floor-to-ceiling wrought iron contraption protruding out into the room between, on one side, a closed piano with three large tabbies curled up asleep on the top, and on the other, a four-seater sofa, seemingly almost entirely upholstered in yet more sleeping cats.

Poppy pulls open a door in the cage and closes it deftly behind her without allowing a single feline to follow her inside it. Then she flings open a wooden door in the wall, and bellows, 'Dawn! Daw – awn! We're ready for Pebbles now. You can bring him down. We'll go out through the front.'

Before she shuts the door behind her, Poppy turns and calls back into the room, 'You'd better come this way too, Vivienne. And you, of course, Ann. I can't risk any of Pebbles' brothers or sisters getting out. Not till it's all over. Cats are such sensitive creatures. They'd be terribly upset by the funeral.'

'She's not always as emotional as this,' whispers Vivienne as she and Ann attempt to cross the floor without stepping on any of the precious tails or paws.

They manage to ease themselves into the cage without any of the creatures slinking through at their heels. Once she has closed the door of the cat-room behind them, Ann looks up and sees Dawn poised at the top of a narrow flight of stairs, silhouetted against a sunlit window on the landing, her shoulder-length blonde hair forming a silver aura around her head. She looks like an angel on a mission, standing there with a dark, rectangular object balanced across her outstretched forearms, held a few inches away from her body as though it is too sacred to be clutched against her chest. She bends her head, then cranes to her left, peering down over the side of this box towards her foot, which she lowers cautiously onto the top step. Her right foot is about to make contact with the step below this when Poppy calls up to her, 'Do be careful, Dawn. We don't want you to fa…'

Dawn's head jerks round to her other side and down towards Poppy. Her foot lands awkwardly and as it teeters on the edge, she grabs the banister with her right hand. The other arm is flung upwards in a vain effort to prevent the object from slipping out of her grasp. As it hits the tread of a step several feet below, Ann can see that it's a picnic basket with its lid flapping open like the wing of some strange bird. Out tumbles a bundle of shining white fabric that gradually unravels as it bumps its way down and deposits the stiff corpse of a mottled beige and chestnut cat at Poppy's feet.

Not *Alice in Wonderland*, thinks Ann in the ensuing chaos of screams, tears and stifled laughter. That's not surreal enough; this is more like *Through the Looking Glass*.

Hong Kong 1930 - Ivy and Shing Mui

Chapter 15

'So, Annie, what d'you make of Poppy?' asks Dawn, as the two of them set out together along the path back to Vivienne's house. 'Quite something, isn't she?'

'She certainly is,' laughs Ann. 'I wouldn't have thought she was my mother's type, though.' Then she sighs and adds, 'I'm beginning to wonder if I ever really knew her at all, or my grandmother.'

'Did you say you've only just found out about Vivienne's real dad?'

'Yes. Grannibelle – that's my grandmother – she never told me, or Vivienne. Not while she was alive. It was all in some letters that her friend, Ivy sent her. And a sort of journal. How she was in love with a man called Rupert. And then her husband, Jimmy, the one who was meant to be my grandfather, he found out about the affair and made her promise never to see Rupert again, so they came back to England and that was that.'

'Yeh, that's what Poppy told me. Dead romantic, yeh?'

'I suppose it is – to other people – but to be honest, I really don't know what I think - my brain's in a total whirl.'

'Not surprising,' says Dawn, looking at her closely. 'Guess you must be dead tired - takes ages for the jetlag to wear off. I'll leave you to chill out, soon as we get to your mum's place.'

It feels strange to Ann, walking around Vivienne's house on her own. It's been comforting to have Dawn's company for a while, someone with no emotional involvement in the story, but now she wants to read the letter that Ivy wrote to Belle – the one from Lugard Road in 1971. She wants to discover for herself whatever else she needs to know, before her mother comes home.

My dear Belle

You will be surprised, I am sure, to receive this letter from me after so many years of silence. By the time this reaches you, there will be no opportunity for us to speak together, so this must serve as a one-way communication from myself to you.

It is my dearest wish that once you have absorbed the content of this letter, you will allow yourself to accept my most sincere apology, and even, perhaps, find it in your heart to forgive your former friend. I say, 'former' since I have long ago forfeited any right to claim your friendship.

Oh Belle, my fear of my own impending death is greatly increased by the knowledge of how I have betrayed your trust in me, and, by doing so, have inflicted harm on the man we both loved so dearly. My only justification, if it can be called such, was my fear that I had not at that time fully supplanted the place you held in his affections, and that if I had allowed him to receive that final letter from you, he would have followed you to the ends of the earth.

I have changed in many ways since our times together in Hong Kong, as, no doubt, have you. When I look back now on some of our activities, I recoil with shame to think how lightly we regarded the danger in which we placed our immortal souls. As I recall, we even expressed some doubt regarding the existence of the soul, and of Almighty God Himself! Praise be to Him, it was not long after your departure that He drew me back into the fold, enabling me to be born again in His love.

My intervals of strength and lucidity are becoming shorter and more infrequent, and the doctors have told me that the cancer is so far advanced I can expect no more than two or three months on this earth. As I approach the hour of my death, I must contemplate as steadfastly as possible the true facts of the situation. So while I cannot deny that I acted wrongly in opening, and then destroying, your letter, I must also ask myself what purpose it would have served had I acted otherwise. Would your little daughter have led a happier life had she grown up with the knowledge of her mother's adultery and its consequence? You had already chosen to sacrifice your own desires for the sake of little Harry, and poor Jimmy. What, indeed, would have become of you had you not made that timely return to the straight and narrow path, rather than continue blithely along the primrose way? As for my dear Rupert, (God bless his soul) although it was I who deprived him of any knowledge of, or contact with, his daughter by you, it was I who gave him the joy of his other little girl.

No, Belle, this child, whom we named Poppy, was not the fruit of my womb. As you had already suggested to Rupert after you ended your brief affair, he did indeed ask me to marry him, once he had been given a more permanent position at the Hong Kong office. You will no doubt remember seeing the announcement in the Times newspaper. Our quiet wedding ceremony took place in 1932, a year after your letter announcing the birth (and the true paternity) of little Vivienne. However, although we made every effort to have a child of our own, the Lord did not bless us in this way. Upon examination by not one, but three separate specialists in the field of gynaecology, it became apparent that I would be unlikely ever to bear a child.

But there is more to tell that relates directly to you, Belle. First though, you must picture me: a bride of three short, happy weeks, still scarcely believing of my good fortune. Rupert was so kind and attentive to me, I had persuaded myself that his affair with you had been but a brief infatuation from which he was fully recovered. As for material goods, I wanted for nothing: Rupert had made a good name for himself in the Company and by the time of our marriage, he had attained a senior management position with an excellent salary that enabled us to occupy a fine house on Lugard Road. How you would have loved that, Belle! The heavenly views! The only cloud on my horizon was the loss of the *friendship we had shared. Apart from that, I was supremely happy in my ignorance, convinced that Rupert had chosen to marry me, because it was I whom he loved, in spite of your more immediately seductive beauty. This happiness came to an abrupt end when I was innocently searching his bureau for some fresh writing paper. By chance I knocked against a catch that opened a hidden compartment and saw an envelope addressed to him in your distinctive hand.*

Do you remember what you wrote to him about me? How I was 'a good sport' and 'a dear'. Imagine then what I felt, discovering that my marriage was founded on falsehood - that Rupert had been following your instructions to the letter: he had indeed 'convinced' me that he had 'really set out to marry' me. Not for one moment had I thought he had made me his wife because, as you so cogently put it, he had to marry somebody sometime, so 'it might as well be a somebody' who may at least not bore him to tears. It was like a knife in my heart. That knife still turns, even now. So, yes, I read through all your letters. And I was glad, I tell you. Glad to read of your suffering. For a while I even hated you, but God in His mercy eventually softened my heart.

But that was not the only discovery that shook my world that morning: yours were not the only letters he had kept and treasured from a former paramour. I remember only too well my own horror and disgust as I slowly took in the meaning of a second collection of letters and other papers. There was a photograph of a young Chinese woman, barely more than a girl. She appeared respectable enough, and at first I thought she must have been a clerk or secretary at his office, for his firm employed several Chinese, though I had never been aware of any women employees. But gradually, with mounting horror, the full story presented itself to me through her series of pitiful letters to him, and then the formal papers, dating from a period two years before that evening which you, too, will surely remember, when he introduced himself to us at mother's hotel. Those papers gave details of a monthly allowance that was to be paid to her 'for the support of the child'.

One item that at first had seemed so innocuous I had almost overlooked it – a few scribbled lines on company paper, in Rupert's hand - turned out to be the clearest evidence of the sort of place that he - my <u>husband</u>! - used to frequent. Dear Lord in Heaven! I nearly collapsed in a heap on the floor as my poor brain took in the meaning of the words I was reading. Poetry, he had called it! Poetry! A word that encompasses the highest form of art – the noblest of sentiments! That he could have kept - treasured even - this translation of crude verse! What must this say about the debased character of this man who was now my husband?

I do not know how I managed to compose myself and mask my feelings, before Rupert returned from work that evening - not only was I filled with bitter disappointment for myself, and rage against you, I had to come to terms with the fact that my own husband had consorted with a Chinese woman of ill-repute, and that she had borne him a child.

Somehow, I resisted acting on my first impulse, which was to destroy everything I had discovered in his bureau that morning. Instead, I removed every scrap of paper that bore your hand, together with the photo of Poppy's mother, that vile piece of verse and just two of her letters, and hid them away in a secret place of my own. The rest of that day, I spent in prayer and reflection, which led me to conclude that I should not judge my husband too harshly for his youthful misdemeanour. I have heard it said that there are some men who are burdened with physical urges beyond the average. It may be, then, that for such men, when they are still in the bachelor state, it is less harmful to others if they turn for the relief of the more animal side of their natures to that type of woman who has already fallen into disgrace.

Two years later, when I received the results of the final test performed by my third consultant, I knew I must accept the Lord's *decision that I would never bear Rupert a child, and I began to feel that it was God's hand which had led me to the discovery of the existence of the first little daughter. It did not take much ingenuity for me to raise the subject, in order to suggest the possibility of officially adopting the child, and to persuade him that we would easily be able to contrive some suitable reason for this choice that would avoid any risk of scandal. I tearfully confessed to him how I had come across the packages, and how I had been so frightened and shocked by my discovery, that I had subsequently burned all the papers but those few relating directly to the birth of the child, and the arrangements for the payments he was making to support it. As you see from the enclosed, this was not the strict truth, but I felt compelled to keep these items, thinking that one day I might share this knowledge with you, and allow you to decide what information to impart to Vivienne about her older sister.*

As for dear Poppy, she was but six years old when we journeyed to Shanghai to bring her back to live with us in Hong Kong. The mother had been able to give up that shameful trade, thanks to the monthly allowance from Rupert's account which continued to be paid for several years after we had removed her daughter from the unsavoury district in which she was being brought up, in what I can only describe as a hovel, crowded as it was, not only with that woman and little Poppy, but with the two grandparents, and even a great grandmother, as well as the woman's two younger sisters and a little brother. Nonetheless, she did not appear to be suitably appreciative of her good fortune. To tell the blunt truth, my husband had paid more than one thousand times over, for the services that woman had freely sold to him as a naive young bachelor all those years before.

After a period of adjustment during which the child refused to be comforted, and continued to sob and scream in that strange language for most of the waking day, stopping only when exhaustion lulled her to sleep for an hour or two together, she gradually became accustomed to our ways and learned to appreciate her good fortune in being brought up by Christian English parents, of good birth. I have to admit that I found the child's display of ingratitude hard to bear, since it seemed interminable at the time, but could not, in fact, have lasted for more than a week, because she swallowed not a morsel of food during the entire sorry episode, from which, I am happy to say, she has suffered no lasting effect, apart from a brief interlude during that stage of life which is now called the teenage years . Indeed, I can make no complaint of the dear girl, now herself the mother of a young man, my adopted grandson, George, for though most of her adult life has been spent in the south of England with her husband, as soon as she received the news of the severity of the decline in my health she has been living here in Hong Kong with me, returning for brief visits to her husband from time to time.

Far be it from me to come between a wife and her duty to her husband, but Poppy, at the age of forty three, must be allowed to make her own decisions regarding her division of duty between her husband and the woman who has been not only a devoted mother to her, but the instrument of her removal from a pagan slum-dwelling to a life of plenty, in which she has enjoyed all the benefits of not only a Christian, but an English, upbringing and education.

Soon, if the Good Lord wills it, I shall fall into a sleep from which I will not wake again in the light of this earthly sun, but oh it is my strong and only hope, dear Belle, now I am stumbling through the valley of death itself and am afraid – so afraid, I do hope and pray that I will wake to the glorious light of the risen Son

Pray for me Belle. Please do not think harshly of me – we did have good times you and I
forgive Ivy your friend
yes friend

Poppy! That poor little girl is Poppy! Has Vivienne shown her this letter from Ivy, her adoptive mother? What a sanctimonious old cow she seems to have been. All that phoney god-stuff. She hadn't sounded like that sort of person in Grannibelle's letters and journal. And the photo of the young Chinese girl – is that Poppy's mother?

As she replaces the final page of Ivy's letter on the bed, Ann's fingers touch the corner of another small sheet of paper. Drawing it out from beneath the scatter of pages, she sees that this must be 'the vile piece of verse' that had caused Ivy such distress.

Memorandum
The Asiatic Petroleum Co. (South China) Ltd
                                         Shanghai 1927
attempted translation of Chinese poetry written on wall
above spot where bed was placed

Desert grasses, flowers wild   *(Chinese for sing-sing girls*
                                                    and whores)
flourish in thousands, yet my child   *(lit: ten millions)*
better re-enter your own doors and sleep with your wife:
though the ways of the girls twixt the dusk and the
                                                        dawning
 allure, and their charms are so many
and "this is the life",
yet the wife of your heart when it comes to the morning
won't ask for a penny.

Ann feels a sudden sympathy for this unknown woman, her grandmother's former friend, alone in her house, innocently rummaging through the belongings of the man she loves, gradually piecing together a series of clues that lead to a discovery that shakes her whole world.

For a brief moment, Ann is twenty two years old. She has just let herself into Max's flat with the key he gave her at the start of their…affair? No, this isn't an affair. There's no wife to get in their way, no obstacles. They're in love. He's crazy about her, 'Not pretty! Who gives a toss about 'pretty'? You're the sexiest woman I've ever known. No, of course it's not just the sex. You're a wonderful person. I adore you.' It's only a matter of time before he starts talking of rings and wedding bells.

But there's someone in the flat. Someone who shouldn't have been there yet.

Not nice, is it, finding out uncomfortable truths about the man you love?

Ann shakes her head and claps her hands together, 'Piss off, Max,' she mutters with a grim little laugh. Then she opens out a single sheet of pale cream paper, folded over and over into a small note that could easily have been slipped, unobserved, from hand to hand.

The ink is faint, and she is unable to make out what must have been a Chinese form of expressing the date in the top right hand corner. Several phrases have been enclosed in brackets in a seemingly random manner, but the hand-writing itself is that of an educated person.

$?^{th}$ of moon (Chinese)

The Manage

Dear Sir,

Since you departed from me (I am) thinking of you all the time (even) in my dreams

(I told you) I would send you my photo, (but) regret (to say) they are not ready yet (to be sent off)

I will send you by and by.

Shing Mui

(Those inside bracket are what I added to get its English meaning)

The second letter covers two small pages and several words have been crossed out, evidently in an attempt to clarify the writer's meaning as she struggles to express herself in English. The numbers in the place for the date are impossible to decipher.

Dear Sir

When I saw you, my love began. Many thanks for your kind treatments to me, therefore I was able to talk to you, and as I found you were really love me therefore I greatly pleased and allowed you to have my room prepared for you. I hate that heavens could not give us a favour of a long time for you to stay here, and so each now is on his way.

If I could I would cut the big mountain down and make the rivers as dry level lands in order to see you easily even in a far distance and to come quickly to you. But these are all in vain.

If I try to remember the words you were talking to me, my heart suffers a great deal. (Chinese words really means my stomach breaks).

I cry to say I was not born in a rich family and therefore I am obliged to live on such business.

Oh, heaven! If there is any one who can pick me up from such dark valley, my world is once again bright.

Herewith I enclose my photo as a remembrance and hope you will let me know when you have got it.

I should be much pleased by an answer and don't let me suffer more.

Shing Mui

Ann sniffs loudly and dabs at her eyes with the back of her knuckles. How could Ivy have read these letters and remained unmoved by the plight of this poor girl? And the cause of it all, that man, Rupert. Her grandfather. No doubt about where Vivienne's callous streak has come from.

Hong Kong 2008 - George

Chapter 16

'So, this Rupert person – yours and Poppy's father. My real grandfather. I presume he's long dead by now?'

Vivienne turns her head and glances around her. It's 10.30 in the morning and the ferry is almost empty as it chugs away from the pier. 'Yes. He died in '41. The Japanese invasion. At least, that's what Poppy was told.'

'Told! I know how much credence can be given to "told", don't I?' Ann mutters, staring at the receding shore-line. Today, the sea is flat and grey under a low sky. After a moment, she adds, 'So where was Poppy at the time?'

'At boarding school in England. I believe she spent all but the summer holidays with Ivy's sister in Worthing. Then Rupert wanted Ivy to go back to England too – he was worried about the worsening situation with the Japanese.'

'And what else was Poppy told, I wonder?' muses Ann. 'I mean, she must have remembered something about her own mother and living with her Chinese family. The way Ivy describes that in her letter – this poor little six-year old, not a word of English, sobbing and screaming.'

'She did speak some English, Poppy's sure about that. But she has only the haziest memory of those years. They told her that her mother had been Rupert's secretary in Shanghai and she'd sent her to live with them in Hong Kong so she could get a good education. When, after her first year with them, Poppy hadn't stopped asking when her Mummy was going to come to take her home, they sat her down and told her she'd gone to heaven to be with baby Jesus and the angels.'

'And had she? Died, I mean?'

'I think that's unlikely – but who can tell? Poppy never did find out.'

'Oh, the poor little thing - that's awful!'

'Yes,' sighs Vivienne, 'Poor Poppy.'

'But I suppose… in those days… well, the fear of scandal and all that stuff?'

'You're right. Things were very different then. But Poppy did know that Rupert was her real father before she was sent off to boarding school. She'd have been eleven or twelve then.'

'Quite the opposite of the usual adoption revelation,' says Ann with a wry smile. 'I wonder how they explained that in a socially acceptable way.'

'I'm not too sure about that, but they'd have had to find a way of explaining her parentage. It's very clear in photos of her as a child that at least one of her parents had oriental blood in their veins. Whatever they'd told her, Poppy created a background for herself that she could feel comfortable with. She discretely let it be known to one or two selected friends, in strictest confidence, that her mother was the daughter of a Chinese nobleman, who had cut her off without a penny when she married the youngest son of a Scottish aristocrat. Her mother had died giving birth to her, so she couldn't be expected to have any memories of any Chinese relatives. She got through her school days by playing on her romantic and exotic origins.'

Ann laughs, 'From what I've seen of Poppy so far, it's not hard to imagine what she'd have been like as a girl – very flamboyant and eccentric.'

'Precisely. The best survival strategy in her circumstances. She seems to have enjoyed her boarding school, and I wouldn't be at all surprised if she'd begun to believe the story she invented about her mother's origins.'

'But she knows the truth now, though, doesn't she? I mean…'

'Truth!' sighs Vivienne, and turns her head towards the window. They've rounded the tip of the main island and are now chugging eastwards along its north coast. 'She knows what she's been told. That's as far as it can go. All the original letters and documents - the ones Ivy had read on that day when she found your Grannibelle's letters to Rupert – all those were lost years

130

back, during the war. All except the ones I gave you to read, and the photo of her mother, Shing Mui. She told Poppy more or less what she'd written to Belle about all that. Everything except the minor detail of me, her sister!'

'So if you hadn't turned up in Hong Kong, and if Grannibelle hadn't written *her* deathbed letter to you, neither of you would have...'

'Exactly. And that's why Poppy wanted me to show those letters to you. "Life's too short for secrets," is what she said. And I heartily agree. Can you imagine how I felt, nearly thirteen years ago, finding out that my whole life had been based on a lie?'

'I think I've got some idea, yes,' says Ann dryly. Her tone is steady, but her head is spinning – *All those years, when she could have known about George, her cousin!* Her next words spill out unchecked, 'But *you* knew how it felt, Vivienne! How could you have kept me in the dark till now? Thirteen years - a secret like that! You could've written, couldn't you? Made copies of everything?'

'You're right, Ann. There is no excuse... But I didn't want to just...and then, as I said, I kept thinking I'd be coming over to England soon, and I'd look you up, and we'd -'

'You did come to England, remember! Edward's funeral. I know I was making it hard for you, but you could have stayed around a bit longer and tried again. At the very least you could have left all that stuff for me to look at later, couldn't you? Couldn't you?'

Vivienne flinches, leaning away from Ann as far as the window will allow. A moment later, she recovers her composure, 'I do remember the funeral. Very clearly. That package was in my hotel room, ready to show you. But you were so...so...Let's just say you made it quite clear that you didn't want to hear anything I might have to tell you. Not ever. As for leaving the papers with you later, I was afraid you'd refuse to look at them – tear them to shreds, burn them, the state you were in...'

'But how was I to know...?' says Ann lowering her voice. 'Yes, I was in a state, but that's not exactly unusual at funerals is it? I was upset. I'd spent nearly two years nursing Edward, while you...And then at the end, hearing him babbling about you, begging you not to leave him...' she stops, and takes a few deep breaths, looking deliberately at a fair-haired little boy, trotting down the central aisle.

A long silence hangs between them, and then both speak at once,

'Ann... I am sorry...'

'I must've been really...'

They turn to face each other, and each mouth breaks into a cautious smile.

Ann speaks first, choosing a safer subject, 'So, getting back to Poppy – how did you meet her in the first place?'

Vivienne laughs, 'Funnily enough, she was Stuart's friend, to start with. As you know, we moved out here in the early eighties. His father worked for Jardine Matheson, and Stuart was born here. He'd always intended to move back at some stage, but I wanted to wait till Colin was old enough to come and visit us on his own. Brighton was quite far enough away from you both as it was.' She pauses and clears her throat. Ann is aware that her mother has turned towards her, but she keeps her eyes fixed on her hands, clasped together in her lap.

'Well,' continues Vivienne, 'as you'll have seen from that letter, Poppy was already in Hong Kong, looking after Ivy in her last illness. After that, she more or less stayed put out here. George would have been in his twenties. He'd already made a home of his own with his English girl-friend in Brighton. Poppy had inherited quite a tidy sum of money from Ivy, along with the house on the Peak. She made some very astute investments in property and was able to do more or less whatever she pleased with her life.'

'Wasn't she lonely, though?' asks Ann. Collecting huge numbers of stray cats seems to her to be something the sad and lonely might fill their time with.

'Lonely!' laughs Vivienne. 'My dear Ann, surely you don't think that the mere presence of a man in the house will

132

automatically keep loneliness at bay? Or that a woman is doomed to loneliness without one?'

'Of course I don't!' she retorts, then, under her breath, 'Must you always twist my words like that?'

If Vivienne heard that muttered comment, she's choosing to ignore it. 'You've seen the type of character Poppy is, even now – larger than life – and the life and soul of any party. She was in her early fifties when I met her, and she was well able to hold her own in any sort of company – male or female, young or old, she could out-drink, out-talk, out-dance, out-play, out...'

'OK! OK!' laughs Ann. 'I get the picture.'

'It was her amateur dramatics, though, that brought her into contact with Stuart. You might remember that's how I met him too.'

Ann remains silent, clenching her hands more tightly together, willing Vivienne to carry on talking about Poppy. Grannibelle's story and its link with Poppy is more than enough to deal with at the moment.

Vivienne glances at Ann again, and then continues in the same, light-hearted tone, 'So, Poppy – yes, she seemed to have taken to Stuart. She took to me, too, straight away. I was flattered – she had a reputation for being extremely selective in her choice of friends. Anyway, she invited us to one of her famous parties. That was before she'd sold the house on Lugard Road. We'd inherited a flat on Mid-levels from Stuart's father. I liked it there. High enough for a good view, and not far from all the best shops, the restaurants, the entertainment.'

'So why did you all move to Lamma?' asks Ann.

'Blame Stuart for that. He never could resist a gamble. It took a few years, but his inheritance eventually ran out. Property on Lamma was a good deal cheaper. Poppy was horrified at first. Not a place for any self-respecting, upper class Chinese to live. Even though she thinks of herself as English through and through, Poppy shares several of the Chinese attitudes.'

'Surely that could as easily have been good old English snobbery?' laughs Ann. 'But actually, it's that woman, Ivy, I can't understand. I mean, for a start, not letting Rupert know that you existed - that her so-called best friend, Belle, had a baby daughter and he was the father – *your* father! That must have been such a shock for you.'

'It was, yes,' murmurs Vivienne. After a moment's pause she smiles and says, 'Well, the good part was finding out that Poppy was my sister. Wasn't it fortunate that we'd become such close friends already? After all, one doesn't necessarily have to like one's own relations.'

'Yes. Very lucky. A best friend to confide in…' says Ann slowly. Unaccountably, her chest has tightened. In her whole life, there's only ever been one person she could call a 'best friend', apart from Grannibelle: Carol Andrews - Carol Taylor from school. They'd not been real friends in those days, of course - Ann had never been anyone's best friend. They'd met again at ante-natal classes and had both been surprised at how well they got on together as adults. Carol was plump and jolly and always there, only ten minutes walk away. Graham liked her too, and her husband, Brian. When their children were little they'd all gone on holiday together, renting caravans on the same cliff-top site near Cromer.

Who can she confide in, now that Carol's gone? It isn't just because Louise has started university that she's recently been feeling so… yes, face it, so lonely. She'd been quite unprepared for the bombshell last September – Carol and Brian, going to live in Sydney, where their daughter, Janie, only a couple of years older than Lou, had settled down with her Australian husband and new baby.

'Ann. *Ann*?'

'Sorry! Miles away,' she says, summoning a quick, bright smile, 'You were saying?'

'Relations. Felicity. Sisters or half-sisters. She never was much of a sister to you, was she?'

'But we weren't actually related at all. She just happened to be the daughter of your husband.'

'I almost turned Edward down, because of her,' muses

134

Vivienne. 'Did I ever tell you?'

'Because of Felicity! Was she really that awful to you?'

'Not to me, no. At least, not then. I got my share of her mischief-making some years later. So, no. It was you I was worried about. She had a rather superior manner - a sharp tongue. I thought she might tease you.'

'You were right there. She did. Still, could've been worse. And I dare say it wasn't brilliant for her, either.'

'I should never have done it,' sighs Vivienne.

'Done what? Married him, or left him? No, don't answer that,' she adds, and manages to smile as she continues in a lighter tone, 'There's a good result for me, too, in all these dramatic revelations - my weird and wonderful new aunt and my new cousin, George.'

Vivienne seizes the olive branch, 'You really did get on well with each other, didn't you?' she says eagerly.

As quickly as it came, Ann's mood of self-pity evaporates in a flash of excitement: *George!* 'Eventually, we did,' she laughs. 'Poor man, I don't know what was worse for him - realising he was going to have to spend the whole flight sitting next to a dangerous lunatic, or later, trying not to spill the beans about his mother's secret sister.'

With her limited experience of friendship, Ann has never considered the possibility of having a man in the category of close friend. She's shared more of her own self with Carol and Grannibelle than anyone else. Your children, even when they're adults, are always your children first and foremost, however well you might get on with them. Before Graham became 'husband', was he ever really 'friend'? And Max? No, there was never a warm, comfortable trust with Max-the-Bastard.

A first cousin, though - almost a brother, but with no history of sibling rivalry seething away under the surface – no friendship could be closer, or safer, than that. Unless, of course, she'd imagined that instant rapport between them.

Chapter 17

Ann follows her mother through the turnstiles, and becomes aware that she's scanning groups of people near the exit for a glimpse of George, as though one part of her has expected him to remain in the place where she parted from him two days ago.

'You wouldn't believe the changes I've seen here in the last twenty years or so,' says Vivienne, slowing to a halt, halfway along the gleaming grey-white tiles of a walkway that stretches above a long narrow lawn and slow-moving rivers of traffic. 'All this, for example,' she says, waving her hand in a wide sweep. 'And look, over there - that gigantic, rather phallic building. Apparently, the offices on the highest floors are the same altitude as houses on The Peak.'

She sounds like a tour-guide, thinks Ann, as Vivienne resumes her brisk stride towards a shopping mall at the end of the wide path. Her mother's display of enthusiasm is taking her by surprise. 'This place is brand new – and a cut above anything you'd find in England, especially the public conveniences. Molton Brown soap and hand cream, floor to ceiling mirrors, vases of fresh lilies, changed daily – the full works! '

'Maybe you should write a 'Good Loo Guide to Hong Kong,' smiles Ann.

'You may well laugh, but you wait till you get to my age,' retorts Vivienne. 'They're not called conveniences for nothing, and since they're becoming a rather more frequent necessity of late, a touch of luxury is more than welcome. '

As they stride through the mall Ann is almost disappointed by its rather Western appearance. Although they are somewhat cleaner and smarter, in essence most of the shop fronts aren't so very different from the new developments in the centre of Birmingham.

She stifles a yawn as she follows her mother down an escalator and out onto the corner of a crowded pavement. The pedestrian lights turn green, and a piercing *ta-ta-ta-ta-tat* urges the jostling stream of shoppers and business men across the street. Ann pauses as they reach the other side. She's beginning to wonder what kind of progress they'll make if they have to force their way through crowds like this all the way up to where George's shop is situated.

'Just thought you might like to see what goes on at street level, before we carry on up. I do walk all the way sometimes, and the some of the smaller roads aren't so crowded, but I think today, we'll give our legs a bit of a rest.'

As they climb a dingy flight of stairs leading up at right angles from the pavement, Ann wonders if her mother has been joking about resting their legs, but soon they're stepping onto the first section of a glass-roofed escalator that has somehow been constructed to run high above the tarmac of a steeply sloping road.

The escalator itself is spotlessly clean, with gleaming metal struts and rails, but its gliding passengers are hemmed in by the frontages of flat-roofed buildings, several stories high, a pavement's width away on either side. Most of these walls, windows and balconies are blighted with mildew and soot. The mere sight of them, as the moving stairway carries her past, makes her skin feel invaded by dirt, but she soon becomes engrossed by glimpses of crowded side streets that branch off at regular intervals. One minute she's peering down onto a grimy jigsaw of dull green tarpaulin and grey-striped canvas crammed together along the full length of a narrow road; the next minute, it's pavement café tables and bright parasols. The common feature of all these streets is the forest of Western advertising slogans and huge banners in Chinese script suspended on long metal poles above the bustle of people below, and, as everywhere else that she's seen so far, the bright and varied shapes and sizes of colourful paper lanterns.

'You'll soon get used to all this,' says Vivienne as they leave the final escalator. 'The contrasts. These extremes of wealth and poverty, new and old. It's the essence of Hong Kong. We can browse around some of the antique shops in Wyndham Street and Hollywood Road before we meet up with George for lunch, and then maybe look for some smart shoes in the mall near the ferry, if we're not too exhausted by then.'

Though the sky is still a mass of low grey cloud, the air between the buildings is muggy and warm. *Exhausted!* thinks Ann, gloomily wondering at her mother's stamina as she forges ahead again up a steep narrow street, composed entirely of wide grey steps. Vivienne pauses at a stall displaying garish posters of tropical fruit. 'I don't know about you, but I could do with some light refreshment,' she says. 'They do the most wonderful freshly squeezed fruit juice here - any combinations you can think of. My favourite is mango and orange.'

'Well, I had orange for breakfast, so...'

'Breakfast! O dear, that reminds me... Now you mustn't be cross with me, Ann.' Vivienne doesn't look in the least repentant as she continues, 'I quite forgot to tell you that Graham rang this morning, while you were still asleep. At least, I thought you would be. In any case, I didn't want to disturb you.'

Another of these disconcerting jolts through space and time. *Graham!* Ann sits down on one of the white plastic stools, beside a picture of a bunch of bananas about twenty times larger than life. Her mouth is dry as she asks, 'Won't he be expecting me to ring him back? How was he? What did he say?'

'Oh, he was fine. Once he'd properly understood what I was telling him.'

Ann stares down at a couple of polystyrene cups and a scatter of coloured paper straws near her right foot. 'I don't think I want to hear this,' she groans.

Vivienne turns back from the counter with a smile, 'I told him that I couldn't possibly spare you until at least your planned departure date – that if there were to be any changes in your schedule, it would be a matter of delaying your flight, rather than bringing it forward.' In almost the same breath she says, 'What about mango and pineapple?'

'Oh! Yes. Whatever you think,' says Ann, barely aware of what's she's being asked. How easy it's been to let Graham slip from her mind for hours on end.

'Of course,' continues Vivienne smoothly, 'I wouldn't want your husband to think I'm attempting to keep you for myself, so I suggested he comes out here to join you. I mean, as I said to him, after this Friday he won't have to be constrained by any demands from his former employers. The world is now his oyster and he should embrace it with gusto,' she finishes, raising clenched fists in a dramatic gesture of defiance.

'Oh my God! Did you really say all that? Tell me you're joking.'

'But that would be a falsehood, Ann. Surely you're not asking me to lie to you?'

'For goodness sake! You're a fine one to talk about lying!' she laughs, struggling to mask her exasperation.

'Ann, dear, there's no need to get so worked up,' Vivienne's calm voice does nothing to convey reassurance. 'I'm not completely insensitive, you know. I did realise that he might be a little concerned about his loss of income so I finished off by saying I'd be delighted to extend my hospitality to him. All he has to do is get back to us once he's decided on a date and time he'd like to travel, and I'll pay for his ticket, no expense spared.'

'This is my favourite place in the whole of this area,' Vivienne says, pushing open the door to yet another exclusive antique shop of the kind that Ann would never have ventured into by herself. 'The owner's a friend of George, and I've got to know her quite well in the last few years. Lucia has encyclopaedic knowledge of Chinese textiles, and she's one of the few people I know with an infallible eye for style and colour.'

Ann dislikes Lucia before she has even set eyes on her. She has contained herself in a frenzy of impatience through the previous half hour, wondering how Vivienne could expect her to show an interest in expensive antiques, when her new cousin's shop is no more than five or ten minutes walk away.

This one seems more like a gallery than a shop, with its artistic displays of embroidered oriental hangings and court robes that could have come from the film set of The Last Emperor, except for the fact that the most recent of these items are more than a hundred years old. While Vivienne glides across the polished floor to the foot of the stairs, Ann hovers just inside the door, pretending an interest in the contents of a glass cabinet. After glancing at a shelf of exquisitely carved 19th Century ivory fans, she finds herself distracted by an embroidered pair of tiny, high-heeled wedge shoes. Doll's shoes, she assumes at first, then gasps as she reads the accompanying description.

'Barbaric custom, wasn't it, that foot-binding?' At the sound of the woman's voice, Ann is immediately made conscious of her own appearance. This must be Lucia-of-the-Infallible-Eye. She shuffles round to face the speaker. Yes, here it comes, the usual reaction from friends or acquaintances of her mother. However hard they might try to disguise it, it's unmistakable: the sudden widening of the eyes, the almost imperceptible shake of the head, then the stiff smile. This Lump, this Ugly Dumpling is *Vivienne's* daughter!

Lucia, of course, is slim and elegant. She could be any age between late thirties and early fifties. Her voice is friendly enough, but there's something about the tilt of her head and the shape of her face that reminds her of Felicity. Heart-shaped, is what people used to call it, when trying to analyse Felicity's particular type of beauty.

Ann suddenly feels drained of any inclination to go anywhere, meet anyone. Least of all, George. What has she been thinking of, expecting him to be pleased to see her again? His dull and dumpy cousin. Right now, she'd like nothing more than to be transported instantly back to her bed on Lamma, where she'd sleep for a week.

'So how long have you been in Hong Kong, Ann?' asks Lucia.

Ann closes her eyes for a moment. How long? She has no idea what day it is, even.

'Tuesday,' says Vivienne. 'You arrived on Tuesday, didn't you? Just the day before yesterday. Somehow it seems much longer ago than that.'

'And I expect you've been keeping her busy ever since she

landed, haven't you, Vivienne?' says Lucia with a laugh. 'You're incorrigible, people of your generation – you and Poppy. I find it hard to keep up with you at the best of times.'

The words drift through to Ann down a long tunnel. Maybe she should just lie herself down here. The floor is beginning to tilt slightly. Has anyone else noticed?

'Jet lag,' Lucia is saying as she puts her hand under Ann's elbow and guides her towards the stairs. 'There's a nice little sofa up there. You can curl up and have a short nap. It's the only thing, once it's taken hold like this – the jet lag.'

George's shop is not quite as intimidating to Ann as Lucia's, but it still falls into the category of Too Expensive And Too Smart. A young Chinese man in a neat, dark grey suit steps forward to greet them as the doorbell jangles.

'Good morning, Paul,' says Vivienne briskly. 'Can you let George know that we've arrived.'

'Of course, Miss Vivienne.'

Ann is pleased to note that the young man appears to be unaware of who she is. Or, if he does know that she's Vivienne's daughter, his face reveals nothing of what he might be thinking. She's been feeling better since her nap, but now she finds that her heart is thudding and her hands are clammy.

A door at the back of the shop is flung open, and George steps through. He pauses for a moment, his face partly masked in shadow, so Ann can't read his expression until his mouth widens into a smile and he is crossing the floor in long strides. She shuffles back a few inches as Vivienne holds out her hands.

George takes them in both of his and plants a light kiss on her cheek, 'How are you, Aunt?' he says with a cheerful grin before turning to Ann, 'No need to hide from me, cousin, dear!' he laughs, letting go of Vivienne's hands and reaching out for hers. 'Come here and let me see you properly, you mad woman.'

'You may be my nephew, George, but I'll thank you to treat my daughter with a little more respect, isn't that right Ann?'

'I don't think you need to worry, Vivienne. From what I've

seen of Ann so far, she's well able to stand up for herself. Seriously, though,' he adds moving closer and putting an arm across her shoulder, 'I've never had a more entertaining companion in all my years of long haul flights. And then to find out that we're related! Well, that gives us both the right to tease each other a little doesn't it?'

Ann laughs. 'I'll have to brush up my teasing skills, then. They've got a bit rusty over the years.'

'That's OK,' says George. 'I'll do the teasing, and you can just run me over with a trolley from time to time.'

'Children, children!' says Vivienne in mock severity, then her eyes widen as she stares at them both.

'What is it, Vivienne?' asks Ann.

Vivienne reaches out and cups her left hand under George's chin, and her right on Ann's. 'Peas in a pod. No doubt about where these two come from. You've seen the photos of your grandfather, George? And you, Ann. That album that Ivy sent to Grannibelle ?'

'Oh!' Ann wrinkles her nose. 'Rupert McFarlane!' She almost spits the words.

'That's right,' says Vivienne a little sharply, 'My father.'

'Our grandfather,' says George firmly. 'Yours and mine.'

He removes his arm from her shoulders and positions himself in front of her, studying her face. This intense interest is so unexpected and so obviously kindly meant, that she does not flinch when he brushes the tip of his left forefinger across the dent in the middle of her hated chin. 'See. Just like mine, but not quite so pronounced,' he says, jutting out his jaw and raising her hand towards it. She hesitates a moment, then laughs as she unclenches her fist and lets him place her finger into the cleft.

'Looks better on you,' she murmurs. 'Mine's been the bane of my life.'

'Poor Ann,' laughs Vivienne, 'I have to agree, though – that chin does look better on a man.'

Ann lets her hand fall to her side and takes a step back. For a moment, she'd been unaware of her mother's presence. She feels her cheeks grow hot, and turns her head, pretending an interest in the prints displayed on the wall behind her.

'Time for lunch, I think,' says George, and Ann feels at once relieved that he hasn't prolonged that topic of conversation, and at the same time, disappointed that he didn't leapt to her defence at her mother's comment. 'You choose, Ann,' he continues. 'Posh restaurant or authentic workman's caff. The Chinese version. The real McCoy.'

'That scruffy little hole?' says Vivienne. 'I don't think Ann would like that.'

Who can claim to know her better, George, whom she met a couple of days ago, or her own mother? 'The real McCoy, please,' she says promptly, then adds, 'So long as you don't mind, Vivienne?'

'Splendid!' exclaims George, 'I guessed as much. Don't worry, Aunty Viv, we'll do the posh nosh another time. I just thought it might appeal to my eccentric cousin.'

Eccentric! Ann savours the word as they leave the shop. Is that how he sees her? Not ordinary – not dull. *Eccentric!*

Through the steamed-up window Ann sees that the restaurant itself is tiny and all the tables appear to be occupied. But just as George pushes open the door, three men file out onto the pavement, preceded by a rush of spicy smells and the din of clattering pans and a high-pitched gabble of voices. The men's appearance, all of three of them short and wiry with paint-speckled, dark blue shirts, leathery faces and wide, gap-toothed smiles, is matched by many of the other diners, though there is also a scattering of young office workers, male and female.

'It's getting a bit too popular, this place,' sighs George, leading the way through the crush towards a small round table near the far wall. As soon as they've sat down a wizened little woman in a black top over wide trousers, bustles up and places three small tumblers on the white paper cloth. She returns a moment later with a battered metal teapot, fills their glasses with pale amber and leaves it in the middle of the table.

George, after a brief consultation, orders congee for the three of them. Vivienne smiles and pats the back of his hand before turning towards Ann, 'It's what we always have whenever we come here,' she explains. 'Fish soup. It doesn't look very appealing, but you'll like it. I know you will.'

Ann is torn between a desire to please George by trusting his judgement, and an impulse to contradict Vivienne's assumed knowledge of her likes and dislikes. She takes a sip of tea, glances across at the glass-fronted metal counter, with its stacks of china bowls and huge steaming containers, then looks at George, 'That's fine by me,' she smiles.

And Vivienne is right. In spite of its grey and gelatinous appearance Ann does like it. Even before she raises the china spoon to her lips, the aroma snags at her memory. She lets her eyelids close as the silky liquid, hot, but not too hot, glides around her tongue and slips down her throat. Then the aftertaste kicks in – spicy and sharp. She's in Grannibelle's kitchen. The mussel shells are in the bin by the sink with the fish heads and spines, now that these have rendered their full flavour into the stock, and the succulent flesh has been salvaged to float with bits of fennel, green chillies, ginger and one hundred and one other secret ingredients. 'That's for me to know, and you to find out,' comes Grannibelle's refrain. The cat has nudged open the door from the back passage and is sniffing the sides of the bin. Any minute now, Vivienne will be pushing back her chair, saying 'Out you go, you dratted cat,' while Grannibelle will chuckle and say, 'Poor Shortbread. He's not harming anyone...'

When she opens her eyes, Ann finds that they're stinging at the edges. 'Hot!' she exclaims, dabbing at them with the paper napkin.

'Do you like it?' George's voice is anxious. 'I think they've used a little more pepper or chilli than usual.'

Vivienne's expression is part quizzical, part smug as she says, 'Well, Ann? What did I tell you? I expect you thought your Grannibelle's Sunday Special was an old Norfolk recipe - am I right? And now you know it was just one among many other things she picked up from her stay out East.'

Chapter 18

George and Ann are on their way to the Botanical Gardens, strolling side by side past a high curving wall on which a sprawl of tangled tree roots reaches nearly to the pavement. At first, Ann was relieved when Vivienne announced that she was going back to Lucia's shop to discuss some business proposition and would meet them later. In Vivienne's company, especially when there's a third person present, she can't help seeing herself through her mother's eyes.

But now, on her own with George, she's wondering what they will find to talk about for the next hour or so. It's one thing to make conversation with a total stranger on a plane, knowing you're unlikely to ever see each other again. You won't be held to account for your words – nor will you have depleted your entire store of mildly entertaining anecdotes. Has she really got anything in common with this man beyond a shared plane journey and a grandfather?

Neither has uttered a word since George gestured towards a large brick building a little way from his shop. 'The old police station. Not many of these original structures left,' he'd sighed. The noise of revving engines, horns and brakes, and blasts of music from car radios provided an acceptable excuse for the lack of conversation, but the street they are in now has less traffic and the wide pavement is almost deserted. How long should she let this silence last before she feels impelled to break it?

She has slowed her pace almost to a halt, and George turns back towards her. 'Amazing, aren't they?' he says, gesturing at the roots spread-eagled across the steeply sloping surface of grey stone. 'I think these are banyan trees, but don't take that as gospel. It's about the only tree name I know out here, apart from 'palm', and that seems to cover a multitude of different shapes and sizes.'

'How about English trees?' she asks.

'Hopeless at those too. Oak, maybe? So long as there are acorns on the ground nearby. Holly is fairly unmistakeable, if you happen to bump into it. Everything else is either a fir tree or deciduous and that's about it.'

Ann laughs, and tells him about Sutton Park, and her surprise on her arrival on Lamma when she remembered how Vivienne taught her the names of all the trees she knows.

'You don't have a very warm relationship with her, do you? I mean, none of my business, of course, but…'

'You're right. But it's hardly surprising. We haven't exactly seen a lot of each other since…well. You know.'

'Sorry,' he says quietly. 'I shouldn't have raised the subject.'

'No. It's OK. I don't mind at all. It's just…'

'Of course. Anyway, we're here now,' he adds, pointing to a flight of stone steps rising diagonally along the side of another steep wall ahead of them, ' Maybe we'll talk about that some other time, if you feel you'd like to.'

For the next half hour they stroll along the winding paths between high wire-mesh enclosures, shaded by lush vegetation. They laugh at the gibbon, hugging its blanket like a toddler, and the macaque monkeys swinging from branch to branch in a nearby cage.

There's no shortage of topics of conversation: their immediate surroundings lead quite naturally to Belle's journal and letters. Ann can picture her walking hand in hand with Rupert as the two-year old Harry trots ahead. Would he have seen huge porcupines like the ones in front of her, bizarrely sharing their enclosure with ring-tailed lemurs?

'Maybe,' says George. 'I don't think there've been many changes to this park, not compared to the rest of the area.'

Ann gazes around her. Through the trees she glimpses huge blocks of shining windows – these towers look as though they've been constructed entirely of glass. One of her favourites from the book of fairy tales Grannibelle used to read her featured a glass mountain, unscalable to all but the pure of heart. She is finding it hard to reconcile her idealised picture of her grandmother with the story that was revealed only yesterday, and which still seems to belong more to fiction than reality.

When she ventures to voice this thought, George says, 'I can see it must have come as a shock. It was enough of a surprise for me when I found out about my grandfather's affairs and my real grandmother. Rupert died long before I was born, so he was just a shadowy figure for me. At least, everyone assumed he'd died in the fall of Hong Kong, though it never was officially confirmed.'

During the brief pause, Ann says, 'You mean, Rupert McFarlane could still be alive?'

'Not very likely,' he laughs. 'For a start, he'd be about a hundred and one by now. Anyway, Ivy and Poppy came back here after the war, specifically to try and find him, but not a single trace was ever found. What came as the biggest shock to me was the fact that my mother had let me believe that Ivy was my real grandmother. True, she never explicitly told me that, but she didn't attempt to enlighten me, either.'

'But Vivienne says that Poppy had made up some story about Chinese nobility when she'd been packed off to boarding school in England.'

''Oh, that!' he laughs. 'I get the impression that she changed her tale a few times since then. I was told that Ivy had a Chinese emperor somewhere in her background. She must have colluded with that final version. It's what most people believe even now. To be fair to Ivy, I think she genuinely regarded Poppy as her own flesh and blood, and she herself always referred to me as her grandson – not that I saw very much of her. '

'So you really do know what it feels like to find out that…'

'That you've been lied to about the identity of your grandparents?'

'Sort of, yes.' She smiles. 'Though in your case it was your mother who was concealing the truth..'

'Mmm…concealing. That sounds a bit kinder than lying, doesn't it? And of course, your mother didn't even know the truth herself, whereas Poppy chose not to inform me that she'd been adopted. So, it looks like we have your mother to thank for the truth coming to light at last.'

'Truth! Whatever that means. I'm getting totally confused. ' says Ann. The sun has penetrated the layer of grey cloud, and they're sitting on a bench enjoying its warmth. From here, Ann can see that the gibbon is still hunched on a wire platform, hugging its bit of cloth. 'It makes you wonder if we've actually progressed very far as a species, doesn't it?'

George follows her gaze and laughs again, 'I take your point. Reminds me of that Walt Whitman poem – 'I think I could turn and live with animals.'

'Something about them not forever snivelling about their condition?'

'Gee, thanks! With friends like you, who needs…?'

'Relations?' she smiles. 'And I wasn't accusing you of snivelling! But yes, I tend to think of that poem myself when I'm in one of my navel-gazing moods.'

'I'd never really given much thought to relations before Vivienne dropped her bombshell. All I knew was that I haven't got many. I was conscious of being an only child, and from time to time I thought vaguely that a brother or sister might be nice, but that's as far as it went – apart from a brief spell between the ages of about three and seven when I had an imaginary friend. He was so real I was almost convinced I could see him…'

His voice tails away, as though he's said too much and he glances sheepishly at Ann. 'Nothing to be ashamed of,' she says. 'Isn't it meant to be a sign of intelligence – a vivid imagination?'

'I can't lay claim to more than mediocre level of brain-power. Scraped through with a third in history.'

'That's one up on me,' she says, 'All I managed was a C in Eng Lit A level. And I've achieved virtually nothing since then.'

'O, come on! A feisty woman like you! I bet you've got some tales to tell.'

'Feisty!' she exclaims with what sounds like a snort. 'First 'eccentric', and now, 'feisty''.

'I'm sorry, Ann. I didn't mean to offend you,' he says, looking anxiously at her.

When she returns his gaze, he realises that she is attempting to suppress a bout of laughter, 'You have no idea how far…how *very* far from the truth…' she splutters, but any further words are drowned in waves of deep belly-laughs.

'Got it right first time, didn't I? Mad trolley-woman!' he chuckles. Then, before his own laughter overtakes him, he adds, 'I just hope it's not a gene you've inherited from our esteemed grandfather. I might be harbouring it myself. '

An elderly couple walking past a moment later look hastily away and quicken their pace. 'Stop! Stop!' gasps Ann, doubling over as tears stream down her cheeks,

Eventually their guffaws subside into hiccups and giggles. Wiping her eyes with the back of her hand, she says, 'It's not something I've done much of, these last few years – laughing, I mean.'

'Me neither,' he says. 'We must be good for each other.'

'Or bad,' she puts in, 'depending on how you look at it. Or who's doing the looking.'

'My staff in the shop here would certainly be surprised.' After a short pause he adds, 'And my sons. My ex-wife too. Not to speak of my mother. Your mother…'

'Old Uncle Tom Cobbley and all.'

'It's a sobering thought, isn't it? Our lack of spontaneous laughter!'

'Don't start me off again, for pity's sake!' she giggles.

'Quick, think of an antidote – who would have been the most shocked to see you making such a public display of yourself?'

Ann's smile disappears at once. She feels herself go tense.

'That bad, is it, your relationship?' he says gently.

'Vivienne, you mean?'

'Who else?'

She remains silent, looking down at her shoes.

'Not Vivienne, then,' he prompts in the same quiet tone.

Another silence. Saying the name will conjure his presence more forcibly still.

'Oh!' murmurs George. 'He's called Graham, isn't he? Your husband?'

'I didn't say… I didn't mean…'

'I know. I know.'

'Graham's OK. He…he's kind and…Oh, it's not *his* fault. Over the years I've just let myself sort of…'

'Don't say another word. I don't want you regretting things later. You're a good person, Ann. Loyalty isn't that easy to come by, these days. I'm really glad to have you as my cousin.'

'Me too,' she smiles. 'I've got some second cousins in Australia, I think, and one in Canada too, but I've never met them. My own dad was an only child and my Uncle Harry never had any children, as far as I know, so you're my only first cousin. Odd, isn't it, the way blood relationships seems so significant.'

'Odd, but nice,' he says. 'Or rather, it can be nice. As we both know, it can also be very unsettling when it comes to family secrets.'

Ann nods. She feels no need to speak.

After a few moments of comfortable silence, George says, 'Let's take a break from our forebears and wander across to the other part of the Gardens and look at some nice safe plant life!'

'Sounds like a good idea,' she replies, jumping up from the seat and reaching for his hand to pull him up. 'Come along, lazybones.'

She's barely aware of the fact that they're still holding hands, swinging their arms in time to their footsteps. All she's registering in her conscious mind is a feeling of well-being. Sunshine always lifts her spirits.

They are descending a wide and elegant stone stairway that would not have looked out of place in an eighteenth century stately home. All around them are magnificent trees, maple, perhaps, and acacia, interspersed with flowering shrubs. The huge ferns and various palms with hairy trunks and broad or ragged leaves add to the dreamlike quality of the day. The contrasting ugliness of the modern fountain ahead of them, with its garish tiles and central spouts of water like gigantic dandelion clocks, seems completely out of keeping and therefore, in a surreal way, entirely appropriate to her mood.

Sensing her appreciation of the view, George pauses, and they stand in silence for a moment, still hand in hand. Ann is about to share her thoughts about the scene when George tightens his grip, and then abruptly withdraws his hand. She follows the direction of his eyes.

'I do believe that's...yes! It's Stuart,' he murmurs. 'Over there by the fountain. It looks like he's heading this way. Would you prefer us to ignore him?'

'Yes!' is her first reaction, then, 'I...I don't know.' To her surprise, Ann is suddenly overtaken by a wave of anger. 'You're absolutely sure that's him? It's more than thirty years since I last set eyes on him. '

'Yes. That's Stuart all right. I've spent a fair amount of time in his company over the past few years. I think he's seen us too. Or maybe not – he's turning back to the fountain.'

'Good,' she says. 'Either way, he won't be ignoring us for much longer,' and she almost runs down the remaining few steps to where he is standing with his back to her just out of the range of stray droplets from the spouting water.

She stands a couple feet behind him for a moment, wondering if he can feel her gaze boring into the back of his neck. 'Hello, Stuart,' she says in a steady voice.

He swings round and his face registers no recognition, 'I'm sorry,' he says smoothly, 'I don't think...'

'I expect that's truer than you imagine,' she retorts. 'A thinker tends to have some awareness of the wider consequences of his actions.'

'I have no idea who you are or what you're talking about,' he says, stepping to one side, clearly intending to walk away from her. Ann is determined that he shall not, so for the next few moments they are engaged in the kind of dance that occasionally takes place on a narrow pavement as two people side-step to avoid each other, but continue to misjudge the other's intentions.

Exasperated, Stuart barks, 'Will you get out of my way,

woman? You have clearly mistaken me for someone else. I have never seen you before in my life. Good *day*!'

Ann executes another little skip, and blocks his path once more. Fixing him with a cold stare, she says, 'Have you really no idea of who I am? I'm well aware that I bear no resemblance to my mother, but, even so…'

'Your mother?' he says, a cautious expression on his face. 'Look, em… I'm afraid there's nothing *I* can do …but I'm sure…if you stay here for a little longer… you'll find…*some*one to help you.' He is speaking with the slow and level tone a postman might use when a large, growling dog with bared teeth has placed itself between him and the front gate. At the same time, he is gradually edging away from her, keeping his head steady, but glancing around out of the corner of his eyes.

He's not worn all that well, she thinks, studying the rather puffy cheeks and drooping jowls. On the one of the few occasions when she'd seen him face to face, a few weeks after the Betrayal, she'd been dismayed to find her heart give a sudden lurch as he'd opened the door to the flat. She was holding Colin's hand and had been glad of his presence, providing a brief distraction that allowed her to turn away until the red in her cheeks died down. Later, she had to admit to herself that her reaction had nothing to do with the stress of the situation, and everything to do with the effect of his penetrating blue eyes and twisted little smile. Why else would she feel that tingle somewhere in the region below her belly button whenever she replayed that scene? What was it she'd mumbled at the time? 'Oh! We've come to see my mother, not you. Did you know that she's virtually old enough to be your mother too?' How angry Vivienne had been. On all subsequent occasions when Ann had accompanied Colin on the long train journey down to Brighton for the monthly access visit, Vivienne had come on her own to meet them at the station, and Stuart had absented himself from the flat until Ann had left.

Ann realises she has let herself lose concentration. Stuart has already taken a couple of strides away from her and she calls after him, 'I'm not surprised you don't want to talk to me, Stuart. I'm

Ann, Vivienne's daughter.'

For a moment he pauses, as if about to turn back, but then he gives a shrug and calls over his shoulder, 'Sorry, Ann. Late for an appointment. Maybe we'll meet up some other time.'

Ann laughs in triumph as George descends the final step and Stuart finds his way barred once more, 'Stuart, my friend! I see you've just met my cousin. I don't think I could have heard you correctly just now. It didn't sound very friendly. Ah, here you are Ann. Stuart is suggesting we sit on that bench for a few minutes and have a quiet chat about Vivienne. Noisy scenes in public places are so distasteful, don't you think?'

'It'll have to be quick, then. I really am extremely busy.'

There's an empty bench near a flower bed full of colourful shrubs. Ann places herself at one end and George at the other, so Stuart is forced to sit between them.

He folds his arms and crosses one leg, angling his body away from her as he says, 'Well, Ann? Maybe you can come to the point now, after that rather childish bit of game-playing.'

Ann senses that George is about to leap to her defence. Before her unexpected rush of adrenalin can seep away, she says quickly, 'I won't keep you long. I have no desire to spend more time in your company than is absolutely necessary. I never expected to bump into you, but since you're here, there are just two things I'd like to say – first, it was absolutely despicable what you did back then, breaking up our perfectly happy family...'

As she draws a breath, Stuart breaks in, 'What rubbish! You...'

'Just listen! I haven't finished yet. That was all in the past. But now! Deserting Vivienne after all those years! It just proves what a thoughtless, selfish jerk you are.' With that, she rises to her feet, adding, 'There! You can get back to your busy life now. Shall we return to the more congenial company of the gibbons, George?'

'That'll suit me fine,' smiles George as he stands up.

'Not so fast, little Miss Innocent, *if* you please,' Stuart almost snarls, swinging one foot as he looks angrily up at Ann. 'Things might have worked out very differently if you hadn't been so - '

153

'Let's go, George,' she says. Her heart is pounding and her breath is coming in short, shallow bursts. She feels herself go hot, and then clammy and cold. 'I don't have to listen to that…that *apology* for a man,' she gasps taking George's arm and letting him lead her away.

'Give my best wishes to Viv when you see her,' he shouts after them. 'She's worth ten of you, Ann. You need to take a long hard look at yourself, before you start lecturing others about wider consequences of their actions.'

Chapter 19

'My new-found niece, spending the evening on her own? Stuff and nonsense!' exclaims Poppy. 'I won't hear of it. Where is the dear child? Leave it to me, Vivie. I'll soon talk her round.'

Ann gives an inward groan, wishing that she had already sneaked up to her bedroom before Vivienne opened the front door.

'What's all this I hear, Sweetie Pie! Not coming with us?' chants Poppy, pounding across the room to the glass-topped dining table where Ann is rising to her feet. 'So you've already eaten? Why should that matter? By the time my stomach starts rumbling, you'll have space for a few more titbits.'

Ann finds herself enveloped in a bear hug, this time being clasped against a scarlet velour top and matching trousers, 'I...I...' she falters, taking a step back and managing to extricate herself before Vivienne strides to the rescue.

'Poppy!' she laughs, 'Ann has had a busy day. She's too...'

'Tired? Of course she is! How thoughtless of me. It's a long haul, all the way down to the village and back again. Never mind. We'll all stay here instead,' she declares, flinging her arms wide, 'Leave it to Poppy, I always say!'

'Er, Poppy. It's not quite - '

'Oh Vivie! There's always plenty of food and booze in this house, isn't there? Constantia can knock up a meal in no time – or I'll ring Ignatius and he can arrange for some dishes to be sent up from the village. What do you say, Ann, darling? That'll suit you better, won't it?'

'Actually, Poppy, I - '

'And if you do nod off in the middle of canasta or back-gammon, we'll just tuck you up on the sofa, or carry you up to bed. I refuse to leave you here all on your lonesome,' she continues, shaking her forefinger at Ann in mock severity, 'Vivie, it's time to put your foot down. Tell her! There are only the two options - she comes with us, or we all stay here and have fun together.'

155

'I've already been scolded by Lucia today,' Vivienne laughs. 'And Ann's well able decide on her own bedtime.'

Ann throws her a grateful look. She is more than happy to let her mother assume that her dazed, almost wordless state ever since George had delivered her back to Lucia's shop has been caused by jet-lagged exhaustion.

She'd not been able to trust herself to do more than nod and smile at George when he'd said, 'I should be able to finish my jobs by lunchtime tomorrow. Maybe we can make arrangements for another outing. I'll ring you in the morning, if you'd like that?'

'Early bed tonight for you, my child,' Vivienne had said gently, putting an arm around her shoulder in the closest to thing to a hug that Ann could remember. With Stuart's parting words still buzzing in her ears, she had stiffened a little at this impulsively maternal gesture. *Vivienne's worth ten of you, Ann*

Her heart was still thudding in her ribcage and it was as much as she could do to keep her lower lip from trembling as George had stepped out onto the street again. He'd not mentioned their meeting with Stuart. Was this an intentional omission, or might he suddenly remember, and turn back with a casual, 'Oh, by the way, guess who we bumped into just now?'

Which is safer - the present or the distant past? Ann wonders, alone at last, looking at the bundle of papers by her bed.

Now that she has the house to herself, she finds that the overwhelming desire for sleep has suddenly vanished, leaving her mind racing. Stuart. No doubt about it – his petulant attack on her was proof that he was at least partly ashamed of the way he had treated Vivienne. Should she tell her about this encounter? If so, how will she manage to broach the subject? No point fretting about this now. She'll ask George for advice when she sees him tomorrow.

Meanwhile, there's Grannibelle's journal entry from that August – the year of the Betrayal. And there's her letter to Vivienne, all those years later, written just a few days before her

156

heart slowed right down, and then, finally, stopped. 'Three a.m. as near as dammit,' the doctor had said as he'd filled in the form that morning. 'She'll have been fast asleep, my dear. You needn't worry. I hope I go as peacefully myself, when my turn comes.'

It's the letter that Ann picks up first.

Penn's Lane, Sutton Coldfield 1995

My dear Vivienne

What can I say? How I wish I could speak to you face to face. No, this is not a reproach – the fault is mine entirely.

I have always despised this type of correspondence – the sudden, last minute disclosure of previously withheld information. Wallowing in regret has never been my style – a decision, once taken, should be upheld. Now, though, I find that 'never' and 'always' are merely words. They have no meaning beyond the moment in which they are uttered.

Words, in themselves, cannot undo the past or change the present so I will keep this as brief as possible. What you will make of these letters and journal entries, and how you will judge me is entirely beyond my influence. I can only hope that these disclosures do not disturb you too greatly. In keeping from you the identity of your real father, I did what I thought would cause the least pain to others. At the time, I assumed that I would somehow know when you had reached an age at which I could tell you the truth. I should have realised that the right moment would never present itself.

This letter of Ivy's, which I also enclose, could have given me the opening I had been waiting for. But you will see from the date that it coincided with that dramatic turning point in your own life. I confess I was angry with you when you did what I, all those years ago, chose not to do. Who is to say that yours was not a wiser and more

157

courageous decision than mine? My dear, I do hope it has brought you lasting happiness.

I expect your reaction to these disclosures will be one of anger and contempt towards me. You will be totally justified in these feelings – I have not been a good mother to you. Would your life have taken a different course if I had been able to show you more affection while you were growing up? Useless speculations, aren't they - 'what if..?' and 'if only...'?

Once your initial feelings have softened a little, as I believe they will, you might like to know that my own later years have been, on the whole, contented.

I will finish now, though this feels to me a cowardly way of ending – I should have spoken to you many years ago. It is still possible that you will come in time, but the attacks have been more frequent of late. Dr Bailey has been so disappointed at his lack of success in making suitable adjustments to my medication. Poor man, he has made it a personal challenge to keep me going for a year or two longer.

I am tired now, Vivienne, my dear.

Ann turns the page, but the reverse side is blank. She sniffs loudly and fumbles for a tissue. Grannibelle sealed this letter and placed it with all the other items into the large and bulky envelope on which she had written Vivienne's name. These are the last words she ever wrote. No mention of her granddaughter.

Oh, come *on*! Quit the self pity. She didn't need to write to me, or about me. I was *there*! What would Vivienne have felt, reading the opening lines, 'How I wish I could speak to you face to face'?

She sits for a long time with the letter in her hand, seeing that bedroom in her home in Penns Lane as it was then, thirteen years ago, before it had become Graham's study. It overlooks the road, and beyond that, the playing fields and the trees that edge the golf course. There'd been a small writing table that fitted snugly into the bay, and during those last few weeks of her life, Grannibelle had spent more time sitting up there and gazing out towards the trees.

How strange, she thinks, picturing that room in that same house now: a black, Ikea desk, too large to fit into that bay, stationed against the far wall; the computer, with its clumsy-looking monitor - *perfectly good still, no need to rush out and buy a flat-screen*; the metal filing cabinet; the floor-to-ceiling shelving stacked with the yellow spines of the National Geographic dating back to the early seventies, and the thirty-six volumes of Encyclopaedia Britannica, obsolete now, with instant access to information on the net; the dominating black-leather swivel chair; and, in the bay, replacing Gran's writing table, a black tin trunk containing Graham's father's bat and cricket whites. Not a trace of Grannibelle's presence remains in that room.

As she reads through the letter once more, she is struck again with pangs of self pity – almost resentment. Ann had condemned Vivienne for not rushing back to England when she'd written to her with the latest prognosis from the doctor: 'she might well have another few years in her, but I have to tell you that her heart could equally well cease to function at any moment', but secretly she was convinced that her mother's arrival would have done more harm than good. She, Ann, could satisfy Gran's every need. Now she must accept that this intimacy was one-sided - an illusion.

Half reluctantly, she reaches for the scraps of paper torn from a discarded journal. There have been more than enough surprises already.

Samphire House, Norfolk, August 1971

It's a very long time indeed since I've been moved to record my feelings in any form beyond the occasional poem or my scribbled stories and aborted scraps of novels.

Days, months – years even - have melded into each other with only the slightest undulations of mood. And now, for the whole of this last week I've been plunged into such…what? Gloom isn't strong enough. Despair? Maybe. Turmoil and confusion? Certainly.

One moment, it's a perfectly ordinary day in the middle of August – a perfect day, in fact. Look! There I am – whoever 'I' am - half way down the path to my front gate. That elderly, respectable woman, Mrs Belle Rivers, is 'she' really 'me'?

I stoop and dig my thumb nail into a stem of lavender, snapping off a fading head. I poke the ragged stalk-end through the gold band on my finger then lift my hand to inhale the rush of scent.

'Morning, Mrs Rivers. Something from foreign parts for you today,' says Bert, reaching a flat package towards me over the gate.

'Glorious day, isn't it?' I say, adjusting the canvas duffel bag on my back before striding towards him, holding out my hand.

One moment, I'm entirely focussed on the day ahead with its promise of fine weather, my thoughts engaged on the challenge of trying yet again to capture with paint and water the elusive light of the wide skies, the sand dunes, the salt marshes. The next moment, as I take in the stamps and postmark and that neat, sloping handwriting, I give an involuntary gasp.

'I'm absolutely fine, thank you Bert,' I say, catching his worried look. 'A surprise, that's all. Someone I've not heard from for...oh! It must be forty years.'

I turn and walk slowly back along the path, my arms stretched out in front of me, the brown-paper parcel balanced on my open palms like an offering. I place it on the worn step as I fumble under the bush of scarlet fuchsia for the key, then open the front door and blink as my eyes adjust from blazing sunlight to the gloom of the hall.

On the way to the kitchen, I shrug off the bag and let it land with a muffled thud on the tiled floor by the coat stand. It remains there, untouched for days.

160

So here I am still. I've not been out at all, not even into the village. From time to time, I've been aware of the phone ringing. I haven't picked it up. Not once. Thoughts have been swirling round and round. I've barely slept.

Rupert.

To find out now that he has been dead all these years! In cold reality he has been as good as dead to me since the moment I chose Jimmy instead of him. The bereaved talk to their dead, don't they - believe their loved one is looking down at them from heaven or some such place – can see and hear them? Hardly a day has passed when I haven't thought of Rupert. But my thoughts have been active messengers, transmitted across the globe to a real, living person – they weren't directed at a few random specks of atoms floating around in outer space.

Reading through this last sentence, I realise that it sounds decidedly bizarre. Fortunately, I've never attempted to confide these ideas to any of my friends, dears though they are. I've never believed in telepathy, exactly – or at least, not at such a vast distance. Nonetheless, I've been comforted by the idea that Rupert might be thinking of me with affection from time to time - that he, too, might have a permanent place for me in a secret corner of his brain – that he, too, might look from his window at night, or rise in the morning and calculate which stage of the unseen moon or sun will, at that same moment, be casting its light onto my sleeping or waking form.

Why should I be feeling as though my whole life has been turned upside down? There has been no material change in my situation – I already knew that he'd taken me at my word and had married Ivy soon after I returned to England with his baby growing inside me.

Oh Belle! It's staring you in the face. Your thoughts of Rupert weren't limited to a few happy times in the past, or some guesswork as to his day to day existence in the present. He has always been there as a possibility for your distant future... your 'one of these days...'

Yes, Ivy was right in thinking that I'd have heard about their marriage, but I didn't learn about it from the Times. Left to myself I would have remained in my chosen state of blissful ignorance. No - hardly blissful. 'Numbed' would be a more accurate word to describe the state of mind that cocooned me for more than a year after V's birth. I was incapable of feeling anything, mental or physical – neither pleasure nor pain.

But someone had decided that I needed to be told. I received the cutting from the South China Morning Post three weeks after the wedding. The handwriting on the envelope was identical to that which had penned the warning letter for Jimmy about the moral danger I was in. I never did discover who this was, though Mrs Parker was at the top of my list.

The identity of the writer was irrelevant. There was no explanation – merely the folded square of newsprint – the slightly blurred photograph with its brief caption. Ivy was smirking at the camera. I could not make out the expression in his eyes, though I held Jimmy's magnifying glass above it, again and again.

Would I have attempted to make contact with Rupert, once poor Jimmy was gone, had I not known about the marriage? And if I had known about his early death, would I have opened my mind to other possibilities?

Enough. Enough, Belle. You have indulged yourself for far too long already - skulking here like a wounded animal – or a spoilt child. A good bracing walk – that's what you need. Then back to your life again. This time, focus on the living, not the long-ago dead.

Your own daughter, for a start. She surely has a right to know about the existence of her sister. And Ann – poor child! Her special birthday. What will she think of me?

Ann lets the pages drop onto the bed. She leans back, resting her head against the pillows and stares across at the lacquered chest against the wall. Above it hangs a mirror in a bamboo frame with a delicate pattern of gold leaves on black. Blinking her eyes till the moisture clears, she sees the white expanse of the bed cover

162

and the dim shape of her upper body rising from the hill of her knees. From this distance she can't make out the details of her features – she could be anyone.

Nineteen seventy-one to ninety-five - that's twenty four years! Grannibelle kept secret this knowledge about Poppy and George all that time. How could she have done that to her own daughter? And her granddaughter!

When Ann first read through Ivy's letter she'd been focussing on Poppy's part in this story – and her own relationship with George. She'd still been reeling from the revelations about Belle and Rupert. Now she's been given a brief glimpse of a quite different perspective.

She's always thought about Time through the traditional metaphor of a river – one along whose banks she's free to wander, dipping in and out of her own past at will. But it's different with the past of others. Why should you expect to have first-hand knowledge of that, when you can't read the minds of those around you in the present? We merely suppose that what's going on in their heads will match our own perception of the world.

Ann gives a rueful smile as she wriggles down under the cover. Will this thought make any sense in the cold clear light of day? If she does meet up with George tomorrow, she might pluck up the courage to ask him.

She's drifting on the edge of sleep when another thought hits her like a bucket of cold water – Graham! Tomorrow is Friday, his last day at work.

Chapter 20

'You don't honestly expect me to accept charity, do you, Ann? I mean, we're not exactly destitute. If I did want to fly out to Hong Kong, or anywhere else, for that matter, I'd pay for my own ticket.'

'It wouldn't be charity…' she begins in the brief pause, but Graham continues, 'Your mother might have meant well, but I have to say, I didn't like her tone of voice. She - '

'But Graham! Dear. She was genuinely trying to - '

'You're right there. She certainly was trying. Very trying.' He gives his usual snort of satisfaction at this tired joke. 'And if you think I'm about to fly halfway round the world for the pleasure of her company, you've got -'

'Another think coming,' Ann's voice mirrors his words. 'Look, it isn't like that. I know you must be feeling upset, but that's not her fault. Or mine. It's just - '

'I know. I know,' he sighs.

'I just thought, you know, a change would - '

'Do me good? His sudden laugh is more bitter than amused. 'I'll tell you what might do me some good, Ann, and that's knowing that you care enough about your husband to be with him at this crucial turning point in his life.'

The silence that follows bears down on her like a solid weight.

'Ann? Are you there still?' his voice sounds almost shaky. A fault on the line? His next question is loud and clear, with the slightest pause between each word, 'Can you hear me?'

The spell is broken. 'Yes, Graham. I'm still here. Of course I'd want to be with you now, but I've already explained the difficulty about leaving Vivienne just yet, so…' she lets her words hang in the air for a moment, before adding in a rush, 'It'd be so nice if you could come here. You'd love it. I know you would.' She's surprised to find that her enthusiasm is genuine, and warms to her theme, 'I mean, I wasn't expecting it to be anything like it is, it's so… beautiful - '

'I've said I'm not coming Ann,' he says, oblivious to her change of tone, 'If I wanted a foreign holiday, I'd choose somewhere in Europe. Don't worry about me. I'll manage perfectly well on my own. Anyway, this phone call is costing a fortune. If do you want to give me any news, maybe you can find the time to send me an email.'

With a guilty start, Ann realises that the next phone call, an hour later, is considerably more welcome.

'The Peak Tram? Oh, yes please! That would be lovely. I expect it'll have changed a bit since Belle and Rupert's time, but even so…'

'Yes indeed,' agrees George. 'That's just what I thought. Re-tracing our grandparents' footsteps – our shared grandfather - '

'And my grandmother!' Ann puts in with a little shiver of delight.

'I'd hoped we'd be able to have lunch together somewhere, but it looks like I won't get away till mid-afternoon. What if we meet at my shop at three, explore the Peak, and then I take you out for supper this evening? I'll be staying with Poppy for a few days, so we can get the ferry back to Lamma together.'

'What a nice idea,' says Vivienne, smiling benignly. 'I can't tell you what pleasure it gives me to see you two young people getting on so well with each other.'

'Young!' Ann laughs. 'You know very well I'm on the wrong side of fifty!'

'You'll soon discover that age is a concept invented with the sole purpose of controlling one's offspring. Beyond that, it has no meaning at all. It's purely relative. Besides, I'm far too young to have a daughter in her fifties!'

Ann contemplates her mother's face with its high cheek-bones, small, straight nose and the firm, neat line of her jaw and almost-perfect chin, with only the slightest hint of sagging flesh. Even the crows' feet around the wide-set, darkly luminous eyes, and the deeper lines from the base of each nostril to the upturned

165

corners of the smiling mouth, seem to enhance the effect of humour and strength of character – the lived-in face of a still beautiful woman.

When Vivienne frowns suddenly and bites her lip, Ann realises that she must have been frowning herself. 'Oh!' she exclaims, her hand jerking up to mask her mouth, 'I wasn't…I mean, I was just thinking…'

'You were thinking, what a vain, pathetic figure your mother is,' Vivienne says dryly. 'I know perfectly well how old I am. I merely choose not to dwell on it, that's all.'

'No! No, that isn't it. Far from it. Actually, I was thinking, well, how…' she hesitates a moment, 'How *beautiful* you are still. It's just a different kind of beauty. Like Grannibelle – even in her nineties she was still beautiful too.'

Vivienne's mouth twists into a smile again as she sighs, 'I see you haven't lost that gift, Ann.'

'Gift?' She's alert again now, waiting for the cut of her mother's sarcasm. 'What gift is that?'

'Hitting the bull's-eye. Getting straight to the heart of the matter. You always could find the weak spot, couldn't you? The best place to stick the knife in – and always with such an elegant turn of phrase.'

'What do you mean?' she asks in genuine puzzlement. 'I meant it as a compliment. You are still beautiful. And when… when have I ever…?' her voice trails away.

Vivienne sighs again, 'I'm sorry, Ann. Take no notice. I'm sure you meant well. You just happened to identify the real issue, which, unfortunately, is something neither of us can alter - it's the link between my type of beauty now, and my ninety-year old mother's. You, my dear Ann, have not been blessed with physical beauty – if indeed it can be called a blessing - but you have what I can never have again - relative youth. The gap between someone in her seventies and her fifties, is almost as unbridgeable as that between a woman in her thirties and a child of ten.'

'Ohhh,' murmurs Ann, 'I see.' She doesn't ask for further enlightenment on the occasions when her words have hit the mark.

Ann has just reached the bottom of the steps by the bakery. She's about to stroll along the main street to send an email to Graham before she catches the ferry for her meeting with George. Once that task is out of the way, she'll be able to relax fully and enjoy her afternoon.

The sky is an almost cloudless blue, the air warm on her bare legs and forearms, while the trees lining the steps and the steep, narrow paths down from her mother's house have been full of the shrill or melodious twittering and warbling of mainly unseen birds. Her spirits have lifted since that somewhat awkward exchange with Vivienne, but the puzzle of finding the best way of wording her email to Graham, telling him about Rupert and Belle, Poppy and George, is acting like a tether, preventing her mood from soaring to its full height.

She slows her pace as she approaches the small, open-fronted café where she and her mother ate custard tarts on her first evening, and an unexpected rapport flickered between them for a while. There's a young Chinese man behind the counter, deep in conversation with one of these tanned, slim creatures who manage to look simultaneously unkempt and elegant, with their blonde, tangled manes, frayed denim shorts and poised, confident air. The girl is laughing and as she casually turns her head sideways, Ann sees that it's Dawn. She hesitates, wondering whether to interrupt their conversation by calling out a greeting, but Dawn has caught sight of her now and Ann feels a sudden rush of warmth at the girl's unfeigned delight, 'Hi there Annie! That's amazing! I was just thinking of you.'

'Me?' she mumbles almost shyly.

'Yeh, you. Don't look so shocked! We're mates, aren't we?' Dawn thumps her lightly on the shoulder with the flat of her palm. 'The do for tomorrow night, yeh? My birthday. Start off about nine at the bar by the deli – then back to my little shack for a bite to eat - chill out with music – whatever - y'know?'

'Er...it does sound fun. But I'm not sure what Vivienne's plans are yet, so - '

167

'That's cool. Poppy's coming along for a bit and I'll be asking Viv of course. Poppy says her son will be here too. George. You met him on the plane, didn't you? That was amazing! Poppy told me before all about him and her dad, and Viv and your gran and all that. Totally ace, isn't it. Make a great film, it would, I reckon. Yeh?'

'Erm, well, I don't know…' Ann is taken aback by this public reference to her family's cupboard-full of long-buried skeletons.

'You want an ice-cream or a smoothie or something, Annie? I just ordered a pineapple juice.'

'That's very kind, but no, I'm on my way to send an email before I catch the ferry.'

'Cool! They let you do that right here,' and she waves a hand towards a flat-screen monitor perched like a some strange, square flower-head on its stem of long, curving metal that is rising up from behind the high round table. Looking more closely, Ann sees that this is made from a segment of tree trunk, its varnished surface scratched and stained, and the yellowing keyboard equally grubby.

Nevertheless, she lets herself be seated on a tall stool while Dawn orders her a freshly squeezed mango and papaya. She realises that it'll be virtually impossible to write a detailed message to Graham with Dawn around. Never mind. She'll just express her sympathy and give a little of her news. 'Vivienne is bearing up quite well under the circumstances, but she's looking very pale and thin. She has a dress shop here on the island and has bought me a few clothes.' Careful – this mustn't look like accepting charity. 'She said she owed me too many birthday and Christmas presents and I think she enjoyed making up to me for her years of neglect.' What else can she safely say without having to go into the whole story, and yet not risk being accused of keeping things from him? 'Vivienne has introduced me to a friend of hers called Poppy. It turns out that she is some kind of relation, but it's so long and complicated I'll wait to tell you the whole story next week when I come back.'

'So you're meeting up with George later?' says Dawn. 'If

you've finished with the email, how about we take our drinks outside in the sun for a bit. We can easily watch for the ferry from here.'

Once seated, further conversation between them is delayed until Dawn has greeted a series of passers by who stop for a quick word before moving on, after giving individual variations on the theme of, 'Nice to meet you, Ann. See you tomorrow night, OK?'

At last, as the flow of people-known-to-Dawn subsides, Ann asks, 'Your birthday, you said. Is it a special one?'

'You mean, like, eighteenth, or twenty first? Nah! It's an in-betweener. Twenty-two tomorrow. Not too fussed, to be honest. Just an excuse for a party. Sixteen was the real big one for me. That was when I, like, lost it, my...y'know...Tell the truth, couldn't see what all the fuss was about. Found out soon after, though. Wow! Didn't I just?' she giggles, then adds with a grimace, 'Next milestone, thirty.'

'Thirty,' muses Ann. 'How young that sounds.'

'Like sixteen sounds to me now, I guess. Just a kid, I was. And I thought I was so grown-up then! D'you remember what it was like for you at sixteen?'

Ann flinches as if she's been struck by a physical blow. She feels a wave of heat sweep up from her stomach to her throat, her cheeks, and her forehead. The next moment, she's shivering violently. She leans down and fiddles with the heel of her sandal. Dawn has noticed nothing untoward. Maybe there's something funny about this drink, though it tastes delicious – smooth and sweet and cool, with a just hint of a sharper edge - unripe cherries or raw gooseberries .

'You OK, Annie?'

'Yes. Yes, I'm fine. A bit of an itch on my ankle,' she says, slowly raising herself up. She reaches across to the low table for her drink, straightens her back and continues, 'Sixteen...what that was like for me?'

'Yeh, boyfriends, parties, all that stuff.'

'Oh, boyfriends!' she smiles ruefully. 'I was rather a late starter in that department. And as for parties, well, on the whole they were more of an ordeal. Sixteen wasn't exactly the best time of my life - that was the year when Vivienne deserted…I mean, went off with Stuart…' Ann bends towards her glass and closes her lips around the plastic straw.

'Ohh!' says Dawn softly, ' So Vivienne…I mean, like…well, Poppy mentioned that Viv's bloke has just left her, but I'd sort of assumed…or rather, I hadn't thought…'

'Of course not. Why should you? Anyway, it's a bit complicated. My own father died before I was born. Vivienne married again when I was little. Then just a week before my sixteenth birthday she left us – me, my little brother, Colin, and my stepfather. Quite a birthday present, eh?' To Ann's surprise, she finds that now she's voiced this, she feels a little more in control of herself.

Above the babble of voices from the restaurant tables under the striped awning to their left across the wide path, comes the strident cling-clang of bicycle bells and the whirring of wheels as three chattering cyclists zoom past, within a couple of feet of them.

After the din subsides, Dawn mutters, 'Just before your birthday an all! That really sucks, that does.'

'Oh, I got over it,' Ann says more brightly. 'I suppose it was worse for Colin – he was only seven. And for Edward, of course. My step father. Such a good, kind man. He was absolutely devastated.'

'No wonder you're not that close to Vivienne,' says Dawn turning her head. As she catches Ann's eye she gives a warm, easy smile.

As though we're real friends, thinks Ann, realising that she is smiling back.

'Don't reckon there's ever a good time for parents to split up,' muses Dawn, staring at the narrow stretch of grubby sand and the flat, gleaming sea beyond the railings on the other side of the path . 'They sometimes wait till the kids go to uni, but that can be tough too. It happened to one of my mates and she was really cut up about it. I'm lucky, though. My mum and dad are, y'know, well, they seem to actually still be kind of in love. And they've been together, like, forever!'

'That's nice,' she says, feeling, for a brief moment, unaccountably bereft. Louise would never be able to make a statement like that about her mum and dad. *Graham*. Had they ever been 'in love'? If not 'in love', then, yes, there was a kind of love. And now…?

'D'you mind if I ask you something?' Dawn asks.

'Fire away,' says Ann, wondering what could be so intrusive that this uninhibited young woman should feel hesitant of asking.

'You're still married to your kids' dad, right?'

'That's no secret,' laughs Ann.

'Nah. That's not the question. What I want know is, what's it like, being with same man all your life – staying faithful, or whatever? I mean, if you are – have been…'

'Faithful to Graham?' Ann is silent for a moment. The idea of anyone ever finding her interesting or attractive enough to…! Dawn might as well have asked her if she'd ever entered a beauty contest, or considered applying to appear on Big Brother.

'I'm not too sure that I know what *faithful* means,' she says slowly. 'I mean, it sounds like a virtue, doesn't it? Something worthy of praise. Can a person be considered faithful if they've never been tempted to have sex with anyone else? I assume you're talking about sex - but can't there be other ways of judging faithfulness or lack of it?'

'Yeh, I guess so. I was just asking, you know, if a person would get a bit, like, bored? '

'There're plenty of ways of being bored,' says Ann. 'It's not just limited to the bedroom department.'

'Maybe that's partly what I mean, "the bedroom department". It sounds so…As if that's the only place you can…' Dawn's words trail away into a low giggle.

Ann turns her head, pretending a sudden interest in a couple of small children who are chasing each other round an empty pushchair while their Filipino nanny is chatting to a waiter outside the restaurant to their right.

171

'It's OK, Annie. No way am I asking for details about your sex-life with your husband! I'm not that cheeky! Nah, it's just, well, my own mum and dad seem to be the exceptions – still together – *and* happy to be, after more than twenty years. Look at your own mum, and even your gran, as you've found out. I'm sort of trying to work it out for myself – kinda research, I guess – asking different married people. Maybe I'll find that there are actually more happily-marrieds than I thought. At the moment, though, I can't ever see myself tying my whole life to one bloke.'

'It's just that you've not met the right person yet,' Ann chuckles, but even as she speaks, the words have a hollow ring to her. *Faithful! The Right Person!* What does this mean, in real life?

Chapter 21

As Ann settles herself onto a seat at the front of the ferry her thoughts to stray back to Dawn's first question about being sixteen. Her initial reaction had startled her – going hot and cold like that. After all, that birthday, her sixteenth, had almost passed unnoticed.

But surely, at that age, birthdays would still have meant something to her. 'Sweet sixteen and never been kissed.' Eileen's parents had hired a marquee and a live band – it was really for Eileen's big brother's eighteenth, but their birthdays were within a few days of each other and he'd agreed, for the first time since he'd reached the age of eight, to let this be a joint occasion. He was a friend of the drummer and so they were performing cheaper than usual. They were real professionals and did night clubs as well as eighteenths and twenty-firsts, and they all had sideburns, and hair down to their collars. The whole class had been invited. Eileen was the oldest in the form, and that birthday fell on the first Saturday of the new school year. The invitations had been handed out on the final morning of the summer term. Eileen had burst into the classroom before registration with a pile of envelopes. She'd skipped along the rows of desks, dropping a thin white rectangle onto each in turn. Ann had absorbed herself by rummaging in her satchel, practicing an expression of indifference in case hers was the only unselected desk. She was the youngest, and would still be a childish fourteen until the last day of August. The second youngest, Carol, was already fifteen-and-almost-a-quarter.

The prospect of that party had dominated Ann's thoughts throughout that August – even during the usual fortnight in Norfolk with Grannibelle, when they'd always pack up picnics and go out to the Point for the day on the seal boats. The high tide had to come at the right time though, letting the sea rush into the Pit and fill the muddy maze of creeks with swirling water so that the two or three broad-bellied craft, owned by cheerful, burly locals, could chug right up to the rickety jetties at Moreston, or Blakeney harbour. Other days, Gran would drive her along the coast to Holkham Sands, or Ovary Staithe. Vivienne and Colin were there too, of course, and Edward came for the second week, and he'd take them sailing, or bird-watching, or into Norwich if it was too wet to do much else.

'Of course she must have a new party frock for her first grown-up dance,' Grannibelle said one day towards the end of that second week, 'It'll be her birthday present from me.'

She was snipping stems of lavender for the house while Vivienne was selecting some of the dark red, strongly scented roses. Ann had just opened the door into the living room and paused, half way across the threshold at the sound of voices through the wide open window, 'But she's still only fourteen, for goodness sake. Plenty of time for that sort of thing. She's got a perfectly suitable dress that still fits her, and what's more, it actually looks quite passable on her. It's not exactly easy, you know, getting something that doesn't make her look like Mr Potato Head in drag.'

'Oh, Vivienne! You can be so cruel. You'll give the poor girl a complex if you're not careful. She's not bad-looking at all, and she has such a sweet nature. Looks aren't everything, you know.'

'So you always told me, Mother dear. At length. And often. I couldn't fail to be aware that my nature is anything but sweet,' Vivienne laughed, but it didn't sound like a real laugh to Ann, whose hand was grasping the round, brass door knob so tightly that her knuckle was almost white. *Potato Head.* The taunt that had sent her home from school in tears, her first term at the Girls' School. She would never, never tell Vivienne anything ever again.

It was only because the following morning was grey and threatening rain, and Grannibelle had insisted on Norwich as the destination for the day's outing, that Ann got her new dress.

Vivienne had already mentioned it while she and Grannibelle were preparing the evening meal. 'When we get back home, I'll take you in to town, Ann, and we'll see what we can find.'

'That won't be easy, will it?' she'd muttered, dropping the final segments of sliced runner bean into the metal colander on her

174

lap, and then pushing back her chair. As she flung open the back door she turned and snapped, 'Anyway, what's the point in new gear when I've got something 'quite passable' already, Mother *Dear*?'

Just after the door slammed shut behind her, Ann felt a brief flash of satisfaction at hearing Vivienne's startled, 'Oh Christ! She heard me. What on earth do I do now?'

Later that evening, Ann was hunched on the bed in her room - her old room from The Norfolk Time that was still her very own - idly turning the pages of 'Anne of Green Gables' when there was a light tap, tap on the door, followed by Vivienne's voice, 'Ann. I'm so sorry. Don't take it to heart, I was just - '

'Just telling the truth about the way I look,' Ann called out. 'It's a wonder you didn't drown me at birth. Bet you would of, if Grannibelle hadn't stopped you.'

'Oh Ann, dear, don't be so silly …' there was a pause and as the handle of the door turned, the chair that she had tried to wedge under it tumbled to the floor and Vivienne's head appeared.

'Go away! Can't you see this is a private room and I don't want you in it?'

'Look, Ann. You must understand that people often say things carelessly about others, without really meaning what they say. That's where that old saying comes from - eavesdroppers hear no good of themselves.'

'I wasn't eavesdropping. I couldn't help it that you were in the garden and the window was open. Anyway, you can't pretend you didn't mean it. That's not the first horrid thing you've said about me.'

'Darling…'

'You needn't 'darling' me. I'm not going to jump off a cliff or anything, just cos my own mum hates the sight of me. If I do decide to go to Eileen's party I don't care what I wear. And it certainly won't be anything you've bought me.'

'Very well then, Ann. I've done my best to explain, but if you're going to insist on taking that line, I might as well save my breath.'

But Grannibelle wasn't going to let anything deflect her from her chosen mission. In spite of the gloomy weather, Edward had chosen to go off bird watching, so, once the four of them had arrived in Norwich, it was easy enough for Grannibelle to manipulate the situation: she would spend the morning with Ann, while Vivienne took Colin to the Castle with a promise of exploring the battlements and the dungeons.

'First stop, Jarrolds,' Grannibelle said, once they'd parted from the other two. 'We've got all the time in the world, and I'm not going back home until we've bought you a nice dress for your special party.'

'What's the point? 'Ann said, morosely, 'Vivienne shouldn't have said it, but she's right - I do look like Mr Potato Head.'

'You can stop that right now, Miss,' Grannibelle's voice was stern, but the arm across Ann's shoulder was comforting. 'What's said can't be un-said, but I can detect a good old-fashioned wallow when I see one. Or rather, hear one.'

She put her other hand on Ann's upper arm, stooped down, and gently drew her round until they were face to face. 'I know that Vivienne can sound unkind at times, but she has problems of her own. One thing I do know is – she cares very deeply about you, and doesn't want you getting hurt.'

Ann opened her mouth to protest, but Grannibelle went on, 'Believe it or not, beauty is a mixed blessing. In its own way, it can make life difficult for a girl growing up. I won't say any more about that just now.' As she spoke, she lifted her right hand to the crown of Ann's head, rhythmically stroking her hair, down to the base of her neck, over and over. 'What is more important, Poppet, is for you to realise that you do have a choice in life – you can either make the best of what you have – and of any situation you might find yourself in - or you can wallow in self pity and eat worms. It's as simple as that. Come on now, let's have a big smile!'

The noise of the engine changes as the ferry slows, and Ann looks around her at the passengers beginning to rise to their feet and make their wobbly way along the aisles, grabbing the backs of the seats as the floor tilts from one side to the other. She's glad, now, to be able to focus on the present, even though she's a little apprehensive about meeting up with George. Will they slip back into that easy companionship again?

She doesn't want to contemplate the birthday of the year that followed her fifteenth. The gulf between the two is like... like that between her, now, in Hong Kong, and the Ann she left behind at Birmingham Airport, just a few days ago. Her fifteenth birthday, and the days immediately before and after, had been redeemed by the gift of that expensively simple and stylish party dress, and Vivienne's brief spell of tact and kindness towards her.

She must have looked quite nice, or at least normal, in that dress - and maybe a year or two older, because Eileen's brother himself had actually asked her to dance. Brendan, his name was, and he had blue eyes and wavy black hair that curled down below his ears. Well, not 'asked' her exactly - she was standing with Carol by the drinks table, giggling over a glass of fruit cup which had vodka and wine and all sorts in it and was already making her head a bit fuzzy, and he'd grabbed her hand, and she'd let herself be tugged on to the crowded wooden square of dance floor as he roared along with the lead singer, 'Let's spend the night together.'

'Lucky you,' said Carol, as Ann, flushed and panting, jostled her way back to retrieve her drink as the song came to an end and Brendan's girlfriend returned from powdering her nose and reclaimed him.

A couple of other girls from her class, who usually either ignored or taunted Ann, sauntered across to pour themselves a drink and she heard one whisper, in a tone of amazement, 'How did *she* manage to get a dance with him?' to which the other replied, 'Must be the dress. Ask where she got it. If Pudding-Face can manage to look half-way decent in that, just imagine...'

For a while after that party, Ann found herself being allowed to hang around the fringes of the group that held second place in the pecking order of the class. Not the top group, of course, but not the bottom, either. She'd somehow been included in a trip to the cinema and another party that Christmas, and then, in March, the biggest miracle of all: Carol had told Ann there was one seat left on the coach they'd booked to take them to Coventry to see the Rolling Stones, and she might as well come too if she wanted. *Wanted?* To breathe the same air as Mick Jagger!

Although nothing that followed could match that experience, Felicity, with her jibes and jealousies had left home at last. Life was…not bad now! It was actually…yes, most of the time, it was actually OK.

Then all of a sudden, Vivienne was gone, and everything changed.

Her sixteenth birthday passed unnoticed by anyone, even Grannibelle.

Chapter 22

As Ann lifts her left hand from the metal rail of the shifting gangway and steps onto the solid concrete of the ferry terminal, a long-forgotten image from her childhood-reading pushes its way into her mind: The Faraway Tree with its succession of strange lands, a different one arriving each week, providing a new adventure for those lucky children who lived on the edge of the Enchanted Wood. Grannibelle didn't hold a high opinion of the books of Enid Blyton – 'I'm afraid they're rather poor fare, compared to the real classics for children. They're all very well, as far as they go,' she would say, 'but the trouble is, they don't really *go* anywhere – they don't stretch the mind.'

'Don't *go* anywhere!' eight-year old Ann would think, as the next chapter brought yet another land for her to scramble onto from the topmost branches of the magic tree.

She smiles to herself as she saunters out into the sunshine – it'll be enough of an adventure for her to find her way to George's shop, unaided.

'No, I'm afraid this wouldn't be the very same carriage that our grandparents rode in,' George says, pausing as they exchange glances at this reference to the closeness of their relationship, 'Still, theirs would have looked pretty well exactly the same as this.'

They are sitting side by side, wedged close to each other on a narrow wooden seat on the right hand side near the front, waiting for the tram to start its journey up to the Peak. George points out the varnished wood panels on the ceiling and around the windows, 'They've added a second carriage since the first tram was built. These are both replicas of that first one. They're trying to maintain the feel of the original – inside the carriages at least.'

Ann has read and re-read Belle's journal and letters so often by now, that she knows them almost by heart, so when the tram starts to pull away up a rather gentle slope she wonders how her grandmother could have even pretended to be afflicted by vertigo on her trip with Rupert. She's about to express this thought to George when the gradient suddenly increases, and she finds that she has to lean forward and grab the top of the bench in front of her in order to keep her spine at an angle that will maintain a conventional relationship with the towering buildings rising up above the trees on her right. From the ferry, it was easy enough to take in the geography of the island, with its high ridge running along the centre, dividing the south edge from the more built-up north, and even when she'd made her way up the series of escalators to George's shop, a considerable height above the ferry terminal, there'd been no question in her head about the structural soundness of the tall buildings around her. Now, however, as the tram hauls itself up the vertiginous track, it seems like a miracle of engineering to have built anything larger than a dog-kennel on these steep wooded slopes.

A few moments later, the tops of those skyscrapers are below them, and only dimly visible through a gathering mist. Soon, the tall, moss-covered trees on both sides of the track give way to walls of glistening rock, speckled with lichens and dripping ferns, and almost close enough to allow an outstretched hand to touch them.

'Bloody rain!' exclaims George. 'I'm really sorry, but I'm afraid that's put paid to your chance of those famous views from Lugard Road.' He sighs as he adds, 'If I'd realised that the sun wouldn't last , I'd have re-arranged things and taken you out this morning instead.'

His expression is so mournful that Ann can't help laughing, 'It's not your fault that it's the Land of Rain at the top of the tree today. If you want an adventure, you have to step onto whatever country happens to come round.'

'Would the Mad Trolley Woman like to explain what on earth she's talking about?' he says, a sudden grin transforming his face.

'The Faraway Tree mean anything to you? Enid Blyton?'

'Nope,' he shakes his head. 'My dear Mama wouldn't give her house-room – on a par with comics as far as she was concerned.

180

The Rupert Bear Annual was the closest I got to those when I was little - apart from what I picked up in friends' houses. Maybe it was the atrocious rhymes and archaic wording that gave it an air of respectability?'

'Grannibelle was just the same,' Ann puts in, then adds with a trace of bitterness, 'Knowing what I know now, I'd say, for her it was because it gave her the chance to speak his name out loud in front of everyone – her lover's name. And to think I used to ask for it, night after night! Disgusting really. It's quite spoiled that memory now.'

George gives her knee a gentle pat, letting his hand rest lightly there for a moment. She feels its warmth through the soft denim of her skirt, 'Don't say that, Ann,' he says in a tone more concerned than critical. 'Even if that was part of her reason for choosing it, it didn't mean she loved you less. It must have been very hard for her, you know – giving him up for the sake of her little boy – and her husband too. I get the impression from all those letters and journals, that Belle was the true love of Rupert's life, and he of hers.'

'Sorry! That wasn't a nice thing to say. I don't know what got into me just then.'

'Don't apologise to me! It's all been a great shock to you, coming out here and having all these revelations thrust on you - and to cap it all, to find yourself lumbered with me for a cousin!'

'That's been the best part of it all, silly,' she laughs.

'Me too,' he replies, then in a lighter tone, 'Enough of all that. I'm in danger of revealing my true colours as a die-hard romantic. And that's in spite of Biggles.'

'Biggles?'

'He followed on from The Bear. I devoured every one of those books. "It may be trash, but at least it's manly trash," my father used to say. Eventually, he weaned me on to G.H. Henty and John Buchan, and I gobbled those up with equal enthusiasm.'

'The 39 Steps! Greenmantle! I was in love with Richard Hannay when I was about eleven.'

'Eleven. Mmm. I think I was still in my anti-girl phase then,'

George laughs, 'Though maybe that was only the real, flesh and blood variety. To be strictly honest, I think I was more terrified than anti.'

'Me too, as far as real-life boys went. Didn't help, being at a girls-only school. And I found most of them frightening enough.'

They become aware that the tram is slowing to a halt, the rain against glass has ceased and the window is now revealing the brightly-lit interior of a small station.

'Another culture shock for you,' laughs George as they find themselves being funnelled, along with all the other passengers, into a wide exit tunnel lined on each side with particularly gaudy souvenir stalls. 'Goodbye to the world of Belle and Rupert for the time being, eh?'

'Yes,' says Ann with a little sigh, 'I could easily imagine them on the tram – especially when it was going through those huge walls of rock and no buildings in sight.' *Strange*, she thinks, how she can smile indulgently at the thought of those faraway lovers, at how she and George are retracing some of the footsteps their grandparents took on their secret outings together, long before she was born, and yet, when she conjures up a real scene from her own past it evokes quite a different set of feelings about her grandmother.

As they turn a corner, Ann sees several youngsters taking snapshots of each other in front of a wide colour photograph, that, for a brief moment, she perceives as a true window, revealing in the foreground the tops of the highest skyscrapers, and below these, across the narrow stretch of the channel that is the harbour, the built-up area of Kowloon, and the outline of mountains in the distance, topped with white clouds in a blue sky.

'You'd be amazed how realistic this appears in the photos. Anyone could be forgiven for thinking it's the actual view,' George says, wandering over to where she is standing. 'Sadly for us, it's the nearest we'll get to that view this afternoon.'

'Never mind,' says Ann. 'The tram ride was worth it for its own sake.'

'Just as well you feel like that,' he grins. 'There's not much inside this place that's worth the time spent getting here!'

They have emerged into the heart of a shiny new shopping mall, where he gestures towards a series of escalators criss-crossing up and up across the lofty central space. 'This is the new Peak Tower,' he explains. 'It's only been here, what, about five years? Six stories high, with a viewing platform on the roof. Not too much point in going up there today though.'

Ann gazes across at a vast expanse of curving white wall and then realises that it's not made of opaque plastic, but glass which has been rendered temporarily opaque by the mist or rain outside.

'We can still make our way up to the top, if you'd like,' George says. 'You never know, but if this is mist rather than rain, there could be some clear sky up there, even if there's nothing else to see.'

'OK, let's do that. I rather enjoy escalators,' she says. 'That sensation of gliding uphill with no effort.'

'So long as you don't try to go up the down ones, or vice-versa,' he laughs. 'I wouldn't put it past you.'

'Can't imagine how you might have got that impression of me,' she says primly, then makes for the foot of a stairway that is descending towards them, and adds, 'Shall we? Bet I could beat you to the top.'

'Go on then,' he says. 'But I maintain the right to disown you.' Then, as she pretends to put her foot on the moving strip he places a hand firmly below her elbow and steers her through a gaggle of schoolchildren towards the upward one, saying loudly, 'Do excuse us! My poor sister has only just been discharged from hospital. She's in rather a confused state today.'

Ann laughs and pulls away from him, taking the steps three at a time. In a mere few seconds she is waving down at him from her vantage point on the next landing while George grins up at her.

A blast of chilly air greets them as they step out onto the wide concrete area of the viewing platform. 'What a contrast with the weather on Lamma,' says Ann, wriggling into her light rain-proof jacket. 'I was actually getting a bit too hot, sitting in the sun outside that little cafe place on the waterfront, and now….Brrrr'

'Here, let me give you a hand with that,' says George, as she struggles with the zip. It seems quite natural to let George take over. Somehow he manages to be supportive, rather than controlling. Comforting, instead of irritating.

After they have stood shivering for a few moments in the swirling mist, and George has taken a photo at the request of four giggling Chinese girls, they set off on the downward journey.

'What's that song about the Grand Old Duke of York?' asks George as they step onto the third flight of escalators, 'You know - the one about going up and down a hill?'

'And when they were up, they were up,' sings Ann, her low voice almost masked by the hubbub around them.

'That's it! Knew I could rely on you for useless scraps of information!'

The song, repeated several times, lasts them all the way to the ground floor. When they step off the final escalator Ann suddenly becomes aware of herself again, and her hand jerks up to cover her mouth. She turns towards George and as their eyes meet, their laughter breaks out.

'All those people gliding past us!' he exclaims, 'Did you see their faces?'

'And you're the one who calls me, mad!'

'It's all your fault. I was a sober, upright citizen till you barged into me.'

'We obviously bring out the worst in each other,' she gives an exaggerated sigh, and then bites her lip.

When they reach the huge exit doors, they stand side by side, staring out at the driving rain. 'So, what now?' asks George. 'I don't suppose you want to walk along Lugard Road in this weather. Shall we just call it a day?'

'Oh! If that's what you'd prefer, then ...' her voice tails away.

'I didn't mention my personal preference, Ann. This is your outing, not mine,' his voice is stern, but his brown eyes are glinting with amusement. 'Go on,' he adds with a laugh, 'You decide. It really is up to you.'

'You'll probably think I'm mad, but -'

'"Definitely" would be nearer the mark, if you're telling me you'd like to get sopping wet and frozen solid? So be it. Lead on, MacDuff.'

Ann takes a step towards the door, 'Hang on a minute, woman. It's all very well for you, with that jacket, but what about me in my shirt sleeves? Do you want to kill me off?'

She follows his glance towards a plastic tub full of umbrellas, and laughs as they make their way towards it.

The start of Lugard Road is only a few paces from the brash, noisy structure of the Peak Tower, but as they round the corner onto the wet tarmac under arching trees, Ann experiences, yet again, the sensation of stepping into a different land. The wind can't reach them here, and the only sound is the shush of steady rain on the trees around and above them, with the intermittent patter of heavier drops that have forced their way through the green canopy onto their raised umbrellas. The fact that she and George appear to be the only ones to have ventured out into this grey, inclement afternoon adds to the feeling of timelessness.

After a few minutes have passed in companionable silence, they come to a halt beside a wooden notice board with pictures of some of the birds that, on a clearer day, they might have seen – or at least, heard. 'Chinese Bulbul,' reads Ann. 'Bulbul sounds like something from the Arabian Nights. And how about this? Black-throated Laughing Thrush –I'd love to hear that,' she adds with a smile. 'Have you ever?'

They are standing at the railing in the fine drizzle, looking over the edge at the tops of wet trees below, poking up through the shroud of mist. 'Heard a laughing thrush? Pass! I'm no better on birds than I am on trees. Cuckoo –yes, probably. Owl, maybe? Anything else - wouldn't have a clue.'

'Can't hear any birds at the moment, anyway,' says Ann, tilting her head. 'Come to that, can't hear anything. Even this rain is like a kind of silence.'

She glances across the road at a high stone wall, with huge ferns clustered along its broad top, and clumps of thick bamboo and broad-leaved, jungle-looking trees rising behind it. 'It's so narrow, it's more like a path than a road,' she says, as they resume their walk, side by side along the centre. 'Do cars really drive along here? I'd not have thought there'd be room even for a small one.'

'They do, I believe. But as you'll have noticed already, there are very few houses along this stretch, and I think most of the traffic is limited to other end – Lugard Road becomes something else, Harlech Road, I think, and it goes full circle round Victoria Peak. Most cars would start from the other direction.'

Rounding a gentle bend, they find the road becoming narrower still as the vegetation on each side encroaches onto the tarmac – these plants are like dream-objects in their strange familiarity. Ann recognises them as giant versions of the stubby, pot-bound specimens found in bathrooms or on kitchen window sills, or their healthier, somewhat larger relatives that might flourish in a neat conservatory or sunny porch. Ann is looking down at the side of the path, silently attempting to identify the long, jagged leaves, or huge, smooth, broad ones, when George suddenly stops.

Looming ahead of them in the mist, draped at head-height just above their path are curtains of trailing strands, the thickness, perhaps, of baling twine. These, together with a vast tree trunk on the left, and thick stems descending on the right from its overhanging branches, form a tunnel-like shelter. Standing beneath it, Ann closes her umbrella and as she look up she sees that each of the stringy, dangling roots has a creamy white tip.

'Oh look! It's as if they're deliberately searching for somewhere to burrow down into the earth and grow themselves into new trees.'

George laughs. 'I'm sure that's just what they are doing, but I'd hesitate to credit them with conscious thought!'

'You know what I mean,' she retorts, as George shakes the drops from his umbrella.

After a moment's silence, she continues, 'It's just… well, this place! The mist – no sight or sound of anyone else around. No hint of any buildings – let alone skyscrapers. It's not spooky, just…'

'Don't worry. I do know…It's getting to me, too, a bit,' and he puts his arm around her shoulder pulling her towards him in a quick, brotherly hug. 'My grandfather – and yours, of course - I can't help wondering what he'd have thought if he could ever have guessed that grandchildren of his, all this time later, would be standing here, thinking of him.'

'And Belle. Would they have stopped under this same tree, do you think?' she says, looking at the width of the trunk, and the numerous thick roots twining around it.

'It looks like it's been here for a hundred years, but things do grow fast in this climate. Whatever, they must have passed this very spot if they did the whole circular walk.'

They stand for a while without speaking, shoulders and arms so close that the fabric of his sleeve is touching hers. The rain starts up again more heavily beyond their shelter - white noise that seems to bind them closer.

Ann is certain that Rupert and Belle paused in this very same spot, feeling more comfortable in each other's company than either had felt with anyone else before, or since.

Chapter 23

'It's Poppy's, really, the flat,' explains George as the lift bumps to a halt and they step out onto polished boards on the fourteenth floor. 'She virtually never uses it, but she insisted on keeping a bolt-hole here on Mid-Levels when she moved out to Lamma.'

Their footsteps echo along the corridor for a few yards, George's with a light *clunk, creak, clunk , creak,* and Ann's making a softer, squelching sound. While he slides the key into the lock of a solid oak door, she wriggles her toes inside her sodden shoes and becomes aware of the drips falling from the hem of her skirt onto the floor. She gives a little shiver as she follows him into a large, L-shaped room with a high ceiling and plate-glass windows that open onto a narrow balcony.

Once the door has closed behind them, she shivers again, 'I don't want to ruin your carpet,' she mutters, stepping back onto the doormat, 'but if I take my shoes off, my feet'll be just as mucky, I'm afraid. There'll be black footprints all over this spotless cream wool.'

'For goodness sake! Just look at you, you poor drowned rat. And shivering, too! What'll I say to Vivienne if you end up with double pneumonia?' he laughs, kicking off his own shoes, and padding back towards her.

She smiles at the sight of his big toe poking out through a dark green sock, and then he's down on one knee and fumbling with the buckle on the damp canvas strap. 'Come on, off with these,' he says, 'and don't let me hear another word about mud on the carpet!' Moments later, still on one knee before her, he is gently lifting the bare soles, one after the other, away from the scratchy mat. The thick pile feels like a caress against her skin. She looks down at the dark crown of his head as he arranges her shoes neatly side by side, and there is something about his quiet concentration on this small task that reminds her of their first meeting at Schipol airport. She holds her breath, willing him to stay in that position long enough for the sudden rush of blood to drain from her cheeks.

He seems in no hurry to rise. She watches in a daze as he reaches out again towards her. She feels the weight of a broad hand across the top of each foot, 'Pretty little things,' he mutters, almost to himself, his thumbs reaching to the soft hollow of the insteps while his fingers trace the outline of the feet, down to the toes. Another shiver runs through her and he glances up, 'Cold?' he murmurs, transferring the hands to his own bent knee and hauling himself up.

'A bit,' she says, with an awkward giggle. Then more briskly, 'I'll be fine, though. Really.'

'Don't get me wrong,' he says, 'but how about I run you a nice hot bath? I can wash the mud off your skirt and stick it in the tumble drier – your shoes, too. Your top's still dry, isn't it?'

'We..ell. Ye…s,' she falters; then, regaining her composure, 'Sounds good to me.'

Any awkwardness she might have felt has vanished completely by the time she and George are perched on high stools at the breakfast bar, sipping mugs of hot chocolate to the accompanying sound of her denim skirt, jacket and canvas shoes flopping and thudding in the tumble drier with George's black chinos.

He has found her an emerald-green silk house-coat of Poppy's with purple dragons embroidered on its sleeves. 'She keeps a few of her things at the back of the wardrobe "just in case",' he explained, as he handed it to her through the bathroom door.

'Suits you,' he'd said when she'd eventually emerged after she'd managed to wipe off enough of the steam from the full-length mirror to get a flatteringly soft-focus image of herself. She'd had to hitch the garment up with the aid of the belt which had circled her waist twice round, and still left two long ends dangling almost to her knees, while the hem of the robe trailed along the floor in her wake.

'Seems almost a shame to have to go out again this evening,' George sighs, standing up and looking across at the now silent tumble drier. 'There's nothing much round here, and I thought

189

Soho would be fun, but -'

'It's OK, I can make my own way back to Lamma. You don't have to take me out for a meal. I'm sure Vivienne will have something, or - '

'Don't be daft, woman!' he laughs, letting his hand rest on her shoulder. 'I only meant, well... I'm enjoying being in my mother's flat with my favourite cousin. It's never felt so...I don't know...so much like a proper home.'

It's dark by the time they step out of George's block, but it's no longer raining. Ann feels refreshed, exhilarated, even, as she and George stroll along the stretch of road from Poppy's flat towards the top of the escalator. 'Oh, yes, let's do that,' she'd replied earlier, in response to his suggestion, 'I'll see more that way than I would from a taxi.'

'OK – if you're sure you're not too tired,' he'd said, sounding doubtful, 'We're at the very top, here in Conduit Road and it really is a long way down. Still, as you can see, there's only one moving stairway – up first thing in the morning, then down in the evening so at this time of day at least we won't be knackering our knee joints on the paved steps!

In the light of a solitary street lamp, he points out a high sloping wall on the other side of the road, 'Just a few, low-rise blocks of luxury flats up there, and then it's trees and rocky crags all the way up to where we were this afternoon. Shame the weather was so foul. It changes so quickly at this time of year.'

'Bad as England,' laughs Ann looking up at the sky, clear, apart from a few scudding clouds, and bright with stars.

'One of the things I like about having a flat right up here – it's almost as good as Lamma, in terms of light pollution. Down in Central, you'd hardly know that stars existed.'

The entrance to the escalator from this end does not announce its presence very clearly. If she'd been on her own Ann might have overlooked the low, narrow structure with its curved glass roof. *Down we go from the top of the Faraway Tree*, she thinks, smiling to herself as she steps onto the moving metal.

Each separate stretch of escalators seems to have a character of its own, some with occasional wafts of jasmine and glimpses of trees and bushes in the shadows between the buildings that they pass, and wide flights of tiled steps running parallel on either side. Others are hemmed in so closely by small, brightly-lit shop-fronts or bars, it feels like being in a tunnel.

'What an amazing structure! Any idea how old it is?' she asks as they pause at the end of a connecting passageway traversing a main road. They are leaning against the railings peering down onto the next strips of escalator snaking away far below between towering blocks of flats and offices. The sections of curved glass roof give out a strange glow from the dim lights underneath them and the brighter ones reflecting down from surrounding windows and winking neon signs. This could be a huge, fluorescent monster, with articulated panels on its back. Or maybe a narrow glacier plunging steeply at the base of a deep gorge.

'Not sure – Fifties, maybe? One thing I do know – Rupert wouldn't have brought your grandmother down this way!'

Almost unconsciously, she lets him link her arm in his as they move on. Thinking about this later, she can't be sure which of them had instigated the gesture – it had taken place so naturally.

'This place is Northern Chinese, Harbin District - I think you'll enjoy it, Ann,' George says, pushing open the door and stepping into a smart but cosy restaurant, with a low babble of voices, clinking of cutlery, and a mixture of tantalising, spicy aromas. A rush of saliva reminds Ann that it's a long time since she's eaten and she glances around eagerly for an empty table, enjoying the sensation of hunger that will soon be satisfied.

A moment later, her mouth is dry. She swings round and grabs at George's arm with a clammy hand, tugging him out onto the bustling pavement, where she hurries him along to the next junction and crosses over to where loud music is blaring from a bar on the corner, and groups of chattering, laughing young people are spilling out of the packed doorways onto the street. As she slows to a halt, George puts an arm around her shoulder, 'What is

191

it, Ann? Are you ill?' his voice is anxious. 'I should have insisted on a taxi… if you can just wait here a moment I'll get one now.'

'No, I'm fine. Really. I'm OK now,' but her faint voice belies her words.

Trust Stuart to spoil everything, she thinks, letting George lead her down a narrow, brightly-lit street with more bars and restaurants than shops. The reserves of pent-up energy that have carried her along all evening like a surfer on a never-ending wave are totally depleted. Her legs feel unreliable as Play-Doh and heavy as lead. Half way down the road, she stumbles and leans more heavily on George's arm.

'This'll have to do, for the moment,' he says firmly, and she makes no protest as he gently propels her through the doorway of a restaurant on their left and into the bay window where he sits her in an armchair upholstered in red plush. Now that she's able to relax, she finds that her knees are trembling uncontrollably and she has to blink her eyes to prevent tears from escaping.

Still standing, George asks, 'Do you like Middle-Eastern food? I've not been here before, but I've heard it's good.'

Ann manages to keep her voice steady, 'I like pretty well everything – just don't ask me to make any kind of choice! I'll have what you're having.'

She looks up from her almost empty plate on the low table between them and sees him watching her with a quizzical expression, 'You had me worried for a while back then,' he says.

'I'm feeling fine now. It was just…'

'It's OK,' he breaks in. 'You don't have to talk about it.'

'You didn't see them, then?'

'See who?'

'In that other restaurant. My mother's friend, the woman from the shop, Lucia. With Stuart.'

'Lucia and Stuart?' George pauses, and then laughs 'I don't think there's anything to worry about there. I quite see that Vivienne would feel upset if he's left her for one of her closest friends, but I'm sure Poppy would have told me that. And anyway,

I don't think Lucia is that sort of person.'

'That sort of person,' she repeats, mulling over the words. 'Isn't that just the point – there's no such thing as 'that sort of person'? It seems that anyone will betray their nearest and dearest, when it comes to "lurv".' Aware of the bitterness of her tone, she stops abruptly.

'Ouch!' George says with a wry smile, 'A touch close to the bone, that.'

'Oh I didn't mean - '

'I know. I know you didn't. And you're right – there isn't a 'that sort of person' – not really. Though I was thinking more in terms of loyalty to friends. I've known Lucia for years and I like her a lot. She's very straightforward. Says what she thinks – no beating about the bush. She was a friend of Stuart's as well as Vivienne's – it's always a bit tricky when a couple splits up – trying to remain friends with both.'

'I suppose,' she sighs. 'I won't say anything to Vivienne, though. I didn't tell her about bumping into Stuart yesterday either. I wasn't sure how she'd…well, she hasn't spoken to me about him – seems to be avoiding the subject.'

'That doesn't surprise me. She's always struck me as a very private person. But I'm sure that just having you here is a comfort to her. That's what brought you out here in the first place, isn't it?'

'I thought I'd find her in pieces,' she says. 'How wrong I was. She's certainly a tough old bird – I'll give her that. You know Stuart. What do you make of him?'

'I'm not too sure. He seemed pleasant. And devoted to Vivienne. Always very attentive and they did seem to have a lot in common – they're both artistic, independent-minded, enjoy the countryside – in spite of Vivienne's elegant appearance, she can stride up a hill faster than I can! I must say, I was surprised when Poppy told me that he'd left her. But then, I suppose…the usual cliché … bloke, getting on a bit …flattered by the attentions of an attractive younger woman…That's more or less my own story, I'm ashamed to say.'

Ann looks away, pretending an interest in a group of youngsters linking arms as they stroll past the window. She doesn't want to hear about George's 'attractive younger woman'. Lucia could also fit that category.

'Jill and I were going through a bit of a tricky patch. She was feeling unsettled after the boys had left home...Lonely, I guess, though I didn't realise at the time. Probably the hormones too. She seemed to have lost all interest in me – and then along comes Patty...' he sighs, then adds with a laugh, 'Men can be very dense, when it comes to reading the real message in the long silences and short answers.'

'Wouldn't life be so much easier if we all said what we meant – men and women too?'

'On one level, it might be. But on the other hand, saying what you're really thinking could be disastrous. Doesn't it always depend on the circumstances?

Ann is silent for a moment. How often does she disclose her true thoughts to anyone? Maybe she could, with George.

'I mean, take your grandmother, for instance,' he goes on. 'She couldn't have stayed with your grandfather if she'd let him know she was still in love with Rupert. Her journal makes that pretty clear. And as for 'she shouldn't have let herself fall in love in the first place...'

'I didn't say that!'

'Not in so many words, but I wouldn't be surprised if you feel like that.'

'I... I don't know.'

He has that quizzical look on his face again, 'See? It's not that easy, is it – saying what you think?'

She bites her lip and frowns, then laughs as she says, 'Maybe it's because half the time I don't really know what I think – maybe I *don't* think!'

'You're not the only one. Most of us go through life on auto-pilot – you know, stock responses we've imbibed from parents and teachers – It's not till we're confronted with events that challenge us that we have to question our attitudes.'

'Mmm,' Ann sighs. The little restaurant has been filling up since they arrived and the hubbub of voices has almost drowned out the sound of plaintive Arabian music. 'I've not had much to challenge me during the last few years, and now…'

'Now you've had the rug pulled from under you?'

'Yes. Yes that's it exactly. Finding that the person who had the greatest influence on me in my life wasn't in fact the person I thought she was.'

'But how does that change things? You are the person you are, partly because of your grandmother's influence on you as a child. Her life before you were born… her affair with Rupert…that can't change the way she was with you… the effect that had on you.'

Ann shifts in her seat and glances around. A waiter is weaving his way between the tables, bearing a hubble-bubble pipe on a small round tray and places it in the middle of a chattering group of young men in smart casual clothes. George follows her gaze, and indicates another group, further away, where a pretty European woman, Spanish, maybe, or Greek, is sucking at the mouthpiece as the water bubbles in the jar.

'Don't look so shocked,' he laughs, 'It's not opium. I think it's just tobacco – a cleaner way of smoking. Looks rather exotic, though, doesn't it?'

'An opium den would be a bridge too far for my entrenched attitudes!'

'I wasn't suggesting - '

'I know you weren't. But you're right all the same. I shouldn't be condemning Grannibelle – after all, she didn't desert her family.'

'Unlike your own mother?'

Ann gives a deep sigh, 'Betrayal. It's not easy to forgive when you've been on the receiving end.'

'Poor Ann,' he murmurs, reaching forward and taking her hand in his, squeezing it gently. 'It can't have been easy for you at the time…you were, what, fifteen, sixteen? No wonder you couldn't bear the idea of being in the same restaurant as Stuart… It wasn't just the thought of him being involved with Lucia, was it? I think you were in a state of total shock…just as you must have been when you first discovered that he and Vivienne…'

Yes, thinks Ann, George is right. A state of total shock. No wonder, when Vivienne had just walked out of the house forever and didn't even say goodbye.

Chapter 24

Ann yawns and stretches her arms wide, luxuriating in having an entire double bed to herself. She doesn't have to think too hard to discover the source of the light, bubbling feeling that is pushing her mouth into a broad smile. George. Her cousin George. Closer than any brother could be. She's never experienced a male friendship – never even thought such a thing might be possible. It's their shared blood that's helped to forge this bond - without it, she could never have let herself open up to him in the way she's doing. That's the added joy of this new relationship – it's totally safe and above board. No-one, not even Graham, could raise any objection.

She pads across to the window and steps out onto the balcony. Far below, boats are slowly drifting on their moorings in the bay. A ferry is chugging towards the pier. A couple of dark brown birds are circling above the harbour. Their long, outstretched wings have jagged tips. *Kites*, Vivienne told her, *Eagles of the sea*. In between the distant screech of bicycle brakes, the twittering of birds, the sudden deep-throated bark of a dog, she registers the underlying hum of the power station. *The heartbeat of the island*, she thinks, and for a moment Lamma itself seems like a living entity.

Today is Saturday. She should ring Graham. She'll phone as soon as she's dressed, chat to him amicably for a bit, ignoring any attempt on his part to weigh her down with his worries, while still maintaining a sympathetic ear, and then, duty done, she can focus on the day ahead.

The day ahead! This is her fifth day and she still hasn't fully adjusted to the time difference – she'll get short shrift from Graham if she rings at what, for him, will be the middle of the night. She'll send an email instead – that'll be easier. He'll find it waiting for him when he undertakes his Saturday morning task of sorting junk mail from the few genuine messages. She can plan her words carefully and he can appreciate her concern before they actually speak.

Vivienne has suggested a trip to the beach if the weather remains warm. George has already said he might be able to join them later, once he's spent time with Poppy. Then, in the evening, there's Dawn's party.

The only party Ann can remember with any pleasure is Eileen's sixteenth – the year of The Dress, when she'd just turned fifteen and Eileen's brother had selected her to dance with. She never anticipated enjoyment at any other party since then, and was never proved wrong.

Never ? Surely this can't be true, she muses as she lets the hot shower-water cascade across her shoulders and down her back. What about functions she's been to with Graham during their life together? Nothing memorable springs to mind, neither especially good, nor bad. Before that time, during the years that followed the Betrayal, invitations were more a source of worry than pleasure – what should she wear? Would she know any of the other guests and would they want to talk to her?

At twenty two, she'd begun to wonder if she was doomed to remain a virgin all her life – a dry old spinster. Then the miracle at the office party: Max, the new Manager, promoted from the Solihull branch, choosing her for the clichéd kiss under the mistletoe! Eight months of bliss, followed by an equal period of desolation.

Bliss? Only if the frequent interludes of suffering a knotted stomach, plummeting heart and hours of waiting by the phone could be included in a definition of that word

The end had come almost as a relief: using the key to his flat that Max had given her at the start of their relationship ('I can never be sure what time I'll be able to get home, and I wouldn't want you waiting on the street for me.' 'Darling, of course I'm not ashamed to be seen out and about with you! It's just so much cosier here – and I can ravish you whenever I want without any risk of upsetting the waiters!'); grasping that key, turning it in the lock, her heart thudding against her rib cage, and her stomach melting at the thought of what they would do this time, when, and how often; turning the key till the lock gave its familiar little click, and the door made its soft shushing sound as it grazed the carpet; the lamp on the shelf by the fireplace, left on as usual, casting its welcoming glow so she won't have to fumble for the light-switch in the dark; the usual throbbing starting up between her thighs as she crosses to the bedroom where she will find the outfit he has laid out on the bed for her…

But this evening he's left his bedside radio on – a play of some sort – a woman's guttural laugh, 'You naughty boy, you'll have to make it up to me for that.' A heartbeat pause before the man responds, 'My pleasure, Ma'm, whatever you desire.' It's Max's voice.

There'd been two or three other men in the years between Max and meeting up with Graham again, but these encounters had been brief and had only served to reinforce her perception of herself as plain, dull and unworthy of love. She'd never again dropped her guard enough to give the slightest hint of that side of her nature that Max had coaxed out into the open. It had been a joyful revelation to her, the person she became when she was alone with him – every pore of her skin opened to his touch. Her skin *was* her. But nothing could be worth the shame and bitterness she'd felt at the end.

Her first outing with Graham? That had been a party, of sorts. His firm's annual Christmas Dance, for which he had needed a partner. He'd been living in London all those years and had moved back to Birmingham after inheriting his father's house in Penns Lane. He'd found himself sitting opposite Edward on the homeward train from New Street, a few weeks before Christmas. 'You must come to dinner, my boy. You remember Ann, of course. My step-daughter. Stayed with me all these years, bless her.'

Graham had been the ideal antidote to Max: courteous and kind, and above all, he was a link with Norfolk, telling her of his bird-watching holiday that summer, and all the other summers, while she chatted happily about her early life there with Grannibelle, and then, after The Move, having to make do with the annual summer fortnight and a week or so at Easter. He was still recovering from the recent break-up of his own marriage to a seductive Turkish girl he'd met at a conference in Brussels – a marriage of convenience, as it turned out, to his dismayed realisation on returning from work to find her bulging wardrobe empty, and a curt little note on the pillow.

Poor Graham, Ann finds herself murmuring, as she steps from the shower and reaches for the towel.

Vivienne has suggested that she stops off on her way to the beach at the café-cum-bookshop where she'd sent an email to Graham on her first day. Their progress down the main street is slowed by constant pauses as Vivienne exchanges a laugh or a few words with friends and acquaintances.

'Don't forget about the picnic, Julian,' she calls across to where he is seated at a rickety table by a food stall on the corner of a side street, under a mould-speckled canopy. 'You and Pete have your orders to join us tomorrow for lunch on our boat.'

'How could I possibly forget, my dear?' he drawls, 'The invitation is engraved on my heart.'

Vivienne laughs and raises an eyebrow as she glances down at a mangy looking mongrel asleep on the litter-strewn concrete under a nearby chair.

'The best Dim Sum on the island,' he says, then turns to his companion, a wizened old Chinese man with a long white wispy beard sprouting from the end of his chin. 'Is that not so, Charlie?'

The man looks up from his newspaper, which he folds with slow deliberation and places on the table before saying, in a voice that rivals Julian's in its rounded vowels and clipped consonants, 'Why else would I be sharing my valuable time with an old devil like you, Julian?'

As Vivienne and Ann laugh and continue down the street, Dawn calls out from the doorway of Poppy's shop, 'See you both later, yeh?'

'Oh, yes, of course! Happy birthday, Dawn. What time was it you said? And where is it we're meeting?'

'Kick off at nine. This bar next door, right here. Then off to my place after, for a bite to eat 'n stuff for anyone who doesn't have to be in bed by midnight.'

'You'll have to count me out for that part, I'm afraid. Poppy too, I'd imagine. We've got our picnic to organise. You'll be welcome to join us on the boat if you're not manning the shop.'

'I am, worse luck. You know Poppy – bit of a slave-driver,' laughs Dawn. 'Still, can't complain. I'm having a great time here and I'm even managing to save a bit of money.'

'Nice girl, that,' says Vivienne, after they've waved goodbye. 'Got her head screwed on the right way. Poppy's lucky to have found her.'

It's not just Dawn she likes, thinks Ann as the narrow road becomes an even narrower concrete path that takes them past the last few shops of the village, and winds its way between railings of the standard dark-green, with a marshy patch of lush vegetation on one side and a few tall trees and low houses on the other. There've been several youngsters, both European and Chinese who have waved at her or called out from pavement tables or shop doorways, 'How you doing, Aunty Viv?' 'Hi, Vivienne. You OK?'

'I tend not to think about age at all, most of the time,' says Vivienne, when Ann comments on this, 'and it's easier out here where there's more respect for older generations. It's an attitude of mind, as far as I'm concerned. I've known a lot of these youngsters since they were babes in arms. A few of the parents have seemed old and staid for years – and then, look at Poppy! She acts more like a delinquent teenager half the time!'

'You're beginning to make me feel like Saffy from Absolutely Fabulous,' says Ann and is disconcerted to realise that her laugh has sounded bitter and humourless, almost proving the point.

Vivienne's laugh erupts so loudly that a flock of small birds in a nearby tree takes to the air with shrill cries of alarm. 'Oh,' she splutters at last, 'Patsy and Edina! Just wait till I tell Poppy!'

For the rest of the walk, Ann remains silent apart from the occasional monosyllabic response to Vivienne's comments about the films and TV programmes that she and Poppy have watched together, though not always with equal enjoyment.

What does she really know about this woman at her side – her mother, who is able to establish an easy rapport with twenty and thirty year olds, yet has had no time for her own grandchildren, or her own daughter. She's wishing she'd never voiced that similarity to the somewhat self-righteous TV character, for whom she's always had a soft spot. No doubt Vivienne and Poppy will start adopting those names for themselves, and she'll be stuck with Saffy.

It's not until they step from a line of dark, feathery conifers onto the wide sandy beach, that Ann realises she's forgotten to send the email to Graham she'd been writing in her head since she got out of bed . It must have been the conversations with Dawn about the party, and all those others who spoke to Vivienne as they walked through the village, that pushed all thought of Graham from her mind.

When she tells her, Vivienne just laughs, 'Don't look so worried! You can do it on the way back. He'll be asleep for hours yet. Now just relax and look straight ahead and to your left but don't turn to the right until I tell you.'

As she focuses on the sight in front of her, Ann catches her breath. The sky is a hazy blue, paling almost to white where it meets the horizon, while a deeper, cornflower-blue soars high above the range of hills to the left of the bay, and is reflected in the glassy water. The still air is heavy with heat, while occasional tingles of cooler currents waft towards her from the unbroken surface of the sea. Anchored about fifty yards from the shore is a broad-bottomed wooden craft that looks as though it could have drifted here from a hundred years ago. It is painted dull green along the water line, and the tarpaulin covering the high flat roof is a similar green. Ann is surprised at her sudden urge to sketch this scene, to have a pencil in her fingers that can move across a pad of thick white paper and replicate the angle of the long narrow prow and the sharper angle of the stern.

'Beautiful, isn't it?' says Vivienne proudly. 'It reminds me of the Greek Islands – the colour of the sea and sky, the curves of these hills, the rough scrub and rock near the summit, the green of bushes on the lower slopes. No sign of human habitation. Where in the world would you find a more beautiful beach?''

Before Ann can do more than give a sigh of satisfaction, Vivienne laughs as she says, 'Now turn to your right!'

The contrast is overwhelming. Instead of a tumble of smooth grey rocks edging the blue water, rising to the green slopes of another range of hills, the vegetation has been replaced by a colony of huge metal constructions: squares and cylinders, with rungs of ladders up their sides, metal walkways between them, squat, smoking chimneys, monstrous cranes.

Ann had forgotten about the view from Vivienne's flat, the tops of tall slim chimneys appearing above the low green hill. These had seemed almost serene in their simple grey lines, like sculpture, giving no indication of the extent of the activity below them, on the other side of the hill. *The power station,* Vivienne had said, but those words had conjured no image of anything industrial that she might have seen around Birmingham. It would have been as ludicrous, as sacrilegious, even, as imagining a group of concrete cooling towers on Blakeney Point.

'So how would you describe this beach, now?' asks Vivienne, almost smugly. 'Is it still beautiful?

Chapter 25

Should she raise the subject of Stuart, Ann wonders. Vivienne is lying stretched out on her stomach on the raffia matting beside her, a large straw sunhat covering her face. Neither has spoken much since they towelled themselves dry, and applied sun cream. The last person Ann can remember helping with this task is the teenaged Louise, her back and thighs firm and smooth. Placing tentative finger tips onto her mother's shoulder blades, feeling the bone so close beneath its loose covering, seemed to Ann almost an intrusion.

'Come on, girl, you can rub it in a bit more vigorously than that,' said Vivienne with a low chuckle. 'It might be a bit thin and dry, but it is skin, not egg shell!'

Several minutes have passed in silence, broken only by the occasional, 'Mmm, this is nice,' from Ann, followed by a sigh of content, and Vivienne murmuring, 'Are you hungry yet?' or 'There's water in the picnic bag if you're thirsty.'

Ann rehearses various opening gambits in her mind: 'Colin told me you'd said... ' 'So, what about Stuart, then?' 'Erm, I don't think I mentioned that George and I saw...'

Impossible! It hadn't felt right to be rubbing sun cream into her mother's spine just now - any questions about her current state of mind would be more like rubbing salt in. If Vivienne wants to tell her anything, she will.

At this very moment, there's a low moan from beneath the sunhat. Ann holds her breath. Is Vivienne dreaming? Another moan, then muttered words, at first unintelligible, then a clear, 'Bastard. You bastard.'

Ann sits bolt upright, then swivels round onto her knees, looking down at her mother's sleeping form. No, not sleeping now. Those small intakes of breath are stifled sobs.

She is reaching out her hand towards her when Vivienne mutters from under the hat, 'Take no notice. Bad dream, that's all. I'm fine.'

'Mummy?' she whispers. The word slips out before she can hold it back. 'You always made me wake up properly after a bad dream. So that I wouldn't slip right back into it... remember?'

At this, Vivienne rolls over on to her back and sits up with a shaky laugh. 'Time for lunch, I think,' she says, unzipping the plastic cool-bag. As she hands Ann a square slice of pizza, purchased from the bakery on their way to the village, she says, 'You mustn't worry about me you know. Most of the time I'm absolutely fine. Really, I am. To be honest, it was almost a relief. We had a lot of good times together – wonderful times - but once he'd hit sixty, things went rapidly downhill. He became old, almost overnight. That was four years ago. I was in my seventies, but I felt more like fifty – forty, even - full of energy, wanting to expand my business, travel more, learn new things, while Stuart seemed to be shutting down, losing interest in everything and everyone, not just me. He's always been subject to occasional low patches - slight depression from time to time - but it was never that serious – a tablet or two from the doctor used to put him back on track.'

Vivienne is looking out to sea as she talks in a low voice, almost as if she's unaware of her audience. Ann examines the pattern made by strips of green and red pepper interspersed with black olives and anchovies. She feels that if she catches her mother's eye, the words will come to an abrupt halt.

'This might sound strange, but actually, we get on better now than we have for ages - now he's come out into the open about Lindy.'

'Lindy!' exclaims Ann before she can stop herself. So Colin was right, there was another woman. And George was right, too: it's not Lucia. *We get on better now.'* Does this mean they're still in touch?

'Frankly, she's welcome to him,' continues Vivienne, seemingly unaware of the interruption. 'At least, the way he's been acting recently. He'd become an utter bore to have around the house, day in, day out. I wouldn't have had the heart to throw him out. I could have, if I'd wanted to – it is my house, you know. He has a weakness for the horses – and not just the horses,' she pauses to bite into a slice of the pizza, then continues, talking as she chews, 'There's never any shortage of things to bet on out here.' Ann smiles to herself. *Don't talk with your mouth full* - one of the constant meal-time refrains from both Grannibelle and Vivienne. 'The Chinese will put money on anything that moves. Lost virtually everything his father left him, including the flat we were in when we first came out. I think I told you, that was one of the reasons for moving out to Lamma – cheaper property.'

She pauses again, and Ann watches out of the corner of her eye as Vivienne licks each finger in turn before taking another mouthful, 'What I miss is what we once had together – there was so much! Sense of humour, passion for life, and for art, and - strangely for a committed townie - a love of the sea and the countryside. So, there you are,' she finishes briskly, lifting the final morsel to her mouth. 'Good, this, isn't it? Have some more,' she adds, passing the box to Ann.

'Thanks,' she says, 'it's delicious.' For a moment it seems that this is the end of the conversation about Stuart, but Vivienne hasn't finished with the subject yet.

'I don't blame Lindy, really. She's the daughter of one of his old college friends. His god-daughter, in fact. The friend lived in London and they used to come and visit us quite often when we lived in Brighton – Lindy was only a child then, of course, and in her teens by the time we moved to Hong Kong. There was absolutely no hint of anything untoward at that stage.

'We came here to sort out Stuart's father's affairs after his death. I wasn't expecting to stay here long. I mean, I know you virtually never visited, but at least – being in the same country - there was a chance you might...' Vivienne falls silent, and then helps herself to a second slice.

Without looking at her directly, Ann senses that Vivienne has turned her head towards her. She keeps her own head bent as she plays with an olive, rolling it up in a strip of red pepper. Concentrating hard, she makes another little package with an anchovy.

'Anyway, if truth be told, there was a different reason why Hong Kong seemed like a good idea back then. Stuart has a roving eye. I've always been aware of that – and I've been pretty sure that during all those early years he did nothing more than look. But there was another danger, closer to hand...' she pauses, and this time Ann meets her eye.

Vivienne sighs and lifts her hand to cover her mouth. 'I probably shouldn't be telling you this, but since I know there's no love lost between her and you...'

'Oh!' Ann gasps and stares at her mother, 'You mean... Felicity?'

'I told you she was trouble, didn't I? Shortly after Stuart and I... Well, I thought she was just curious, wanting to see who it was that her wicked step-mother had run off with – but even then, there was more to it. She was positively throwing herself at him, but she was wasting her time at that stage, when he was still deeply in love with me.'

Ann draws in a sharp breath and turns abruptly to look at a group of children splashing at the water's edge near a small outcrop of rock further along the beach.

She feels a childish urge to block her ears, but Vivienne seems not to have noticed her reaction, 'Not a single word from her for years after that, then all of a sudden, there she is again, a beautiful thirty-five year old, on the rebound from a broken relationship. She didn't say that, of course. It was, "Down on business for the day. Just thought I'd pop in and see how you both are." But Stuart began to have late meetings and occasional trips up to London...'

London. Felicity. Stuart. Perfectly plausible. Likely, even, knowing Felicity. Never content until every man in the room was looking at her. She'd never liked Ann, the plain little step-sister – but how she must have hated Vivienne!

At thirty five, Felicity would have been in her prime, while Vivienne, twenty years older...and Stuart, closer in age to the younger woman...

It was his dark eyebrows, sloping upwards above the bridge of the straight nose and almost meeting in the middle. The way he'd raise them, one a little higher than the other as he fixed those deep blue eyes on you. Amused. Knowing.

What did he know about her? Nothing. Nothing at all. She'd barely met him. Detested him, of course.

It was revolting. Disgusting. Doing that with Vivienne, a woman almost old enough to be his mother. Had they really expected her to just…?

'So, once we were out here,' Vivienne continues, still gazing at the horizon, 'Well, it suited Stuart, and I must confess, I was ready for a new challenge myself, so…'

'So you decided to stay put. Enjoy the good life.'

Ignoring the hint of sarcasm in Ann's tone, Vivienne goes on, 'It wasn't what you'd call a decision, as such – not a decision to stay. It was more a case of never deciding when to leave. There was always something – Colin coming to visit – Stuart being offered a temporary lecturing post…'

'Lecturing?'

'History of Art. You know he paints. He taught at the art college in Brighton for years. Paints rather well, actually. Watercolours. Very delicate.'

'I didn't know. I wasn't exactly interested in him,' Ann lets her voice trail away as she flicks grains of sand from the beach mat with her finger and thumb.

'I suppose not,' sighs Vivienne. 'Why would you be? After all, he wouldn't exactly have been a father-figure for you.'

'Edward was the only father I needed,' Ann says sharply, and then adds in a gentler tone, 'At least I can thank you for him.' *If nothing else.* The implication hangs in the air, unsaid.

'He was a good man, Edward,' murmurs Vivienne. 'Too good for me, in many ways.'

Ann draws her knees closer to her chest, hugging her arms tightly round them. She watches thin puffs of smoke curl up from the stubby chimneys on the huge metal constructions to her right, then slowly turns her head till they disappear from her peripheral vision and she is gazing at the shimmering sea, edged by the green and brown hills, with a further, fainter range beyond, which seems to merge into the pale blue of the sky.

Feeling calmer, she says, 'So, this Lindy – when did she come here? You said you don't blame her...I suppose it was his fault, then?'

'Why must blame always be one-sided - weighed like a lump of lead against a handful of feathers? Her fault. His fault. Your fault. Mine.'

Like a skipping song, thinks Ann. 'Hang your washing on the line,' she chants in a sing-song voice.

For a moment, Vivienne looks startled, and then she laughs, 'Oh! I see! *What's the time? Half past nine...* Shouldn't that be 'knickers', though?'

'I didn't want to shock you, mother dear.'

'The boot's on the other foot, isn't it?' Vivienne says dryly. 'When it comes to the blame game, we both know...'

'I thought we were talking about this Lindy person,' puts in Ann hurriedly.

'Lindy. Yes. Well, to cut a long story short, she was going through a messy divorce. Her son was here on a gap year, teaching in the New Territories and she came out to visit. It seemed the most natural thing in the world for her to stay with us for a bit after she'd spent a couple of weeks with him. I was only too glad to have her in the house - it perked Stuart up no end. Little did I know quite how perky he was becoming! They'd always adored each other, and for Lindy, it seemed the perfect relationship – she could confide in him, weep on his shoulder, drag him out for long walks – all in absolute safety – until the inevitable happened...'

'Inevitable? It didn't actually have to happen, did it? Not if he'd...'

'Life's not that simple, Ann. Or rather, it is. Me Tarzan, You Jane. Sex. It's one of the driving forces in life...'

'Yes, yes. I know that. But we're humans, not animals – we're supposed to be able to exercise control, aren't we? No one has to give in to animal impulses.'

'I agree that things might be a good deal simpler if everyone kept to the rules that their particular society lays down, but...'

209

Vivienne gives a deep sigh.

Ann sneaks a quick look at her mother's profile. The bright sunlight is etching more deeply the shadow that runs from the base of the nose to the edge of the closed mouth, and other lines she hadn't noticed before, scored into the sagging skin above and just below the jaw line.

'Anyway,' says Vivienne with another sigh, 'All I do know is that the older I get, the less I feel inclined to judge. Let's just say that any intimate relationship between a man and a woman is more likely to develop a sexual dimension than not. The real question is, does it matter?'

'Well, of course!'

'Of course it matters, or, of course that's the real question?'

'I'm getting out of my depth,' says Ann after a long silence. 'This time last week, back at home, I suppose I'd have been absolutely clear about this sort of thing...'

'And now?'

'Now?' Ann slowly shakes her head. 'It seems as if I don't know anything.'

Chapter 26

'Bed? Go home to bed?' bellows Poppy from her perch at the bar, resplendent in a gold sequinned tunic over black satin trousers. 'My dear Dawn, I'm long past the stage at which sleep could enhance my beauty. Or indeed, when a lack of it could cause any noticeable deterioration. That's one of the great joys of being an octogenarian, as you youngsters may discover one day. Of course I'm coming back with you, Dawn! I'm certainly not going to miss out on the rest of your party.' She grips the edge of the bar as she wriggles down from the high stool. 'My beautiful sister, on the other hand, is still in her sprightly seventies so she owes it to her numerous admirers to be asleep before midnight wherever possible.'

'Poppy, you're incorrigible,' laughs Vivienne, as Julian helps her into her tailored jacket of dark purple silk. 'Ever since I've known you, you've used the age card to justify doing anything that happens to suit you at the time, or avoiding anything that doesn't. Just make sure you don't try it on with me, tomorrow lunch-time! You are joint-hostess after all, and I'm relying on you to be gracious to Lindy, if Stuart decides to bring her along. That might be a bridge too far for me!'

Ann's eyes widen. *Vivienne has invited Stuart to join them on their boat!* She bends her head and fiddles with the handbag on her lap, hiding her face until she can regain her composure.

As she rises to her feet, George is at her side, ready to slide back her chair, and he leans towards her murmuring, 'Your mother really is something else! She never ceases to surprise me.'

'Me too,' says Ann with a rueful smile.

'My own dear mother is the same, though – totally unpredictable. I was supposed to be escorting her back to her house myself, but if you're going on to Dawn's as well, I'll come with you.'

The fifteen minute walk is conducted in almost pitch darkness,

211

once they've left the lamps of the village behind; the canopy of trees overhanging the concrete path is obscuring the faint light from the stars and the waning moon. The warm air is electric with the rasping of cicadas and Ann takes deep breaths, relishing the alternating wafts of oleander, jasmine and pine. She'd like to pause for a while on her own, away from the chattering, laughing throng of Dawn's friends a few yards ahead. Perhaps she'll get the chance of a quiet walk on another night – with her mother, perhaps. Or George.

Another night! This one will be the fifth of her seven nights in Hong Kong. How quickly the time is passing. It's her own fault; she had wondered how she'd survive a week of Vivienne's company, after all those years. Graham's suggestion of a fortnight being the minimum stay for a journey of that length had made her stomach lurch in a sudden panic. *Ten days away will be plenty*, she'd countered, after working out how much of that time would be taken up by the journey.

'I should have selected more sensible footwear,' sighs Poppy, coming to an abrupt halt under a solitary street lamp on the edge of a clump of trees. *Like Narnia, through the back of the wardrobe*, thinks Ann, then notices the wooden bench. 'You two young people can go on ahead. I'll just rest here for a few minutes.'

'Don't be silly, Ma,' says George, sitting down beside her and patting the space on his other side for Ann. 'Apart from anything else, you're the only one who knows where Dawn's place is.'

'*Silly*, he calls me! See what I have to put up with, Ann?' laughs Poppy. 'No respect for his aging mama. Anyway, you do know where it is, Georgie – I've given Dawn use of the cabin while Jazzie and Dillon are away.' She leans past her son and adds, 'A nice young couple. Jazzie helps out in the shop for a few months in the summer. They're saving on rent as they're hoping to buy their own flat. Somewhat primitive, but it does at least have electricity and running water now.'

George gives an exaggerated shudder, 'Can you imagine? She could have bought a proper house right from the start, but she chose to camp out in utter squalor!'

'Don't exaggerate! I'd already got a house here. The cabin was an investment. I bought it for virtually nothing – the price of a night or so at the Mandarin. I've never actually stayed here myself.'

'OK. OK!' laughs George. 'I have to admit, it was a shrewd buy, as usual. Anyway, about your feet - would you like me to ring Ignatius and tell him to get hold of a V.V?' He turns to Ann, adding, 'I don't expect you'll have noticed, but all the trucks on Lamma seem to have the same letters on their number plates: V V.'

'Oh! I didn't realise they carry passengers.'

'They don't, as a general rule,' puts in Poppy. 'But it has been known for me to - '

'Has been known!! Come off it, Ma. You've got your own tame drivers who take you up the hill every time you have a night out.'

'Only when I'm wearing the wrong shoes! Talking of which, I think I'm ready to hobble along to Dawn's now. I don't mind making a discrete departure in a V.V., but I'm not going to let myself down by arriving in one.'

From this point on, there is a lamp every fifty yards or so lining the path and revealing swampy vegetation on one side and trees on the other, with no signs of habitation. Now the hum of cicadas is masked by the steady thump, thump of bass notes, and shrill wild tones above, faint at first, then louder and louder until the lights of a low building with a wide veranda come into view.

'Here we are,' says Poppy with a flourish, indicating a squat construction that is more a shack than a house.

'Poppy!' shrieks Dawn, leaning towards them over the rickety wooden railing. 'You've made it! And you Annie. And George, too. That's cool!' A moment later she's helping Poppy up the short flight of stone steps, past an open-sided lean-to shelter, its roof of thick sheets of yellowing plastic supported by a framework of rough wooden poles. As Ann follows, she realises that the narrow space is serving as a makeshift kitchen, with an old electric cooker against the wall of the house, next to what looks like a top-loading washing machine, and a large stone sink with a single tap.

The next half hour or so passes in a haze. Most of the action - eating, drinking, smoking, dancing and above all, talking - appears to be taking place outside on the veranda and on the path below. Poppy and George have been swallowed up by the throng, and as Ann hovers in the shadow, leaning against the pitted plaster on the corner of the building, she glances around for faces she might recognise from earlier in the evening. There's the German woman who runs the deli, and has lived on Lamma with her American husband for nearly twenty years. She's talking to the young English couple who stopped off at Hong Kong on their way back from Australia and decided to extend their stay for a few weeks. And there's that pleasant Dutch man who sells second-hand books from a roadside stall, talking to Julian's Chinese friend, Charlie. Among the disparate group of thirty or more guests, the one common factor is the lack of conformity: the ages range from late teens to eighty and there seem to be almost as many nationalities as there are people present, each in a different style of dress or undress.

But there is a common factor! The realisation strikes her like a revelation: everyone here is at ease with themselves. Tall or short, dumpy or scrawny, old or young – smart, scruffy, long hair, no hair - white, brown, black, pink, tanned and freckled…Ann's mouth stretches itself into a wide smile. She feels almost dizzy as the words shout in her head: I'm the same as everyone else…*because* I'm different. Because I'm *me*!

'Hey, Annie! You look like you're on something pretty strong there,' says Dawn with a grin. 'You gonna let me in on the secret?'

'Oh! You made me jump!' Ann blinks and shakes her head, but she's still smiling, 'Secret?' she asks.

'You're high as a kite and you've not been drinking much, so…'

'Two white wine spritzers, that's all.'

'I thought you must have had a splif or two, at least. A couple of the guys here have brought along some real good shit…' her words fade to a halt as she searches Ann's face, then she steps forward and gives her a big hug, 'Oh, Annie! I do love you! You're just so down-to-earth…so *nice!* Come on, let me show you the inside of my palace!'

'I'm glad you think I'm nice,' Ann laughs, as she lets herself be led towards the open doorway, 'I like you, too!'

Dawn halts on the threshold, spreads her arms wide, and declaims in a mock-posh voice, 'Now, if Madam would like to step inside and view the interior… The open-plan design of the ground floor is ideal for the minimalist taste, where rugs and cushions can be viewed to best advantage. Note how the futon-type bed (it's just a mattress, really) will ensure plenty of head-room when sleeping on the mezzanine floor, which is accessed by a compact wooden stairway (ladder, to you). Actually,' she finishes in her normal voice, 'I adore this place. It's really cool.'

Ann looks around the room. In spite of an almost total lack of furniture, it seems homely and welcoming. The walls are covered with brightly printed lengths of fabric – sarongs, perhaps – while a collection of paper lanterns shaped like fish or dragons hangs from the ceiling. 'It's lovely,' she says, 'But living out here alone! So isolated! Don't you find it a bit… well, scary?'

'Nah! Not at all. Did think I might, at first, but people are so friendly here on Lamma. I 'spect you've found that too. I've only been here a few weeks and as you can see, I've made loads of friends already. Bit of a change from some parts of good old England, eh?'

'You could say that,' she says with a laugh.

'It must be extra strange for you, what with finding out that stuff about your grandmother and then Poppy and George. He's a sweetie, isn't he? Quite fit, as a matter of fact. Blokes around my age can be so immature! You two seem to have hit it off pretty well, don't you?'

Ann feels her face go hot, and turns her head, pretending an interest in watching the dancing as she says, in a casual tone, 'Yes, we do get on well, but I suppose it's not that surprising, when you think how closely we're related.'

'Dunno about that. You're first cousins, aren't you? I've only got two cousins and I'm not that close to either of them. Oh, look! There he is. *She* certainly seems pretty keen on him.'

About ten feet away, beyond a couple draped around each other in a slow shuffling dance, Ann sees George leaning against the railings, deep in conversation with a slim, attractive woman in her thirties. From her eyes and the shape of her face, she looks Chinese, but there's something about her wide mouth and perfect teeth that suggest an American upbringing, or dentist, at least. No doubt she's intelligent and cultured, as well as good-looking, Ann thinks with a pang.

'Look! Now there's Poppy waving at you,' says Dawn. 'Actually looks like she's on her own for a moment! S'pose I better go 'n mingle for a bit. Catch up later, OK?'

Poppy is sitting on a green plastic chair, the opposite end of the veranda from where George is standing. The arm that is not waving frantically in her direction is resting on a wide slab of stained white marble that has been balanced on the wrought-iron base of an old Singer sewing machine. In front of her, there's a large plate piled with food.

As Ann treads her way past a chattering group of men and women sitting cross-legged on colourful rugs and lounging on cushions, her mind is doing somersaults: a few minutes ago she'd reached a stage of blissful certainty about her place in the cosmos, while just this afternoon, in conversation with Vivienne, she has been forced to question some of her most fundamental principles, and now…Now, she decides, she feels like a piece of driftwood in the middle of the ocean.

Poppy has shifted round to face her, 'Ann, sweetheart! Grab yourself some food, then come and sit here next to me,' she booms above the thudding music, wrapping one arm around Ann's waist, and reaching up with the other hand to pull her down until her chin is resting awkwardly on the gold covered shoulder, and the crown of her head is being stroked like a cat. 'I've been waiting for a chance for a proper tete a tete with you all evening, my little munchkin,' she coos, releasing Ann at last.

She gestures to a wooden table behind her, on which is a

wobbly stack of assorted plates, several large bowls of various salads, an earthenware dish of brown rice and a huge metal pot whose spicy contents are hidden under billows of steam.

'Lamb or goat or something,' says Poppy. 'It's delicious.'

Ann is grateful for the break in conversation while they eat. She chews slowly. Ruminating. It might be nice to be a cow. *I think I could turn and live with animals...* George, on the plane. How quickly they'd established common ground. A real rapport. Soul mates.

She tries to anchor herself by conjuring a picture of Graham, happily chatting with the group on the floor nearby, sprawling on the large, brightly covered cushions, but her eyes drift back towards the doorway, and the Graham-image refuses to lower itself into a sprawl. It stands by the telephone table in the hall with the usual stiff, morning posture, just before he turns to step into the porch and walk briskly up the hill towards the station. He has already entered the world of work. His features are expressionless – no, that's not accurate, the blank eyes, straight mouth, rigid chin, these are all part of a mask which lives on a shelf named, 'Give-Nothing-Away'. Ann herself, shuffling towards him in a pair of Louise's discarded Snoopy slippers to receive the ritual goodbye kiss - she's an integral part of the scene: husband leaves house to catch train to work.

Ann blinks and shakes her head. Her view of the doorway is blocked by two young women, arms around each other's shoulders, spare hands raising beer bottles to their lips. What will Graham do with himself, now that he's been banished from the world of work? The sudden tightness in her throat takes her by surprise. Poor Graham. How will he know who he is?

'So, Ann dear, tell me all about this husband of yours.' Ann gives a start as Poppy's plump, warm hand descends onto her wrist, almost clamping it to the table-top.

'Your mother tells me he's a bit of stick-in-the-mud,' she chortles, 'but that's Vivienne for you. I'm sure he's perfectly charming, really.'

'What would Vivienne know? She's barely set eyes on him,'

Ann retorts.

'Ah ha! Leaping to his defence. So he's a good man. I thought as much. She's not exactly the most astute of judges when it comes to men, is she?'

Ann shifts in her chair and stiffens her fingers. Poppy withdraws her hand and as she does so, Ann picks up her fork and prongs a piece of meat, 'You're right about this, it is delicious,' she says, more calmly than she feels.

Poppy gives a loud laugh, 'Well said!' she exclaims, 'That puts me in my place firmly and kindly. Husband and mother out of bounds to interfering old aunt.'

In spite of herself, Ann joins in the laughter, 'No! Not really. Vivienne did warn me that I might find you a little…em, frank. Not to be taken aback by anything you might say because you mean well - heart of gold and all that.'

'I'm fully aware that I'm not everybody's cup of tea,' she says dryly. 'That doesn't bother me in the least. But seriously, my dear, I don't want to go upsetting you. I have been so looking forward to meeting you. As far as I know, you're the only niece I've got.'

'Actually, Poppy, I was just saying to Dawn, since arriving on Lamma I'm not too sure what I think about anything any more. There's been such a lot to take in all of a sudden and…'

'I know, dear. I do know.' Poppy reaches out her hand again and pats Ann lightly on the shoulder.

'Vivienne, for instance. I just can't understand what's going on. I came out because Colin told me she was completely distraught about Stuart leaving her, and now I find that they're still friends, and he might even bring his…his-'

'Floozie? Is that the word you're looking for?'

'You tell me. From what Vivienne says, it doesn't sound as though that's the best word to use. What did you think of her, Poppy?'

'Scheming Minx sounds about right, though Vivienne won't have it. Won't hear a word against him, either. I'd have given them short shrift, myself, the pair of them.'

'It does seem very strange to me. I mean, after what he's done to her – and after she'd made that woman welcome in her own home...'

'There's a lot more to Vivienne than meets the eye, you know. I'm most reluctant to voice this suspicion, but I'm beginning to think she's been deceiving me all these years. She's developed that tough outer layer of devil-may-care cynic to keep her real self hidden. I believe that under it all, there's a quiet, kind, heroic saint.'

Ann's fork clatters down onto the floor, 'Saint!! Vivienne, a saint! I can't believe I'm hearing this.' Her voice emerges as a high-pitched shriek, and nearby heads swing round with curious stares.

'Sorry, Poppy,' she says at once in a lower voice. 'It's just...just too much! After what she did to me... to us. She ruined my life, you know. Going off like that without a backward glance... '

'That's all right, my dear. I understand how you must feel,' Poppy's voice is very gentle as she adds, 'But are you absolutely sure that she deserves all the blame?'

Chapter 27

'We'll walk, thank you, Ma. Unless you'd prefer to hitch a ride, Ann?' says George. 'There's certainly not room in the V.V. for all three of us.'

'The walk will do me good, after all that food,' says Ann, suppressing a giggle at the sight of Poppy, sitting bolt upright on one of Dawn's cushions on the floor of the truck, gripping the metal sides with both hands, and trying unsuccessfully to stretch her legs out straight in front of her, now that the driver has raised the rear section and bolted it back into place.

As the ungainly vehicle jolts away on its enormous wheels towards the darkness beyond the street lamp, Poppy's head and shoulders sway and bump from side to side and up and down, on a level with the back of the driver's chair, his own dark head and padded blue shoulders towering above her.

'Safe, journey, Ma!' calls George, then, spluttering with laughter, 'This little piggy went to market, this little piggy...'

'George! You shouldn't be so...' gasps Ann, before giving in to her own explosion of laughter.

It's a while before either of them attempt to speak; they can sense each other's ripples of mirth that threaten to break to the surface. At last, Ann says, with only a slight giggle, 'I do like Poppy! She's great fun, isn't she?'

'I'm so glad you like her. Some people find her a bit overpowering and I know she's really taken to you.'

'It's weird, isn't it – us not meeting till now? I mean, I can sort of understand why Grannibelle never got round to telling us all about Rupert and everything, but Vivienne has known since 1995! My own mother, not even writing to me about it. I'm going to find it very hard to forgive her for that, on top of everything else she's done to muck up my life.'

'She probably thought she should tell you face to face.'

'Too right, she should! But she didn't have to wait thirteen years to do it.'

'But if you never went out to Hong Kong, and she didn't go to England...'

'She did, though. She came to Edward's funeral three years later. Bare-faced cheek, if you ask me, the way she'd treated him! And even coming back to his house for the gathering afterwards!'

'I admit, it does seem a bit strange that she didn't tell you then, at least. Haven't you asked her why?'

Ann feels her cheeks grow burning hot and is grateful for the deepening darkness as she mutters, 'Sort of – but she didn't really have much of an answer.'

None of the scattered houses that they've passed in the last few minutes has shown any signs of life, and the street lamps on this stretch of the path appear not to be working. The surrounding trees are clumped more thickly together now, and Ann slows her pace almost to a halt as her eyeballs strain to see more than a yard or so ahead.

George stops and links her arm through his in such a way that her hand is nestling in his palm, 'Don't worry, our night vision will kick in soon. It's not as dark as it seems.'

As they stand side by side, it feels to Ann that the darkness has a physical texture in which they are cocooned. 'Like twins,' she murmurs, unaware, until she hears herself, that she has voiced the thought.

'This darkness ...' he murmurs back. His hand tightens on hers and he says with a laugh, 'Come here, Twin,' as his other hand draws her round until her cheek is resting on his shoulder and his fingers are lifting her hair and gently kneading the thin skin of her scalp just above her ear, over and over, like a massage.

Like a lover?

She feels herself go rigid, and pulls away with a tight laugh, 'You'd've had me falling asleep on you, if you'd carried on much longer!' Peering around, she adds, 'You were right, I can see better now. Amazing how the eyes adjust, isn't it?'

They step apart, no longer touching. 'Mmm. Eyes fascinate me,' he says. 'How they work, I mean. How the brain processes the information they give. And how it can distort what it sees, to

221

suit what it's expecting to see.'

For the next few minutes the conversation continues safely with this and similar topics: optical illusions; reasons for the unreliability of witnesses; cultural influences on ideas of beauty...

'I mean, just look at the gathering this evening,' says George. 'They come from all over, and I bet they'd nearly all make similar judgements about what counts as beauty.'

'You're probably right. The white and European ones, anyway.'

'And not just them. People world-wide are open to the same influences via the media. The Caucasian-European-American ideals. It's sad, in a way, don't you think?'

'Sad?'

'The lengths some women will go to – mainly women, anyway. It's becoming fashionable among some Chinese to have plastic surgery on their eyes and noses, to make them look more Western.'

'That is sad! Terrible, actually. Do you know, I was just thinking earlier how at ease with themselves all those different people seemed – and not many of them would qualify as good-looking in that ideal way. It made me feel so happy – you wouldn't believe! One of the few times in my life I've felt perfectly comfortable in myself – in my physical body.'

They have reached another street lamp; with his hand on her elbow he leads her into the bright centre of the pool of light, then stepping back, he looks her up and down with a quizzical gaze. 'Nope! Nothing wrong with your body – two legs and feet - arms, hands; average height – usual arrangement of features - nothing wrong at all.'

'Very reassuring,' she laughs.

As she walks on up the gently rising slope, he falls into step beside her again, 'Your physical body is part of *you*, Ann,' he says in a level tone. 'You as a whole person. A person I happen to like, rather a lot.'

'Thank you, kind sir. And I quite like you, too.'

After a slight pause, he continues, 'I'm glad I'd got to know you before I realised you were Vivienne's daughter and my cousin - it means my judgement wasn't coloured in any way. From the very start, you struck me as being a genuine original – that's my name for people who seem content to be themselves wherever they are and whoever they're with.'

She smiles, biting her lower lip and shaking her head. 'Nice of you to say so, but that's not me at all! Think about it. Even now, Vivienne can turn heads – Grannibelle was just the same when I was little – and then, having Felicity foisted on me as a step-sister – only a few years older and absolutely stunning…It's not as though I chose to be an outsider. I had it thrust upon me,' she finishes with a defiant grin, raising her hand to tap her forefinger against her outstretched chin.

'But I love that chin!' he laughs. 'I have to, since it's just like mine! Seriously, though, people do tend to change somewhat as they go through life.'

'Yes. Of course. To a certain extent, anyway.'

'I think we sometimes let ourselves be defined by other people – the ones who've always known us. They kind of lock you in to the person they think they know – the one they met in the first place, however long ago that was. Maybe that's one of the difficulties with families – siblings, parents, wives, husbands - they make you carry on defining yourself within the limits they've placed on you.'

'You're right!' says Ann slowly, 'I've not really thought about it like that. It's different with your own children, though, isn't it? It has to be, or they'd never grow up.'

'You've said it!' he laughs. 'Maybe that's the reason for the number of great big babies, male and female, wandering around in adult bodies. Stuart probably comes into that category. I've not met Lindy, but I'd guess she does too. "I want what I want and I want it now!" Vivienne seems to be coming out of all this as the proper grown-up - though I have to say, it does seem a little strange to be inviting them both to join us all tomorrow. I don't need to ask what you think, do I? I saw your face back there in the bar… Quite a picture!'

As the path levels out, he slows down and nods towards the house on their left, 'Here already – Poppy's Cattery! There're still lights on downstairs. Would you like to come in for a drink, or a mug of cocoa or something?'

'Better not,' she says. 'I don't expect Vivienne will be waiting up for me, but you can never tell. Thanks for walking me back. I'll see you tomorrow.'

As she turns to go, he puts his hand on her arm, 'You don't think I'm leaving you to go the rest of your way on your own, do you? Anyway, I want to hear what you've got to say about Stuart before we see him again tomorrow. I'm intrigued to know how it all started – him and Vivienne – They never actually married, did they, though they'd been together longer than a lot of married couples. You said that Edward was her second husband. That marriage can't have lasted all that long.'

'Seven years. You could say it was the seven year itch, I suppose. She wasn't exactly going to confide in me, was she? *Don't tell Edward, but I've been having it off with…* I only caught sight of him once or twice. Never suspected a thing. The first I knew was when Edward told me she'd gone. Just like that!'

'Just like that?'

'Just like that,' she repeats in a monotone. 'Still there, when I went to bed. Gone in the morning.'

'And you were only, what? Fifteen? Sixteen? That must have been hard.'

'You could say that. I did actually meet him a couple of times in Brighton, when I had to take Colin down to visit her. It was horrid. Gruesome! The way he smiled all the time. Let's all be friends, shall we? Friendy-wendy - pally-wally…' she is suddenly aware that her voice has risen to a squeak, and her chest is so tight she can hardly breath as she whimpers, 'I don't want to see him tomorrow. Don't want to see him.'

George's arm is across her shoulder and she lets herself be drawn towards him again. They stand very still. She closes her eyes, and as her breathing slows it becomes deeper. The murmured words reach her from a long way off - Grannibelle's voice, 'You'll be all right, sweetheart. I'm here now. I'll take care of you. It'll be all right, all right …All right now?' says George, relaxing his hold as she straightens and takes a step back.

'Yes. Yes, I'm all right,' she says, with a small shake of her head, and then, more steadily, 'Don't know what got into me just then. Probably a bit tired…Better get moving again. Sorry!'

'No need to apologise, Ann! And no need to worry, either. I'll be taking care of you. This boat trip will be part of our family history trail! We've done the Peak already, and this'll be another of Belle and Rupert's outings. I'm not letting anyone upset my favourite cousin - and that's a promise. Gold-standard guarantee, OK?'

'OK,' she laughs. 'But 'favourite' isn't much of a compliment - you've only got one other cousin, and you haven't even met him yet.'

'Oh! Your brother, Colin. I forgot. Well, you're the favourite till I do meet him, and then we'll have to see.'

When they reach Vivienne's high wooden gate, Ann says, 'I can't see from here if the lights are still on downstairs, but if you'd like to come in for a drink, I'm sure Vivienne -'

'No. Better not, thanks,' says George with a smile. 'If Poppy's still up and about, I'll need to pack her off to bed. She has a tendency to potter round in the cat-room half the night and then sleep all morning. Aunty Viv won't be too thrilled with that.'

'I'll see you tomorrow, then. And thank you for walking me home and everything.'

'And everything?'

'You know. Being so…so kind! Putting up with all my silly -'

'If I can put up with being run over by a trolley, I - '

'Ok. Ok.' She laughs. 'I can see I'm going to have to think up something really outrageous, if I don't want the trolley-thing brought up six times a day.'

'Can't wait!'

'And I can't hang around out here all night,' she says, fumbling with the catch on the gate, 'So, see you tomorrow, Ok?'

'Goodnight, cousin, dear! ' he says as the gate swings open.

'Night, then, George. And thanks again.'

'Thank *you*, Ann.'

She lifts her hand in a quick wave, then steps through into Vivienne's front garden. From the tree above there's a rustling and a sudden short twittering as a bird stirs.

'Sleep well,' calls George, in a stage whisper.

She takes hold of the edge of the gate, preparing to push it shut, 'Sweet dreams,' she calls softly.

Walking the gate back towards its post brings her closer to where he is still standing on the path. She can't just shut it in his face without a word.

'Night, night. Sleep tight,' she chants.

'Don't let the bugs bite,' he calls back. 'If they do, get your shoe...'

'And knock their little heads in two,' they chant together, their voices rising to a shout, as the gate bangs shut between them.

A moment later, Ann swings round towards the house; an upstairs window is flung wide open and a man's voice hisses loudly, 'Who the devil's making that bloody racket out there. Have you no consideration for others? It's three o'clock in the bloody morning.'

She turns back to the gate and slowly pulls it open enough to let her peer out onto the path, where George is doubled over, one hand clasping his stomach, the other clamped across his mouth as he tries to stifle his laughter, 'Did you see who that was?' he splutters in a half-whisper, 'It sounded to me remarkably like Julian – and if I'm not very much mistaken, that's Vivienne's bedroom window!'

Chapter 28

Ann wakes to pellets of rain smashing themselves against the window. But it can't be raining. This is the day for the picnic on the boat. She rolls over onto her side and fumbles for the bedside clock. Five twenty-five. Still the middle of the night. There'd been no hint of rain on the way home, and hadn't there been stars in the sky?

She remembers the almost tangible darkness under the trees. Perhaps it had been cloudy then. That darkness! She pushes her fingers through her hair, above her right ear, along the skin of the scalp where his fingers were... She can feel them now –

Her hand becomes a fist as she thumps it down onto the sheet. She swings her legs over the edge of the bed, and sits for a few moments, her back straight, drawing in deep breaths. She stands, switches on the light and tiptoes across the floor to the adjoining bathroom. Her mouth feels dry and stale. She forgot to clean her teeth before tumbling into bed. Can she do this now, without waking her mother in the room below?

Vivienne's window! George was right. And it had certainly been a man's voice. But which man? What if it's not Julian? That could be embarrassing enough – her mother, with yet another man! But Stuart?

Will she have to face him over the breakfast table? Will she bump into him on the stairs, his tanned legs and feet bare, his short, black silk dressing gown gaping open at the top, half slipping off his broad shoulder. That chest – its bear-like pelt. Will it be greying now, like his hair?

Hell! Where's all this coming from? What's got into her? Surely this can't be another symptom of jet-lag. She's only just got over that, and she'll be flying back into another dose before she knows it. The Tuesday evening plane - the day after tomorrow.

No, she's only had a couple of hours' sleep so far – it doesn't count as Sunday morning, yet.

'Can't be nine, already, Vivienne,' groans Ann, pulling a pillow over her head as she feels a light hand on her shoulder.

'You'd clearly had a very good evening, Ann,' comes Vivienne's sardonic voice. 'Actually, I decided to let you sleep a little longer. It's half past ten now and I've brought you some breakfast. Things are a bit chaotic downstairs. Sunday's Constantia's day off.'

The pillow thumps to the floor by Vivienne's feet as Ann sits bolt upright. 'Half past ten!' she exclaims, 'I didn't realise I'd gone back to sleep. Thought it was just after six. Oh, and thank you for the breakfast. I'll get up now and eat that when I'm dressed.'

'No panic,' says Vivienne, as she places the tray on the dressing table. 'Change of plan. You'll have heard the rain in the night? It's slacked off a bit now, but it's still blowing a gale.'

'So the picnic's off?' Ann feels a sudden lightening of her shoulders, but composes her expression into one of regret. 'What a shame. I was looking forward to seeing your boat.'

'We might still manage to go out later this afternoon – though it'll probably be better to wait till tomorrow, now. But we're not giving up on the picnic altogether – not after all Constantia's hard work in organising the provisions. And Poppy's man, too.'

'But the rain…?'

'It'll take more than a bit of bad weather to deflect Poppy from any plan involving a party of some kind! Everyone's coming here.'

'Everyone?'

'Pete and Julian, obviously. Then there's Poppy and George, you and me – that's six. Three or four more from here in the village, maybe a few more than that, now we're not limited to numbers for the boat. And then of course, the ones who'll be coming over on the ferry - a boat trip of a sort, regardless of the weather – I can't deprive Lucia of her outing – she's bringing a couple of friends of hers with their little girl.'

Ann holds her breath as Vivienne adds, 'Right! Up you get, then, Lazy Bones.'

Vivienne turns as she reaches the door, 'Stuart rang just now to see what's happening. Lindy had been going out with other friends, but that's been called off, so…'

'So you're letting that woman...'

Vivienne sighs, her hand on the door frame. She hesitates for a moment, and then comes back into the room, shutting the door behind her. Ann watches as she walks slowly to the window and pulls up the blinds. Staring through the rain-speckled pane, she says, with another sigh, 'Lindy's not a bad person. A bit scatty – not terribly bright, but actually, I quite like her, even now. And Stuart too…'

'But still, you know…I mean…'

Vivienne sits down on the end of the large bed and twists round to face her daughter, 'I'm not saying it's easy, Ann. It's not. But life's too short…' The edge of her lip curves up into the familiar lop-sided smile and she shakes her head, 'And it gets shorter with every day that passes! You'd be surprised how wonderfully this concentrates the mind. Time really is the best bullshit detector – I'd make a fortune if I could find a way to patent that notion. Make it concrete in some way.'

Ann's mind races. What answer can she make to that? 'I...I'm not sure that I…'

'Agree? Approve?' says Vivienne crisply, straightening her back.

'When have you ever needed my …'

'Your approval, Ann?' she cuts in, 'You'd be surprised.'

Ann bites her lip, and then says in a kinder tone, 'No. I meant, *understand*. I'm finding it hard to take in how you could...'

Vivienne's face softens, 'Of course you are! We get so used to living with complications, anything simple is hard to accept. The simple facts in this case are, in no particular order: no one human being has any god-given rights over another. Would you agree with that, Ann?'

'I, em. Yes. Of course.'

'You don't have to agree with everything I say!' she smiles. 'To be perfectly truthful, I'm working this out as I go along. I can't even be one hundred percent sure that I'll agree with everything I

229

say myself, so I can hardly expect you to!'

'Right, then,' Ann says, lifting her elbows above her head, and then stretching out her arms as she gives a wide yawn. 'How about –"it's possible to hold two or more contradictory viewpoints at the same time"?'

'I like that. It sums things up pretty neatly. In fact,' she says, glancing at her watch, 'since this topic could probably last us all morning, maybe we should leave it at that for the moment.' Then, in one quick gesture, she tugs the duvet down to the end of the bed, adding with a laugh, 'And maybe you should get yourself decent before everyone arrives.'

Ann rises from the bed and stumbles to the bathroom, rubbing her eyes. Before Vivienne turns the door knob, she looks back into the room, 'Just one more thing I need to say – Stuart and I, we go back a long way. I'd rather remain friends than cut off all ties. I am still fond of him. Those kinds of bond are not so easy to break, you know. And if that means accepting Lindy as part of the equation, so be it.'

'I think I can understand that. In a way…'

'Oh, and one other thing before I leave you to your shower – Julian is a dear, good friend. I don't want to shock you, Ann, but I know that you know he spent the night with me. One doesn't necessarily lose one's libido after one's seventieth birthday – or one's eightieth, if Poppy is to be believed.

Bloody hell! thinks Ann, as she stands under the cascade of hot water. My mother!! What would Louise say to that? Ann can't imagine herself discussing a topic like this with her daughter. Though come to think of it, no doubt there'll be something about Sex and the over Seventies in Lou's university course - explicit details of research projects conducted in sheltered housing complexes and old people's homes – part of the module on Aging she'd told her about at the end of her first term.

Louise! That email, yesterday afternoon, waiting in her inbox when she'd dropped in on the internet café on the way back from the beach: *Dad says don't worry about not getting hold of him. He's gone to Norfolk for the weekend. He'll be back on Tuesday evening at the latest, so he'll be able to pick you up from the airport on Wednesday morning, as arranged. He sounded really perky when he called me just now. He'd made a snap decision after he left work on Friday – needed to celebrate his freedom after years of toil and he was going to do his bird-watching in style. Bit of a surprise for me, I can tell you - I nearly dropped my phone into my yoghurt and blueberries – Dad, a snap decision! Wow! What next?*

Oh, and he'd just got back from buying himself a top-class pair of binoculars!

Reading this, Ann felt a wave of relief that he was managing perfectly well without her - but when she read further, something more like resentment rose to the surface : *Anyway, he said that since you weren't there to celebrate with him, he was going to push the boat out for a change and he'd booked himself into the Morston Hall Hotel for three nights. I Googled it as soon he put the phone down and I could hardly believe my eyes. I mean, Dad! All those years of caravans on the cliff top near Cromer! The nearest we ever got to a hotel was that B & B in Cornwall one year. Even out of season, I'd guess his stay at that place won't be far off the cost of your entire trip.*

So much for Graham's worries about their finances! She'd hinted more than once that it might be nice for them to stay in a hotel, now that the children no longer joined them for the summer fortnight on the coast. Or maybe they could break out and do something really daring, like crossing the channel!

'But you love Norfolk, don't you?' he'd say. 'And we've always enjoyed the caravan - being able to do exactly what we want, when we want to. I honestly can't see the point in spending good money when there's no need.' And now, actually staying at The Morston Hall Hotel! The most he'd ever managed was to take her there for an occasional dinner.'

Hope you're having a fab time – Can't wait to hear all about it. Lots of love, Louxxxxxxxx

PS I've emailed Danny to keep him up to speed

PPS You and Dad are giving me some useful case-study

material for the Aging module!!

Well, thank you very much, my darling daughter, Ann mutters with a wry smile, letting her hands glide down her upper arms, slippery with Vivienne's passion-fruit shower gel. The skin on the outer sides is still firm and smooth. The same cannot be said for her breasts, but then, they'd begun to droop years ago, when they shrank back to their pre-childbearing size 34 B after weaning Louise. She casts a critical eye downward, but she still has a discernable waist, and her rounded her stomach shows no trace of stretch marks. Case-material for the Aging module! Graham, perhaps, at nearly sixty-one, but surely Middle-aging would be more appropriate for her.

She'd already selected the clothes she would wear for the boat – casual but smart with a nautical flavour – the new white cotton trousers and a blue and white striped T-shirt with three-quarter length sleeves and a scooped neck.

She gulps down the lukewarm tea and munches snatched mouthfuls of papaya and muesli as she blow-dries her hair, managing to get it to look more or less as the girl in Headways had intended, with the help of the hair serum Louise had forced upon her. 'Now you've actually agreed to having a definite hair style, as opposed to a quick snip with the kitchen scissors, you need to make sure you get the best effect for your money!'

'Not bad,' she murmurs to her reflection. 'In fact, I look almost OK - for my age.' The thought occurs to her that women's looks might balance out a bit as they get older – the deficiencies of the plainer ones might not stand out so much when some of the pretty ones start going to pieces. She is surprised at the sudden pang she feels for those women, the ones she used to envy so desperately. It must be hard for them, with so much to lose, whereas she...

Stepping closer to the mirror, she examines her face. It could be a trick of the light, but her chin doesn't seem quite so prominent as usual. My link with George, she thinks, and as she smiles she sees for the first time how the altered shape of her cheeks affects the angle of her jaw.

'Ann! Are you ready now?' calls Vivienne from below. 'George has come to see if there's anything he can do to help.'

Opening the door, she calls, 'Just coming!' then glances back into the room, sees the breakfast tray and hurries across to pick it up. The bed's a mess, and her clothes from the evening before are strewn across the chair, but no-one's likely to see it. There are more important things to worry about than her own appearance and the state of the bedroom. But she's not going to let anyone upset her. No one. And certainly not Stuart.

Her chest is tight she steps onto the landing, clutching the tray with clammy hands. As she pushes the door shut with her foot, she murmurs over and over like a mantra, 'I will be OK. I will be OK.'

Chapter 29

'You're so kind, Ann,' coos Lindy, 'Do you know, I think I'm beginning to feel better already. I've always found the Feng Shui of this room so much more conducive to relaxation than anywhere else in the house. I felt so at home all the time I was staying here.'

As if to prove the point, she wanders into the bathroom, picks up a damp towel from the floor and drapes it over the metal rail, running her hands along it to smooth out any wrinkles. 'I really don't want to hold you up,' she says, turning back towards the bedroom and leaning against the door frame. 'I mean, now it's stopped raining and everyone's going for a walk...'

'I'll be fine - most of them won't be going very far,' says Ann, managing to keep her voice calm as she straightens the quilt and plumps the pillows with more force than necessary. At home in this room! No wonder, when she was having it off with her hostess's partner. 'Anyway, not quite everyone - Poppy's gone back to her house for a rest.'

Lindy gives a tight little smile, 'Well, of course, Poppy... I gather she was up till all hours last night. And now she's leaving it to Vivienne to look after Lucia and her friends and their cute little girl.'

'It was Vivienne who suggested a stroll through the village in the first place, and she was keen to show them Poppy's shop as well as hers.' Ann was clear about this because she'd been waiting to see how the groups would form themselves and was hoping that Stuart would tag along with Lucia, but he'd said, 'I'd rather stretch my legs a little further than that. I've been hemmed in by brick and concrete all week – not to speak of exhaust fumes and all that bloody din of brakes and horns and blaring music.'

To her disappointment, George had said, 'I'm with you, there, Stuart. What if we all wander down to the village together and then the proper walkers can carry on across to the other side of the island – or anywhere you fancy.'

Until then, she had managed to avoid more than a brief

exchange of pleasantries with Stuart; as part of a small group rambling up hill and down dale, it might be difficult for George to protect her from Stuart's tongue: *you need to take a long hard look at yourself, Ann*... It was at this point that Lindy had decided to have her 'little turn', and Ann had offered to take her up to her own bedroom – 'being at the top, you'll hear less noise from up there.' By the time she wanders down to join Vivienne and the others in her shop, Stuart will be striding along a hillside with George.

Lindy has sauntered back into the bedroom and is standing in front of the mirror, 'What a fright I look!' she exclaims, patting her bright yellow frizz of shoulder-length curls. '*Goldilocks*, Stu calls me. I keep on telling him I want to get it all chopped off, but he won't hear of it. Men! They do love their long hair, don't they?'

'They're quite keen on women's too,' says Ann dryly.

'That's what I meant, women's hair. Men think they sort of own it,' explains Lindy, earnestly.

'Joke,' says Ann,

'Oh, silly me,' giggles Lindy. 'I'm not very good at jokes. And of course, I didn't mean...' she falters, as Ann casually raises her hand to her own bare nape.

'Erm... I've just straightened the bed for you. I'll leave you to it, now, shall I?' says Ann, 'If you're quite sure you'll be all right on your own?' she adds. 'I mean, if you gave him a ring, I expect Stuart would be...'

'Oh he would, yes! More than happy. He's so tuned in to all my little moods and fancies. Even more so, now that...' Lindy purses her lips, tilting her head to one side; her closed eyelids flutter as if holding back a secret that is struggling to escape. With one hand spread across her stomach, she glides to the door, peers out, and then pulls it to, until she hears it click shut.

Ann is experiencing a sinking sensation in her own stomach as Lindy moves towards her, 'Just checking that we really are on our own,' she breathes, taking Ann's hand in both of hers before collapsing onto the bed, leaving her no choice but to sit herself down at her side. 'We haven't told anyone yet. I mean, it is a very delicate situation, after all. We wouldn't want Vivienne to hear it through the grapevine – we'd hate her to be upset, she's been so terrifically civilised and understanding - but at the same time, I mean, how do you broach a subject like this with an ex, er...girlfriend ...? So, I said to Stu, what if I have a little chat with Ann first? I mean, as her daughter, I'd thought you... But Stu didn't think it would be a good idea... so then he had to tell me how Vivienne had felt about you at the time of the...you know, about what you'd done... so I agreed you might not be the best one, and perhaps Poppy might ...But you saw how she was with me today, I mean, she couldn't have made it plainer if she'd come right out and called me a fucking bitch, in front of everyone...' her voice quavers to a halt and she sniffs loudly, releasing Ann's hand as she fumbles through the flounces of her mauve and rose-pink gypsy skirt, eventually locating the pocket and drawing out a crumpled man-size tissue into which she trumpets vigorously.

The image of an elephant flashes across Ann's mind; she's glad of the distraction. She is having difficulty with organising her thoughts - or rather, in identifying any conscious thoughts at all under the onslaught of emotions that are tightening her chest. A Chinese burn; that's the nearest to this kind of searing pain. Felicity was good at that – she'd clasp Ann's wrist with both hands and twist them around it in opposite directions, tighter and tighter until Ann could hold out no longer and had to gasp and whimper for her to stop, even if this did mean that she was failing yet another endurance test, and would have to wait at least a month before there'd be the slightest chance of being invited to join Felicity's gang again. Ann was nearly eleven before she realised that not only did these endurance tests grow more impossible each time, but that there was, in fact, no gang to join.

'So you see, it is a bit awkward, ' Lindy is saying, 'Although of course we're both blissfully happy about it all, and Stu can hardly believe that his dream is coming true at last, when of course he'd given up all hope years ago. He sacrificed everything for her, you know – she was about the same age as I am now when she... And though I'd never hear a word said against her, I can't help

236

feeling it was just the teeniest bit selfish not to give it a try, at least. After all, look at me! My boy, Ryan, is nearly nineteen, so I could reasonably have expected all that to be over and done with by now.'

Lindy pauses to draw breath, and Ann realises that her own wave of panic is fading as her brain latches on to the novel notion of Vivienne with a third baby by a third man. Catching Lindy's eye, she gives a wry smile which is evidently taken as encouragement to continue, 'I mean, it wouldn't have been that big a gap for her, would it? Not with a child of seven, or whatever he was then, the boy, Colin. I know you were about sixteen, so it's not as if she was against the idea of a gap, per se. And that husband of hers, her second, wasn't he? He'd got a child already, but poor Stu, only twenty eight, just a lad, really – that's terribly young for a man to cut off all chances of ever having children of his own, don't you think? Between you and me, I think that's why Stu never asked her to marry him – kind of subconsciously keeping his options open, you know? I'd hate that to happen to Ryan when he's that age. Not that I'm criticising Vivienne for that. I think the world of her, I really do. And of course, I'm in the perfect position to totally understand what it's like to be in the grip of an overwhelming passion at the age of forty. Though I have to say, in my own defence, I haven't broken up a marriage, as such, nor walked out on a young child.'

Ann claps her hand to her mouth in an effort to stifle a laugh. This is ludicrous. Surreal! Less than a week ago, she was dreading her first encounter in more than a decade years with her estranged mother, for whom her over-riding emotion has almost always been resentment. Now she is sitting on a bed in Vivienne's house, while the woman, the *pregnant* woman, who has stolen her man, is excusing herself for her own mid-life passion for this man, and, on top of that, she's condemning her predecessor for not having given him a child more than thirty years ago, thereby relieving her of the responsibility for doing so. And now, Ann herself suddenly finds that she's overtaken by an urge to defend Vivienne's behaviour - defend the Betrayal!

237

'On the subject of age gaps,' she says with forced calm, 'Have you ever considered the simple maths involved in your own situation?'

'Maths?' says Lindy, warily, 'I've never been much good at maths. I had such a horrible teacher at school, he put me right off.'

'Well, I suppose you must know how old Stuart is?'

'Sixty four isn't old. Not these days. And he's ever so young-looking.'

'I didn't mean…Oh, well, anyway... yes, sixty four. Vivienne is seventy seven, and you're forty-'

'I'm nearly forty-two,' she says defensively. 'And I know what you're getting at. It's all right for your mother to run off with a much younger man, but when he wants to take his last chance of happiness with a much younger woman, then it's all wrong if the sums add up to a bigger number. And anyway, life's not that simple. It's all right for you to sit there and make judgements, but I've know Stu all my life and we've always loved each other in a pure, innocent way on a higher plane altogether – it's been a spiritual communion of two souls, and nothing physical ever, ever entered our heads – and what we have now is so beautiful because, it's like…like…'

'Like you were made for each other?' says Ann with thinly veiled sarcasm.

'Exactly! I knew I was right about you, Ann! As soon as I set eyes on you, even before we were introduced, I could see you have a beautiful aura, it positively radiates compassion. And it was wrong of me to say what I said just now, about you thinking it was all right for your mother to run off with Stuart, when I know that you only did what you did because you actually wanted to prevent it from happening and - '

'That's all right. That's all right. Stop now, stop. You just lie down here and rest. I'm going out to join the others on the walk – they won't have even reached the village yet and I only came up because I knew I'd left the bedroom in a mess and I didn't want you to feel…'

'You see? I was right about your compassion, Ann. You did

really want to set out at the same time as all the others. I am so sorry for keeping you – and now I feel perfectly fine again, now that you've let me unburden myself of my secret, so maybe a little walk would do me good as well.'

O god. She has to get away. Anywhere. Anywhere away from this torrent of words that's threatening to sweep away years of, layers of…She takes a deep breath and in a steady voice she says, 'Em, well, I don't want to appear unfriendly, Lindy, but actually, I will need to walk fast if I'm to catch up with the others – I might even have to break in to a jog, and in your condition….'

'Oh, yes, you're right, of course, jogging wouldn't be quite… I'll just go and sit in the garden for a bit, now that the sun is coming out. Thank you so much for listening so kindly. And I can tell Stu, can I, that you will find a way of giving Vivienne our glad tidings?'

Ann is already at the door, 'Yes, yes of course I will. Must dash. Bye now!'

She keeps one hand clamped across her mouth, and the other on the banisters as she takes the stairs two at a time, and makes it to the ground floor toilet with seconds to spare, slamming the door behind her and turning on the tap to minimise the chance of Lindy hearing as she falls to her knees and lets her stomach heave its contents into the toilet bowl.

She stands for a moment, gripping the edge of the washbasin as she stares at the water gushing from the tap and swirling down the plug hole, then bends forward and scoops a few handfuls to rinse out her mouth. Her head has stopped spinning and her knees are less shaky but her brain has been replaced by wads of cotton wool. All she wants to do is curl up on her bed and fall into a dreamless sleep.

Sutton Coldfield 1971

Chapter 30

This will do, thinks Ann. The pagoda is empty. She's only passed one small family group on her way up the hill. There is no one around. She could stretch out full length on one of the grey stone benches that run along its edges from corner to corner. The red paint on the pillars that hold up the roof has faded almost to pink. The sky is threatening rain again, but the air is mild. Birds in the trees on the slope below start chirruping to each other. Random phrases of poetry float across her mind, 'bright litter of birdcalls...', 'only an attitude remains...', 'the stone fidelity they hardly meant...'

Fidelity. Duplicity.

'They fuck you up, your mum and dad...' That's a more typical, more relevant piece of Larkin.

Attitude. Hardly meant. I didn't mean...I didn't mean that at all.

Ann can't go back home yet. Colin or Edward will see that she's been crying. Even Mummy would notice that something was wrong. Why couldn't Ann have been given eyes like hers or Colin's? Not merely because they are large and hazel with thick dark lashes, but because they don't have her white-rimmed inner lids that stay red for ages after shedding even a few tears.

No, Colin won't see. She said goodnight to him before she came out and he'll be asleep by now. She peers at her watch: only half an hour since she was hiding behind the wide trunk of the chestnut tree in the holly glade, listening with a thudding heart to the whispering, passionate voices.

Vivienne won't be at home yet, of course. She'll finish what she's doing with the Dirk Bogarde man first. Though maybe they won't actually be doing IT because Mummy had sounded so upset

240

when she had to explain why she couldn't go away with him. And because holly leaves are much too prickly to lie down on – they'd hurt, even if you were sitting on a picnic rug. She and Colin had tried that once when they were being explorers in the Amazon, and Vivienne left the house this evening just in her running clothes and certainly wasn't carrying anything. But anyway, the Dirk-Bogarde-Sydney-Carton man already knew that Vivienne had a child because he'd seemed to think it could all be solved so easily. 'It's not Edward, it's my little boy,' Vivienne said – that was her reason. So Edward didn't count. It was no surprise to Ann that she wasn't even mentioned. But the man did know there was a girl, too, because he'd said, 'Bring him with you,' meaning Colin of course, and then he'd added, 'And the girl', so Vivienne must have let it slip sometime – maybe she'd wanted to put him off when he was trying to stick his tongue in her mouth. 'It's called a French Kiss,' Eileen had explained to a giggling group of girls when they were still in the fourth form. All those germs and spit. It sounded even more disgusting than a French Letter. 'You're far too young and beautiful to have a child of nearly fifteen! I don't believe it!' Dirk would have said and he'd have done a sum in his head to work out if Vivienne really could be as old as all that. But it obviously hadn't put him off at all.

Ann is in a place no one will ever find: an old oak with a huge, gnarled trunk that branches out into three wide limbs, making a snug kind of platform with a shallow dip in the middle and plenty of space to curl up in, at least ten foot above the ground and invisible from below, even if anyone did wander off the narrow tracks that thread the woods between Keepers' Pool and Bracebridge. Most people just stay near one of the many entrance gates, and have no idea quite how big and how ancient this park is.

'Park' is quite the wrong word. It sounds tame and small. She looked it up once – something to do with woods and pasture attached to a country house, or a neat, ornamental enclosure in a town, for public recreation. This is neither. When they came to do the Tudors in History she was thrilled to discover that it was still a wild forest in those days, and Henry The Eighth himself had presented it to the people of Sutton Coldfield for ever and ever. It didn't quite make up for the loss of Cley and Blakeney Point, but it was some consolation to know that she was actually a part-owner of these woods and lakes, even if they were really more Edward's than hers because it was his house and he'd always lived in Sutton.

She loved Edward now. Sometimes she almost forgot that he wasn't her real father and she wished that he was. She hadn't liked him at all at first, because he had dragged Mummy away from their proper home, and she had made Ann come with her, even though she'd begged and pleaded to be allowed to stay with Grannibelle, and even though she knew that Vivienne didn't care tuppence for her and wouldn't have minded at all if she'd left her behind in Norfolk. In spite of this, she hadn't liked what Felicity had said about it: Vivienne was afraid that Edward wouldn't still love her if he thought she'd be prepared to desert her own daughter. And anyway, wasn't he mainly marrying her so she could be a mother to his?

Ha! Felicity was more right than she could ever have guessed. That's exactly the type of woman Vivienne is: a child-deserter. OK, so she's told Dirk/Sydney that she doesn't want to leave Colin, but she didn't even mention her daughter, and she certainly wants to desert her husband. Poor, poor Edward. Vivienne would have taken Colin and run away with that man, quick as a flash. It's only her fear of what Edward might do that's keeping her here. Keeping Colin here. 'He's a divorce lawyer, for god's sake; he'll know exactly what to do.' But would he? Edward, of course, has never talked to her directly about his 'cases', but she's gleaned enough from overheard snatches of conversations to know that these days it's usually the mother who is awarded custody. Custody. Yellow and cowardly. One of those words that sound nothing at all like what they mean. Would Edward really be able to stop Vivienne from stealing Colin away from them?

Ann had been determined to hate the new baby. 'He's not a real brother,' she'd said when Edward had wanted to take her to visit Vivienne in the hospital. 'Felicity's welcome to him – he's got her surname, not mine.' She'd had to go in the end, though.

Edward had insisted, 'I won't have you upsetting your mother like this, Ann. I do understand that it's not been easy for you to share her with me and Felicity, and now this new little soul. But love doesn't work like that, it's not like food, or money, or anything that has to be divided into smaller and smaller portions the more people you give it to. With love, the more you give, the more you have left to give.'

She'd understood what he meant by this as soon as he'd lifted the small blue-wrapped bundle from the Perspex cot next to Vivienne's bed and placed it in her own reluctant arms. Heart melting? Rush of love? All the clichés in the world couldn't describe what she'd felt when the object, much lighter than Grannibelle's cat but surprisingly solid under the layers of wool, squirmed and wriggled, opened its little pink mouth in a yawn, blinked its two, squinty eyes up at her, then gave what sounded like a contented sigh and fell back to sleep.

Luckily, Felicity wasn't with her this first time, so she hadn't seen the soppy smile that fixed itself on her face as she'd gazed down at her baby brother. Her baby. Not Felicity's at all. *Rockaby baby on the tree top*. The words suddenly took on their full meaning: *down will come baby, cradle and all?* Ann would never, never let anyone harm her baby.

In her shallow nest between the branches, Ann folds her arms around her knees, drawing them up close to her chest and shifting her weight so that a different area of bottom is subjected to the hard wood of the tree. When she comes here with her book and an apple or a few broken biscuits, she stuffs the picnic rug into her satchel so that she can fold it into fours, cushioning her from the knobbly bark. She hasn't yet brought Colin here. He'll need to be a bit bigger before she can help him to scramble up this high.

How will she bear it if he is taken away? When she was little, she'd sometimes lie awake at night playing out different tragic scenarios in her head. The best one was at her own funeral, when she had died rescuing two-year old Colin from a blazing building, or snatching him from under the wheels of a huge lorry, and everyone would be sobbing their hearts out, especially Vivienne because now that it was too late, she'd realise what a wonderful person Ann really was, and even Felicity would be crying buckets. At other times, she'd experiment with someone else's funeral, to see whose death would make her cry the most. Colin's was always top of the list, even above Grannibelle's, but there were times when she could hardly squeeze out any tears at all at the thought of Vivienne in her coffin. Deep down, though, she'd always known that in real life she would cry.

'You dumbo, this isn't doing any good', Ann mutters, then gasps as a bird in a branch overhead gives a sudden squawk and beats its wings to regain its balance, sending down a flurry of bits of twigs and acorns. After what she'd heard in the holly glade, she'd backed away as quietly as she'd come, taking quick, shallow breaths, because of the sharp pain behind her breastbone that was trying to push its way up into her mouth and burst out as a scream. The next thing she knew, she was standing at the base of her tree without any thoughts in her head at all. She'd run all the way here as though her legs were doing the thinking for her.

As she looks around, she realises that the light is already beginning to fail. She can't stay here much longer. Colin will be fast asleep by now. Edward doesn't know that she's not in the house in her own bedroom. If Vivienne is back now, she'll have other things on her mind and won't give a thought to her daughter. It'll be easy to sneak up to her room unnoticed. It's important not to let herself rush into anything. She'll need to think it all through very, very carefully. Life has been a lot better since Felicity went off to London and isn't even home in the holidays much. Now that it's only the four of them, it feels more like a real family. School hasn't been too bad either, recently. Perhaps the man will go away, now that Vivienne has said she can't come with him.

Ann will keep her eyes and ears open, and her mouth firmly closed.

But the man hasn't gone away quite yet. She knows his name now. Stuart. Stuart Darling. What kind of a name is that? It seems to fit in quite well with things like Never-Never Land and people who won't grow up; though in the book, Mr Darling is Wendy's father and a proper adult; it's Vivienne who wants to run away from responsibility. Stuart is an actor. That's his hobby, anyway. His job is teaching English at the Boys' Grammar. At least, it was last term. But it was only an infill post. He's got a proper promotion now, in a posh school in Brighton where he's got his own flat and he'll be moving down there in just a few weeks. When she hears this, Ann's heart gives a little leap: so everything's going to be all right, after all.

Vivienne is so calm and cool when she introduces Stuart to Ann that for a moment she almost wonders if she'd dreamt the incident in the holly glade. Maybe that overheard conversation hadn't really happened. After all, she'd found herself at her oak tree without being aware of how she'd got there – that's the kind of thing that happens in dreams.

That day, the day she finally meets him face to face, she and Colin have been at Keeper's Pool as usual in fine weather, especially at the start of the holidays. They took a picnic lunch, planning to be out till tea-time, but Colin was stung by a wasp before they'd even had a swim and they've come home to get the tube of sting-relief which she'd left on the kitchen table. Colin started screaming again as soon as they reached the gate.

Of course, Vivienne has to comfort Colin before she can explain what Stuart is doing in their kitchen at half-past eleven on a Monday morning. 'He's a member of the Highbury. You know - the little theatre in Sheffield Road? Where I help out with sets and things like that sometimes? I'm going to be auditioning for a part in the autumn play. A big part. The main female role, in fact. Stuart's just dropped round to give me a few tips.'

'Nice to meet you at last, Ann,' he says, holding out his hand and giving such an open, friendly smile, it seems as if he really is genuinely pleased to see her. Close up, he's even better looking than Dirk Bogarde. Those eyes! There's more to it than that though – a screen image can only work directly through the senses of sight and sound. When a man like this is standing close enough to shake your hand, and every pore of your skin, even under your clothes, is prickling with a kind of electricity that connects your whole body-space to his, and there's a tingling pain at the bottom of your stomach and between your legs and you're breathing a strange, animal scent and you can't tell whether it's coming from your own body, or his...

Someone is shaking her shoulder and an anxious voice is saying, 'Ann? Ann. What are you doing here? Are you all right?' and she struggles up from where she's been lying curled on the stone bench in the corner of the pagoda on the hill above Vivienne's house on Lamma Island. And it's early March, well into the twenty-first century, not late July, nineteen-seventy-one.

'What is it, Ann?' says George again, bending down and grasping her hands, 'You're frozen, woman! However long have you been here? Come on, let's get you back to the house.'

Her feet are planted on the tiled floor, but her leg muscles refuse to co-operate with George's efforts to pull her up. She shakes her head slowly, 'Sorry,' she murmurs. 'Just give me a moment.' She glances towards the narrow mud track between the trees and shrubs, 'Where is everyone? Will they be...?'

'It's OK,' says George, sitting down at her side, 'Stuart's with Lindy. Charlie and the other two stopped off at Poppy's shop on our way back. I came to look for you. You don't mind, do you? I mean...if you'd rather...'

'No. Stay. It's just...'

'You don't have to talk, you know. Silence is fine by me...'

She looks down at her lap where her left knuckle is pressing into the white cotton of her trousers just above her knee. She seems unaware that George still has hold of her right hand which is resting in his palm, bridging the imperceptible space between their thighs.

After a long silence, she slides her hand away and lifts the other to join it, rubbing her palms together and twisting the linked fingers from side to side.

'And..?' prompts George. 'It might help to just let whatever it is spill out. We're more than just cousins, aren't we? Friends, I

246

mean. Close friends.'

'Of course. Yes. Friends.'

'It seems like I've known you for ever. I don't think there's anything you can say that will shock me. I mean, after the way you introduced yourself, I could see you'd be capable of virtually anything,' he adds with a laugh.

Ann stares down at the ground, fixing her eyes on a jagged stone and a small beetle that is trying to burrow underneath it.

'You don't know me,' she says flatly. 'You don't know what I'm really like. Things I've done. Things I've…things I've pretended not to know…' her words trail away into a sigh. The beetle has shifted a few grains of earth. If she focuses enough, she might hear its tiny legs rasping and grating.

Her voice is almost inaudible as she mutters, 'I got so good at pretending … after a while it wasn't pretence any more - I actually *didn't* know.'

Another silence. Ann is drained of words.

At last, George murmurs, 'And now you do?'

'And now I do.'

Chapter 31

This summer, the Norfolk fortnight has been messed up. Edward always drives them to Grannibelle's on the Friday afternoon, then leaves them there on the Sunday while he goes back to work for a week. Then he joins them again the next Friday and stays with them till the end of the holiday. That's how it's been, every year since The Move. And now Vivienne wants to change it all.

'It's not fair! We always - ' begins Ann, her stomach plummeting, her voice rising.

'That's enough, Ann,' Edward cuts in. 'Your mother is too busy during the first half of August, and I can't switch my weeks around at this late stage. Vivienne will take you both for another week a little later. You'll be having two shorter holidays instead of just the one –'

'But Mummy might change her mind again, when it's her turn to take us. I bet there'll be other 'really important' rehearsals.'

'There won't be,' says Edward smoothly. 'Everything will have gone quiet again towards the end of August. You have my word on it.'

'Your word, Dad! What difference can *your* word make if *she* -?'

'I said, that's enough, Ann. Subject closed.'

She turns on her heel and stalks out of the room, biting her lip, holding her breath. She runs up the two flights of stairs with her eyes screwed almost shut, finding the handle of her bedroom door through a watery blur. He knows, she thinks. He must know. But if he does, how *can* he just say nothing?

Since that episode in the holly glade, nine days ago, Ann has felt as though she's been treading water. She's good at that - it's easy to stay in the sea for ages, so long as you don't get too cold. All you do is swim out a bit till your feet can't reach the bottom. Your arms and legs don't get tired because you're just dangling there, paddling them ever so slowly, and your head is bobbing on the water like a lost beach-ball. Sometimes a seal will pop up close by and stare at you with its spaniel eyes. You feel kind of free, like you belong, really belong. Like a bird might feel when it's gliding high up in the blue sky. But you must always, always check the tide first. It has to be on its way in or you can get dragged out towards the horizon and drown.

July has changed into August and still she is keeping her head above water, saying nothing. She knows that Edward knows about Stuart's existence, if nothing else, because Vivienne comes out with his name at supper, bold as brass, on that same Monday when Colin got stung by a wasp. 'Wasn't it kind of Stuart to pop round this morning?' she says, and Ann is so startled she has to look down at her plate to hide her red cheeks. 'He thinks I'm in with a very good chance of playing Gwendolyn,' she continues, with the girlish giggle she usually keeps for when there are other men around.

Edward merely nods as he chews his mouthful of cold ham, but Vivienne continues, 'You know, Importance of Being Ernest?'

'Yes Vivienne, I am familiar with the characters in that play. I saw the early fifties version of the film with Edith Evans as Lady Bracknell. You might recall that shortly after we first met, I commented on your similarity to Joan Greenwood, an actress whose poise and beauty I've always admired. It's entirely apt that you should be taking the role that she played.'

'We did it with Miss Oliphant,' says Ann, relieved that the conversation has been steered away from Stuart. 'It seemed a pretty dopy play to me. All that fuss about a name. Anyway, I thought Gwendolyn and the other soppy girl weren't meant to be more than about eighteen. You're far too old for that!'

'Ann, that sounded very rude. Not only rude, but inaccurate. On stage, your mother would certainly make a convincing eighteen year old.' He turns and smiles at Vivienne, then adds with a cold edge to his voice that Ann has not heard before, 'I've not had the pleasure of his acquaintance yet, but there seems to be no doubt that young Stuart would have excelled in the role of Mr Worthing. What a shame it is that he won't be here to perform with you.'

Vivienne is overtaken by a sudden fit of choking, and covers her mouth with both hands. Her cheeks are flushed and her eyes are streaming as she pushes back her chair and rushes from the room.

Too late, Ann realises that her own comments have made matters worse. She is no longer treading water in a calm sea. From now on, she'll keep quiet - do nothing that might break the surface, cause a storm. Only about three more weeks, and *he* will disappear from their lives and everything will go back to normal. She'll keep out of Vivienne's way. Ask no questions about her auditions and rehearsals. Never mention Stuart's name.

She thinks about him, though. It's impossible not to. Especially when she's in bed. It gives her that lovely shivery tingling. But there's something not quite…Her own mother's…boyfriend? So she tries not to use his name, even in her head. He's a made-up man, like a film star, or someone in a book, who just happens to have eyes like his, a voice, a mouth …

It's odd being in Grannibelle's house while Vivienne is left behind in Sutton Coldfield. It wouldn't feel so strange to Ann if it was just her and Colin. That's happened once or twice during the Easter holidays, or the occasional long weekend, and it's been like the old days, the proper Norfolk Time, except that Colin wasn't even born then. But being here with Edward, and Mummy not being with them – that gives her a hollow feeling in her stomach.

On the first morning, she overhears Grannibelle asking, 'Are you quite sure you want to go through with this, Edward? It must be so very hard for you, wondering if she…' Her voice trails away and during the silence that follows, Ann imagines Edward stiffening his back and turning towards the window to avoid meeting Grannibelle's gaze, 'I'd be more than happy to have the children for the whole week if you'd prefer to go back and keep her company.'

'I know you would, Belle. Thank you. And I'm also grateful that you have made the effort to understand what I'm doing. I really do think this is the only way. Even the strongest of storms will eventually blow itself out. She's so …so…*Vivienne*!' he gives a tight little laugh. 'Fire and water. It's my own fault. At one level, I knew it right from the start – I thought I'd be able to make it work. And I will. I will. If we can just ride this out.'

The rest of the week passes more slowly than usual. But it's not the good kind of slow, where each day is so full of different activities that when you lie in bed at night and run through everything you've done since breakfast, it's hard to believe that what happened in the morning really was a part of this same day.

Edward's moods veer from glum silence to forced jollity. Grannibelle seems to have a worried frown on her face whenever Ann catches her on her own, and then insists there's nothing wrong; she was just thinking about what to cook for supper, or should she hang the washing out, because it looks like rain.

By the time they pack the car ready to go back home, Ann is in a fever of impatience. She's had a couple of quick phone conversations with Vivienne, but the last of these was two whole days ago. She'd sounded bright enough and said how well the rehearsals were going, and how no-one could believe she'd never acted before. But was that just an act she was putting on – lulling them into a false sense of security?

By the time Edward draws up outside their house, switches off the engine, pulls on the handbrake till it gives its little screech and click, then opens the door and steps onto the pavement, Ann isn't sure if this hot and cold feeling in her chest and stomach is car-sickness or fear.

Then all three of them are in the hall, and Vivienne is leaning against the kitchen door frame, with that tilted little smile as she drawls, 'How nice to see you all again, my darlings,' and Colin lets go of Ann's hand and hurtles towards his mother with such speed that she gives a proper laugh as he flings his arms around her hips and nestles his head against her stomach. Then Edward steps forward and puts an arm across her shoulder and kisses her cheek, and says 'Hello, old girl,' in a funny, thick kind of voice, and a great surge of anger seems to knock Ann sideways so she can hardly breath.

Now that the August fortnight has been split into two separate weeks, Ann's birthday, her sixteenth, will be celebrated in Norfolk. She's glad of this, because it means she doesn't have to worry about whether or not to have a party, and what if no-one wants to come? It couldn't be even half as good as Eileen's, and there'd already been lots of other sixteenth parties or special outings this year – most of which hadn't included her. Grannibelle said she'd arrange a trip to a matinee at the Theatre Royal in Norwich and then a special supper at that lovely restaurant in Blakeney, and Edward will come, and Vivienne and Colin, of course, and perhaps Ann would like to invite that nice girl they'd met last summer who'd moved into the big house just outside Holt.

Ann's not thinking about her birthday now though. She's concentrating on getting through the next ten days. Once they've managed to get Mummy into the car with them, and they're on their way to Norfolk again, it'll all be over. That man – she won't use his name now, even when she's not in bed and letting her mind wander where it shouldn't – that man will have vanished from their lives forever. Vivienne would never leave Colin behind. That's one thing she can be sure of now. That's why Mummy was still here when they got back from Norfolk. She's bound to be sad for a bit, after *he*'s gone away to Brighton, but she'll have her big role in that play to keep her busy. Edward will stop looking gloomy all the time and they'll all be able to relax.

They nearly make it. They nearly ride it out.

Edward's movements are as predictable as clockwork. He always catches the same train every morning, and any slight variation on the time he arrives back home is due entirely to the ups and downs of British Rail. But during supper on the Tuesday before the weekend when they're going back to Grannibelle's, he says, 'I'm afraid I shall be very late home tomorrow. Grenville was meant to be meeting a client at Stafford but he's gone down with some kind of stomach bug. It's a complicated case, and he'd arranged a series of meetings that have had to spill over to the evening.'

Ann looks up from the sinewy meat she's detaching from the

chicken leg, and glances across at Vivienne, whose eyes have widened suddenly. She seems to be biting back a smile as she says in a casual voice, 'Will you be eating there, or shall I keep a meal for you?'

'I expect I'll have eaten before I set out, but I'll give you a ring at lunchtime. I should have a clearer idea of how the land lies by then.'

'That's fine – I've not got anything much on for tomorrow.'

'Mummy, you *have!*' squeals Colin indignantly, 'You're taking us to 'Willie Wonka and the Chocolate Factory' tomorrow.'

'Don't worry, Colin. Of course I haven't forgotten that!'

But after breakfast the next morning, there's a slight change of plan. Vivienne has received a phone call from the 'Ernest People', asking her to come to an urgent meeting that afternoon. Ann will have to take Colin to the film on her own. Vivienne will drop them off at the Odeon on her way, and she'll make sure they're in plenty of time for the other short film and all the trailers and advertisements and the ice cream break. It'll still be broad daylight when it finishes at half past five, and they can walk home on their own. They'll be ready for some fresh air after being cooped up in the stuffy cinema all afternoon.

'I'm really sorry I can't come with you,' she adds. 'It's just that - '

'That's all right, Mummy,' says Ann, keeping her voice light and making sure she's smiling with her eyes as well as her mouth. 'It's really important, your play, especially with you being Gwendolyn. Anyway, it'll be quite fun with just Colin and me, won't it, Col?'

His bottom lip stops quivering as he sees an opportunity, 'Can we have popcorn *and* ice cream *and* a drink *and-*'

Vivienne bends and scoops him up in a hug that lifts his feet from the ground, 'You can both have whatever you want, so long as you're not sick,' she laughs. Then she puts Colin down, pats his head and turns towards Ann with a strange expression on her face. There's a slight flush on her cheeks and her eyes are bright with little sparkles of what could be tears. 'Thank you, Ann,' she says.

253

'I really do appreciate that.' She glances across at Colin, happily arranging his Dinky cars in a line under the kitchen table. 'I didn't want him to be upset.'

She's talking to me like a grown up, thinks Ann with a sudden rush of pleasure. Like she talks to Grannibelle or Edward, even. But the thought lasts no more than a second. *She won't catch me out like that again, Mrs Nicey Nicey'*

Ann keeps her head down, pretending embarrassment as she gives Vivienne a quick hug, and mutters, 'It's OK, Mummy. We'll be fine.'

When the phone rings, Vivienne and Colin are out. They've taken some stale bread to feed the ducks.

'So what is the message you'll be giving to your mother?'

'I'm not stupid, Dad,' says Ann with a laugh. 'I don't need to write it down. That man who had the tummy bug is feeling better now. He'll take over the work in Stafford and you don't have to go back to your office today, so you'll be home early. Anyway you don't need to fuss - she won't even be here when you get home – only it won't be cos of the cinema. She's got to go to a meeting now instead.'

'Oh!' he says, and there's a long pause before he carries on in a brisk voice, 'Nonetheless, I want her to know I could be back home by four. It's very important, Ann. You won't let me down, will you?'

'Of course I won't,' she says.

The hall seems full of echoes as she replaces the receiver. The sunlight filtering in through the stained glass window above the door is flecked with motes of dust that shimmer and glow in the slanting rays of red and green and blue. She's never noticed before how it makes the oak panelled walls seem dark and sinister in contrast. It feels as though she's standing outside of her self; as though she's someone else, someone in a film or a play.

The feeling intensifies as she tiptoes up the stairs, letting the banisters take some of her weight, so the usual steps don't creak. She's the nameless heroine in 'Rebecca'. She'll have to make sure

Mrs Danvers doesn't see her as she turns right onto the landing that leads to the main bedroom instead of carrying on up the next flight to her own room.

Vivienne hasn't yet got round to making the bed this morning. The sheet is tangled up with the blankets and trailing onto the floor. The pillows haven't been shaken and plumped up to their full fatness. The one on the far side is where Vivienne's head would have rested – and that's the dent made by Edward's balding head. Would Stuart's head have left a similar hollow? *Stuart*. Ann finds that she can say his name here, in the room where he probably slept with Vivienne on every one of the seven nights when she and Colin and Edward were all at Grannibelle's. 'Slept with'! How much *sleep* would they have got?

There's a buzzing noise inside her head.

Will Stuart lie here with Vivienne this very afternoon, while she and Colin…?

Someone is squeezing the breath out of her lungs.

The stabbing pain in her chest ebbs away as she hears the kitchen door bang, and Colin's voice from downstairs shouting, 'Annie, Annie, We're back!'

She's pausing at the top of the stairs when Vivienne strolls into the hall and calls up to her, 'Any phone calls?'

Ann feels completely detached from her own voice, which is saying, 'Yes, Dad rang a few minutes ago. He said to tell you he won't be needing supper. He'll be back late.'

How can a mere few sounds made with lips and tongue and breath make such a difference? Words can slip out so easily - why can't they be as easily unsaid?

The rest of the morning Mummy is at her nicest. Colin's new friend, Tim from three doors down, has come to play, and while the two boys are out in the garden Vivienne asks Ann almost shyly if she'll help her practice her lines. 'It's a scene with Cicely, so I thought perhaps you could…?'

For the second time that morning, her words emerge without her conscious volition, 'Oh all right,' she says, instead of 'Sorry,

255

I've got stuff of my own to do.'

Over the next half hour or more, Ann shifts from one role to another: Cicely, Jack Worthing, Lady Bracknell. How they both giggle as Vivienne and Ann reverse their own roles of daughter and mother. 'Actually, you're really rather good, you know,' says Vivienne. 'Maybe you should audition for a part in the next play.'

She's like the sea on a calm sunny day, thinks Ann, pulling herself up yet again from being lured out into dangerous currents. It would be so easy to forget what she'd overheard in the holly glade. Even though she can't pretend that never happened, maybe it really is all over now? Maybe she has got it out of her system, like Edward is hoping.

Then she remembers Stuart's face. His physical presence.

Will Vivienne really choose Edward, with his long nose and domed forehead and all those wrinkles round his eyes and hardly any hair left, and those old fashioned clothes?

How can she bear to be in bed with an old man like Edward, if she's had Stuart lying on top of her, and that tragic, passionate mouth moving down onto her lips?

'Do you mind if we stop now?' she says abruptly, putting the script down on the table. 'I'd like to get a bit of fresh air since we'll be inside all afternoon.'

'Of course I don't mind. I'm so sorry, dear. That was rather selfish of me, but I was so enjoying working with you like this. We must do it more often.'

In what seems like one swift movement Vivienne glides across the room and draws Ann towards her in a hug. 'I'll ask Tim's mother to let Colin play at their house tomorrow, and we'll go shopping for some really nice clothes for a special sixteen-year-old.'

Ann finds it almost impossible to swallow any of the lunch that Vivienne has prepared for them. Luckily, Colin has insisted on eating in the garden, so it's relatively easy to hide most of it under the prickly shrub next to the bench.

There's still time for Vivienne to sneak away with Colin before Stuart goes to Brighton to start his new job. Or maybe she'll bide her time for a bit longer and Ann will come home from school one day and find them gone.

She lets Colin sit in front with Mummy on the way to the cinema, to make extra sure that her own unruly tongue doesn't blurt out the truth about Edward's phone call. If Vivienne isn't lying about her theatre meeting, then there'll be no harm done. The worst that Ann will have to face is finding an explanation for how she managed to get his message so wrong.

But if Vivienne is lying, if she and Stuart…

Well then. Edward needs to know.

It'll be their own fault, not hers.

If anyone should ever ask her what she thought of the film itself, she'll not be able to tell them a single thing about it. Colin polishes off all the popcorn and more than half of her vanilla tub. She spends every minute of those hours in the darkness concentrating on not being sick.

Chapter 32

There's a long silence as Ann's voice trails to a halt, and her mind jolts her back from the stuffy cinema and the red-cushioned seat beside her little brother, to this hard stone bench where the small creatures flitting in the darkening air beyond the pagoda are now more likely to be bats than songbirds.

Her shaky attempt at a laugh doesn't quite mask the bitterness in her tone, 'See? I said you'd be shocked. What price my moral high-ground now!'

'Poor little thing,' says George, rising to his feet and pulling her towards him. How quickly, in just these few days, she has become accustomed to the comforting feel of his arms around her and the steady sound of his heartbeat against her left ear.

After a moment, he says, 'I take it Edward caught them in flagrante?'

'How could I just not remember about my own part in all that? It doesn't seem possible!' she mutters into his shoulder, then lifts her head and tries to pull away from him. 'I've always thought of it as *her* betrayal of *us*! What a terrible, horrible thing to do. And that's who I am. That's the real me!'

'Nonsense!' he says. 'You were no more than a child then. You can't be expected to have understood all the complexities of adult relationships. After all, how many adults ever achieve that level of maturity – especially once sex has been added to the melting pot?'

'Don't know,' she mumbles.

'Well, there you go. You start off with a base stock of ignorance - add in a dollop of teenage hormones, and a pinch of bad luck or bad timing, and hey presto! Disaster!'

'How am I going to face Vivienne now? After all I've said and thought about her, when really…And, oh! Poor Edward! To think what I did to him, and he never once confronted me with… '

'There now, there now,' he soothes, stroking the crown of her head, as she tries to stifle her sobs, 'Just let yourself go, love. It's

Ok to cry. It really is.' With his other hand, he draws out a large handkerchief from his trouser pocket, 'Good old-fashioned cotton,' he says with a laugh as he thrusts it into her hand. 'Crumpled but unused.'

'Thanks,' she says with a sniff, then, 'Sorry about all this.'

'Don't be silly. I'm glad you've been able to confide in me. It must be really traumatic, suddenly having to re-evaluate key facts like that.'

'Not nice at all, finding out what an unpleasant person I really am.'

'Now then. None of that. We've all done unpleasant things at some stage in our lives, but one swallow doesn't make a summer. Not that swallows are unpleasant,' he adds with a chuckle. 'Nor summers for that matter, but you know what I mean.'

'I suppose so,' she says, 'But - '

'But nothing! You've had a shock, that's all. It doesn't change anything. You're still the same person, Ann - the same lovely person. It's going to take more than a couple of minutes to get to grips with something like this.' He pats her shoulder then pulls her closer to him, while the other hand smoothes the hair on the nape of her neck.

Now his fingertips are pushing through the strands of hair above her ear, massaging her scalp. The amplified sound is like waves, shifting over sand. Her breathing slows, and she lets herself relax into the rhythm of his touch. All she wants is to stay like this until she feels herself again. The self that George has discovered, a woman who laughs spontaneously and can chatter away for hours on end and feels perfectly comfortable inside her own skin.

A sudden, dull ache settles in the pit of her stomach – she is not that self. She never will be. In The Norfolk Time, she'd often tried to identify the exact moment when the sea shifts from its state of slack water to the tidal ebb or flood. She knows it's the same sea, but to her, it has a quite different tang and smell to it.

This sudden change of mood has nothing to do with the present or the past - the near future hits her with such force that she jerks backwards, pushing her hands against his chest. Before she can take more than a step away from him, George grabs hold of her wrist, 'Steady on, pet!' he exclaims.

'Sorry! I'm sorry, George,' she says, struggling to regain her composure. 'It's just a reaction to, you know…It's been quite a day, hasn't it?'

'Maybe I'd better take you back now,' he says. 'You must be tired. And hungry too. I didn't see you eating much at lunchtime.'

'You're probably right,' she replies, glad of the darkness as she blinks back her tears.

They walk down the path in silence, hand in hand. When they reach Poppy's gate, Ann slows down and glances towards the house.

'No,' George laughs. 'I'm not deserting you here. I'm taking you all the way. Unless, that is, you'd like…?'

'No. You were right first time. I do love Poppy, but I don't think I'm up to facing her just now! I'll see her tomorrow.'

'Tomorrow,' muses George. 'Monday. I've got to pop over to the shop for a bit in the morning, but I should be back by mid afternoon. Unless you'd like to meet me in Central?'

'I'd better wait and see what Vivienne's plans are,' she says. 'There's this rather difficult conversation looming up, but I think I'll save that till I've had a good night's sleep.'

'Not a bad idea. Just make sure you don't forget the important thing - you were a confused teenager trying to save your family from splitting up. That didn't make you a bad person at the time – and it certainly doesn't make you one now, more than thirty years later! I repeat: you're a lovely person, Ann.'

'Thank you,' she says with a light laugh. 'Just goes to show what a kind person you are!'

As he opens the gate to Vivienne's house, he squeezes her hand and plants a light kiss on her cheek – a brotherly gesture. 'I'd better get back to Poppy now. Tell Vivienne I'll see her tomorrow. And you, of course.'

'Goodbye, George,' she says, and manages to keep her voice level as she adds, 'Thanks for everything.'

'My pleasure,' he says, then, almost in a whisper, 'I mean it,

Ann. You *are* a lovely person. Lovely and lovable.'

'Oh, what a shame! You've just missed Lindy and Stuart,' says Vivienne, glancing up from the sofa as Ann hesitates in the doorway, her shoulders stiff and her hands tightly clasped. 'They left a few minutes ago to catch the ferry.'

'Oh,' says Ann, unable to think of a suitable response.

'So, what did you make of Lindy's news, then?' continues Vivienne, raising her eyebrows. 'She said she'd told you.'

For a moment, Ann struggles to remember anything that Lindy has told her, apart from...

'The baby. *Their* baby,' says Vivienne. 'Hers and Stuart's.'

'Oh,' mumbles Ann again. 'Oh, the baby. Of course.'

Vivienne focuses her gaze on Ann's face, 'Are you all right, Ann? You look as though you've seen a ghost. Come and sit down,' she adds, patting the cushion beside her, and then holding out her hand.

As if in a dream, Ann lets herself collapse on to the sofa. Her eyelids are so heavy, it takes a huge effort of will to force them apart, but she can't summon up any words beyond, 'Tired. Sorry. So tired.'

'Food,' exclaims Vivienne briskly. 'You just sit there and I'll heat up some soup.'

The warm, spicy liquid revives her enough to take in what Vivienne is saying, 'So, what else did Lindy tell you?'

'It wasn't so much what she told me…She didn't actually say anything. It was more like, I don't know, like turning on a tap. It all came flooding back. Edward's phone call. The trip to the cinema…'

'I see,' says Vivienne, turning to look at her, with solemn eyes, 'So now you know what happened?'

'I know what I did,' sighs Ann, clenching her fists and angling her knees away from her mother, 'I know it was all my fault.'

'No,' says Vivienne. 'It wasn't your fault. I never wanted you to think that. Nor did Edward. It was my responsibility. The whole sorry mess. Can you bear to hear about it now? I'll understand if you'd rather not.'

'I...I... Oh Vivienne, I don't know. I just don't know,' Ann picks up the large white linen napkin from her lap and crumples it into a ball with both hands. 'It's all so...'

'I know. I know. I'm not trying to make excuses, but I think it'll help you to hear this. And me too.'

'Ok. I'm feeling better now with that soup inside me. So if you want...'

'I do want to. And a glass of wine won't come amiss for either of us.'

'So, here we are then,' says Vivienne with forced jollity as she comes back to the sofa and places two brimming glasses of red wine on the low table in front of them, 'It's Listen with Mother time! Are you sitting comfortably? Then I'll begin.'

Chapter 33

Vivienne had deliberately chosen that Wednesday for her trip to the cinema with the children. It might help to keep her mind off Stuart. He was catching the ten thirty from New Street and would be arriving in Brighton at around the same time that she and the children were being ushered into their seats at the Odeon. Colin was bound to have his usual supply of whispered questions that would need her instant attention. Focus on Colin.

When it came down to it, this was the stark choice: Colin or Stuart. Her son or her lover. Tuesday was the final test of her resolve. Thanks to the rather dowdy Mrs Ibstock, and her over-anxious little Timothy, Vivienne had been able to leave Colin and slip out to the park for an hour that afternoon. Ann, of course, was only too pleased to be left to her own devices.

Goodbye, not au revoir. That was to be the truth of it, though she couldn't let Stuart know that. Not yet. Even to herself, she had barely been able to face the likelihood that they would never see each other again. After all, he was still more boy than man - he hadn't learnt yet to accept the unacceptable. She'd have to help him through it. One step at a time - that was the way it worked.

'I'll be able to think up a reason for travelling down to London for the odd weekend,' she told him. And he could come back to Sutton for the half term break, and then there'd be all those long school holidays. What was the point of playing a major role in The Importance of Being Ernest, if she couldn't dream up a suitable Bunbury of her own? Their love would survive the long separations, and eventually Colin would be old enough to be allowed to choose between his parents, and of course he would choose her. Or maybe, before that, Edward might, totally painlessly of course...

From one minute to the next she veered between belief in what she was telling Stuart, and what she knew in her heart to be true: a clean break was the only way. She'd managed to give up smoking when she became pregnant with Colin. The desperate, almost

263

constant craving had taken her by surprise, but she'd stuck to her guns. People got used to the loss of a leg or an arm. Even their eyesight. Put your mind to it, and you can adjust to anything, in the long run. If you have no choice.

Maybe she'd be able to pretend that Stuart was dead. She could deal with death.

It was Stuart's pain that was so hard to bear: the look in his eyes as he said in a choked voice, 'I'll never stop loving you, you know.' The way his Adams apple bobbed as he swallowed hard and blinked his eyes fast, and then the little sniff and cough as he turned on his heels, shoulders back, head erect and walked away through the trees.

She has no right to feel sorry for herself. After all, she'd known from the start that this mad involvement with Stuart couldn't last. The age gap was only one of the impediments between them. She'd resisted for weeks, but his persistence had worn her down. He might be younger, but he was far from being a child and should be allowed to take responsibility for his own actions. It was flattering too, a welcome antidote to reaching the depressing side of forty. A bit of fun would do her more good than harm. In the long run, it might even restore some excitement to their marriage. Not that there had ever been an excess of that, even before the wedding.

She'd never intended to get in so deep. Foolish woman! As if emotions can be weighed out precisely and arranged in little packets to be taken off the shelf and used in sensible quantities that never go beyond the bounds of reason.

So, she's got herself rather badly burned. Tough luck! Hard cheese! She'll just have to apply some psychological Acriflex and hope that the scars aren't too visible.

And now, out of the blue, this: Edward is presenting her with the possibility of one final afternoon of passion. '… very late home tomorrow… complicated case…series of meetings that have had to spill over to the evening.'

Oh, the depths and complexities of self–deception! To think that she'd even felt a little rush of pride in her own fortitude as she watched, dry-eyed, while Stuart disappeared into the trees.

By the time the meal has ended, Vivienne has managed to regain control of herself. Her initial reaction has startled her – the way her stomach suddenly turned to water, the stab of pain down there – the way her brain leapt into action like a greyhound after a hare, weaving this way and that through the obstacles that might prevent their union. Oh, to lie in bed together one last time! The joy of it will be worth the agony of yet another final parting.

It comes almost as a relief to realise that Edward's change of plan for the next day has been announced too late. Even if Stuart were to be able to delay his departure, how can she contact him to let him know? Too risky by far to phone his lodgings from the house at this time of the evening. And anyway would he be able to speak without being overheard by the headmaster or his family? Nonsense! Of course she'd manage to make herself understood. That old cliché: Love will find a way! She can walk into Sutton and use the payphone in the shopping centre! But didn't she use her last few coins on a packet of chewing gum this very afternoon, before going to collect Colin from Mrs Ibstock's house? Edward hates it when he sees her chewing, but it's got to be better than taking up smoking again. Raid Colin's money box for a few coppers? That would be not only risky, but utterly despicable.

No chance. No choice. Forget it. She takes a few deep breaths as she stands at the sink, and stares at her image in the darkened window pane. Although the kitchen light is on, it's not quite dark outside yet. Fresh air. That's what she needs. And time on her own. She'll never settle now without a brisk walk.

She wipes her hands on the drying-up cloth and opens the back door as Ann steps through from the hall. Taking a gamble, Vivienne smiles and says, 'Oh, Ann! I'm just popping out for a quick breath of air. Would you like to join me?'

The girl hesitates for a moment, and Vivienne frowns, giving herself a mental shake. Her own daughter! Why should she recoil from the idea of Ann's company? She takes a step towards her and holds out her hand, 'Come on, it'll do you good.'

'No thanks. Just came to see if you needed help with the

265

washing up.'

'Oh, that was kind, but it's all done now. Tell Edward I'll be back in a few minutes, will you?'

She slips out through the side gate and onto the pavement where she hurries towards the park. There's far more daylight outside than you'd guess from inside at this time of the evening. There's a thin line of dark pink just above the treetops and above that, an expanse of pale lemon melding into lime green, colours so crisp and pure, so tangible, she can almost taste them. They always, even now, make her want to shout for joy. Or is it pain? This loss.

Wrapped in her thoughts, she doesn't notice the figure lurking beside the hedge of the final house before the corner. He steps into her path and she gives a startled gasp, before she sees his face and lets herself be drawn into his arms.

After a few moments of frantic kisses and endearments, she breaks away and whispers 'Go to the park. Quick. I'll follow you.'

'I couldn't keep away,' he says, once they've reached the safety of the trees. 'I had to see you one last time. I've been walking up and down your road for ages, just *willing* you to come out.'

'Thank god you came. Thank god!' she says, tears of relief scalding her eyes. The eleventh hour stay of execution. Of separation. The unexpected gift of another afternoon. She can't not tell him now.

'Feeling better?' says Edward, glancing away from the television as she enters the room. 'You certainly look more yourself again.'

The flush on her cheeks could easily be explained by exposure to the cooler evening air, but she'll have to keep a check on the tell-tale smiles that try to sneak onto her lips.

She hardly sleeps that night, see-sawing between excited anticipation and guilt at the prospect of telling yet more lies to the children. This will be the only compensation for losing Stuart - an end to all the lies. She's well aware this small gain will weigh like a feather against the weight of loss, but it might help ease the pain a little if she remembers how she felt each time her glib tongue delivered another falsehood within range of Colin's guileless eyes and Ann's searching gaze.

Ann is turning up trumps this morning. Her reaction to the 'urgent meeting' has shown not a hint of resentment, or worse still, suspicion. And the dear child has really been most helpful in hearing her lines. Not just helpful, but fun, too. She can't remember ever having felt so close to her daughter – a real sense of companionship. Could this be the start of things to come? Will Ann, at sixteen, blossom into a relaxed and pleasant companion, one who does not seem to be forever judging her and finding her wanting?

Poor Ann. Things can't have been easy for her in this house – leaving Norfolk and her beloved grandmother, not to speak of enduring Felicity's sharp tongue. But it was more than just the move. Her own state of mind after Lesley's bloated body was recovered from the sea – weren't there theories about the effect on the foetus of a mother's distress? She and Ann had never 'bonded', but the poor little baby couldn't be blamed for that.

She sighs as she removes the tray of sausage rolls from the oven. Colin's favourites. In other circumstances, it would have been nice to be sitting between the two of them in the cinema, surrounded on all sides by the ooohs and aahs and rustling sweet wrappers of other children, and Colin's sticky hand on hers, and his giggles of delight, and Ann smiling, in spite of her grown-up self and wanting to see 'The Go-Between' instead of the babyish Chocolate Factory. Now, Ann will be the one to revel in the role of mother, something that has often caused Vivienne a pang of envy in the past. How mean-spirited is that? From now on, she'll turn over a new leaf – build a proper relationship with her daughter. Learn to appreciate all that she has, instead of crying for the moon.

But first, there is the final, final taste of bliss to come. She'll savour every precious moment and after he's gone, she'll play them over and over in her mind, and in the weeks and months and years that follow, they'll be a source of consolation for her as she lies in the dark next to Edward, remembering Stuart's body moving on hers.

So beautiful! He is so beautiful it hurts. She closes her eyes, the better to lose herself in the physical sensations. There is all the time in the world. She draws his head down, licks the salt from his upper lip, and explores his tongue with hers...

The last thing she remembers of this part of her life is the sharp, animal smell of him and the roar that explodes from the doorway, 'Bitch, you fucking bitch, you stinking whore, you harlot– get out – get out of my bed – out of my house get out *now*! Out! Out! Out!'

Vivienne is in shock as she lies sprawled on the bed, while Stuart raises himself on his hands and cranes round towards the door, then tries to clamber off her, but his legs get entangled in the sheet and he tumbles awkwardly onto the floor. It takes Vivienne a few moments to comprehend that this is Edward's face advancing towards the bed, scarlet and still bawling, 'Out! Out!' as he bends to pick up one of Stuart's shoes.

As she sits up and slides her legs over the edge of the bed, hugging a pillow against her breasts, one half of her wants to giggle at the ludicrous, farcical scene. The other half is cold as stone.

Edward is the first to slip back into his civil self. He gives an embarrassed cough, clears his throat, jerks back his head and says in a dull monotone, 'Vivienne, you leave me no choice. I had hoped we could avoid a situation like this, but it seems you are determined to humiliate me beyond the point of endurance. I will not stand in your way. I shall go downstairs now and wait in the sitting room. You have thirty minutes to pack a suitcase and leave the house. The rest of your belongings will be sent after you, if you choose to leave a forwarding address. My son, of course, will remain with me. I doubt that you will want Ann to join you in your love nest, and you may rest assured that I look on her as my own daughter.

'As for you, you turd,' he snarls, rounding on Stuart who is hopping on one leg as he struggles into his underpants, 'May you rot in hell. Flogging is too good for you, and I will not demean myself by laying a finger on your lily-white skin. Now remove yourself from my premises at once, before I change my mind and thrash the living daylights out of you.'

Hong Kong 2008

Chapter 34

'He really thought I'd staged the whole event, you know - just to bring matters to a head. Too much else had happened by the time we'd both realised what you'd done, Ann. There was no going back.'

Ann has listened in a numbed silence as Vivienne tells her part of the story, and now she leans forward, elbows on her knees, and buries her face in the crumpled napkin, her whole body shaken with sobs.

For several minutes they sit there side by side without speaking, Vivienne's open palm resting on her daughter's shoulder. At last she says, 'That's enough now, dear. You needed to know, but you don't need to blame yourself.'

Ann sits up and blows her nose loudly.

'That's right, ruin my best table linen!' says Vivienne with a laugh, 'Now then, why don't you go and wash your face while I pour us both another drink? You've heard the worst part. Now I need to put you back together again, you silly goose. All that was a lifetime away.'

By the end of the evening, they are both giggling as they try to mount the narrow stairs with their arms draped round each other's neck.

Ann's mind is a kaleidoscope of emotions as she snuggles under the quilt. It has taken Vivienne nearly an hour to haul her from the pit of self-loathing, but eventually her words have sunk in. Some of these have echoed what George told her: she was a confused teenager, doing her best to save the family from breaking up. She was afraid of losing her little brother.

But Ann knew this was only part of the truth. The small voice in her head insisted on being heard, 'It wasn't just Colin. It was much, much worse than that. I told that lie because…because I was jealous.'

'That's quite understandable, darling,' Vivienne laughed.

'No, you don't understand. It's something really awful…disgusting. I was jealous of…'

'Jealous of me. I know. Of course you were. How could you not be? Stuart was what you'd have called a 'real dish', back then, wasn't he?'

'But…but…'

'Listen Ann. You were a child, not quite sixteen. I was forty. Which of us was old enough to know better? I think I said to you a couple of days ago that allocating blame won't help a situation. In a way, the whole thing was an accident waiting to happen. An act of god, if you like,' she finished with another laugh.

She went on to talk about the early days with Edward. How kind and thoughtful he was. How nice it was to be adored, at first. The relief of knowing she would be looked after for the rest of her life. The excitement of moving to the outskirts of a large city, with the opportunities this might bring – meeting new people, finding a rewarding career. London, of course, would have been better, or even Norwich itself, but there weren't exactly queues of even half-way suitable men beating a path to her door; her youth was slipping away with increasing speed, so…

And that was the first step towards what happened, seven years later.

To be fair, the first two or three years were as good as could have been expected. A difficult step-daughter and a resentful eight-year old didn't exactly help at the start, but things settled down, and then, of course, there was the baby.

She'd felt a pang of guilt at the love that engulfed her when Colin was placed in her arms, and she realised for the first time what she had been supposed to feel for her first-born.

On the eve of her thirty-ninth birthday, Vivienne had spent the afternoon in the park. It was a cold, dank January day and she'd walked through soggy leaves under the dripping trees, immersed in self-pity. She had set her life on a course that promised no change beyond her own and Edward's gradual decline into old age and eventual death. She'd laughed as she told Ann this. 'What a pathetic, selfish creature I was!'

It was the December of that year that she'd met Stuart. In an effort to bring new interest to her life, she had joined the nearby amateur theatre group and was allotted tasks behind the scenes. Stuart was starting a temporary teaching job at the Boys' Grammar the following term and was looking around for ways of filling his spare time.

The day after her fortieth birthday, they'd bumped into each other again in Sainsbury's ('Yes, literally! Our trolleys collided.'). A few weeks later, they were lovers.

She felt alive again.

Hindsight always seems to clarify, but how do we know that it doesn't equally distort? As for herself, of course Vivienne regrets the pain she caused. She will never get over the guilt for what she did to Edward, though that has to include not only the ending of the marriage, but her agreement to marry him in the first place. And how could she, or Edward, regret the step which led to Colin's birth? Ann, perhaps, has suffered more than anyone, and sadly there is nothing Vivienne can do to make up for it.

She has to admit though, that in spite of what she feels now, at the time she had felt utterly betrayed when she and Edward had discovered Ann's malicious lie. They were communicating mainly through her solicitor by then. Edward, of course, was conducting his own case.

'I have to say, Mrs Morgan, that many people would consider Mr Morgan to be acting very fairly in the circumstances. After all, there's no denying that you deserted the marital home, and made no attempt to take your children with you. I need to advise you that almost any of the judges you might come in front of will find your husband's suggestions for access arrangements entirely reasonable, and in the boy's best interests.'

This was a bitter pill: only one weekend a month, and a week in each of the school holidays. And no, she did not blame Ann for visiting so rarely. She herself might have done more in those early weeks and months to bring about a reconciliation with her daughter, but Vivienne was racked with her own guilt and grief, and there was precious little to build on, in the way of a mother-daughter bond.

Regret now, at this stage in her life? No. She could not, hand on heart, wish that this had never happened. Nearly thirty seven years with a man you love? How could any woman regret that?

There'd been hardly a dull moment, except in the last two or three years, with the increasing frequency and severity of Stuart's depressive phases. Even then, she had her own activities - developing the shop, the boat, her friends, and of course, Poppy. If anything, she should be thanking Ann for forcing her to take the leap into the unknown.

At Vivienne's bedroom door, Ann had hesitated before continuing up the next flight of stairs.

'Friends, are we, now? Do you think?' said Vivienne, almost shyly, as she reached forward and lightly stroked the back of her fingers across her daughter's cheek.

A short while later, Ann, on the verge of sleep, smiles as she thinks about that moment. *Friends! How amazing is that?*

She wakes in pitch darkness a few hours later. She's lying awkwardly, half on her front, half on her side, sprawled across the scattered pillows, but her lips are slightly parted in a smile, and there's a warm glow behind her breastbone. Her right arm is bent and almost covering her face while her palm is cupped over her ear and her languid fingers tangle with her hair. She lets her hand slide down onto her cheek, and is surprised to find it wet with tears.

The tide has turned again - here comes that dull ache in her stomach, that sharp lump in her throat. Tomorrow is Tuesday, and she'll be flying home to her other life. Her real life with Graham.

Real?

'It wasn't just the sex, you know,' says Vivienne, pausing near the brow of the hill to let Ann catch up with her. She'd stopped to admire the view of the sea far below them, shimmering under the clear blue sky, but Vivienne had not noticing her lagging behind till she called out in a mock-whine,

'Wait for me, Mummy! Wait for me!'

They both laugh, and then laugh again as Ann says, 'Were we discussing sex just now? I thought this was a tree-focussed outing. Some kind of nature walk.'

'Well, birds and bees, you know. Yes, you are going to find out something very special about trees – but actually, Stuart was the one who first opened my eyes to this particular phenomenon. Though ears would be more accurate - but you'll soon see what I mean. Or hear, rather.'

'The little I saw of him, he struck me as a real townie.'

'Not really. We both enjoyed lots of things about city life - still do enjoy, in fact - the cultural aspects, theatres, exhibitions and so on. Then there's the shopping, the restaurants, sitting in cafes watching the world go by. Brighton was good for all that, and so is Hong Kong, in its own very different ways. It wasn't just a matter of economics that brought us to Lamma, the cheaper houses, it was all this space,' she says, gesturing towards the sea below, the further hills ahead, and the trees they are approaching on their left.

'It is beautiful,' says Ann. 'Not at all what I'd expected of Hong Kong.'

'There's been a lot of development here since we came, of course, but there are quite strict building regulations, I believe. Next time you come, we'll take you to the New Territories on the mainland. There are stunning ranges of hills that seem to go on forever, and beautiful, deserted bays and thick woods where you can see monkeys playing in the trees. You can walk for miles and not see a soul.'

Next time, thinks Ann and her heart gives a little leap. Might she come here again? Spend time here with George again?

'So you see,' Vivienne is saying, 'I want you to understand why I welcomed them into my home, and will continue to do so.'

'Em…Stuart and Lindy?'

'Of course. I'm still very fond of Stuart. As I've said before, bonds like that aren't so easy to break. I was only with Edward for seven years, but I must tell you, I was amazed at how I missed him, once the worst part of the whole divorce business was over. Things are never straightforward when it comes to relationships. He wasn't ever going to set the world on fire, but he was a good, kind man, and he deserved better than me. Do you know, your Graham always reminded me of Edward in a way?'

'Oh,' says Ann. She doesn't want to think of Graham just yet. Not before she has to. 'So what about the baby, then? What will you do when it's born?'

Vivienne stops at the edge of the path. They've reached a small wood, and she steps onto a narrow track between low shrubs, then turns back to Ann with her crooked smile, 'I expect you'll think I'm being ridiculous, but if I still feel the same as I do now, once it's born, well, it already feels to me like a kind of surrogate child – or maybe, grandchild.'

Oh, these emotions, thinks Ann as a wave of anger hits her.

Vivienne sees her expression, and her hand flies to her mouth, 'Oh god! What am I saying! Ann, I'm so sorry.'

Ann gives a rueful smile, 'It's OK, Vivienne, it was just....'

'I know. I know. Your Louise and Daniel. I haven't forgotten them. Nor Colin's two. My own grandchildren - my own flesh and blood!' she gives a deep sigh, then shakes her head, 'I really have made an almighty mess of things, haven't I? Terrible mother and even worse as a grandmother.'

'It's all right. It's all right,' mutters Ann. 'I suppose I didn't exactly make it easy for you. I could have sent you photos and stuff over the years. I just didn't think you'd be interested.'

'Spilt milk, and all that. Water under bridges,' says Vivienne with a shrug. 'After all this time, we can't expect everything to fall into place, all in one go. Maybe we should both just go easy on ourselves – leave the past where it belongs. I can't have very many years ahead of me now, and I don't want to waste what's left to me in pointless disagreements and regrets. And that's why I...well, Stuart...Lindy, you see?'

'I... I'm not quite sure,' mutters Ann, following Vivienne as she takes a few more steps along the track.

'It's about conventions, really. Our ideas of what's acceptable and what isn't. What we're supposed to think and feel in certain situations – or what we think we're meant to feel.'

'Ye...es?'

'I mean,' Vivienne continues, pulling a large, broad leaf from an overhanging branch, 'the supposedly normal reaction to desertion by a long-term partner - especially when the other woman was a guest in my home, and her impregnation undoubtedly took place in that very house.' Abstractedly, she begins to tear the leaf into strips along its veins, 'Well – any self-respecting woman in these circumstances would rather see the pair of them hanged, drawn and quartered than let them step across her threshold ever again.' The remains of the leaf flutter to the ground. 'Unless, perhaps, the faithless partner sends the trollop packing, and crawls back on his knees, wearing sackcloth and ashes, ready to do penance for the rest of his days,' she finishes with a laugh, swiping her palms against each other, scattering the final fragments of green.

She turns and starts walking further into the wood and Ann follows. The path is a little wider now, and the ground-cover of low bushes has given way to scrubby strands of yellowing grass and scattered layers of brown leaves. The tall, slim trees are wide apart and the thin canopy of waving green allows bright glimpses of clear sky.

'So you're not a self-respecting woman, then?' laughs Ann, falling into step beside her.

'More self-protecting, than self-respecting, I think. What's in it for me, if I behave like that? I still care for Stuart. I miss having him around. As I said, it wasn't just the sex for us; it was more about companionship - though he wasn't much of a companion towards the end. Before Lindy came out here, he was down in the village, drinking, most evenings, and often didn't come home till mid-morning.'

'So why...?'

'Why did I put with it? ' she says with a rueful smile, 'Why do

276

any of us put up with certain behaviours from our life-long partner – our nearest and dearest, once the initial flush of 'in love' has turned to something else?'

Why indeed, thinks Ann, and draws a sudden breath as Vivienne says, 'I'm sure your Graham doesn't behave like that, but I'd hazard a guess that you occasionally find him somewhat insensitive – dominating, even?' After a short pause, she adds, 'No, I don't expect an answer to that! But whatever the truth of it, I'm pretty certain you'd be devastated if he upped sticks and left you. And you would never in a million years, leave him.'

Before Ann can think of a suitable response, Vivienne has slowed to a halt again and is gazing around from tree to tree. She steps purposefully towards one with a trunk as thin and almost as high as a telegraph pole before the first of its many leafy branches spreads itself towards a neighbouring tree.

Ann watches in bemusement as her mother stands up close beside it, pushes back her hair and presses her ear against the smooth, grey-green bark, one arm around the trunk,.

Her eyes are wide open and staring straight ahead. She appears to be listening, and for the first time Ann notices the background twittering of small birds. She shuffles her feet a little and bites her lip as she looks around, avoiding catching her mother's eye. After a minute or two, the sound of a sudden intake of breath draws her back to her mother's face. It is lit with an expression of delight.

'Here, Ann,' she whispers 'Put your ear against this tree.' She steps back and guides the bewildered Ann into her place. 'Be patient,' she says. 'You might not hear anything at first.'

'But what -?'

'Shh! Trust me. Just listen.'

The bark is hard and slightly grainy against her ear. All she can hear is distant birdsong, and then, oh, this must be the pulse of her own blood. A moment later, there's a distinct 'clunk, click,' from inside the tree, and then a gurgling sound, 'Whoosh, chug glugg glugg whoosh,' on and on, like a faulty radiator.

Vivienne has read her face and laughs delightedly. 'It's the sap, rising. Isn't it amazing! There must be valves inside that help

277

to siphon it all the way up the tree. You know, for photosynthesis.'

'Shh,' says Ann and waves her hand. She doesn't want a biology lesson. She wants to listen and listen to the most astonishing sound in the world. All the years she's been on this earth, and she's never heard this before, never known it could be possible!

Chapter 35

'You can hear it at night, too,' says Poppy, 'the sap coming down. Some Chinese won't go near a wood after dark, because that's when the tree spirits talk to each other.'

'Really? That's so cool,' says Dawn.

'Cool is exactly how I feel, all of a sudden,' laughs Vivienne. She turns up the collar of her emerald silk jacket and hunches her shoulders as she clasps the lapels together under her chin.

The five of them are sitting at large, round table under the brightly lit canopy of the restaurant where Ann first met up again with Vivienne, just a few days earlier. The almost-empty dishes crammed onto the circular turntable in the centre are evidence of the large meal they have just finished.

A chill breeze has sprung up from the bay, and the red paper lanterns strung along the sea side of the canopy begin to jiggle and sway.

'Look, sea spirits!' laughs Dawn.

'It's a good thing they've got electric lights inside, not candles,' says Poppy.

'Whatever they are, I think they're giving us the signal to move somewhere warmer,' says Vivienne, placing her hands on the edge of the table and preparing to rise to her feet. Before she can do so, George has lifted his own linen jacket from the back of his chair and is draping it across her shoulders, bending to whisper something in her ear.

Ann sees Poppy swivel round, and give a little nod towards the waiter who has been hovering in the doorway. Instead of approaching their table, he disappears into the restaurant. Getting the bill, thinks Ann with a pang. It has been lovely, sitting out here in the balmy evening air, looking at the reflections of lights on the still water of the bay, and basking in the companionship of these four people. She doesn't want this meal to end. Her last supper. Her last night in Hong Kong. This time tomorrow, she'll be on the plane.

As George sits down again the waiter re-appears with a tray of glasses and a bottle of champagne in an ice bucket.

'I know that this might have been more appropriate at the start of the meal,' announces Vivienne, 'but we didn't want to draw attention to a gloomy subject too early in the evening.'

'It's a tragedy!' says Poppy in a doleful voice. 'Just when I meet my dear niece at long last, and start to get to know her, she's about to disappear to the other side of the world.' She turns to Ann who is sitting beside her, and clasps her right hand in both of hers. 'At my age, who knows if I will ever see you again my poppet?' she quavers, then withdraws one hand and dabs at her eyes with her napkin, sniffing loudly.

'Come on, Ma. I'm sure Ann will be back here again soon, now she's seen how easy it is. And anyway, there's nothing to stop you from jumping on a plane to England yourself, as I keep on telling you.'

'See how he treats me! Even when I'm in my eighties, he has no respect for my white hairs.'

'That could be because you've never given them a chance to show themselves,' laughs Vivienne.

'Black hair or white, it makes no difference to the pain I'm feeling in my heart. It's such a shame you can't stay longer, Ann. *Such* a shame,' Poppy squeezes Ann's hand, and chokes back a sob, which turns into a hiccup.

'You can see now why we've waited till the end of the meal, Ann!' laughs Vivienne. 'I'm not too happy about your departure myself, but Poppy does have a tendency towards histrionics, given half a chance.'

With a final sniff, Poppy straightens her back and says, 'I'm not ashamed of showing what I feel. Better than being a cold fish, like you Vivienne.'

'Stop squabbling, you two,' says George with a grin. 'There are no cold fish at this table; we just have different ways of expressing our feelings.'

'Nicely put, George,' says Vivienne. 'I know that we will all miss Ann, but for me, in a strange way, that's actually a source of happiness as well as sadness.' Her voice falters as she smiles across the table at her daughter, then continues more firmly, 'Now, let us raise our glasses and drink to Ann – May she have a safe journey, and a speedy return.'

A series of toasts follow, and a few minutes later the bottle is empty. Before they leave the restaurant, there's a brief discussion about their next destination. Dawn is meeting friends at a bar further along the main street, and Poppy is in favour of them all staying down in the village for a little longer, 'The night is yet young,' she exclaims, when Vivienne suggests that the four of them go back to her house for a nightcap.

'What price your white hairs, now, Ma?' laughs George then turns towards Ann. 'What would you prefer? A quiet drink at Aunty Viv's, or a rowdy one with Dawn and her friends?'

Ann glances at her mother and realises that she has no choice. 'No offence to you, Dawn, but those bars are a bit noisy. I'd like to spend the remains of the evening with my mother and my new relations in a place where we can hear ourselves think!'

'That's my girl,' smiles Vivienne, and places an arm across her shoulder in a quick hug, before following Poppy along the street.

The phone is ringing in the narrow hallway as Vivienne opens her front door, and she reaches it as Constantia bustles in from the kitchen wiping her hands on her apron.

'Oh! Graham! What a nice surprise! Ann is right here beside me. We've just got back from a farewell meal.'

Ann can almost feel her brain turn itself around in her head as she reaches out her hand to take the receiver. She counts to three before she places it against her ear. 'Hello, Darling!' she says, in a bright voice, and then pauses. There's a hollow echo on the line. Let him speak. Give herself time to readjust.

'Hello! Ann! Is that you?' Is she imaging the undertone of impatience?

'How are you Graham? Are you still in Norfolk?'

'Of course I'm not. Didn't Louise tell you? I said I'd be back on Monday. Three nights at those prices was more than enough,' he finishes with a laugh.

She lets that last statement hang in the air, wondering if it was amusement and not sarcasm she'd heard in that laugh. 'So, was it nice?' she ventures, 'Did you have a good time?'

'I did, actually. Very nice indeed.' He sounds almost smug and is clearly waiting for her to coax from him the source of his satisfaction.

It's bound to be some rare bird or other. Even as she asks, 'So, did you spot anything special?' she knows that whatever rare species of bird it might be, it belongs to the feathered and winged variety, not the human, without a shadow of a doubt. Why should that thought feel so depressing?

'Special's not the word for it! You'll never guess what it was!' In spite of herself, Ann has to smile at the excitement in his voice. 'In all these years I've never been closer than a couple of hundred miles away, when a sighting's been reported.'

'Go on, then, tell me!' she says, and her smile now evident in her tone.

'Guess, Ann. See if you can guess.'

He's not worrying about the cost of phone calls, now, she thinks. 'Graham, you know I won't get it. The only birds I know the names of round there are Redshank and Canada Geese. Everything else is just a plain seagull.'

'I'll give you a clue,' he persists, 'It's a really exotic bird.'

'Sorry Graham. That doesn't help me at all.'

'Well, how about this: it's got these unmistakable black and white barrings on its wings.'

She plays along with him, knowing that he wants to delay the moment of revelation for as long as possible. His version of foreplay, she thinks, and has to stifle a giggle at the thought of an erotic phone-call service laid on specifically for birdwatchers.

'A hoopoe!' she echoes, as he reveals the secret after feeding her each little fact of its appearance in the same piecemeal manner. The word itself triggers the memory of a picture in one of Danny's nature books, in the section, Exotic Visitors to Our Island Shores.

'Oh, and you've been having a good time with your mother, I hope?' he says, almost as an afterthought. 'So, I'll pick you up on Wednesday morning, then. Nine thirty. You won't need to worry if there's a delay from Amsterdam. I've got all the flight details and I'll check the state of play before I set out.'

As she draws her breath to say goodbye, he delivers his closing words, 'It'll be nice to have you home again, Ann. I've missed having you around.'

Ann has no idea how much time has passed since the phone clicked, severing contact with that strange but so-familiar place, where it's only half past one in the afternoon and the whole evening still to come. She stands in the hall staring down at the rug on the polished tiles, her hand resting lightly on the receiver, her mind in turmoil.

'Are you all right, Ann?'

It's George. She hadn't even heard the door opening and closing again behind him. 'I'm fine,' she says. 'Just struggling a bit with getting my head round this Time-thing.'

'It hits me like that too,' he laughs. 'Horribly confusing, isn't it?' As he reaches the door of the cloakroom, he turns back to her and says, 'What would you say to a breath of fresh air, in a moment?'

'Em… How about, "Hello"?'

'Ha ha! Very funny.'

'Alright then, I'd say, "yes".'

Back in the living room, George says, 'Ann's taken it into her head that she'd like to go and commune with the tree spirits. Any other takers?'

'I'll pass on that one,' says Vivienne. 'I've done quite enough walking for one day.'

'Me too,' says Poppy, 'I think we can let the two youngsters, take care of each other, can't we?'

'I would hope so,' says Vivienne with a laugh.

'We won't be long,' says Ann with an anxious glance at Vivienne.

'We'll be fine, Poppy and I. Stay out as long as you want.'

'Yes, do. It'll give us the chance to indulge in the really juicy gossip,' chuckles Poppy. 'Off you go, now, the pair of you.'

George pauses when they reach the track that leads to the pagoda.

'Cold?' he asks, as Ann gives a little shiver.

'Not really,' she says, 'Goose walked over my grave, that's all.'

'That's a rather macabre expression!'

'I suppose it is,' she laughs. 'It was one of Grannibelle's.'

'Shall we sit there for a bit?' he says, gesturing towards the dark, angular shape beyond the bushes. 'It should be quite sheltered. I don't want you to get cold.'

'I'll be fine,' she says.

They sit side by side in the same spot where they'd been the previous evening.

After a few minutes of silence, she says with a hint of a laugh, 'I hope you're not afraid of tree spirits?'

'No,' he says, then, 'Oh! Would you rather go to that wood and listen for the sap?'

'No, I'm fine here.'

'That's good. Me too.'

Another long silence. Must she be the one to break it, again? Does silence always have to be broken? It occurs to her that it would be a kind of vandalism to destroy this one. It seems so fragile. She's almost afraid to breathe…

When her right hand reaches out towards him, his left hand meets hers halfway.

They both laugh.

'Great minds think alike,' says Ann.

'We do, though, don't we? Think alike,' he says, and then adds, almost in a whisper, 'That's the trouble, isn't it?'

'Yes.'

'What are we going to do?'

'What *can* we do?' she says.

They're on the edge of another silence. This one has to be

284

broken. In a flat voice she says, 'I'm flying home tomorrow evening. I land in Birmingham at half past nine on Wednesday morning. Graham is picking me up from the airport. He'll drive me to our home. Then we'll - '

'You don't love him, do you?'

'No,' she says. 'Not *love*...'

He releases her hand, and for a moment, she feels a mixture of relief and disappointment. Then that same hand is resting on the back of her head, and his other strokes her cheek as she lets him draw her face towards his.

It's that tiny feeling of relief that stops her. It comes from somewhere deeper and closer to the truth of who she is. The slightest resistance is enough, her neck becoming less flexible, the tightening of her jaw. He lowers his hands and leans back against the stone wall.

She can hear his breath gradually become more regular. In the darkness she senses that his hand is reaching out for hers, and again they meet halfway, but this time, everything has changed.

'So now we know,' she muses. 'In a funny way, I feel better now.'

'Better because we know what we both feel? Or because we know we won't do anything about it?'

'Both, I suppose. What do you think?'

'Do you really want to know?'

'Yes. But I think I can guess.'

'Go on then, Miss Clever Clogs,' he says with a warm laugh.

'You feel happy about the first part, and not so happy about the second?'

'In a nutshell, yes. But at the same time, I do realise that we could have spoiled everything just now. I wanted to take the risk, but it wouldn't have been right for you. Not yet.'

She raises his hand to her lips and places a light kiss on each knuckle bone. 'Thank you!' she says.

'What for?'

'For understanding. That's what's the most important thing to me – the fact we understand each other so well.'

'Me too. Favourite cousin,' he says, and he kisses her hand in his turn. 'We won't be saying goodbye, tomorrow, you know. It'll be au revoir. No one can object to first cousins emailing each other and chatting on the phone…'

'And you'll have to come to visit us. It'd seem very odd to Graham if you didn't want to meet him as part of your new-found family. And Louise will definitely want to meet you. I could come down to Brighton and stay with her.'

'You'll come out here again too. You'll have to. It wouldn't be fair on the old dears…'

As they dawdle back towards Vivienne's house, hand in hand, they weave a narrative of the times they can spend in each other's company. No one can object. No one will be hurt. They are first cousins – almost like brother and sister.

Not. As Dawn would say.

No. Not at all like brother and sister. But they'll keep that side of things in check. They won't *do* anything. Now they both know, now it's out in the open between the two of them, it'll be easier to manage. They won't discuss it. It'll be their secret, the way they both feel about each other. And a secret between two people binds them more closely together. A bond more intimate than sex.

All their friends and relations will be intrigued by the story of their shared grandfather. Louise and Daniel will be thrilled to find out not only about George, but about their great aunt, Poppy and George's two sons. Wouldn't it be fun to have a family reunion out in Hong Kong, with all the descendants of Rupert McFarlane and their wives or husbands? They can leaf through that album of Grannibelle's that she left for Vivienne – those black and white pictures of Belle and Rupert and Ivy, and they'll laugh at the chin that she and George inherited from Rupert, proving their kinship. Colin would have to come over from The States, and maybe Marlene would bring the two little ones. Vivienne could start to build a relationship with Lou and Danny at last. And Stuart and Lindy's baby would be born by then, and from the way Vivienne was talking, she'll regard all three of them as part of her family…

The only person Ann finds it hard to imagine at this future, happy family gathering is Graham.

But maybe she is being unfair to him. He produced a surprise of his own last Friday, booking in to the Morston Hall Hotel. If he does agree to come out here sometime, who is she to say that Hong Kong might not work its magic on him too?

If you have enjoyed *Paper Lanterns,* **and** *the Dangerous Sports Euthanasia Society* by Christine Coleman you will also enjoy:

<u>**FROZEN SUMMER**</u> by *Crysse Morrison* **(Hodder & Stoughton)**
"absolutely stunning — a really brilliant, unputdownable book"
— *Katie Fforde*

"the kind of book that will never go out of fashion: a good psychological thriller pacily told... Morrison's debut proves her a superb storyteller" — *The Times*

"had me completely absorbed from the first page"
— *Joanne Harris*

AND

<u>**SLEEPING IN SAND**</u> by *Crysse Morrison* **(Hodder & Stoughton)**
"As intense and absorbing as her first book, this novel must not be missed. Confirming her reputation as one of the finest psychological writers of today, lyrical yet spare, delicate yet powerful."
— *Kirsty Fowkes*

"Morrison's talent is in rendering the ordinary extraordinary and in making every detail of a life, indeed, every life, seem important and noteworthy. The end is truly spine-tingling."
— *Writers News*

"Crysse Morrison has done it again—produced a book which tantalises till the last page."
— *Sue Jones*

Order Crysse's books via www.cryssemorrison.co.uk

You will also enjoy:

STAR GAZING by _Linda Gillard_ (Piatkus)

Short-listed for _Romantic Novel of the Year 2009_

"A joy to read from the first page to the last … Romantic and quirky and beautifully written."
— _www.Lovereading.co.uk_

"Touching and perceptive." — _Daily Express_

"A read for diehard romantics with a bent towards environmental issues." — _Aberdeen Press & Journal_

EMOTIONAL GEOLOGY _by Linda Gillard_ (Transita)

Short-listed for the _Waverton Good Read Award 2006_

"Lyrical, intriguing and haunting." — _Isla Dewar_

"Complex and important issues are played out in the windswept beauty of a Hebridean island setting, with a hero who is definitely in the Mr Darcy league!' — _www.ScottishReaders.net_

"The emotional power in these novels makes this reviewer reflect on how Charlotte and Emily Brontë might have written if they were living and writing now." — _Northwords Now_

A LIFETIME BURNING by _Linda Gillard_ (Transita)

"An absolute page-turner! I could not put this book down and read it over a weekend. It is a haunting and disturbing exploration of the meaning of love within a close-knit family … Find a place for it in your holiday luggage!" — _www.Lovereading.co.uk_

"Gillard wrote well in her first novel; she writes even better in her second … Absorbing, clever and touching."
— _West Highland Free Press_

For more information visit **www.lindagillard.co.uk**